The Eye of Heaven

CLIVE CUSSLER
and RUSSELL BLAKE

PENGUIN BOOKS

PENGUIN BOOKS

UK | USA | Canada | Ireland | Australia
India | New Zealand | South Africa

Penguin Books is part of the Penguin Random House group of companies
whose addresses can be found at global.penguinrandomhouse.com.

First published in the USA by G. P. Putnam's Sons 2014
First published in Great Britain by Michael Joseph 2014
Published in Penguin Books 2015

001

Text copyright © Sandecker RLLLP, 2014

The moral right of the author has been asserted

Set in 11.25/13.57 pt Garamond MT Std
Typeset by Jouve (UK), Milton Keynes
Printed in Great Britain by Clays Ltd, St Ives plc

A CIP catalogue record for this book is available from the British Library

B FORMAT ISBN: 978–0–718–17873–4
A FORMAT ISBN: 978–1–405–93273–8

www.greenpenguin.co.uk

PENGUIN BOOKS

The Eye of Heaven

Clive Cussler is the author of a great number of international bestsellers, including the famous Dirk Pitt® Adventures, such as *Poseidon's Arrow*; the NUMA® Files adventures, most recently *Ghost Ship*; the *Oregon* Files, such as *Mirage*; the Isaac Bell historical thrillers, and the recent Fargo Adventures. He lives in Arizona.

Russell Blake is the author of twenty-nine acclaimed thrillers, including the Assassin, JET, and BLACK series. He lives on the Pacific coast of Mexico.

ALSO BY CLIVE CUSSLER

The Eye of Heaven

Prologue

Somewhere in the Labrador Sea, AD *1085*

Flashes of lightning seared the turbid night sky, illu-minating the drawn faces of the men heaving on the long wooden oars of the Viking longship as it fought against the ravages of the unforgiving sea. The captain swayed in time with the relentless swell as he watched the wall of towering waves pounding the stern.

Sheer cliffs of black water driven by the icy wind threatened to capsize the hardy craft with each passing minute. Sheets of rain lashed the grim crewmen as they strained at their task, their survival depending on their unflagging effort. The captain eyed them with determination, his brow furrowed as the deluge tore at his skin, water running along the faint white battle scar stretching from the corner of his left eye to his blond beard. He'd grown up on the ocean, one of a hardened race of adventurers and plunderers, and nature's untamed violence was nothing new. Countless nights he'd hurled oaths on the treacherous North Sea, but, even for him, this was a once-in-a-lifetime storm.

The wooden vessel was now badly off course, driven

north as it ran with the seas. Had it pressed on its intended route, one of the mammoth waves would have assuredly broken over the bow and capsized the ship, bringing certain death. The best the captain could do was to steer the boat with the wind at his stern and ride out the fury of the gale.

A flare of brilliance streaked through the roiling clouds, glowing momentarily before fading back into the gloom. Salt water dripped from his bearskin cloak as the muscles on his powerful arms bulged from the effort. Another bright flash lit the night. The glowering profile of a carved wooden dragon reflected the light just aft of the captain's head, soaked with the spray blowing off the angry sea.

From among the exhausted oarsmen, a tall man with skin the texture of leather and an untamed red mane lurched his way forward, his footing sure on the coarse oak planks beneath him even in these miserable conditions.

'Thor is venting his fury tonight, eh, Vidar?' the captain shouted to his mate over the howling wind.

'He is indeed, sir. But I think the worst is past. The swells seem smaller than a few hours ago.'

'I hope you're right. My arms ache like I've been wrestling a bear all night.'

'I know the feeling. You've seen my wife.'

The two veteran seamen exchanged humorless smiles, and then the mate edged next to the captain and took the rudder staff from his grip.

'So much for trying to sleep in this nightmare. How are the men holding up?' the captain asked.

'As well as can be expected. Cold. Tired.' Vidar didn't say 'afraid.' It wasn't in these warriors to admit fear.

'They've spent enough time quaffing ale and enjoying the native hospitality. This will give them something to think about in case they've softened like a maiden's robe.'

'Aye, Captain. It's definitely putting them to the test –'

A deafening explosion shook the deck beneath them. Both men gazed at the dazzling pyrotechnics with eyes seasoned from a lifetime on the ocean and in battle.

The captain glimpsed a shape rising behind him and turned instinctively. They stared as the stern split a massive wave, the rush of the breaking sea the only sound. After a brief moment suspended at the crest, they gradually eased down the back side, the black monster disappearing into the darkness.

'Could you imagine if we'd hit that one square on?' Vidar asked in a hushed voice.

'Or amidships. We'd all be on the way to Valhalla by now.'

Their eyes drifted to the mast, now shattered and useless, the top half torn away like a twig, along with a major portion of the sail – victim of the stealth with which the storm had hit. That had been a costly miscalculation. He should have lowered the woven wool sheet before the wind could rip it loose. But he'd been trying for every bit of speed possible. His men's arms were strong, but after almost twenty-four hours of rowing, even in shifts, they were reaching their limit.

Among the most impressive longships ever launched, *Sigrun* was built to exacting standards for a crew of ninety, with rowing positions for up to eighty men, two to each of the ship's forty oars, and a detachable mast fifty feet in height. She boasted a length of a hundred and twelve feet and a beam of sixteen, a keel hewn from one massive oak, and square stones for ballast. *Sigrun* could travel at a speed approaching fourteen knots under sail in calm conditions, but during a winter storm of this proportion, in the farthest reaches of the North Atlantic, speed wasn't an issue – staying afloat was.

The *Sigrun* had a typical Viking lapstrake, double-ender hull, but with a taller gunwale for open-sea expeditions, and its stern and bow were sculpted with identical dragon heads. Ships like *Sigrun* had a solid track record, navigating some of the most dangerous oceans on the planet, and their seaworthiness and speed were legendary. But even the most durable craft had its limits, and the storm had pushed *Sigrun* and her crew far beyond anything they'd been through in all their years together.

Long hours passed, and as dawn's first glimmer fought through the heavy gray clouds the seas began to flatten. The captain called out the order for the exhausted oarsmen to rest now that the most dangerous part had passed – and then his eyes spotted a new menace: ice. Fifty yards ahead, an iceberg loomed in the haze, easily the size of a small hill. He twisted to the crewman manning the rudder and yelled a warning.

'Ice! Ahead!'

The ship had a shallow draft, but, even so, the churning waves could push them too near the submerged mass, which would shatter the wooden hull and sink the longship, the icy water killing all hands within minutes. The bow swung slowly, the steering sluggish as it resisted the surge of the following seas. Another rolling swell pushed them nearer – too close for the captain's liking.

'Put your backs into it. Pull, damn you, pull or we're done for.'

The ship glided past the brooding ice as silently as a wraith. The captain's eyes roved over the frozen monolith, an island of desolation in the middle of the ocean. He offered yet another silent prayer to the gods. If the ship was in the ice, the storm must have blown them farther north than he'd feared, and the overcast would make it impossible to plot a course using the primitive means at his disposal.

'Bring one of the ravens from the hold,' he ordered.

Vidar relayed the command to the nearest crewman, who scuttled away. The storm surge was nearly spent, and it was time to use one of the Viking seafarers' secret weapons: birds.

Two men heaved a deck hatch open and descended into the forward cargo hold. Moments later, they emerged carrying a rough wooden cage with a large, agitated black form in it. The taller of the two men carried the cage to the captain's station at the stern and set it down on the deck. With a final glare at the sea, the captain squatted on his haunches and eyed the raven.

'Well, my friend, it's time. May you fly straight and true. Don't let me down. Our survival depends on your instincts. Let Odin guide you.'

He straightened and gave the crewman a curt nod. 'Release it, and wish it Godspeed.'

The crewman lifted the cage to chest height as Vidar approached and, after fiddling with the leather binding that held the access door closed, pulled the door open and reached in. The raven flinched, but the fight was out of it, and Vidar easily cornered it with cold hands. He withdrew the bird, and then, with a prayer of his own, tossed it into the air.

The raven circled the ship, finding its wings, and then flew to port.

'Be quick about it. Bring the bow around. Follow the raven.'

Their gazes trailed the black speck as it disappeared into the distance, and they quickly aligned the prow's fearsome dragon head to the bird's flight.

'How many more do we have, Vidar?' the captain asked.

'Only one. We lost the other two from shock.'

'I know how they must have felt. That storm was one we'll be talking about around the fire when we're old and gray.'

'That's the truth. But we made it. And now we know where landfall lies.'

'The only question is how far away.'

'Yes. And how hospitable.'

'Probably not warm beaches and willing maidens, I'd wager, judging by the ice and the dropping temperature.'

'I suspect you're right.'

The men fell silent, lost in their thoughts, their course uncertain for now. Once they found land and the clouds had parted, they could use the sun to plot the way home.

'Order the rest of the men to the oars, Vidar. We need to make speedy time while it's light. I don't want to spend another night on the open sea with icebergs waiting to sink us.'

Vidar turned to the resting men, who were slumbering wherever they could find space on the deck. 'Time to earn your keep. To the oars, Vikings, to the oars!'

By late afternoon, they could make out snow-covered mountains in the distance, perhaps half a day ahead at their present speed. The welcome sight galvanized the exhausted men, who redoubled their efforts now that a destination was within reach. Vidar manned the rudder, and the captain looked landward from the helm, keeping a sharp eye on the water. As the ship drew nearer to land, the sea was filled with smaller chunks of floating ice, as well as the occasional massive iceberg.

'What do you think?' the captain asked, his face pallid from two days of relentless stress.

'It's land, sure enough. I say we find safe harbor and put up for the night and then devise a plan once we're rested.'

'The men are surely at the end of their rope. We can improvise some repair for the mast. It will be a long trip home if we have to row all the way.'

Vidar nodded. 'That it will be.'

'Look – a fjord. If we follow it inland, we should be able to find a suitable spot to make camp,' the captain said, pointing a gnarled finger at the gap along the coastline. 'With any luck, there may even be an open river.'

'Could be,' Vidar agreed, squinting to better make it out.

'If there is, that would mean fresh water. And possibly animals.'

'Both welcome guests to our diminishing stores.'

'We should follow the fjord and see how far it goes,' the captain said. 'I don't see any better options, and it will be dark again soon.'

'Anything that gets us out of this wind. At least the cliffs will provide us shelter from the worst of it.'

'Make for the fjord.'

Vidar fixed the oarsmen with a determined glare. 'Come on, lads. Pull. We're almost there.'

The only sound was the oars creaking as the men strained at their task. There was no other sign of life, no evidence that they weren't the only living things on Earth. There was nothing to indicate that they hadn't been blown to a freezing purgatory in some remote netherworld.

'Steady, men. Steady . . .' Vidar called out as they weaved around the ice floes toward the blue-white cliffs on either side of the fjord. He leaned toward the captain. 'Can you make that out in the distance? It looks like a narrow channel.'

'Yes, I see it. It's likely there's another bay beyond it. Whatever the case, we need to keep moving forward until we find a place to put in for the night. It's likely there's no place to land along this unforgiving coast.'

The ship eased through the gap in the shore and found itself in an increasingly dense ice floe. The craggy canyon walls jutted high into the heavens and blocked out the dimming rays of the setting sun. As they continued forward, the area grew darker, but thankfully the worst of the weather had been left at the channel's mouth and the water was still.

The captain pointed to a spot ahead.

'There. By the base of the glacier. It might be tight, but it looks like we can get the ship at least partially beached, safe for the night. We can then take a party and see what awaits us on land at dawn tomorrow.'

Vidar squinted at the sliver of flat ice and nodded. He leaned his weight against the rudder and turned the craft's bow to the sloping indentation. The slim remaining light wavered across the surface of the ice-strewn inlet, and the men expended their last resources driving the longship the final distance. The curved bow scraped on to the frozen crust with a jolt, and the crew leapt out to heave the vessel farther ashore so it wouldn't float away with a rising tide, using their battle-axes to secure grips in the ice. They were able to get half of the mammoth craft out of the water – a testament to the design and lightweight construction of Viking vessels. The captain gave the signal to cease; they'd done their best, and, with the final glow of the rapidly dwindling dusk, would do better to conserve their strength and make camp on deck for the night.

The captain gazed skyward at the tapestry of stars and offered a silent plea to the gods that they aid him in guiding his men to safety. Tomorrow they would mount an expedition armed with their longbows and, with any luck, bag venison for food while they repaired the shattered mast. While it was not impossible to use the oars to carry them east to their homeland, even a partial working sail would increase the odds of delivering their priceless cargo.

His final thought before drifting off was that no matter what, he had to make it back. He'd sworn a sacred oath to the expedition's leader, who had died in a land so far from home.

The new dawn revealed an ominous gray backdrop of sky. Vidar shifted, his cloak crackling as a thin veneer of ice shattered along its surface. He forced his eyes open to find the entire ship dusted in white – snowfall from a midnight flurry that had entirely blanketed the craft. The captain stirred several feet away from him and then rose. His eyes roved over the slumbering crew before settling on what had been water and was now frozen solid. An ominous horizon of storm clouds brooded over the ocean. He watched as the dark line approached, and moved to where Vidar was struggling to sit up, his limbs stiff from the cold.

'I fear another storm is approaching. Have the men unfurl what's left of the sail,' the captain ordered, 'and we'll use it for shelter. Judging by the look of those clouds, we're not out of it yet.'

Vidar nodded as he squinted at the heavens. 'We don't have long before the storm returns.'

The captain turned to his crew. 'Men! Up with you. Get the sail free and spread it over the deck for cover. And be quick about it. Unless you want to be up to your necks in sleet!'

The groggy crew pushed themselves into action, and by the time the freezing deluge fell they'd crafted a makeshift tent and were huddled beneath it. The first wave of hail hit with the force of a blow against the fabric, and to a man they were grateful for the captain's quick thinking as the weather tore at the vessel with the fury of a demon.

On and on the storm raged until midday. Eventually the hammering ceased, and the only sound was the heavy breathing of the men, their exhalations warming the enclosure as the blizzard abated.

When the captain pushed the edge of the sail aside

and moved into the now-still air, the landscape was blinding – white as far as he could see, the ship now buried up to the top of the gunwales. He considered their alternatives, which were bleaker by the moment. They were trapped, the ship immobilized, and there was little to encourage him on their chances of survival.

Vidar's head poked out beside him, and then, slowly, the crew moved the sail aside, the men pausing as a group to take in the vast expanse of the Arctic wasteland. The captain scanned the surroundings and then squared his shoulders.

'All right. The worst is behind us. Form an exploratory party, and let's take the measure of this place while we have a break in the weather. Report back before dark. I want to know what we're facing.'

Vidar turned toward the men, his face stoic, his jaw set with resolve. 'Thirty of the best archers among you, gather your bows and swords, and take sufficient provisions for the day. We depart as soon as ready.'

The crewmen scrambled, energized at the chance to finally get off the ship, and there was much good-natured argument over who was the better bowman and thus more deserving of the duty. After a brief outfitting, the Vikings tromped through the fresh snow, a slow line of shaggy forms moving toward the glacier, searching for a route to ascend from the water's edge. Finally Vidar cried out and pointed to a narrow gap in the ice where a jagged outcropping of rock jutted from the steep face. The column diverted to the promising area before disappearing, one by one, from view.

Dusk had darkened the sky when the captain saw Vidar's familiar red beard approaching across the ice, returning from the gap, trailed by the plodding archers. When Vidar arrived, he gave the captain a curt nod, and the two men moved to the stern of the ship, where they could converse privately.

'We went for hours. It's nothing but ice. Didn't see even a bird.'

'It can't be endless. What about the surroundings?'

'There are mountains in the distance on either side. I think our only chance is to try to reach them tomorrow. Where there's land, there will be life, and, if we're lucky, we can hunt something down and return with it.'

The captain considered his mate's words.

'Very well. At first light, form two parties. Forty men in each. You take one, I the other. Split up and we'll make our way off the ice in opposite directions. That will improve the odds of at least one of us finding food. We'll leave the rest of the men with the ship.'

The following morning, the men set off at dawn, a long file of brave warriors with no enemy to vanquish but cold and hunger. Once they were on the glacier's surface, the captain clasped a strong hand on Vidar's shoulder and embraced him.

'Good luck to you. May your game bag be brimming by day's end,' he said.

'And to you as well. When we've hunted all we can carry, we'll return to the ship.'

The captain nodded, looking deep into Vidar's eyes. Both men knew that their future was uncertain, with no guarantee of anything ahead but misery and starvation. But they were Vikings and they would forge ahead until there were none left standing. The captain took a bearing on a far peak and pointed, his voice measured and strong.

'Onward, men! There are streams of clear water and fat elk eager to make your acquaintance. Let's not force them to wait.' And with that, he took the first long steps toward the distant mountains, moving with the grace of a predatory cat, leading as he always had, with the confidence of one born to the task.

I

Cartagena, Spain, present day

The *Bermudez* rocked lazily in the mild swells of the azure sea, tugging at her anchor chain like an over-excited dog on a short leash. The ninety-six-foot steel-hulled expedition boat was more stable than most vessels her size, and she gave the appearance of a commercial fishing trawler rather than a marine archaeology ship. A small red-and-white dive flag bobbed thirty-five yards off her stern.

Bubbles frothed to the surface near the oversize aft dive platform as Remi Fargo emerged from the deep. Water coursed from her black wet suit as she hauled herself up the partially submerged ladder. She pushed her dive mask up on top of her head and reveled in the warmth of the summer sun on her face. Dropping back into the water, she slipped out of her buoyancy control system vest. Sam Fargo padded across the deck and down the steps to her position, pausing for a moment to appreciate her beauty before offering a grin and reaching out to help with her fins and gear.

'And who might this vision of loveliness from the sea be? A mermaid, perhaps? A siren?' he asked playfully.

She eyed him with skepticism and swatted his bare chest. 'Are you getting fresh with me?'

He shrugged. 'I figured flattery was never a bad option.'

'You'll go far, young man. You have a bright future.'

Sam lifted the BC harness with a strong, slightly sunburned arm, the rigid lines of muscle barely strained by the forty-pound rig. 'You find anything more?'

'Nope. I think we've cataloged everything.' More bubbles disturbed the surface, and then another head popped out of the water. 'I see Dominic's arrived.'

The second diver pulled himself on to the platform and shed his tank and gear. Closely cropped black hair slightly fringed with gray topped his lean, swarthy face. He smiled at them and gave a thumbs-up.

'I think we're done, no?' he asked, more a statement than a question. As captain of the ship and the leader of the Spanish team of divers chartered by the University of Seville to explore the shipwreck a hundred and thirty-five feet below, it was Dominic's call. He deferred out of courtesy to his two American colleagues, who were renowned treasure hunters. They had originally discovered the wreck and reported it to the Spanish Department of Maritime History. Sam and Remi's research had concluded that it was probably a seventeenth-century merchant ship that had sunk in a winter storm. It was lying buried in the silt on a ledge, beyond which the seafloor dropped off sharply. The shipwreck had turned out to be the type of vessel in

question, and a group of divers and marine archaeologists had been dispatched, with the Fargos assisting
in exploring the ship to determine its historical
significance.

'Sure looks like we're finished,' Remi agreed as she
ran her fingers through her hair, faint bronze highlights
shimmering as it began to dry. She unzipped the front
of the wet suit and her hand unconsciously moved to
the tiny gold scarab suspended from a leather thong
around her neck. It was a new good-luck charm Dominic had presented to her in an elaborate display when
they'd arrived. And good luck it had indeed brought –
in spite of the depth, the dive had been a relatively easy
one: a week in an idyllic location, doing what they loved.
The captain was charming and the crew courteous and
efficient. If only all of their adventures were so low-key,
she thought, and turned to Sam. 'Where can a girl
freshen up around here?'

'Your cabin awaits. The champagne is on ice, the
chocolates on the pillow,' Sam said with a small bow.

'Knowing you, you drank the champagne and wolfed
down the candy,' she teased.

'I'm an open book to you, aren't I? What was the
giveaway?'

'The brown smear on your chin.'

The low rumble of powerful diesel engines reached
them from across the water, and they turned to watch a
large white private yacht cut its power as it neared to
within two hundred yards. Remi peered at the transom,

but the name and home port were blocked by a long row of dive tanks in a custom-made rack.

'Any closer and we'd be buying each other jewelry,' Sam said as they continued to observe the vessel.

'Big, isn't it?' Remi remarked.

'Probably a hundred and fifty feet at least.'

'Lot of tanks. Looks like they're serious about their diving.'

A crew member moved to the bow of the opulent craft and, moments later, the anchor dropped, its long chain rattling as it lowered into the sea. Two and a half miles away, the rugged coastline jutted into the summer sky; nearer was the Isla de Las Palomas, with its fleet of pleasure boaters and small yachts out for day trips from the nearby marinas. A polar-white cruise ship inched into the Cartagena harbor, a popular port for many Mediterranean cruises.

'Doesn't it strike you as strange, Dominic, that a boat would anchor this close to the shipwreck?' Sam asked.

'Not necessarily,' Dominic said. 'A lot of boats here like to overnight within sight of others, in case they need assistance of some kind.'

'Still, we're a long way from the beaten path, don't you think?' Remi said.

'Maybe they're just as curious about what *we're* doing here,' Sam reasoned. 'After all, we've been anchored for a week, and the dive flag's very visible.'

'That's probably it. Human nature,' Dominic said, apparently unconcerned.

Remi held her hand up, shielding her eyes as she watched the ship play out more anchor chain. 'I just hope they don't discover the shipwreck and disturb any artifacts before the government authorities get here.'

'I wouldn't be too worried about it,' Dominic assured her. 'Most divers know better than to go inside a shipwreck that's mostly buried like this one. Nobody wants to get trapped. A death sentence —'

'You're probably right.' Remi tilted her face up to the late-morning sun and closed her eyes, then opened them and looked at Sam. 'Weren't you in the process of wooing me with chocolates and champagne?'

'It was more of a veiled threat.'

'You should know I don't scare easily, veils or otherwise.'

They made their way to their stateroom after putting away their gear. Their quarters were large by marine standards, paneled in dark hardwood, the mahogany dulled by the years but still retaining a warm richness. Sam took a seat at the small built-in table near one of the cabin's two portholes as Remi entered the bathroom, and soon the shower was steaming forth a luxuriant stream.

'You buy that the boat's harmless?' Remi called from the stall.

'No reason to believe it isn't.'

'There's a lot of very valuable statuary in that shipwreck,' Remi reminded him. The merchant vessel had gone down with all hands, and had been rumored to be smuggling priceless antiquities from Greece to Britain, where there had been a large market for them among the royals and the upper class. Their careful inventory of the wreck had confirmed the centuries-old suspicion, and there were untold millions of dollars' worth of never-before-seen Greek relics in its hold – a different kind of treasure, to be sure, than the usual gold and jewels, but treasure nonetheless.

The hope had been to keep the remarkable discovery quiet until the government could arrange to retrieve the statuary from the sea, and it was always a concern that mercenary treasure hunters could intrude, damaging the site as they attempted to pilfer it, although the likelihood was low.

'There is indeed,' Sam conceded. 'I'm sure the people of Spain wouldn't want anyone to try to make off with their property.' Sam and Remi had agreed that anything they discovered would be turned over to the government – a policy of theirs that had made them welcome additions to many of the most interesting expeditions around the world. They were in the game for the thrill of discovery, not for the money, Sam's fortune having been long solidified by the sale of his company to a conglomerate years before.

'Dominic didn't seem too concerned. And he knows these waters well.' The shower shut off and the door swung open. Remi emerged and wrapped herself in a thick towel and dried her hair with another in front of the bathroom vanity as Sam tapped at the laptop computer in front of him.

'True.'

'I think we should keep an eye on that boat.'

'Aye, aye, Skipper.' Sam's gaze drifted from the computer screen to the bathroom doorway, where he could make out half of Remi as she brushed the tangles from her auburn mane. 'Have I mentioned that you look fabulous?'

'Not nearly enough. Now, where are the champagne and chocolates?'

'I might have exaggerated to lure you belowdecks.'

'It worked. I hope you have a suitable alternative in mind.'

Sam powered down the laptop and closed the screen. 'I have a few ideas . . .'

2

When Sam and Remi returned to the main deck, they glanced up at the second level, where the crew sat around a card table dotted with beer bottles, laughing and tossing money into the pot as they studied their hands, smoke curling skyward from hand-rolled cigarettes. The expedition was over and now it was time to relax, a pursuit at which the Spanish excelled.

Remi watched with amusement as one of the men accused the head of the dive team of cheating. The target's predictable response to the gibe was one of outrage and offended pride, which was suitably soothed with a round of toasts celebrating his integrity. She turned to Sam, but he'd moved to the stern, where he was staring at the horizon. A light breeze from the south tousled his hair and his white linen shirt. Remi joined him, and together they watched as four divers from the visiting yacht donned their wet suits and equipment and then dropped into the water.

'Are you thinking what I'm thinking?'

'That maybe we've been compromised?' Remi asked.

'Actually, I was more leaning toward it being a nice afternoon for a relaxing dive.'

'I can't go very deep. Still need a lot more surface time.'

'I don't think you'll need to. I just want to have a look around and make sure that our suspicions aren't correct.'

'Just because you're paranoid doesn't mean they aren't out to get you.'

'Exactly. So what do you think?' asked Sam.

'That it's time to go back and put on our bathing suits? You're going to owe me some serious spa sessions for this after doing the last dive.'

'You know I'd have gone with you if I could have. The decompression tables don't lie.'

'Which means you have limited dive time, too, Mr Cousteau,' she warned, concern flittering across her face.

'Yes, ma'am. Whatever you say, ma'am.'

'Now, that's a little more like it.'

Five minutes later, they were ready, the crew still absorbed in its revelry, unaware of Sam and Remi's approach to the dive platform.

'Visibility still about sixty feet?' Sam asked as he put his mask in place.

'About that. Maybe a little better.'

'Then we shouldn't need a lot of bottom time. Just a fun, recreational dive.'

'Near the wreck, of course.'

'Seems like the natural place, doesn't it?'

'What about being spotted?'

'We'll dive on a trajectory that'll place the *Bermudez*'s hull above us as much as possible,' Sam explained. 'Besides, if I'm right, they won't be looking up. You know how it is when you're wreck-diving. Tunnel vision.'

Remi nodded agreement. 'Good plan.'

They eased the heavy stainless steel ladder from the platform into the water and, instead of dropping into the sea, carefully lowered themselves until they were fully immersed. Sam gave Remi the okay and she reciprocated, signaling that she was ready.

They gradually descended to sixty feet, moving as they had discussed on a rough course for the wreck. At forty yards away, Sam signaled to Remi to stay put and then swam away, farther into the darkening depths. Ten minutes went by, and just as she was beginning to worry, Sam reappeared, checking his dive timer. He pointed toward the surface.

When they made it to the surface, he spat his regulator out, the big white yacht only fifty feet away.

'Busted. Two of the divers were inside the hull, and the other two were outside. I could see their work lights,' he reported. 'And then five more came out of the wreck. Hauling statuary. So the four we saw were only a small part of the gang. Could be ten or more inside.'

'How? How could they have known?'

'Obviously, they came prepared . . .'

'Which raises the questions, who are they and who leaked the info?'

'Anyone who knows about the wreck could have given them the coordinates. That's a pretty long list of Spanish officials.'

'I suppose so. And as to who these pirates are . . . ?' Remi asked.

'There's only one way to find out.'

She shook her head. 'You're not thinking –'

'The best defense is a good offense.'

'Wouldn't it be better to notify the authorities?'

'You mean the same ones that might have tipped these guys off? What do you want to bet that goes nowhere?'

Remi sighed. 'I suppose this has been way too calm for your tastes so far. I should have known better.'

'Come on. Let's go take a look at how the other half lives.'

'We are the other half.'

'You know what I mean.'

'Yes, Sam. I'm all too afraid I do.'

They approached the interlopers' yacht at fifteen feet of depth, and Sam punched in a waypoint on his dive GPS when they were directly below it. With another glance back at the shipwreck's position, he pointed up at the stern, and Remi signaled that she was ready. Together, they ascended to the dive ladder that hung below the swim step and Sam hauled himself up, followed closely by Remi.

'Let's leave our gear here. We'll look just like any of the other divers. If we're spotted, just wave.'

'I don't know, Sam. I might be a little curvier than the average technical diver.'

'Which is only one of the many reasons I love you.'

'At least I can cross off the worry about you running away with another diver.'

'Running sounds exhausting, especially in flippers.'

Remi swatted him.

After a furtive scan of the empty lower-deck area near the transom, they mounted the stairs to it. The yacht had four stories above the hull. A soft swirling of jazz music drifted down from the second-story deck.

'Sounds like the party's up there,' Remi whispered.

Sam nodded. 'Question is whether we want to join in.'

'Prudence would dictate caution.'

'So we crash it?'

She gave him a knowing look. 'If I said no, would that stop you?'

'Good point. Let's sneak up and see who we're dealing with.'

'Sneak? Wearing a wet suit? On a mega-yacht?'

'I didn't say the plan couldn't use some fine-tuning,' Sam admitted.

She smirked. 'Lead on, O great hunter.'

He hoisted himself on to the second-level deck and found himself facing three extremely tanned young beauties wearing little more than smiles, lying on chaise longues around a hot tub. One of them glanced up and fixed Sam with a frank gaze, then lowered her sunglasses slowly to get a better look.

Four considerably older men sat gathered around a large teak table filled with epicurean fare and champagne, their cigar smoke pungent on the balmy breeze. A fifth, and younger, man stood at the portside railing, watching the *Bermudez* with binoculars. Sam regarded the seated group, and one of the men rose – an imposing figure, wearing a brightly colored Robert Graham shirt, ivory Armani silk-and-linen pants, and Prada loafers. Sam smiled and locked eyes with him. The man's face registered shock for a few seconds, but quickly settled into a practised grin, as genteel as the cream panama hat cocked rakishly on his head.

'Sam and Remi Fargo. What a pleasant surprise. How good of you to drop in,' he said, his upper-crust British accent unmistakable.

Sam sensed Remi behind him. Without turning to her, he approached the table with an equally friendly smile on his face and reached out to lift one of the champagne bottles from the sweating silver buckets. He studied the label for a second and then dropped the bottle back into the ice.

'Well, if it isn't Janus Benedict. Still drinking Billecart-Salmon 1996, I see,' Sam said.

'I see no reason to change horses, having already backed a winner. If I might ask, to what do we owe the pleasure of your company?'

'We were over on that other ship, saw yours, and were wondering if you had any Grey Poupon.'

'Ah, the infamous Fargo humor asserts itself. Well met,' Janus replied, his tone steeped in an elegant civility that perfectly complemented his graying pencil-thin mustache.

The other three seated men eyed the Fargos with guarded amusement, enjoying the interlude – it was obvious to everyone at the table that Janus and the Fargos were old adversaries.

The younger man approached Janus and murmured in his ear, 'Janus. What are you doing? Throw them off . . . now. Or better yet –'

Janus silenced him with a curt gesture. He moved him away and spoke into his ear. 'Reginald, stop,' he hissed. 'Stop right now. One should always keep one's enemies close, the better to understand their mind.'

'It's insanity.' Reginald reached toward the rear of his waist, where a pistol was concealed by his loose shirt.

'Reginald, you may be my brother, but you escalate this on my boat and there'll be hell to pay. Think. Just for a second. Bring a weapon into the equation and we're out of options. So stop it, now, and go back to studying your navel while the adults play.' Janus pulled away and returned his attention to the new arrivals. 'Please. I insist. Some champagne. And, Remi, may I say that you look as ravishing as ever . . .'

Remi had removed her dive hood and unzipped

her wet suit. 'Ever the silver-tongued devil, aren't you, Janus?'

'I'd have to be made of stone to be oblivious to your beauty, dear lady,' Janus said, then took his seat and snapped his fingers. A steward in white slacks and a matching short-sleeved shirt with black epaulets materialized from inside the upstairs salon.

'Bring two more chairs for my guests, as well as some proper glasses. And be quick about it,' Janus ordered.

'Yes, sir.'

Like rabbits from a hat, two more stewards appeared bearing chairs and champagne flutes. Remi and Sam took seats at the table. The shorter of the servants poured them both glasses of champagne, which sparkled like effervescent gold in the bright sun.

Janus indicated his entourage with an open palm. 'Allow me to introduce everyone. Pasqual, Andrew, Sergei, meet Sam and Remi Fargo – some would argue the most successful treasure hunters on the planet. Oh, and the gentleman over there, admiring your fine vessel, is my younger brother, Reginald.'

The men nodded at the Fargos.

Sam shook his head. 'Hardly treasure hunters, Janus. We're merely possessed with insatiable curiosity and find ourselves in the right place at auspicious times.'

'Yes, quite – you certainly have Lady Luck perched firmly on your shoulders. But fortune favors the bold, it's said.' Janus raised his glass in a toast. 'To fair weather and smooth sailing.'

Remi raised her glass to meet his, and Sam just smiled.

'What brings you to the Spanish coast, Janus? Not really your stomping ground, is it?' Sam asked.

'All work and no play, dear boy.' Janus's eyes skimmed over the three reclining nubiles by the tub. 'Doctor's orders. Take in the salt air, enjoy the sun. None of us can be sure how much more time we have.' He paused. 'And you?'

'We must have the same doctor. He gave us almost identical instructions,' Remi interjected.

'Yes, well. Great minds and all.'

Sam leaned forward. 'I couldn't help but notice that you have quite a dive shop on this boat.'

Janus didn't blink and merely offered a wan smile. 'Some of my guests are real enthusiasts. One of the prices of entertaining. I had it outfitted so they'd have everything they could wish for.'

'Judging by the empty tank holders, I presume we missed them.'

'Did you? It's so hard to keep track of everyone on a yacht this size. But it doesn't surprise me to hear that they went for a dive. That's one of their passions, after all. Rather keen on it, actually.'

'What is she? Forty meters?' Remi asked.

'Oh my, no. Rather more like fifty-something. I forget exactly. It's only one in my stable, don't you know. A bit of a sod to maintain and not inexpensive, but why do we strive if not to enjoy our little luxuries?'

They spent another twenty minutes bantering, circling gladiators in a verbal arena, probing each other for any hint of vulnerability, but Janus was too smooth to slip up. Even though Sam and Remi knew his game, and Janus knew that they knew, there wasn't much to be done about it aboard his yacht. When Sam grew tired of the exchange, they excused themselves, thanked Janus for his hospitality, and returned to the dive platform.

'Leaves a taste like spoiled food, doesn't he?' Sam commented as they donned their gear.

'Like rotten shark meat.' Remi pulled on her hood. 'He's very smooth, though, isn't he? Butter wouldn't melt in his mouth.'

'He's always been that way. Remember the last time?'

Sam and Remi had run across Benedict once before, on an expedition to locate a lost Spanish galleon off the Normandy coast – a search that had ultimately proved successful, but not before they'd had to contend with suspicious equipment failures they'd believed had been engineered by Janus's henchmen. His name came up routinely in certain circles in connection with stolen artifacts, as well as his primary business: arms-dealing to a who's who of African despots and cartel-affiliated shell companies. His connections and financial clout were such that he'd never been prosecuted for so much as a parking ticket. His network of banks, insurance firms, and real estate development companies secured his position as a legitimate fixture on the United Kingdom's social scene. He'd been invited to more palaces than most career diplomats and swam in the treacherous waters of power with the natural ease of a barracuda.

'We have to notify the university and the government, Sam. We can't let him get away with this. You and I both know the wreck will be picked clean by the time he's done with it,' Remi whispered.

'Yes, I know. But my fear is that he's obviously been able to buy off at least some of the higher functionaries, so by the time they do arrive to secure the cache the Spanish people will be the poorer for it.'

Remi adjusted her dive vest and turned to face Sam. 'I know that tone. What are you thinking of doing?'

'We'll still go through the proper channels, but it may take a little unconventional thinking to guarantee he doesn't make off with anything first.'

'And you're just the guy to think big . . . and outside the box,' she said, raising one eyebrow.

'I'd like to believe I'm more than just a pretty face to you.'

'Well, you do give a good back rub.'

'Subtle hint there?' Sam asked, peering over the edge of the platform at the water below.

'And you catch on quick. I like that.'

She splashed into the sea, and Sam waited until her head bobbed on the surface nearby before joining her, his mind churning over possible ways to thwart Janus on the open ocean, vastly outnumbered by his crew.

3

Dominic paced in the pilothouse as Sam and Remi waited with crossed arms for a response from the Spanish Department of Antiquities on what course of action they intended to take in order to protect the shipwreck from looting. In frustration, Sam glanced at the Anonimo Professionale CNS dive watch Remi had given him for his birthday. They'd insisted on radioing in the threat when nobody had answered their phones – not completely unexpected on a Friday before a holiday weekend.

Dominic cut short his walk to nowhere and turned to face them. 'My friends, we've done everything we can. I'll notify you when I hear something.'

'Isn't there anyone else we can get in touch with? The police? The Coast Guard?' Remi demanded.

'I'll notify everyone and anyone, but there's a limit to how many of these agencies will react. Remember that while this is extremely important to us, to the rest of the world it's low on the priority list. Our best bet is to wait for someone from the university or the government to respond.'

'By which time, they could have made off with most, or all, of the relics,' Sam said.

Dominic shrugged. 'I understand your frustration. I share it. Which is why I'll wait to hear and keep calling whoever I can think of.'

Sam touched Remi's arm and they exchanged a look. Sam nodded and let out a sigh. 'I suppose we have to work within the system. If nobody cares to respond, we can't make them. And we certainly can't sink Benedict's boat, much as I'd like to.'

Remi gave him a dark glare. 'Sam . . .'

'I said I wouldn't. Don't worry.' Sam looked at Dominic. 'You will come get us if there's any word?'

'Of course. The moment I hear something.'

Sam led the way back on deck, where the crew's barbeque celebration had gradually increased in volume as the day wore on. Raucous laughter greeted them, along with shouts of mock outrage as the never-ending card game continued. The surface of the water around the *Bermudez* rippled with golden flashes as the sun slid beneath the horizon. Twilight would soon overtake them, and both Sam and Remi knew that their chances of any action being taken by the authorities were receding with the sun's waning glow.

Back in their stateroom, Remi sat down on the bed and eyed Sam, who had moved to the nearest porthole, from which he was watching Janus's yacht.

'You know nobody's going to respond until Monday at the earliest,' she said.

'That's unfortunately true. Whether it's because Benedict paid them off to be unavailable or because it's

Friday in Spain.' Sam paused. 'I think I know how they're going to make off with the statuary without risking being boarded and arrested, even though it's a long shot. They're not going to load anything on board.'

'Then how are they going to steal it?'

'Ah. With a little sleight of hand, and using Mother Nature to hide their tracks.'

'It's a little late in the day for riddles, Sam.'

'If I were them, I'd wait until it got dark. How long do you think it would take to empty the hold?'

'Just to extract the statues, if you didn't care about damaging the wreck? At least all day. But you might lose a few pieces,' Remi said.

'Right. Their biggest problem will be raising it all from the bottom. They can't do that without being obvious. So my hunch is they'll wait until dark and use the ship's cranes.'

Remi frowned. 'I thought you said they weren't going to load it.'

'Not into the boat.'

She stared at him, puzzlement written across her face, and then smiled. 'You're a sneaky one, aren't you?'

'If you want to catch a thief, you have to think like one,' Sam said. 'They could be done in six to seven hours if they move fast, which you have to believe they will. The work lights will more than compensate for the lack of daylight. I say they'll pull an all-nighter and be ready to steam out of here at dawn, if not before. That's my prediction.'

'But we're going to throw a wrench in that,' Remi said.

'You bet. I specialize in wrench tossing. It was my minor in college.'

'I thought it was beer drinking.'

'You have to have priorities. And they aren't mutually exclusive.'

'What time do you see the party beginning on our end?'

'I'd say around four in the morning. Better to be early than too late.'

'Want to fill me in on how we're going to stop them?'

'I thought you'd never ask.'

The moon grinned crookedly from between scattered clouds, its cool radiance shimmering across the wrinkled sea as Sam and Remi descended to the dive platform. The rest of the archaeology team had long since retired and were slumbering the untroubled sleep of the inebriated. Remi opened one of the watertight lockers and removed two bulky dive masks with night vision monoculars attached – courtesy of Sam's contacts in the Defense Department. They'd used them to great effect inside the hull of the wreck, where the scope would amplify even the dimmest traces of light and illuminate the entire area.

'I hope this works,' Remi whispered as they checked each other's gear.

'It's our best shot. But, hey, what do I know?'

She patted the top of his head. 'You're good on the equipment.'

'You, too.' He stepped away. 'The night vision scopes are state-of-the-art. Worst case, we use one of the flashlights if we need a small light source. If we're careful and limit the beam to the hull, nobody will see it.'

She eyed the gentle swells. 'Did I ever tell you how romantic it is to dive into the cold sea in the dead of night?'

'I was hoping you'd be a pushover for that.'

'You know me like the beating of your own heart.'

They both froze as a creak reached them from the upper level. Sam cocked his head, listening for any hint of movement, and after a few minutes of continued silence they relaxed – it was probably just the wooden deck changing temperature.

Sam took the mask from her and switched on the NV scope, then pulled the strap over his dive hood. 'Hey, whaddaya know? I can see! You ready to go swimming?' he whispered.

'I was born ready, big boy.' She donned her mask and activated the scope and, after a final check of her dive bag, lowered herself into the water. Sam joined her moments later, and soon they were swimming toward Benedict's yacht using Sam's GPS waypoint.

Visibility wasn't as bad as he'd feared, ten feet below the surface, and enough moonlight penetrated to their depth for them to easily see each other. Sam estimated that with the scopes they had a good thirty feet of usable range before everything faded into darkness, which he hoped would be enough for their purposes. Remi glided through the water like a dolphin behind him, and when he looked back he felt a surge of pride in her for agreeing to tackle a difficult task with him, as she had so often, without flinching.

The yacht's hull loomed ahead, and as they drew closer they could make out the expected nets suspended below it by nylon rope, secured to heavy steel eyelets that had been welded to the vessel's underside specifically for that purpose. Sam gestured at the nearest, filled with statues, and they passed in front of it to the bow. As they did, the water hummed with a droning vibration – the engines firing up.

Remi looked at Sam. He indicated the closest net, withdrew his XS Scuba titanium dive knife from its leg sheath, and swam to where one of two lines connected to the hull. Remi did the same and moved to the opposite line, taking a moment to peer at the full nets hanging like pendulous fruit from the ship – easily a dozen or more – disappearing into the darkness along the yacht's length. Sam began sawing at the nylon line. Remi matched his efforts until her side frayed and then snapped, followed almost instantly by Sam's. They watched as the net filled with artifacts sank slowly back to the bottom. When it was out of sight, they swam to the next in the queue.

Ten minutes later, as they were approaching the second-to-last net, the yacht began moving. Sam looked around and pointed at the anchor chain, which was slackening as the vessel eased forward. Remi shot to the side to avoid becoming entangled in the netting as it moved toward her. Sam did the same. The chain tightened as it pulled free from the bottom, and then the vessel paused directly over the anchor as it rose from the deep.

Remi motioned at the two remaining nets. They swam to the two lines and began cutting, aware that they didn't have much time before the ship got under way. If they were lucky, they'd be able to free both and get clear by the time the yacht powered forward again.

Sam attacked his line with renewed vigor. The anchor chain clattered as it rolled on to the windlass at the bow, the sound, even underwater, like the firing of a machine gun. The cutting became more difficult as the stern drifted, pushed by the wind above, the giant five-bladed props turning slowly as the transmissions rested at idle.

Sam's side finally came free, and one side of the nylon net dropped in slow motion; and then, just as Remi was through her side, the huge props began spinning and the yacht lurched forward. Sam cursed silently as he felt the pull of the props dragging him toward them. After a final glance at the remaining net containing a single statue, he kicked with all his might to escape. He'd seen too many photographs of accidents involving propellers to risk a last attempt and he turned his head, searching for Remi, as he dived straight down.

He almost made it. The last net snagged Sam's tank

and for a horrifying moment he was dragged along, all control lost. Facing backward, he found himself staring at a vision crafted from his worst nightmares – the churning of the gleaming, sharp brass propellers only a few yards from where he was trapped.

The surge as the ship gathered momentum pulled him closer and he struggled uselessly to free himself, aware that he had only seconds before the anchor was up and the captain increased speed to where even if Sam got loose, he'd be sucked into the deadly blades. He reached behind him with his dive knife and slashed blindly at the thick nylon net.

To no avail.

In a last desperate bid for survival, he groped for his harness releases and snapped them open as he took a deep breath of compressed air and then pulled his regulator free of his mouth and swam into the deep with all his might.

His left flipper jolted as a prop blade tore through it, and then he was being pushed through the water as though in a jet stream, hurled backward by the prop wash as the yacht accelerated.

After a seeming eternity of being batted around in the wake, Sam broke the surface and gasped in fresh, sweet air, the stern of Benedict's vessel bright in his night vision monocular. He inhaled another huge lungful and then went back under to look for Remi.

She'd got clear sooner than he, and Sam could make out her form gliding into the dark.

Safe.

He dived down to her and took her hand. Remi gave it a squeeze. She turned to him and her eyes widened behind her mask as she saw him without his tank, only the snorkel in his mouth. He gave a thumbs-up, and they both rose to the surface.

'What happened to your rig?' she asked as they floated in the dark.

'The sea gods demanded a sacrifice and it was either the tank or me.'

'Are you all right?'

'Never better. Let's get back to the boat before dawn breaks,' he said, looking over to where the *Bermudez* floated peacefully on the ebony swells.

Back on board, Remi removed her gear, and they both stripped off their dive suits. Their intention was to say nothing about their nocturnal adventure until the shipwreck was under guard. Given Benedict's obvious reach into unknown levels of the Spanish administration, that seemed the most prudent course. No point in tipping him off and eliminating any timing advantage they'd bought themselves.

Sam got a better look at his battered fin, sliced laterally. The prop blade had missed his foot by inches – an unnecessary reminder of how close he'd come. Thankfully, Remi didn't register it in the dark, and he decided not to share his brush with disaster.

'The statue he got away with looked like the full-height one of Athena,' Remi whispered.

'We'll notify the authorities, if and when they arrive. I don't trust anyone on this boat.'

Remi's eyes widened. 'You don't think one of the team . . . ?'

'I don't know what to think. I just know that Benedict's dirty money seems to have bought a lot of indifference to obvious robbery, and I don't want to take any chances.'

She nodded. 'Think we could get another few hours of shut-eye?'

'That's my hope. We'll heat up the phones and the radio tomorrow. For now, I'd say mission accomplished, even if he did get away with one relic.'

'Once it's reported, he'll be hard-pressed to smuggle it anywhere or sell it.'

'Hopefully, that's true, but, as you know, some collectors are pretty unscrupulous.'

'But by the time anyone responds to us, he'll be in international waters. I'd be steaming for the sanctuary of either Morocco or Algeria. It's only a hundred and something miles. Piece of cake for that vessel.'

'It doesn't sound like today's the day he gets his, does it?'

'I wouldn't bank on it. Now, can I talk you into some serious pillow time?'

Janus Benedict stood on the transom deck, his color high, obviously angry, as the head of the dive team reported that the only thing they had to show for their trouble was one statue. Reginald looked ready to strike the unfortunate man, who was nothing more than the bearer of bad news.

'You idiot. How could you let this happen?' Reginald shouted, his silk Versace shirt shimmering in the sunlight.

Janus held up his hand to silence his brother and spoke in a calm, evenly modulated voice. 'Hector isn't to blame, Reginald. This does no good.'

'What do you mean, he's not to blame? We just lost millions because he failed to secure the cargo properly!'

Hector shook his head. He held up a piece of thick yellow nylon rope and pointed to diving gear he'd placed at the deck edge. 'No, sir. All the lines were still attached to the ties. These ropes were cut. Look at the ends. And that dive rig was caught in the netting. This was no accident.'

Janus nodded as he stared at the nearby coast, glimmering like a mirage on the horizon.

'It was the Fargos. Had to be.'

'I knew I should have shot them when I had the chance.'

Janus spun to face his brother. 'Really? That's your solution? Commit cold-blooded murder in front of a host of witnesses? Have you taken leave of your senses?' he asked through clenched teeth, then shook his head and addressed Hector. 'Very well, Hector. Bring the statue up on to the deck and pack it as agreed, and we'll hand it off at the rendezvous.'

An Algerian commercial fishing boat would be coming alongside within the hour to ferry the statue to safety, leaving the yacht to continue on its way to Majorca. In the highly unlikely event it was stopped and searched, there would be nothing to find. It would be the word of the Fargos against his, and with what he'd paid in bribes to lubricate the Spanish system, he was confident there would be no lasting trouble.

'I still say a bullet between the eyes would have solved a lot of problems,' Reginald muttered as Hector left, relieved to be off the hook for the failed expedition.

'How many times do I have to tell you that taking rash action is a fool's game? These are high stakes, and you don't have the luxury of behaving impulsively. We're playing chess, not rugby. It's all strategy, not brute force and silly risks.'

'Says the man who just lost millions by being restrained,' Reginald said, and then immediately regretted it when he saw the cold in his elder sibling's eyes.

'Well, old boy, I make the millions, so they're mine to lose, aren't they? I think you might want to reconsider any further insolence. You're the one who begged to participate in my operations – as I recall, it was you who decided that the life of a playboy had grown tiresome, not I. And you didn't complain about my approach when that young woman filed the police report in Cannes. You were more than grateful that I'm respected enough to arrange for that sort of unpleasantness to disappear.' Janus paused for a moment and sighed. 'Don't push the limits of my patience, Reginald. If you want to be a part of my business, you'll do things my way. Impetuous mistakes only bring grief, whether you believe me or not. This was nothing more than one round in a longer fight. I'm confident we'll see the Fargos again, and, when we do, things will go very differently.'

Reginald gave him a curious look, chastised but unrepentant. 'You say that as though it's fact.'

Janus put a fatherly hand on Reginald's shoulder and gestured to the breakfast bounty laid out on the circular table near the main salon.

'Patience has its own reward. This isn't over. You'll have to trust me on that.' Janus cleared his throat, the subject closed. 'The statue of Athena will bring several million from a buyer in Moscow, so at least we'll cover the fuel and sundries for our little outing, if not much more. So it wasn't a total loss. And remember this: good things come to those who wait.'

They walked to the table and took seats opposite each other, and a steward practically ran to pour them piping-hot dark roast coffee. Another arrived with glasses of fresh-squeezed orange juice, and a third stood discreetly in the background until both had been attended to before inquiring how they preferred their eggs prepared.

Reginald ordered an omelet and Janus an egg-white scramble, and when his younger brother returned his gaze to him, Janus was staring off into the distance, an expression of tranquillity on his refined features, as though the plan had gone perfectly and he had not a worry in the world. Reginald knew Janus and he knew that look. If he said it wasn't over, it wasn't, and Reginald was confident that the meddling Americans would get their just deserts at his brother's hands – for all his civilized veneer, Janus was as deadly as a cobra, and equally silent.

There would be a tally of all debts, and when that time arrived, the Fargos would pay.

Of that he was certain.

4

As morning drifted lazily by, Dominic failed to get any response from his contacts, and Remi decided to take matters into her own hands. She activated one of the satellite phones and called a familiar number. Selma Wondrash answered on the fourth ring.

'Selma? It's Remi. Sorry to call so late.'

'There you are! I haven't heard from you for almost a week. I get worried when you two go dark on me.'

'We were busy with the dive.'

'How did it go?'

'We're finished, but there's a wrinkle.'

'Isn't there always? What can I do to help?'

'What kind of contacts do you have with the Spanish Navy?'

Selma thought about it, processing furiously. 'Spanish Navy . . . let me dig around some. If I don't have an in, I can probably find someone who knows the right people. What did you have in mind?'

Remi explained her thinking and Selma grunted assent. 'I understand. Let me get on this. It's one in the morning here, but I'm still up, so might as well make use of myself.'

'I was afraid I'd woken you.'

Selma hesitated. 'No, I've been somewhat of a night owl lately. Insomnia. Comes and goes.'

'I hate that. You should take something for it – you sleep little enough as it is . . .'

'If it lasts much longer, I will. But for now, it's a good thing I was up. I'll call you back once I have something to report. Is there anything else?'

'Have the Gulfstream fueled and ready for takeoff for tomorrow evening. That'll give us the twenty-four hours we need from our last dive. File a flight plan for San Diego. We're coming home.'

'That's wonderful. Consider it done.'

Sam had purchased a Gulfstream G650 business jet with an effective range of over seventy-five hundred miles from a bank that had repossessed it from an investment group that had fallen on lean times. Since acquiring it, their ability to move around the globe had increased markedly. The extravagance was unlike him, but as the accountants had pointed out, there was never a U-Haul following the hearse at a funeral – you couldn't take it with you. The sale of the company and the ongoing royalties from Sam's latest inventions ensured that they would always have far greater financial resources than they could spend in ten lifetimes.

Remi hung up and leaned in to Sam, who was standing on the aft deck, gazing at the blue expanse of the Mediterranean distrustfully as though Benedict's yacht would reappear at any instant.

'Selma's putting on the full-court press. Knowing her, she'll have the Seventh Fleet here by lunchtime.'

Sam put an arm around her and kissed the top of her head. 'Have I told you lately how lucky I am to have you?'

She turned to face him, stood on her tiptoes, and rewarded him with a long kiss. 'I'm glad you're finally realizing it. Does this mean my spa time and hedonistic pampering start soon?'

'The moment we arrive home.'

They took in the calm sea, a few recreational craft puttering in the distance near the island, and Remi touched her lucky scarab necklace. 'All things considered, this could have been a lot worse. At least we didn't have to take on a small army of guerrillas armed only with a spade and a flintlock.'

'Ah, the good old days. You're right, of course, I just wish I'd got to that last statue in time. Thirty more seconds and we'd have had it clear.'

'I know, but you can't win them all, and I'd say that we did pretty well for a last-minute improvisation.'

Dominic approached them from the pilothouse, a dejected expression on his handsome face, the dusting of a five o'clock shadow and the red bandanna covering his hair lending him the air of a pirate. 'Still nothing. I'm afraid we won't be hearing anything until Monday, but at least the yacht has left the area, no?'

'But it might come back – and the wreck still needs guarding. We've put some things in motion on our end. It's a long shot, but you never know,' Sam said.

Dominic's eyes narrowed as he smiled his infectious Castilian grin. 'That would be wonderful. Everything's closed down at the university, so I'm getting nowhere.'

Half an hour later, Remi's satellite phone trilled and she had a murmured discussion with Selma before disconnecting. 'The cavalry's coming over the hill,' she said.

Sam nodded. 'How long?'

'Two hours. They're going to send a boat from Cartagena, but it'll take some time to get it under way.'

Sam and Remi had returned to the main deck when they heard the distant roar of large engines from the west. Remi scanned the water and pointed at a gray shape bearing down on their position. A two-hundred-foot Serviola-class naval patrol vessel approached from the harbor at Cartagena, and as it drew near she could make out its name: *Atalaya*.

They both stood and watched as it anchored nearby. They were soon joined by Dominic.

'I'd say that should keep any treasure hunters away until a proper recovery of the wreck's cargo can be mounted,' Sam said. He filled Dominic in on the predawn raid on Benedict's boat and handed him a slip of paper with coordinates scribbled on it. 'The nets are at this waypoint. The yacht's divers were kind enough to retrieve them from the wreck, so it should be child's play to raise them from the bottom.' He took another look at the warship and nodded. 'With our early-morning dive, we won't be able to fly until tomorrow. Any chance we could impose one more night?'

'A pleasure – and I'll take you to the mainland myself.'

The next morning they packed their belongings, including the night vision dive gear to return to Sam's source. Dominic shared a farewell luncheon with Sam and Remi. The crew had had a very successful fishing expedition that morning. Enjoying a last glass of the excellent local Albarino white wine, Sam said, 'We appreciate all the hospitality, Dominic. But looking at the time, we need to get ashore. Can we catch that ride you promised us?'

'Of course. Give me five minutes.'

They loaded into a fiberglass skiff, twenty-four feet long with a single powerful outboard, and then they were slicing through the gentle waves, an occasional bump and splash as they encountered a bigger swell sending a curtain of salt spray high into the air. Sam and Remi sat amidships on a hard bench seat as Dominic captained the craft from the stern. Twenty minutes later, they arrived at the commercial port in Cartagena, where, after saying their good-byes, they flagged down a taxi to take them to Murcia–San Javier Airport, fifteen miles away.

Their jet waited on the tarmac. The two pilots, Brad Sterling and Rex Fender, were running their preflight checklists while Sandra, the flight attendant, supervised the provisioning of the sleek plane, watching the catering personnel with a sharp eye as food and drink were loaded aboard. When the Fargos arrived, she greeted them warmly, her week-long vacation in Spain now at an end, and Remi noted that she'd found time to catch some sun in the seaside town, no doubt having a more relaxing time than they'd had on the *Bermudez* with a round-the-clock diving schedule.

'We filed a flight plan and should be in the air within twenty minutes, tops,' Brad informed them. 'Flight time will be eleven hours at forty-eight thousand feet, and it should be smooth sailing – we'll be above any weather.'

Sam and Remi settled into the oversize, hand-stitched leather seats. A separate cabin in the rear was furnished with a bed that occupied most of the width. Sandra had thoughtfully arranged for a chilled bottle of 2004 Veuve Clicquot La Grande Dame champagne and two crystal flutes to ease their wait for takeoff. Sam popped the cork with a flourish and poured them each a portion, which they sipped with relish.

The powerful turbines whined as Sandra closed and secured the fuselage door, and after a brief taxi to the far end of the runway the sleek jet was streaking into the sky in defiance of gravity, climbing at a steep angle over the Mediterranean before executing a gentle bank west.

Once they were at their cruising altitude, the Spanish mainland disappearing behind them, Sam and Remi logged on to their respective computer terminals to prepare for their next outing: an expedition in the northern reaches of Canada to assist in a US Coast Guard–sponsored exploration of the fjords of Baffin Island to study the cataclysmic melting of the glaciers. They'd been invited by their friend Commander Wes Hall, and would spend a week there using Sam's specialized equipment to collect data on the geophysical changes.

They touched down at San Diego International Airport just before 9 p.m., where they were greeted at the charter terminal by Selma, who was driving the Cadillac CTS-V. Remi hugged her while Sam loaded the bags into the expansive trunk and soon they were on their way to their oceanfront home in La Jolla.

'So, did you miss us?' Sam asked.

'Of course. The house isn't the same when you're not there,' Selma said.

'How's Zoltán? Is he being a good boy?' Remi asked. Zoltán was their king-sized German shepherd, brought back from Hungary after one of their adventures involving Attila the Hun's lost tomb.

'You know him. He doesn't know how to be anything but good. Although you can tell he misses you, of course. Remi, you're the love of his life. I really think if he could talk, your husband there would have a run for his money,' Selma joked.

'Hey. He's a handsome beast, but I've got opposable thumbs,' Sam reminded, and everyone laughed good-naturedly.

When they pulled into the garage, Sam and Remi could hear Zoltán barking even with the car doors still closed.

Sam said, 'You go ahead. I'll bring up the rear with the bags. Sounds like your second love is going berserk. Better say hi before he tears the wall down.'

The garage door closed behind them, and Selma popped the trunk while Remi made for the entrance. When she opened the door and stepped into the connecting hall, Zoltán's barking ceased, replaced by a low whine as his sensitive nose detected Remi's presence. She entered the kitchen to find Zoltán sitting obediently, quivering with anticipation but too disciplined to rush her. She approached, got down on one knee, and gave him a long hug, and he reciprocated with a kiss and a nuzzle, in a kind of canine heaven to have the mistress of the house finally back, his lush tail sweeping the floor in a fan of joy.

Selma came in, followed by Sam with their luggage, and Zoltán whined again, his every dream now reality. Sam dropped the bags by the refrigerator doors and clapped his hands together, inviting Zoltán to him, and the dog gladly leapt forward. Sam scratched behind his ears, and Remi joined him, petting Zoltán, as Selma watched the reunion with a smile.

'Do you want me to take your stuff up to your room?' Selma asked.

Remi shook her head. 'Sam will do it. After a week of loafing around, he could use the exercise.'

'That's right. It was nothing but gin and donuts out on the water. I let Remi do all the hard work. Didn't want to pull something or hurt myself,' Sam said.

Selma's poker face didn't twitch. 'Well, then, if you don't mind, I'm going to call it a night. I'll see you both in the morning.'

'Thanks for picking us up, Selma,' Remi said.

'No problem. All in a day's work,' Selma said, and then retired to her suite.

Up in the master bedroom, Remi threw herself down on the king-sized bed with a sigh of happiness, Zoltán already curled up on the floor by the footboard.

'It's good to be back,' Sam said. 'And as an added bonus, the floor's not rocking. I'm going to take a shower. I'll be out in a minute.'

'Relax. We've got nowhere to be.'

'Yeah, but the time difference has got me coming and going. I don't know whether I should be having breakfast or a nightcap.'

Remi sat up. 'Did Selma seem odd to you?'

'Odd? In what way?' Sam asked as he pulled off his shirt.

'I don't know. Subdued. Maybe a little preoccupied.'

'Possibly. But didn't you tell me she's been having problems sleeping recently? I know I get kind of grumpy when I'm short on rest.'

'Kind of grumpy? More like a bear whose hibernation was disturbed.'

'Bears need "me time," too. Maybe you should talk

to her tomorrow. Ask her. As for me, I've got seven thousand miles of travel dust to hose off.'

'I didn't see much dust inside the plane you wing us away on these days.'

'You know what I mean. And soon, squeaky clean as a newborn.'

'I'll be the judge of that.'

5

Selma was already up, the rich aroma of coffee in the air, when Sam and Remi made it down to the research level of the house, where morning sun streamed through the floor-to-ceiling windows. The Pacific's calm blue spread before them like a lapis tapestry, and Selma was gazing out at the view.

'Good morning, Selma. How are you today? Sleep any better?' Remi asked as she poured herself a cup.

Selma turned, seemingly startled by their arrival, a troubled look on her face.

'Oh, Mrs Fargo! No, I didn't. I . . . I'm not good at some things, and I guess this is one of them . . .'

'Selma. What's wrong?' Remi asked. And Sam joined her, both obviously concerned.

'I want you to promise you won't overreact,' Selma said.

'Overreact to what?' Sam demanded, and then softened when Remi threw him a sharp look.

'That's what I was afraid of,' Selma muttered.

'Don't worry about him. He's just grouchy in the mornings. You should know that by now. Just tell us what's going on, Selma,' Remi coaxed.

'I've never said anything before, but my hips have

finally got so bad that I have to have them both replaced.'

'Oh no, Selma. I'm so sorry to hear it,' Remi said.

Selma drew a long breath, as if steeling herself to dive off a cliff. 'I went to the doctor about a week and a half ago, and they say I can't put it off any longer.'

'Selma! Why didn't you tell us? No wonder you haven't been sleeping,' Sam said.

'I know I should have said something. But the timing is terrible. We've got so much going on, and you're leaving in a couple of days. I just don't want to let you down. You're both so busy.'

'Nonsense, Selma. You're one of the family.'

'When do they want to do this?' Sam asked.

'They've scheduled me for surgery in six days. At Scripps.'

'That's one of the best in the country, isn't it?'

'Absolutely.'

'We're canceling our trip to Baffin Island, or at least postponing it, until you're back in the saddle and recovered,' Remi said, her tone firm, moving to Selma and giving her a long hug.

'Oh no. That's exactly what I don't want. Please, just do what you planned to do. I would feel terrible if you canceled your trip. There's nothing you can do, anyway.'

'Yes there is,' Sam replied. 'I'll arrange for the rehab equipment you need to be set up here. You can come home directly from the hospital and we'll find the best physical therapist. You'll have twenty-four/seven care if I have anything to say about this.'

They were interrupted by the bathroom door closing. A young woman with a severe haircut, dyed black with shocking-red highlights, wearing black jeans and an avocado T-shirt, stood looking at them all. Selma pulled away from Remi and cleared her throat.

'I was waiting to introduce everyone. This is my niece, Kendra Hollingsworth. I asked her to come over and meet you. She's going to be helping out while I'm . . . in the hospital and recovering. Kendra? Come meet Sam and Remi Fargo.'

Kendra stepped forward and shook hands with Remi and then with Sam. He noticed that she had a tattoo on her neck and on the inside of her wrist, and a small twinkling dot on her nose – a piercing.

'Nice to meet you,' Kendra said, her voice demure.

'Likewise,' Sam said with a quick glance at Remi, whose face was impassive.

'Kendra recently graduated from USC and she's got some time on her hands, so she graciously agreed to help out,' Selma said, aware of the slight tension in the room. 'I've known her since she was a baby and she's one of the smartest people I've ever met. And an amazing talent.'

'What did you major in, Kendra?' Remi asked.

'Computer science and history, a double major. I wanted to go for mathematics as well, but it was too heavy a load.'

'That's impressive,' Sam said.

Kendra shrugged. 'Not so much, once you start looking for a decent job. At least, not in this environment. It's either programming or going for a teaching credential – neither of which really interests me much. So I was really excited when Selma asked me to help out . . .'

'Have you introduced Kendra to Pete and Wendy yet?' Sam asked.

'Not yet. I was going to do it tomorrow. I wanted to give Kendra an orientation today, being as it's quiet, Sunday and all.'

Remi moved to Sam's side. 'Selma, I want to hear more about your plans. Can you make some time to have lunch with me today?'

'Of course. I want to show Kendra how the systems are networked and take her through everything we're working on right now. But I should be done by, let's say . . . one?'

'That would be perfect. Pick a place.'

'Oh, you know me, wherever's fine.'

'Then I'll think of someplace special and make a reservation. Come on, Sam. Let's leave them to it,' Remi said, and they made their way back up to the living area.

'She seems awfully young, doesn't she?' Remi whispered as the door closed behind them.

'We were all young once, remember? As I recall, I was pretty good at what I was doing at that age.'

'Poor Selma. She looks so down. I mean, she's

putting a brave face on it, but she's got to be in a lot of pain. I know her too well. You can see it in her eyes.'

'I know. Thank goodness she's getting top-notch care.'

'Still, it's . . . I mean, we just take for granted that she'll always be here helping us. And then something like this happens . . .'

'See what you can glean at lunch. And stay positive. Attitude's important. Oh, and of course tell her that whatever she needs, no matter what, she's got it. Any treatment, any physical therapist, wherever in the world . . . whatever. All she has to do is say the word.'

'I will. Knowing Selma, the biggest hurdle will be keeping her from coming back to work too early. You know how she loves it.'

'I do, but Pete and Wendy are no slouches. Between them all, things will be fine. Plus, it's not like we're going to need tremendous support charting glacier shrinkage. It'll be about as exciting as . . . well, watching ice melt.'

Remi walked to the open sliding glass doors and paused at the threshold, a light ocean breeze caressing her hair. 'What's with the tattoos?'

Sam shrugged. 'It's the thing these days. Seems like everyone's got them.'

'I just hope she's . . . stable.'

Sam joined her and put his arms around her, hugging her from behind. 'Maybe that was her act of rebellion in college. We all had our share. Remember?'

'Speak for yourself. I was a good girl.'

61

'You still are. The best. You just don't have particularly good taste in men.'

'I'm willing to overlook your faults. Besides, you smell good.'

'You got me this cologne for my birthday.'

She turned and sniffed his chest, and then gave him a long kiss, before pulling back and looking deeply into his eyes. 'Score one for the lady.'

That night, Remi and Sam enjoyed dinner at the Valencia Hotel, just down from their house, the appetizer of fresh calamari and an entrée of blackened bluefin tuna as good as any they'd tasted. Sam ordered a bottle of 2010 Cobos Reserve Malbec, which was the perfect accompaniment for the fish, complementing its powerful spice-and-pepper seasoning with rich currant and chocolate notes. Conversation revolved around Selma, her upcoming operation, and their misgivings about having to leave on Tuesday morning after only two full days at home.

'Remind me not to pack our schedule this densely next time around,' Sam said as they watched the surf break on the beach before pulling at its sand in a never-ending rinse-and-repeat cycle.

'It's not all your fault. I agreed, remember?'

'So it's *your* fault! After all, you're supposed to be the brains of the outfit.'

'I must have missed that memo, Mr Cal Tech Inventor Guy.'

'Hey, we all get lucky once in a while.'

After Sam paid the check, they meandered through the hotel lobby's oversize mission-style doorway and up the street to the path that cut across the lawn to their house. On the road in front, a figure in a dark sedan focused a telephoto lens and took a series of photos of the couple, their silhouettes framed against the night sky, illuminated by a full moon.

Sam slowed for a moment and leaned into Remi as his eyes roamed over the street to their right. 'Don't be alarmed but I think we're being watched.'

'From where?' Remi asked, her voice low as she continued to match Sam's pace.

'I can't be sure, but I thought I saw movement in one of the cars on the road.'

'That could be anything. Young lovers. A dog. Someone getting ready to start their car or lock it.'

'All true. But usually by this hour, the area's shut down for the night.'

'So what's your game plan?'

'You stop, throw your arms around me, and kiss me, with you facing the ocean. That will give me a chance to scope out the street.'

'Is this some tricky maneuver to get your way with me?'

'I think you've seen most of my moves by now.'

'That's what you always say and then you produce a new one.'

'Kiss me, you gorgeous creature. Now, before I'm another minute older.'

Remi stopped, turned, and, stretching up on her tip-toes, she threw her arms around Sam's neck.

Sam scanned the few cars parked along the sidewalk and spotted the sedan. Moonlight caught the camera lens, which glinted as it moved, confirming his suspicions.

Remi broke from her kiss when Sam squeezed her waist, and they began walking again, now a short way from their house.

'I saw something, possibly a lens, reflecting light, in one of the cars. The good news is that it isn't fixed to a rifle.'

'How do you know?' Remi asked, suddenly serious.

'Because we're both still alive. The not-so-good news is that someone's definitely watching us.'

'That's alarming. I wonder why? Could it be autograph hunters or something?'

'Very funny. Let's get inside and check to make sure the security systems are on. Then I'll go for a little walk and see if I can straighten out whoever it is.'

'Why don't we just call the police?'

'And say what? That I saw something shiny in one of the cars? How seriously do you think that'll be taken?'

'I guess you've got a point,' Remi conceded.

'Even a broken clock's right twice a day.'

Selma had already retired when they entered the house, and after double-checking all the sensors and the alarm from the central control panel Sam deactivated the door on the side of the garage and slipped out into the night. The street was quiet, the only sound the crashing of waves on the rocks at the tip of Gold-fish Point and the distant hum of traffic from Torrey Pines Road. Sam crept on rubber soles around the first parked vehicle and made his way to where the watcher was parked, keeping below the level of the windows just in case.

When he was almost to the sedan, his heart sank. There, in front of him, was an empty parking space, seven cigarette butts on the asphalt the only indication anyone had been waiting there.

Sam stood up straight, hands on his hips, and stared down the street.

The car was gone.

6

Tuesday morning arrived in the blink of an eye, and when Selma dropped Sam and Remi off at the airport for their trip to Baffin Island, they both embraced her for a long time, Zoltán by her side, standing attentively, flinching as jets took off overhead. Remi knelt and gave the German shepherd a kiss and scratched his chin.

'I hate to leave you alone again, big boy,' she crooned in his ear. A tail wag assured her that he understood, and when Remi stood, his gaze followed her with boundless affection.

'Let us know how the surgery turns out,' Sam asked Selma, who nodded in response, clearly embarrassed to be the center of attention.

'I'm just a little nervous, but the doctor said that they do dozens of this kind of procedure every day. It's really nothing,' she assured them.

'I'm sure it'll be over in no time,' Remi said. 'But please, Selma, humor us. Let us know how it goes and how you're doing afterward. We're both very concerned.'

'I promise I will.' Selma cleared her throat. 'Now on to more pressing things . . . The equipment I arranged for arrived in Baffin Island yesterday. I've got a charter flight waiting in Iqaluit to take you to Clyde River

Airport, assuming there are no delays. The runway at Clyde River's way too short to accommodate the jet, so it'll be a prop ride for you on that leg.'

'Sounds like you've got everything covered, as usual,' Sam said.

Selma blushed. 'If there's anything you need I haven't anticipated, Pete and Wendy can handle it. You've got your satellite phone, so you're never more than a call away. Besides, by the time you're finished doing the glacier survey I'll be back on deck, ready for anything, as always.'

Selma looked down at Zoltán and moved to the car. When she opened the rear door, Zoltán shot by her, a black-and-brown furry streak of lightning. 'Looks like somebody's ready to get going. He does so love to be on the road, though he's probably wondering where breakfast is.'

A flight crewman retrieved their bags from the trunk of the car and carried them into the small charter building, where Sandra was awaiting them, perky as ever. She led them on to the tarmac and up the stairs and stowed their things in the cabin while Sam and Remi took their seats. They were airborne in minutes, and, once they hit their cruising altitude, Sandra served a light breakfast of pastries and fruit.

Six hours went by quickly while they both worked on their computers, and when they touched down at Iqaluit International Airport on the southern side of Baffin Island, they were rested and ready for the next stage of their journey. The Gulfstream taxied to the terminal area, where a number of small prop planes sat off to one side. A single-prop Cessna Caravan was parked near the edge of the tarmac, with two men fueling it and preparing it for flight.

'Want to bet that's our ride?' Sam asked.

Remi reached over and squeezed his hand. 'It'll be slow going the rest of the way.'

The G650 rolled to a stop and Sandra opened the door. A blast of Arctic wind blew in, instantly chilling them, and Remi thanked Providence for the winter coats they'd brought. Going from seventy-degree San Diego weather to below freezing was going to be a shock, they knew, but there was no getting around it, and it would be even colder off the eastern coast of Baffin, the fifth-largest island in the world and the biggest in the Arctic Archipelago, much of its shores covered in ice year-round.

'Don't look at me like that. We both signed off on this, remember?' Sam said in response to the glare Remi threw him.

'I didn't really take into account the cold. Or all the snow.'

'It won't be that long. Only a week. And the ship should have heat. At least, I hope it will.'

'I can't feel my feet.'

'Oh come on, we're still on the plane.'

'We're getting out?'

'That's the spirit,' Sam said, and then stepped out

on to the stairs. A frigid gust cut across the runway and hit him like a cold slap and he silently wondered if Remi didn't have a point. 'See? It's like being on Maui,' he declared.

Remi gave him one of her looks and reluctantly trudged after him. The taller of the two men near the Cessna waved and approached. 'Mr and Mrs Fargo?'

'That depends on whether there's heat on the boat,' Remi said.

The man looked at them, puzzled, and Sam tried a grin, hoping his face wouldn't crack.

'That's us. You must be the welcome committee.'

The taller man nodded and extended a hand. 'I suppose so. Let's get your things stowed. We don't want to lose the light. Landing at Clyde River can be challenging even under the best of circumstances. You don't want to do it in the dark. By the way, I'm Rick.'

'Rick, nice to meet you. You sound like you know the area pretty well,' Sam said.

'You could say that. Been flying these parts for over twenty years.'

Rick wasn't talkative once in the air, which suited Sam and Remi just fine. The Caravan droned along on the four-hundred-and-fifty-mile trek, and there was less than a half hour of light remaining when the gravel landing strip of Clyde River Airport came into view through the scattered clouds. The plane touched down without incident, and in moments they stopped in front of a small Quonset hut that passed for a terminal.

Two men exited the structure, wearing heavy jackets and knit caps. As Rick opened the door, Sam immediately recognized Commander Wes Hall, the head of the research mission and an old friend.

'Sam, Remi, good to see you again. Although it would be nicer if this duty was in Fiji,' Hall said as Rick retrieved their bags from the hold.

'Be pretty tough to map glacier melting rates there, though, wouldn't it?' Remi asked with a smile.

Sam nodded. 'Serves you right for not having the foresight to investigate something more fun. Like maybe coral density on the Great Barrier Reef.'

'That's why I'm a simple Coast Guard officer and you're the hotshot adventurers.'

'Right now, I think the word "hot" in any context might be a stretch,' Remi quipped.

'Indeed. This is my first officer, Lieutenant Ralph Willbanks. Lieutenant, may I present Sam and Remi Fargo?'

They shook hands, their breath steaming in the frosty air.

'I've heard a lot about you,' Willbanks said.

'You can't believe everything the commander tells you,' Sam warned.

'I left out the dragon slaying and the ability to levitate,' Hall said.

The group chuckled.

Rick arrived with their bags. Willbanks shouldered both, and Hall waved at a waiting Hummer. Inside, a

Canadian Navy ensign had the diesel engine running and the heat blowing. Remi crawled in the backseat with a sigh of relief, followed by Sam. Hall took the front passenger seat, and Willbanks slid in next to Sam and pulled the door closed.

As the big vehicle bounced down a rutted dirt track, Hall said, 'We're only a few minutes away. The ship's anchored in Patricia Bay. We'll overnight there, and be under way by 5 a.m. The ice waits for no man . . .'

'I don't suppose you've got any Scotch to go with the ice, do you?' Sam asked.

'Actually, once we're up in the fjords, you can make cocktails with glacier ice. Makes everything taste better, I hear. But I'm afraid I'm dry for the duration. Duty calls and all. Don't want to set a bad example, carousing with civilians.'

'As long as there are no prohibitions against the hired help having a bracer now and again, I'm in.'

'If you were being paid, you'd be hired. As it is, helping fund this expedition makes you honored guests, and my motto is to treat guests with all possible hospitality.'

'I like the way you think. How cold is it out, anyway?' Remi asked.

'A toasty three degrees Fahrenheit. But don't worry – it gets up as high as six during the hottest part of the day.'

'I don't suppose you have spa or massage facilities on board?'

'That gets installed after this mission. Sorry, I thought you got the memo,' Hall said.

They rounded a bend and entered the small town of Clyde River, its grim, weather-beaten shacks shabby and uninviting. A few of the houses had lights on, the residents huddled inside against the constant cold, as dusk banished the weak glow of the sun to its nightly refuge behind the surrounding mountains.

'Where's the casino?' Sam asked.

'Floating in the bay. Every day aboard's a crapshoot on a shakeout cruise like this.'

'Oh, is she new?'

'Roger that. The *Alhambra*'s the latest technology, and she was just launched two months ago. A hundred-and-forty-foot cutter with improved light ice-breaking ability. The older Bay-class cutters can handle up to twenty inches of ice. This beauty ups that to nearly three feet.'

'And that's considered light?' Sam asked.

'Compared to her four- and five-hundred-foot siblings, it is. But those would be impractical to take into the fjords. The *Alhambra*'s the perfect fit – agile enough to explore the coast without fear of grounding and hardy enough to break through the ice crust that even in the late spring and early summer coats the surface.'

'Oh, there she is,' Remi said, pointing at the vessel in the bay, the distinctive red racing-stripe logo of the US Coast Guard emblazoned on her white hull near the bow, her lights reflecting off the placid surface of the black water. 'She looks bigger than a hundred and forty feet.'

'She's beamy. Almost thirty-eight feet. And brawny. I like the design a lot. Not great in beam seas because of her round underside, but that's true of almost all ice-breakers,' Hall explained.

The truck slowed to a stop, gravel crunching beneath its oversize tires, and everyone got out. The wind sliced through Sam's and Remi's winter coats like they were made of linen. Remi hugged herself in an effort to keep her teeth from chattering.

Hall nodded knowingly and said, 'I've got two Arctic explorer jackets with your names on them.'

'Thanks, Wes. You're a gentleman. Between you and my husband, you've made this a kind of dream second honeymoon.'

'Sam's always had a soft spot, I know.'

'Truer words were never spoken,' Sam agreed.

Willbanks made a call on his radio, and, after a crackling acknowledgment, a skiff that was tied behind the *Alhambra* started with a stuttering roar and made its way to their position on the shore. Sam and Remi followed the two Coast Guard officers down the sloping bank, and in no time they were cutting across the water to the waiting ship.

'Selma tells me that all the equipment made it in one piece?' Sam shouted to Hall as they slowed near the research vessel.

'It did. I had my techs wire it into our systems and verify everything.'

As soon as they boarded, Hall took them on a tour of the ship and introduced them to the fifteen-man crew, then showed them to their cabin – a snug stateroom with a small bathroom and shower, built more for efficiency than comfort. Remi looked the quarters over without comment as he pointed out the various levers and knobs that controlled everything from an intercom to the temperature, and then Hall took his leave after inviting them to dinner once the men had chowed down.

When the watertight door closed behind the commander, Remi moved to the bed and tested its firmness with a tentative hand.

'It's going to be a long trip,' she said.

'Hey, at least it's got heat. Just pretend we're camping out.'

'Because I so love camping.'

'You've spent enough time in the field with me, roughing it.'

'The key word in all that is "enough."'

'Seven days. Seven short days at sea. It's like a private cruise –'

'Into a frozen hell. Can I get a refund?'

'I'm afraid once you're on the ride, you're on it.'

'I suppose it's too cold to swim to shore.'

Dinner was surprisingly good, and after an hour of

swapping stories and catching up on lost time with Hall Sam and Remi returned to their room, replete but tired after a full day of traveling. They drifted off to sleep, the heavy ship swaying gently in the river's current.

7

The thrumming of the twin diesel engines vibrated the entire ship as the *Alhambra* moved north into the Arctic Circle, plowing through the swells just off the northern coast of Baffin Island. The trip had been fruitful so far, and by the third day the ship had traveled a hundred and sixty miles north of Clyde River. The team had surveyed four fjords, mapping the bottom and measuring the amount of shrinkage of the glaciers. The exploration had settled into a routine – up at dawn, under way within an hour, taking advantage of the daylight that seemed to go on forever.

The rpm's dropped as the vessel approached the day's target, a sliver of blue that faded into icy white before them. A row of mountains loomed on both sides like guardians over a barren, hidden kingdom at the top of the world. The surface of the sea began crackling as they neared the fjord, a thin skin of ice lingering even as spring grudgingly prepared to transition into summer.

Hall stood at the pilothouse windows while the helmsman beside him manned the wheel, pointing the cutter's bow inland to follow the fjord wherever it might lead.

'Cuts through the ice like butter, doesn't it?' Sam

commented. He stood in front of a bank of monitors, where the computers recorded a host of measurements from the specialized instrumentation he'd provided.

'The secret's a low-pressure air hull-lubrication system that drives air between the hull and the ice. It reduces the pressure on the hull and increases the vertical shear, so the ice cracks with far less pressure than on the old-style ships,' Hall explained as he raised his binoculars and studied the area ahead. 'It looks like this forks off to the right. Let's check the satellite footage again.'

Hall moved to a monitor and zoomed in on their location, the technician obligingly focusing on the yellow pulsing icon that represented their position.

'See that? The glacier up ahead used to come down another mile. You can see how it's receded over time.' He peered at the screen. 'What do you say, Connelly? You think we can squeeze through that channel?' he asked, tapping the screen with his finger.

The tech did a quick measurement on-screen and nodded. 'Yes, sir. But it'll be tight. This shows the gap at less than a hundred feet. One wrong move and we'll be on the rocks.'

Remi mounted the stairs as they neared the gap. The ice thickened as they proceeded, and the base of the mountains loomed on either side of them.

'It's magnificent, isn't it?' she said, admiring the incredible landscape and its wild beauty.

'That it is, that it is,' Sam said, keeping his eyes fixed on the screens.

'You aren't even looking.'

'I saw it before, on approach. Now I'm earning my keep.'

She moved forward, a few feet from Hall, and watched as the ship drew near the gap.

'That looks awfully tight,' she said.

'It's one of the reasons we're using this dinghy instead of one of the big boys. Maneuverability,' Hall explained.

The ship eased into the narrow channel, the dark brown rock towering overhead only a stone's throw from either gunwale, and the helmsman pulled back on the throttles even farther. And then they were through, into a long fjord ringed by sheer cliffs so tall they blocked all but the ambient light of the sun.

'See that? Looks like it stretches for another mile and a half and then ends where the glacier meets the water,' Hall said, gesturing ahead. 'According to a study of satellite footage, a thousand years ago the glacier used to extend all the way to where we are now.'

'Well . . . that's strange,' Sam said, leaning forward and studying the display. 'The magnetometer. It's going nuts.'

'"Nuts"? Is that the technical term?' Hall asked.

'It's just weird. The readings are all over the place. Like there's something in the ice.' He stared at the readout.

'An ore deposit?' Remi asked.

'Not like any I've ever seen. I'm getting a signal fifty

yards ahead that doesn't indicate natural mineral readings. No, this looks like . . . It looks like a structure.'

'Out here?' Hall exclaimed. 'Maybe an old fishing boat?'

'That's unlikely,' Sam replied.

Hall asked, 'Can you get a bearing on it?'

'Maybe forty-five yards now, fifteen degrees starboard.'

'Over by that rise in the snow?'

'Correct.'

'Helmsman. Go easy. Get us as close as you can, but don't sink us.'

'Aye, aye, sir.'

The *Alhambra* inched forward, the crackling of the ice against the hull now becoming a groan, and then it ground to a stop. The helmsman backed off the throttles and took the transmissions out of gear and then looked to Hall expectantly.

'What does all that high-priced junk of yours say?' Hall asked Sam.

'That we're about fifteen yards out from whatever it's picking up.'

'Maybe a downed plane?' Remi suggested. 'Or some refuse left over from World War Two?'

'Anything's possible, but this looks fairly deep in the ice. Whatever's down there didn't get there recently.' Sam paused. 'But it's really odd. Unless I'm misreading this, it's not submerged. It's on the surface.'

'I don't see anything,' Remi said.

'That's because the ice increases in depth all along the coast. It's probably twenty feet thick by the time there's actual rock beneath it,' Sam said, studying the area in question through the pilothouse windows.

'Well, now what?' Hall asked.

Sam took a final look at the screens and rose. 'I'd say it's time to go for a walk.'

Hall, Sam, Remi and three crewmen made their cautious way across the slippery, snow-dusted surface. Sam noted the gradual incline as they neared the mysterious target and calculated they'd climbed fifteen feet higher than the surface of the fjord by the time they were on top of whatever it was. The metal detector began screeching like a terrified gull when he swept it over the slight rise. He carefully moved along, dragging his foot, tracing a rough outline where the readings stopped. When he was done, the outline was roughly thirty yards long.

'Can you get some more men here?' Sam asked. 'With tools to dig? Hopefully, you have some on board . . .'

'A few picks and shovels, and a crowbar or two,' Hall said, gazing at the outline.

After two hours of the team's chipping away at the ice, one of the crewmen gave a cry. Sam and Remi hurried to his position.

Sam knelt down and examined the brown material, then stood and considered the outline again. 'It's wood.'

'I can see that. Question is why it registered on your scope.'

'Because there's more than wood down there. Has to be iron, and a variety of other metals.'

Remi held his gaze. 'Are you thinking what I'm thinking?' she asked.

'I don't want to get too excited or jump to any conclusions just yet.' Sam turned to the men, who had stopped gouging at the ice. 'Be careful. Dig on the outside of the wood. You can see the line where it disappears into the ice. Stay on the far side of it.'

More seamen arrived at Willbanks's urging, and soon they were hacking at the frost with whatever they could find – shovels, picks, pry bars, hammers. By the end of the afternoon, much of the buried structure was exposed, and there was no question about what it was.

'A Viking ship,' Remi said, her voice laced with awe.

Sam nodded. 'Indeed. The first ever discovered on Baffin. There've been some finds in Greenland, but never here. This is exciting. It's in perfect condition. The ice preserved everything.'

'What's this? Can you make it out?' she called to him from the middle of the long craft.

'What are you talking about?' Sam asked as he joined her. Remi was squinting into the ice at the interior of the vessel.

'I see something.'

Sam cupped a hand over his eyes and peered into the gloom, then shook his head. 'The light's fading. I can't tell.' He called over his shoulder, 'Anyone got a flashlight?'

Two minutes later, Willbanks arrived with a long black-aluminum light and snapped it on before handing it to Sam.

'Thanks,' Sam said, and directed the beam into the ice, which was opaque in places. The light seemed to disappear as it penetrated the milky parts, and then it shined across the object of Remi's attention. Remi jumped back. Sam continued gazing into the ice.

A man's sightless blue eyes stared into eternity from within his frozen prison, a puzzled, peaceful expression on his face, as he clutched the remnants of a torn sail, his scraggly blond beard plainly visible even with a heavy animal-skin cloak draped over him in a futile, centuries-old bid to stave off the inevitable.

8

Sam and Remi sat in the pilothouse with Hall and Will-banks after dinner, watching the night shift continue its work on the Viking craft, struggling to reclaim the thousand-year-old ship from nature's cold embrace. Powerful portable work lights illuminated the area, and the *Alhambra*'s main spotlight was directed at the stern of the ancient vessel as it emerged in fits and starts.

'This is an amazing find. I mean, really. An authentic Viking longship in flawless condition, with its crew perfectly preserved. I've never heard of anything remotely like it,' Remi said, voicing what was on everyone's minds.

'It is indeed. The research value alone is immeasurable,' Sam added.

Hall asked, 'What do you count? Ten in the boat so far? A ship like that would carry, what, eighty, ninety men?'

'No way of knowing for sure, but if I had to guess, I'd say the boat took shelter here, maybe from the weather. Perhaps the rest of the men went to find an alternative passage back to the sea or went foraging. We might get some answers as we uncover more of the ship.'

Remi shuddered involuntarily. 'Imagine what it must have been like for these last survivors. Starving to death, freezing, knowing they'd never see their homeland or family again, dying in a wasteland . . .'

'The only good thing is that hypothermia is painless,' Hall said. 'You just drift off and at some point your heart stops pumping blood to your brain. So at least it's unlikely they suffered in the end.'

'Still, it's creepy, you have to admit. That one . . . the way he's just staring into nothingness.'

The table went silent as they considered Remi's comment, and then Sam stood.

'With any luck, we should be able to have the entire boat excavated enough to do a more thorough inspection by the end of the day tomorrow. I don't know about you guys but I'm beat. It's been a while since I spent the day on a chain gang.'

Remi rose with a smile. 'I'll second that. Gentlemen, thanks so much for committing the crew to doing this. I know it's not part of the expedition objective.'

'Are you kidding?' Hall said. 'This is part of history. Although you bring up an important point – one I've been thinking about. We'll need to move on, sooner rather than later, and complete the mapping of the fjords and the glacier analysis. Unfortunately, we're on a schedule. While there's some flexibility in it, the *Alhambra*'s earmarked for other duty after this tour and I've got to at least try to stay on track.'

Sam nodded. 'No question the analysis is important.

Let me put my thinking cap on and see if I can come up with a solution. I hate to just leave this to the elements while we wait for someone to get up here and take over the find. You radioed it in, right?'

'Yes. I'm waiting for a more detailed response,' Willbanks replied, 'but the preliminary from the Canadians is that they'll send a team as soon as possible. But that's not as easy as it sounds. They'll need to assemble staff and equipment, find a suitable ship, outfit it –'

'I know the challenges all too well. But it is what it is. We'll make the best of what we have and figure something out,' Sam assured him.

Remi took Sam's hand and pulled him toward the companionway that led to their stateroom. 'Good night. Please make sure that they're careful as they get more of the boat uncovered. Better to work slower and with greater care . . .'

'Message received,' Hall said. 'Good night to you both as well.'

By 3 p.m. the next day, the longship was almost completely excavated. Sam and Remi were undertaking the more detailed work on the interior of the vessel, and they'd agreed to leave the ten corpses encapsulated in a thin layer of ice for preservation.

Remi tapped at the first of the wooden chests lined along both sides of the hull, where the oarsmen sat and which contained the only real storage on the ship other than a small compartment in the hull. They'd discovered the shattered mast lying in the center aisle, where it had been stowed, and only a few of the oars were still there – the absent ones probably used for firewood before the remaining crew had starved and frozen to death.

'Sam? Come here. I think I've got this one clear of ice,' Remi called.

Sam nodded from his position fifteen feet away, where he was chipping carefully with a hammer and chisel.

'You're faster than I am,' he said as he moved cautiously toward her over the slippery deck.

Together, they pried open the top of the chest, and Sam set it carefully aside. Remi reached in and withdrew a small statue of a figure of carved obsidian.

'That doesn't look Nordic,' Sam said from behind her.

She handed it to him wordlessly and retrieved a beautifully painted clay bowl. 'This is . . . incredible. Look at the condition. It's like it's only a few weeks old. I've never seen anything like this before.'

He took it from her and studied it. 'Unbelievable.'

Wes Hall approached from where he was supervising the work clearing the bow. He eyed the bowl that Sam held but didn't comment.

Remi lifted a pounded copper mask and regarded it with practised scrutiny.

'Care to venture an opinion?' Sam whispered, unable to believe his eyes.

'Not an opinion,' she answered in a voice that

betrayed shock. 'None of it's European. All of these artifacts are pre-Columbian.'

'Are you suggesting Aztec?' Hall said skeptically.

Remi shook her head. 'I'm no expert on pre-Columbian art, but I'll bet a bottle of fine cognac that's where they came from a thousand years ago. I'd have to guess the Olmecs, Toltecs, or Mayans. Perhaps another culture from Middle America. This predates the Aztecs, I think.'

'What are they doing on a Viking ship in the Arctic?' Hall asked.

Sam shrugged. 'I can't begin to guess.'

Remi continued inventorying the contents of the chest, noting the number of statues within, most covered with glyphs. This was a treasure trove beyond their comprehension – not of gold or silver coins, but proof that the Vikings had traveled the coast of America and been in close contact with the native groups there. When she was done, she carefully photographed all of the items for future study and replaced them in their original resting places in the chest. Sam returned to the box he'd been working on, and when he'd cleared enough ice from the plain wooden container, he pried the top up.

'More of the same,' he said, holding aloft a delicately crafted orange ceramic urn before giving it to Remi.

The afternoon passed quickly as they opened two more chests, which contained more ancient pre-Columbian artifacts as well as some of the oarsmen's personal effects. Deep in the ship's hold, Sam discovered a heavy stone slab with carvings ringing the edges – a Viking rune stone. Fairly common across Scandinavia, this one was smaller than those used as primitive grave headstones, but neither Sam nor Remi could read the ancient Norse writing, so they photographed it and earmarked it for more detailed examination later. By dinnertime, they had discovered a wealth of artifacts that made it obvious that the ship was a find that would change history.

Sam and Hall agreed to temporarily halt the excavation on the longship now that the scope of the discovery was evident. They spent a half hour on the radio with excited staff from the Canadian Archaeological Association and Waterloo University, as well as the Canadian Historical Association in Montreal. Everyone agreed that an expedition would need to be mounted immediately and that the site couldn't be left unattended, given the importance of the artifacts. By the end of the discussion, Sam had made an agreement that he dreaded discussing with Remi, but there was no way around it.

'You did what?' she demanded, arms folded across her chest as she sat on the bed in their quarters, an expression of incredulity on her face.

'I volunteered us to spend some time camped out on the ice.' Before Remi could object, he added, 'You saw what's in those chests. There's no way we could just continue on with the *Alhambra* knowing that's there.

Come on. I know you. And you know me. This is the kind of thing dreams are made of.'

Remi held her stern frown for a few more seconds and then relaxed, unable to stay annoyed at her husband for very long. 'You really owe me now. It's bad enough to be stuck on this sardine can, but now I have to camp on a glacier? There isn't enough spa time in the world to make up for that.'

'Wes says he has special tents that are insulated. And propane heaters. It won't be as bad as you think,' Sam said, and then reconsidered that tack. The words sounded stupid to him even as he uttered them. Of course it would be that bad. It was five below and they'd be on the ice for at least a week, maybe more. 'But no question that I owe you. Anything you can imagine, I'll do.'

'Anything?'

'Absolutely.'

'I'm going to remember that.'

The next morning Sam and Remi watched as the *Alhambra* backed away and broke free from its position in the ice with a series of staccato cracks. Behind them, a large silver insulated tent with reflective coating stood like a forlorn orphan – their new home, stocked with as much comfort as was available from the ship's stores.

'At least refrigeration won't be a problem,' Sam said.

'Silver lining to every cloud, huh?'

'When you get lemons . . .'

The ship reversed for another dozen yards and then

executed a three-point turn so it could break through the new ice using its bow. They watched as it neared the narrow channel and then sailed out of sight, the fading rumble of its throaty diesel engines the sole trace of its passage other than a jostling trail of fragmented surface ice.

A silence settled over the fjord.

'Finally. I thought they'd never leave.'

'I know. The crowds drive me nutty,' Remi agreed.

'Stupid kids, with their music and parties and everything.'

'Maybe now I can finally get some work done.'

Remi absently fingered the gold scarab on her neck as an icy gust blew remnants of snow around their feet. Sam nodded and turned from the fjord's mouth.

'You really like your good-luck talisman there, I see.'

'It's served us well so far. We just discovered a perfectly preserved longship and we weren't even looking for it.'

'Can't argue with success.'

Remi dug around in her oversize explorer jacket and found the satellite phone. She pressed a speed dial number and waited for the call to connect. Kendra answered on the third ring, and Remi was happy to note that she sounded sharp and efficient.

'Kendra? It's Remi Fargo.'

'Mrs Fargo, how are you? We got the messages you sent about the longship. That's got to be exciting.'

'Yes, it is. It's amazing. One of the most exciting

finds we've ever made. But that's not why I'm calling. How's Selma?'

'The surgery went as planned and she's starting her physical therapy in the hospital. They expect to keep her another two or three days and then she'll be home. All the equipment's arrived so that Selma can continue her PT at the house.'

'Be sure to tell her that we called and are wishing her well.'

'Of course.'

'Did Pete and Wendy have any luck on the research we asked them to do?'

'I'm helping them and we're still running checks, but while it looks like there are a number of reports of Vikings in the Americas before Columbus, there's no evidence on any one of them as being genuine. There are those who claim they were here and others who have alternative explanations.'

'Welcome to the world of archaeology. The good news is that this find will close any further debate. There's no other explanation for the artifacts we're finding. But all of you keep looking.'

'We will. We're all getting along great, and Pete has been especially helpful.'

'That's good to hear. Listen, Kendra, moving and restoring this ship is going to be a huge project. Years back, we had a similar challenge, on the confederate submarine CSS *Hunley*. When Selma makes it back in, would you have her touch base with Warren Lasch, who headed up that project, and see about putting him together with Dr Jennings? They're going to need all the expertise they can get.'

'Of course. Consider it done.'

Remi signed off, wanting to conserve their battery time, and moved back to the Viking ship, where Sam had resumed his seemingly endless chore of picking away at the vessel. They spent the remainder of their daylight hours like that, painstakingly removing ice from chest after chest and making copious notes of their findings.

At night, the specially designed heater kept the temperature in the tent bearable. They fell asleep quickly after a full day working on the ship, which slowly but surely was yielding more treasures.

One night drifted into the next, and it was with some surprise that they realized over a week had gone by. When the satellite phone chirped on the morning of their ninth day camping, it so startled Sam that he almost dropped it in his haste to answer.

'Yes?'

'Sam Fargo? Dr Jennings from Montreal. I'm on my way there with a team. We should make it to the fjord by early tomorrow. How are you holding up?' Jennings was one of Canada's top archaeologists and the head of the group that would eventually be transporting the ship and its contents to a controlled lab in Montreal.

'As well as can be expected. Although I'll admit that sleeping on the ice is getting old.'

Remi rolled her eyes as she continued working nearby.

'I'll bet. We're bringing an entire camp with us. You've been fortunate that no storms have moved through. But it doesn't look like we'll be so lucky. There's a front headed toward Baffin and it'll hit tomorrow in the late afternoon or evening. The first order of business will be to get the camp set up and the longship under cover, and to get you out of there before the worst of it starts.'

'Will you be all right on the ice in a storm?' Sam asked. 'Maybe the ship could wait for a day or two until it passes . . .'

'That's up to you. Depends on your schedule and your level of urgency to get back to civilization.'

'I'll talk to my wife, but it seems like the most prudent course would be to wait it out with you on board after securing the site, doesn't it?'

'I won't argue that, but I can't ask you to do it. We'll see you tomorrow.'

Sam terminated the call and explained their options to Remi, who concurred that they weren't in such a rush to leave that they would risk their colleagues to the brutal force of a storm. Now working with a renewed sense of urgency, they reviewed the contents of all of the chests, each numbered and with the items cataloged, as the ten dead Viking warriors watched over them. They'd had the luxury of taking their time, documenting everything in meticulous detail for later research – something all too rare, given the high-profile nature of many of their more visible discoveries.

When the archaeology team arrived the next morning just after sunrise, Sam and Remi heard the ship enter the fjord before they saw a massive red hull squeeze through the gap with no more than twenty feet of clearance per side. Almost twice the size of the *Alhambra*, the CCGS *Cameron* was a Canadian Coast Guard A1 Lloyd's ice-class two-hundred-and-twenty-six-foot offshore oceanographic science vessel with a forty-eight-foot beam. Entry into the fjord would pose no great problem, according to the bottom-mapping data supplied by the *Alhambra* – the depth varied from sixty to a hundred and forty feet, easily accommodating the enormous craft's fifteen-foot draft.

The *Cameron*'s high bow crushed through the surface ice with ease and slowed to a stop twenty-five yards from the Viking longship's stern. Sam and Remi could make out the captain and his mate in the towering pilot-house, and then a tall man in his forties emerged from the superstructure and moved to the bow, almost three stories above them. He waved and called out.

'Ahoy there! You must be the Fargos.'

'Dr Jennings, I presume. I recognize the voice,' Sam answered, returning the wave.

'And that's the Viking ship. Goodness. She looks like she was just built.'

'It's remarkable. We left much of the hull with ice on it to preserve it.'

'I can't tell you how excited we are about this. It's an honor to meet you both.'

'Likewise, Dr Jennings,' Remi said.

'Please, it's Matthew. It's a bit chilly to stand on pointless formality,' he said, his breath issuing fog with every word.

The archaeology team on the *Cameron* wasted no time. After testing the ice to ensure that it was stable enough to walk on, they began carting tools and sections of temporary buildings to the area by Sam and Remi's tent. It took the better part of the morning and much of the afternoon to erect five structures: a portable field kitchen, a bathroom-and-shower facility, two barracks, and an equipment room with a communications center. The eight-man building crew worked with quiet efficiency as Sam and Remi luxuriated in a stateroom, enjoying their first hot shower in over a week, followed by a massive meal of seafood washed down with beer and white wine, compliments of the Canadian government.

Sam met with the archaeologists after lunch and spoke to a packed house. After a report of their progress to date on excavation and news of their incredible discovery of pre-Columbian artifacts, a spirited discussion ensued.

Jennings cleared his throat and said, 'We know that there was contact between the Viking settlements in Greenland and the one discovered on southern Baffin Island, in the Tanfield Valley. So it's obvious that there was a trade route of some kind, even if irregular. But we've never seen any hard evidence of Vikings journeying farther south. There's been speculation about trips to the Canadian mainland for logging, but nothing conclusive ever surfaced.'

'We'll need to get the ship carbon-dated, of course,' another scientist pointed out, 'but it looks like it's a later type – a dragon ship with a sail.'

Jennings put his pencil down on the desk. 'Which would narrow it to anywhere from AD 900 to 1300. That's consistent with the saga of Leif Eriksson, which has him journeying westward around AD 1000, after hearing about the New World from Bjarni Herjólfsson, when he sailed the Newfoundland coast after being blown off course in AD 986. The point being, this new evidence clearly proves that there were others who ventured south as well as west.'

Remi turned over their notes and the record of their observations, having already entered them into their computer. She and Sam took turns fielding questions from the group. When the gathering broke up, everyone descended to the ice, and the scientists got their first close look at the Viking craft. The team looked like children in a candy store, and the sense of excitement was palpable for the men and women who would spend weeks, if not longer, preparing the boat for transport to Montreal.

The sky darkened as the afternoon passed, and an ominous line of angry clouds moved in from the ocean as the team secured a huge tarp over the Viking vessel to protect it from the elements. Even in late spring, a major storm in the Arctic Circle was nothing to take lightly, and the crew hurried to batten down the little camp and harden it against whatever nature threw at it.

As the procession of gray storm clouds approached, the *Cameron* reversed into the center of the fjord, where it dropped anchor in the deepest portion and waited. Soon after, the wind picked up, and within a half hour a gale was driving sheets of freezing rain through the glacial canyon. Lightning crackled overhead, the baritone boom of thunder shaking the big ship with each explosive volley.

The surrounding mountains shielded them from the worst of it. Sam and Remi could only imagine what the crew of the Viking boat had endured, and gave silent thanks in the wee hours of the morning that they'd been spared the experience of an Arctic storm while in their tent.

They awoke to a fresh blanket of white. Four hours later, the expedition team was waving farewell to Sam and Remi as the *Cameron* steamed slowly toward the gap. Remi inched closer to Sam as the sheer rock walls moved past them and, once the ship was well into the narrow channel, they returned to their stateroom, their part in the discovery now consigned to the history books.

The captain intercepted them on the way inside and shook both their hands with brisk enthusiasm. 'We'll have you back in Clyde River by tomorrow morning.

Anything I can do to make your stay more comfortable, let me know.'

'I'm still trying to get used to the concept of warm water and hot food,' Remi quipped.

'Well, we have plenty of both, and I believe Jennings left a few bottles of excellent wine in case you need something to quench your thirst during lunch and dinner. Again, don't hesitate to ask if you need anything.'

'When will you return for the team?' Sam asked.

'Hard to say. It may be a larger ship that picks them up – something that can accommodate the entire long-ship. Our readings show that gap as being ninety-seven feet at the narrowest point, so we should be able to get one of our bigger boats in – with a little luck and some lubrication on either side of the hull.'

'Thanks for the hospitality. It's good to be off the ice,' Remi said.

The captain nodded. 'I have no doubt. Whenever you like, come up to the bridge and I'll give you a tour. Hopefully, the seas will have calmed down and it will be a smooth ride back to civilization . . . if you can call Clyde River that.'

They shook hands again, and then they were alone. In their stateroom, Remi checked the indicator on the satellite phone, noting it was recharged, and handed it to Sam before plopping down on the bed.

'Give Kendra a call and check on Selma. See about having Rick meet us at the airport. As far as I'm concerned, I've spent about as much time as I ever want to on Baffin Island, even if it was in such charming company as yours.'

'You know you're going to be bored out of your mind after an adventure like this. How are you going to occupy your time now that you don't have to chip ice all day long?' Sam teased.

'I'd say we both have plenty to do now that we know for a fact that Vikings had contact with pre-Columbian America. I'm thinking that we should take a hard look at the lore and see if there's anything that points us in a promising direction. They were there, and the artifacts we found represent a significant treasure for those civilizations. There had to be a reason the Vikings were loaded down with goods from what's now Mexico.'

Sam nodded. 'Great minds think alike. Now that we know —'

'We can get a jump on everyone. And if there's somewhere this thread leads, get there first.'

'Now, that's the girl I married.'

'Then fly that girl out of here on the first plane you can find.'

Sam took the hint. He swung the heavy door closed behind him and made his way to the bridge so he'd have a clear line of sight for the phone to function. Remi had been unflagging and tireless in her efforts, and it wasn't lost on him that he'd need to make it up to her in spades.

After all, a deal was a deal.

9

Antibes, South of France

The sunset deepened to a soft gold hue over the Tuscan-inspired waterfront villa. A lofty shoal of cloud streaks hung like colored smoke, all vivid orange and red, a dazzling kaleidoscope reflected off the Mediterranean as the sun sank slowly until it was nothing more than a glowing ember in the sea. The view from the house was as magnificent as they came, which was the reason Janus Benedict had purchased it almost twenty years before, adding to the grounds a tennis court and pool that would have been the envy of most hotels in the area.

Out on the veranda, Janus sat watching the celestial light show, his raw silk navy blazer unbuttoned as a concession to informality as he sipped a 1923 Fonseca Port. He'd purchased it from a store in Lisbon on one of his wine-hunting forays into the region. The ruby liquid had turned amber from age, and the passage of years had imbued it with secondary flavors that more than justified the exorbitant price the seller had demanded.

A micro cell phone chirped from the circular glass

table next to him. Janus set his Romeo y Julieta Short Churchill cigar in a crystal ashtray and reached over to answer it.

'Benedict,' he said.

'Sir, we have more news on the Canadian find.'

'Yes, Percy. Do tell.'

'Everyone's being tight-lipped about it, but I persuaded one of the assistant professors that his financial woes might be temporary if he could give us something usable,' Percy said, his words clipped, delivered with the precision of a laser. Percy was Janus's go-to man for skullduggery and had performed admirably for decades.

'I'd like to think my generosity knows few bounds.'

'Quite. Anyway, it appears your Fargos have done it again. A most remarkable discovery on Baffin Island. Apparently, it's a Viking longship, the likes of which has never been seen.'

'Interesting, but hardly earth-shattering. And more important, of little use to me. There's not much market for Norse antiquities.'

'Nor should there be, I'd think. Beastly stuff. Axes and pelts and the like.'

Janus could tell from Percy's inflection that there was more, but he didn't rush the man. He'd get to whatever it was when he was ready. 'But it does tend to highlight the incredible success this cavalier couple have in turning up unusual finds.'

'I'll give them that,' Percy said. 'This one in particular

is noteworthy because of what was being transported by the longship.'

'I see. What was being transported . . .' Janus echoed.

'Yes. It appears that it was a hoard of pre-Columbian knickknacks. Pots, statues, that sort of rot.'

Janus sat up straighter, and his heart rate increased by twenty beats per minute. 'You did say pre-Columbian, didn't you, old boy?'

'The very thing.'

'Ah, then I understand what the fuss is all about. That's certainly a feather in their caps. I'd imagine it will cause quite a stir in academic circles.'

'Quite.'

'Brilliant work, as usual, my good man. And if I know the Fargos, this will be only the first step. They have keen minds and move quickly. They're sure to use their newfound knowledge to their best advantage, and, if there's a treasure to be found, they'll be relentless. I think it's time to step up surveillance of them. But more sophisticated than the last idiot you sent. I want no more incidents that could tip them off.' Percy had filled Janus in on the botched photography outside the Fargos' La Jolla home and was livid over the sloppiness.

'Of course. I've already taken steps in that regard. This time, with more, er, subtle approaches.'

'I want to be kept abreast of every move they make, is that clear?'

'Crystal. It shall be done. I'll report on anything that seems pertinent.'

'Where are they at this moment?'

'On their plane. According to the flight plan the pilot filed this morning, headed back to San Diego.'

'Very well. Do whatever you need to do. Spare no resources. My instinct is that watching and waiting should turn up some very interesting results. They don't stay stationary for long, and when they move, I want to be two steps ahead of them.'

Janus hung up and stared at the phone, then set it back on the table and resumed his appreciation of his fine Cuban smoke. The horizon had faded to purple and crimson, the sun's final shimmering on the sea replaced by the lights of other estates owned by the privileged and powerful, stretching all the way to Cannes. He took another sip of the liquid gold and sighed contentedly. Whatever the Fargos had planned, he intended to foil. After their interference with his last project, it was personal. For all Janus's aplomb, that had been a slap to his face, an insult every bit as painful as a blow.

That would not stand.

One of the French doors swung open and Reginald stepped through before closing it softly behind him.

'There you are. You missed the sunset,' Janus said as his brother took the seat on the opposite side of the table.

'I've seen plenty of them. What's that you're knocking back?'

'Bit of vintage port.'

'Any good?'

'Not bad. You might not like it, though.'

'Probably not. Don't see how you choke down that sweet stuff. Like molasses to me.' Reginald depressed the button on a discreetly located intercom on the table and called out, 'Simon, be a good lad and fetch me a Glenfiddich on the rocks, would you?'

After a few moments of silence, a stately voice emanated from the tinny speaker. 'Of course, sir. Very good. Your usual measure?'

'Perhaps a finger or so more. It's been a frightful day.'

'It will be there shortly, sir.'

Reginald stared out at the darkening water and then removed a pack of cigarettes from his breast pocket and lit one. He blew a gray cloud at the overhang and tapped his fingers impatiently. A houseboy emerged bearing a silver tray with a single tumbler of Scotch, three-quarters full, with two small cubes of ice floating in the caramel distillation. Reginald downed a third in one swallow as the servant disappeared back inside.

'Ah. At least the Scottish are good at something,' he observed.

'I see you're in another of your good moods,' Janus said.

'Never better. So what's on the agenda for tonight? Raping and pillaging?'

'Hardly. I have reservations for five at the Carlton at seven. With the von Schiffs.'

Reginald groaned. 'Not them. Anything but that.'

'Behave, Reginald. It's business. You'll put on a brave face.'

'The son's an ass. Takes after his old man. And the missus is a positive gargoyle.'

'Perhaps. But they're very profitable acquaintances to know.'

Reginald polished off the rest of his drink and held it aloft. 'Best to have a few more of these, then.'

'I think not, old chap. Don't want you to make a scene.'

Reginald's eyes narrowed dangerously. 'I'm a big boy, Janus.'

'Yes. Well then, do behave like one, won't you? I can't have you showing up to dinner inebriated, which is where this is going. If you want to pursue your date with a bottle, do so after dinner, not before.'

'Bloody hell.'

'That's the spirit. Go and find a proper jacket, and have Simon bring the car around. Dinner bell rings in a few minutes,' Janus said, dismissing Reginald, already on to something else.

Reginald's sneer was lost on him. The younger man rose, stubbed out his cigarette with a curt stab, and stalked into the house.

Janus smoothed his glossy graying hair and finished the last of his port and then stood, taking care to also smooth his slacks and adjust his cravat. It wouldn't do to appear rumpled to the von Schiffs. The Germans were very judgmental about the little things, and, as he knew, the difference between success and failure often came down to careful presentation.

Reginald was right, though, about the Germans' son being an idiot.

But enduring a couple of hours with the imbecile would pay handsome dividends, so he'd do so with a smile.

The predatory smile of a raptor.

10

The overnight trip back to San Diego was mercifully smooth, and when the G650 touched down with a puff of smoke from its tires, Remi turned to Sam and gave him a tired look.

'Home at last,' she said.

'Hopefully, for a while. Unless you've scheduled something in the dizzy whirlwind of our social calendar and not told me about it.'

'The only thing I've got scheduled is some serious spa time and an appointment with a masseuse to treat my frostbite.'

'That wasn't frost that bit you.'

'Don't get fresh with me. I still haven't forgiven you for volunteering us.'

'Nor should you. I'm hoping some spoiling you rotten might alleviate the worst of the sting.'

'That and more notoriety when they break news of the longship.'

'Maybe you'll get your own reality show.'

'What camera crew would be stupid enough to take that duty?'

'Good point.'

Kendra was waiting with the Cadillac, Zoltán occupying most of the backseat. He caught sight of Remi and let loose a delighted bark as his tail beat the seat back like a spirited metronome. Remi's heart soared when she saw his chocolate eyes trailing her.

'Who's my big, brave boy?' she called, arms outstretched. He vaulted out and ran to Remi and then waited, trembling, as she knelt and hugged him.

Sam waved him away. 'No, no, spend the time with her, not me. I just buy your food. No need to make a fuss on my account.'

Remi rolled her eyes. 'You're jealous!'

'I am not. Okay, maybe a little bit. He's got better hair than me. There. I said it.'

'He's a Hungarian charmer. I've always been a pushover for those.'

'Serves me right for being born in California.'

'Don't worry. Surfer boys are my other vice.'

Kendra filled them in on the research as they wove their way through the early-morning traffic to La Jolla. 'We've compiled an entire dossier on possible items of interest that involve anything that hints at contact with Europeans, pre-Columbus,' she began, 'but it's a fuzzy target. So much of their history is oral traditions that were garbled, or changed by the Spanish. So there's no telling what's invention or what's true. I'm afraid it's going to be good old-fashioned midnight-oil burning to make sense out of any of it. And believe me, there's a mountain of data.'

'We've got nothing planned except digging through it,' Remi said, 'so that's not a problem. How's Selma?'

'She's resting at the house. She really wanted to come greet you, but I told her that would make me too nervous.'

'So she's up and around?'

'Sort of. I don't think she's going to be a hundred per cent for a while.'

'That's not unexpected,' Remi said. 'I know they tell you to figure on at least six months to be fully recovered.'

'It's got to be frustrating,' Sam said. 'I know how much she enjoys being in the thick of it.'

Kendra nodded. 'Let's just say that she's a difficult patient. That's what the doctors said. "Feisty" was actually the word they used most often.'

Remi smiled. 'No doubt.'

Kendra led the way into the house, followed by Zoltán and Remi, Sam bringing up the rear. Inside, Selma was sitting and sipping tea, her walker next to her. Zoltán let out a greeting woof.

'Welcome home,' Selma said, smiling.

'Selma. How are you?'

'Oh, you know, always in the fight. I've got my trusty walker. But I do have to give in to the wheelchair every once in a while,' she admitted.

'The important thing is that you're recovering.'

'I wish it wouldn't take so long. I'm really tired of being so dependent.'

'Kendra has helped out wonderfully,' Sam said, 'and we're between adventures, so you aren't missing anything.'

Remi nodded. 'That's right. We're here for the duration. You just need to focus on your physical therapy and getting better. Don't worry about playing mother hen with us. We're in good hands,' Remi assured her, glancing at Kendra.

'I'll try, but it's become something of a habit . . .'

Sam carried the bags up to their bedroom, and Remi joined him shortly after.

Remi paced in front of the glass wall that faced the blue Pacific beyond the terrace. 'I just want Selma to take her time and not try to rush her recovery.'

'We're all different. We should respect her wishes,' Sam said gently.

Remi stopped and stared out at the ocean, the pristine beauty calming her as it usually did. 'You're right, of course. I just don't want her to overdo things, to injure herself and get into big trouble. That would make her recuperation time even longer.'

'You know what you need? Let's head over to the Valencia Hotel and get you a full spa treatment. The whole deal. That always makes you happy. And then lunch on the restaurant veranda, maybe a Kistler Chardonnay, some blue point crab . . .'

'Why, Sam Fargo. Now I remember why I hang out with you.'

'I thought it was my piano playing.'

'And your lovely singing voice.'

He gave her a skeptical frown. 'Maybe that's pushing it.'

'"To each his own," said the man as he kissed the cow . . .'

They spent the morning and much of the afternoon at the hotel, and when they returned home, Remi was in considerably improved spirits. Sam suggested they begin poring through the archive of pre-Columbian lore Pete and Wendy had amassed.

The whole research team was working harmoniously downstairs, Pete leaning over Kendra's station and pointing at something on her monitor.

When evening came and twilight faded into night, they'd only dented the reams of accounts, many of them conflicting. Sam and Remi agreed that the Toltec society around AD 1000 would be where they'd focus their energy, scouring the accounts for anything that hinted at European influence around that time. When they said goodnight to Selma and Kendra, they were both exhausted but heartened that they'd made at least a small amount of progress in their research.

'Did you see the way Pete was looking at Kendra?' Remi asked as she plumped the pillows in readiness for some well-earned rest.

'Not really. What did I miss?'

'I think he might be taken with her.'

'Pete? Really?'

'That's what I got. I wonder what Wendy thinks?'

'I'll defer to your feminine intuition in these matters. Everyone knows men are the last to know these things.'

'It's one of the endearing qualities of your gender.'

Zoltán watched them from his position at the foot of the bed, his eyes alert, ears pointing straight up.

'At least I've got that going for me,' Sam said.

Remi moved behind him and slipped her arms around his chest. 'I'm willing to forgive you for putting me on ice recently – at least a little, big boy.'

'Don't scare the dog.'

'He's braver than he looks.'

Zoltán, as if following the discussion, closed his eyes with a faint snort.

'Sam, check this out,' Remi called, the morning's second cup of coffee cooling on her desk beside her oversize monitor.

'What am I looking at?' he asked.

'Quetzalcoatl.'

'The feathered serpent god of the Aztecs?'

'Also called Votan by the Mayans.'

'And?'

'He's described as being white, with red hair . . . and cross-eyed,' Remi said.

'Cross-eyed?'

'Yes. More interestingly, in the Viking sagas that were compiled in the fourteenth century, a Viking explorer named Ari Marson, who was a redhead and was cross-eyed, disappeared around AD 980 on his way to Greenland. According to the saga, he was worshipped as a god in a new land ten days' sail from Vinland.'

'Vinland, eh? And where might that be?'

'According to different accounts, anywhere from Baffin Island to the northeast part of the US'

Sam did a quick calculation. 'That would put his landing spot south of the US Which could mean Mexico.'

'Possibly. Some accounts speculate it might have been Cuba. And there are also stories of Quetzalcoatl coming from the east to the Mexican mainland – from Cuba.'

'Interesting. What's that?' Sam asked, pointing at another image on the screen.

'It's an image of Quetzalcoatl as a white man with a beard.'

'But I thought that the worship of Quetzalcoatl was far older than the tenth century.'

'It was,' Remi agreed, 'but there was a great deal of confusion when the Spanish arrived. They got a lot wrong, and that was complicated by the religious climate in Europe. So they simply changed things they didn't like.'

'And the victors get to write the history books.'

'Exactly – and as far as the dates in the sagas go, those are considered unreliable, too. In other words, 980 could have been 1080 and simply been changed during one telling in its oral tradition – or whoever drafted the written account could have remembered it wrong.'

Sam nodded. 'But back to Vikings on the East Coast. Do I not recall a Viking coin being found in Maine back in the fifties?'

'I saw that, too. There's still some debate about whether it's a hoax or not.'

'There's always debate. That's what makes this so much fun. Cutting through all the opinions and guesswork and discovering the truth.'

Remi leaned back. 'If we take this at face value, then it's possible that Quetzalcoatl was, in fact, a Viking.'

'In some accounts, he came from the east in long-ships with shields on the sides. And among the many forms of knowledge he brought was the use of metal – specifically, iron – which the Vikings were expert at. Maybe we should be focusing on this Quetzalcoatl fellow.'

Remi nodded. 'I'm way ahead of you. But this gets even more confusing. A famous ruler of the Toltecs in the eleventh century was either believed to be a reincar-nation of Quetzalcoatl or was deified as a god. Again, that's largely speculative, because the Aztecs eradicated most of the Toltec records. But this ruler, Topiltzin Cē Ācatl Quetzalcoatl, ruled the Toltec capital of Tol-lan, which is now called Tula, in central Mexico. He was credited with bringing all sorts of knowledge to the Toltecs, including growing corn and working with metal, and improving their masonry skills by quantum leaps. And he's referred to in some accounts as being a white man with a beard who favored long robes and animal skins.'

'My head's starting to hurt.'

'I know. It's like trying to grab a greased eel.'

'Still, that's positive as a starting point.'

'Agreed.'

'I'm thinking we pull up everything we can on this ruler Quetzalcoatl and drill down from there,' Sam said, returning to his desk.

'That's as good a plan as any. I'll get the crew on it.'

The next three days were spent digging deeper into the legends surrounding the enigmatic leader of the Toltecs. His reign became the dominant force in central Mexico. The few codices that purported to tell the story of the Mesoamerican civilizations were of limited help and seemed to contradict one another in more than a few places. But eventually a few threads gelled into a common theme. Around AD 1000, a ruler had emerged who transformed Toltec society. He introduced amazing leaps in technology, and was often described as resembling a white man, although other accounts had him native-born.

At ten o'clock in the evening, after another long stint of poring over the data, Sam's pulse quickened as he read an obscure tome that chronicled a legend associated with Quetzalcoatl. He was buried with a treasure unlike any ever seen, with all manner of jade and gold artifacts. The crowning item, a magnificent jewel, was considered as much of a legend as that of El Dorado, the city of gold: the Eye of Heaven, a flawless emerald offered from the Toltecs as tribute to the powerful ruler, rumored to be the size of a man's heart and possessed of magical properties.

The account was long on hyperbole but short on detail, and chronicled numerous hunts by the Spanish to locate the tomb, all of which ended in failure. Over time, the excitement had faded and the rumor was discounted as one of many that the conquering

Europeans had concocted in a bid to secure investors for exploration.

But one thing stood out for Sam: the detailed description of Quetzalcoatl. In this account, he was an old man who died of natural causes, his heavy red beard laced with gray, and he was laid out in a jade-and-gold casket and entombed in a holy place that would forever remain secret.

To an accomplished treasure hunter, the mention of a hidden tomb with undreamed-of riches was like waving a red cape in front of a snorting bull. Sam shut off his monitors for the evening and made his way back upstairs, where Remi had retired an hour earlier. He felt a familiar buzz of anticipation – one that had rarely led him wrong in the past.

He told Remi about his discovery as they sat sipping snifters of Rémy Martin XO cognac by the open doors, the ocean dark other than for the twinkle of distant lights from the occasional vessel working its way north from San Diego Harbor. By the time Sam finished telling her about Quetzalcoatl's lost tomb, Remi was also excited.

Three hundred yards offshore, near one of the vast kelp beds that hugged the shore, a twenty-eight-foot fishing boat was anchored. Anyone scrutinizing it would have seen two men with their rods in the water doing some night fishing. A more careful study might have noted a directional microphone pointed at the open door of a home on the bluff, and noted a third man in the lower cabin, sitting with headphones on, listening to every word being spoken inside the Fargos' bedroom.

But there was nobody to notice the men on the boat. The discussion was being recorded and would later be analysed, along with countless others, and then forwarded to the client. The operatives were seasoned surveillance professionals, well versed in eavesdropping and corporate espionage.

A haze lingered across Mexico City in the predawn glow of a thousand lights. The freeways were already clogged with vehicles on their early-morning commutes, arriving from the dense neighboring suburbs that ringed the vast metropolis.

A tired old garbage truck lurched slowly up a road in the municipality of López Mateos, its engine straining as it made its weekly rounds in the impoverished sprawl ten miles north of Mexico City. Many families lived eight to a twelve-by-fifteen-foot room, and the drug-related violent crime made it one of the more dangerous areas in the region. The truck rolled to a screeching stop when a rumble began from the street beneath. The earth began to shake – at first gently and then with increasing violence.

A nearby brick wall split and collapsed, the top crumbling as the earthquake shook it, and a geyser of water shot from a fissure in the center of the street. The men in the garbage truck watched in horror as several of the two-story cinder-block homes fell in on themselves as though the earth had sucked them into the ground. A few half-naked children ran into the street while the pavement beneath them shuddered. The few working lamps on the building fronts winked out as power cables snapped somewhere down the line. Streetlights rocked before tearing free and crashing to the ground in explosions of glass.

In the distance, the city's high-rises swayed. Even in a region known for its seismic outbursts, this was a big one. The shaking continued for a full minute before the earth settled to stillness beneath the frightened people.

The street resembled a war zone, with huge cracks crisscrossing the remaining pavement and water mains gushing into the air before pooling in stinking ponds also fed by ruptured sewage lines. Doors opened as neighbors emerged to take stock, the calamity only the latest in a seemingly unending string of bad luck visited upon a population born under a dark star.

The sun inched over the surrounding mountains and cast a dim glow through the sediment that had floated skyward from the demolished buildings. The garbagemen surveyed the ruined street for a while longer and then the driver put the ancient truck in gear and executed a shaky turn before heading back down the rise.

Further research into Quetzalcoatl's tomb revealed nothing of use, and by late afternoon of the second day it was obvious to everyone that they'd hit a dead end. Sam's eyes were burning from boring holes through his monitor, searching for the one elusive glyph, a thread that might lead them in a positive direction; now they were out of options. But Sam hadn't earned his reputation by giving up – his tenacious nature invariably drove him to up the ante when the going got rough.

When Selma joined them, Remi stood to greet her as Sam rubbed a tired hand over his face.

'How's it going?' Selma asked.

'Just the usual frustrations,' Remi said. 'Incomplete accounts, vague hints without any substance, partial reports . . .'

'Ah, research, how do I miss thee,' Selma intoned.

'How are you? Feeling any better?' Sam asked, turning from his screen.

'You know. Every day brings its own little challenges.'

'The important thing is that you're making progress,' Remi said.

'Sometimes it doesn't feel like it,' Selma confessed – a rare admission from the woman who was as indefatigable and hard-charging as they came. She stared off at the ocean and then fixed a smile on her face. 'I thought I'd stop in and see how you were making out without me.'

'Not so great, Selma. We're sort of at the end of our rope on our current line of thinking,' Sam said, and then gave her a summary of their progress – or lack of it. When he was finished, she nodded.

'Well, you know what you're going to have to do.'

Sam and Remi exchanged a look.

'No . . .' Remi said.

'Let me make some calls. That won't hurt me. Truth

be told, I'm going stir-crazy, even with the books and TV. I'll call a few people and put out some feelers. It'll cheer me up if I can help in my own small way.'

'Selma –' Sam started, but she waved him off.

'I'll let you know if I hear anything. Now, get back to work. You'll never make it if you keep finding excuses to slack off,' Selma teased, and then without another word expertly turned her walker and slowly made her way back to her rooms with a familiar expression of determination on her face.

Sam exhaled noisily and stood, stretching his arms overhead and rolling his head to get the kinks out of his shoulder and neck muscles. Remi went back to her screen while Sam got his fifth cup of coffee and then pushed one of the glass doors open and moved on to the wraparound terrace for some welcome salt air. Gulls wheeled in the blue sky overhead, riding an updraft from the sea, and a few boats worked the edge of the kelp forest. Gluttonous seals competed with the anglers for the ocean's bounty, and Sam watched as their oily black heads popped out of the water here and there before submerging again for another run at the fish.

Not a bad life, he thought. Simple. Go for a swim, fresh fish for lunch again, then maybe a siesta on a nice rock while the sun warmed you. The seals definitely had it figured out. Better than going blind staring at pictures of ancient ruins, trying to find clues to untangle one of history's enduring mysteries.

With a final glance at the late-afternoon sky, he

reluctantly returned to his computer and continued with his search for the meaning of the unintelligible carvings he'd been studying.

Two hours later, Selma emerged with a look of triumph on her face.

'Congratulations. You've been invited by the National Institute of Anthropology and History in Mexico City to study their inventory of Toltec artifacts. An old friend and colleague of mine, Carlos Ramirez, is in charge of the effort there. He's the director of Antiquities and the cousin of one of the ministers of the interior, as well as being on the university board.'

'Selma! That's wonderful,' Remi said, rising from her seat.

'He's a very sweet man. We collaborated on some research years ago and I don't think he's ever forgotten how well we got along. Anyway, he's got his hands full right now because after the big earthquake a repair crew fixing some broken pipes in the street discovered a new find – a series of subterranean vaults connected by a tunnel system that was exposed by the quake. They appear to be Toltec, but it's all very preliminary because the area near the ruins is still in disarray. He invited you both to fly in and meet with his two senior researchers – and, if you like, to go through the new find together.'

'Selma, you never cease to amaze me,' Sam said, shaking his head in awe.

'Well, it's not all that amazing. All I had to do was

remember what the country code for Mexico was and call in a favor. Let's not make it more than it is.'

'When can we go?'

'Apparently, most of the city is fine, but some areas were pretty hard hit and whole blocks were flattened. The quake measured a 7.8, but the damage was localized. He basically said you could come down whenever you want. Your reputation opens a lot of doors.'

'You didn't tell him what we're working on, did you?' Remi asked.

'No, I just told him that you were researching the Toltecs and Quetzalcoatl and how the Aztecs and later the Spanish twisted the Toltec legends. That gives you a pretty broad canvas on which to paint. But it will also explain why you might be more interested in some lines of inquiry than others.'

'You're a genius,' Sam said.

'Seriously, this might get you closer than doing the digging online. As you know, that only takes you so far . . .'

Remi nodded. 'And then you have to get your hands dirty. We know, Selma.'

'I don't know what to do with myself when my hands are clean for this long,' Sam agreed. 'I'd say it's time to head south of the border. *Ai yai yai!*'

Remi gave him a mock frown and shook her head. 'I'm afraid he might have already been prepping for the trip by nipping at the tequila.'

'Nonsense. I'm sober as a judge,' Sam insisted.

'That explains a lot,' Remi countered, and they all laughed.

'Kendra? Looks like it's time to get the pilots off the beach and warming up the plane,' Sam called out.

'When would you like to take off?' she asked from her workstation near the windows.

Remi and Sam looked at each other, and Remi shrugged. 'Tomorrow morning? Say, at eight? That will put us in Mexico City by noon local time.'

'Will do. How about a hotel?'

'I think last time we were there we stayed at the Four Seasons in the Zona Rosa district. As I remember, it was very good, and centrally located.'

'Consider it done,' Kendra said. She definitely shared the same orderly genes with Selma, they'd discovered, and with time they'd grown to appreciate her quiet, straightforward style. 'Any special requests?'

'Selma will give you the rundown on the usual we like to take into the field on something like this,' Remi said. 'It's pretty basic. She's got the list.'

'Great. Then I'll get right on it.'

The rest of the day sped by as they prepared for their trip, and both Sam and Remi were more than ready for a final celebratory meal at their favorite restaurant in San Diego, an Italian place in the Gaslamp Quarter. They took Sam's newest acquisition, a black convertible Porsche 911 Turbo 918 Spyder Cabriolet that he rarely had time to drive. He dropped the top, and Remi leaned back in the soft leather seat as the warm evening breeze blew through her hair. He worked through the gears with enthusiasm as the powerful engine catapulted them down the on-ramp and on to the freeway.

'Easy there, Hoss,' Remi cautioned as the downtown skyline rose ahead of them.

'Sorry. I keep forgetting how responsive the gas pedal is on this thing.'

'I think we already passed liftoff. You can ease up.'

'Your wish is my command.'

Sam slowed to a sane pace and soon they were handing the keys to a valet and entering the restaurant. The owner greeted them like long-lost relatives and escorted them to the private corner table they favored. His wife came over to say hello and suggested a special tasting menu of the chef's specials for the night, paired with a bottle of 2009 Sassicaia – arguably Italy's foremost Super Tuscan red wine.

The meal was relaxed, each dish perfectly prepared and presented, beginning with a bruschetta to die for, followed by braised sweetbreads, veal ravioli in a truffle sauce, and three preparations of shrimp. By the time Sam and Remi were sipping glasses of limoncello, they were ready to burst, and both agreed that they would sleep well after the wonderful meal.

13

The G650 descended through the cloud covering on the final approach to Benito Juárez International Airport in Mexico City. When they broke through the last of the clouds, the city was a few thousand feet below them. Torrential rainfall blanketed the buildings and roads. As the aircraft touched down, its tires threw a rooster tail of water into the air, and then they taxied to the jet charter building. All around them vehicles raced through the downpour, headlights beaming and flashers blinking, bearing luggage and fuel and provisions for the outbound commercial jets waiting in line for their chance to brave the storm.

A black GMC Yukon waited for them outside the terminal's glass-and-steel entrance. The driver held the door open for them, loaded the luggage, and then circled around to slip behind the wheel. Once they were in traffic, the streets were jammed with vehicles. Water rushed along the surface, potholes the size of televisions filled with ominous black water. The locals shambled down the sidewalks, wearing plastic parkas and toting umbrellas, as they picked their way along the uneven concrete. Outside a discount pharmacy, a forlorn figure wearing a plush chicken suit stood under an overhang, waving a yellow foam sign with *Abierto* printed on it in large red letters.

'If the treasure-hunting thing bottoms out, I could always do that,' Sam commented.

'I'd pay extra to see you in that outfit, regardless of the circumstances.'

'I don't know. It might lower property values in La Jolla.'

'Coward.'

'I am not.'

'Chicken.' She put her hands under her armpits and flapped her elbows. '*Pwuk-pwuk-pwuk . . .*'

He eyed her with good humor. 'Are you trying to tell me something? Because you're getting this rooster's attention.'

'It's either the chicken suit or nothing.'

'If I didn't know you were kidding, I'd be seriously worried.'

'Kidding?' Remi asked with raised eyebrows.

'Never mind.'

They checked into the hotel. After unpacking their bags, they called Carlos Ramirez, who spoke in heavily accented English. He told them that they could come by at any point that afternoon and he'd be happy to introduce them to the others researching the new find. Sam and Remi grabbed lunch in the hotel restaurant and then had a taxi take them to INAH – the National Institute of Anthropology and History – located next to the Cuicuilco Ecological Park in the city's southern-most reaches.

Carlos Ramirez met them at the security desk in a stylish, immaculately cut dark gray suit. He wore his salt-and-pepper hair longish, and a dapper mustache framed his upper lip, which was perpetually curved in a smile.

'Ah, Señor and Señora Fargo. Welcome, welcome. I'm glad you didn't let the weather scare you off,' he said, shaking hands with them.

'Compared to some of the places we've been recently, this is paradise,' Sam said.

'A little rain never kept us away from anything important,' Remi assured him.

Carlos led them upstairs to his office. 'I have a suite here, in addition to one at our headquarters in the historic district. But truthfully, I spend most of my time here. I prefer academia to bureaucracy. Of course, fieldwork is my first love. But there is less opportunity for that now that I'm in a position of responsibility.'

The office was expansive, with a conference table at one end surrounded by burgundy leather-upholstered chairs, and a large oval desk near a bank of windows overlooking the park. 'Please, have a seat, and I'll call the others and make introductions. But before we do that, tell me all about what I can help you with.'

'As Selma might have told you, we're researching the

Toltecs,' Sam explained, 'specifically around the AD 1000 era. We figured since this is where they were located, we should come to Mexico and do some in-person nosing around.'

'Your accomplishments precede you. We as a nation are in your debt for saving the Mayan Codex on our behalf. Anything I can offer you in the way of assistance is yours for the asking.'

'Well, I shouldn't think that this will be nearly as dramatic,' Remi said. 'I'm afraid much of what we're doing is going over old ground. But it's all part of the job, and we prefer to be thorough.'

'Yes, of course. Where would you like to start?'

'We'd like to look at the existing collection of artifacts and any documents you have that pertain to the Toltecs . . . or their most famous ruler, Quetzalcoatl.'

'Absolutely. Unfortunately, there isn't nearly as much as we'd like. The Aztec priests destroyed most of the records of his accomplishments. To complicate matters, the Spanish, whether deliberately or accidentally, further distorted the records until what we know about him is likely wrong.'

Remi nodded. 'Then you understand the problem we've been having. We're hoping you have material that's not online, which might shine some additional light on Toltec civilization, as well as their leader.'

'Actually,' Carlos said, 'you couldn't have arrived at a better time. From what we can gather, the newly discovered crypts that surfaced after the earthquake promise to provide exciting new information about their civilization. Of course, it's far too early to tell, but we're hopeful. This looks like it was hidden underground deliberately, which the Toltecs only did with their most valued sites – and it's well south of Tula, so completely unexpected.'

'We'd be honored to see it as soon as possible,' Remi said.

'Let me call in the archaeologists who are heading up that dig. You'll be working closely with them. They're two of our best.' Carlos dialed his phone and spoke a rapid-fire stream of Spanish. 'They'll be here shortly. Maribela and Antonio Casuela. Brother and sister. Remarkable intellects and experts on the Toltecs.'

A soft courtesy knock sounded through the door a couple of minutes later. A tall woman in her early thirties entered, followed by a man around the same age. That they were siblings was obvious from their facial features. What neither Remi nor Sam was prepared for was how physically arresting they were. The woman's long ebony hair seemed to gleam from its own light source, highlighting her smooth caramel-colored skin, high cheekbones, pearl-white teeth, and flashing chocolate eyes. The man was equally stunning, his strong jawline and rugged profile resembling that of a model or a cinema star rather than an academic.

The woman spoke first, extending her hand to Remi. 'Señora Fargo. How nice to meet you. I've followed your exploits with delighted surprise for years.'

Carlos beamed at them. 'Remi Fargo, this is Maribela Casuela.'

'The pleasure's all mine,' Remi said, her eyes roving quickly over the woman's flawless form, her sensible black slacks and red blouse hugging her curves in a way that most women only dreamed of.

'And you must be Sam Fargo,' Maribela said, offering her hand to Sam, her palm cool to the touch, her voice musical.

Sam could have sworn that a small electric current passed between them when their skin touched and quickly turned to the brother. 'Antonio, right?'

'It's a thrill. A real thrill,' Antonio said as they shook hands.

'But, please. Use our first names. I hate formality,' Remi said as the newcomers took the offered seats next to Sam.

Carlos filled them in on what the Fargos were interested in, and their eyes lit up at the mention of the recently unearthed crypts.

'It's remarkable,' Antonio said. 'We've both been inside, and the carvings alone will make for years of study. It seems as though there's an interconnected series of tunnels to at least four burial chambers. We've already removed the mummies. The insight that this undisturbed find should offer is unique. I'm sure you'll find touring it an amazing experience.'

'And, of course, you're welcome to review everything

we have on the Toltecs and Quetzalcoatl,' Maribela added, 'although most of it is well covered in the academic journals, so there won't be many surprises.'

'How is the area around the new discovery?' Sam asked.

Carlos frowned. 'It's controlled chaos. We've cleared the entry point and there are police guarding it, but the neighborhood is still a disaster area. Over a hundred people lost their lives in that *colonia* alone. Rudimentary services have yet to be restored, and there's been some looting. Rescue teams are working through the buildings, but it's not a good situation.'

'Is there any danger of pilfering of the tombs?' Remi asked.

'The hope is, no,' Antonio replied, 'but the police are very poorly paid, so anything is possible. We've cataloged all of the precious items, and have an effort under way to move them here, but it's slow going because we want to adequately document the state of the find. There's a fine line, as you know . . .'

Remi nodded. 'First, do no harm.'

Maribela eyed her. 'And what is your background, may I ask? I think I read that you're an anthropologist?'

'That's correct, a physical anthropologist, although it's been years since I was involved with academia. I much prefer being in the field, too.'

'Of course. There's nothing like the thrill of being first, is there?'

'No. I've been very fortunate that my husband here shares that passion,' Remi said, clasping Sam's hand possessively.

Antonio and Maribela gave them a tour of the artifacts and photos they'd amassed in the basement of the large building. Many of the items were already familiar to Sam and Remi from images on the Internet.

'One of our frustrations,' Maribela remarked, 'is that the Toltecs didn't have a written language, so any history is oral tradition recorded at a later date. And sporadic pictographs. But you can see by the glyphs they had an elaborate grasp of symbolism, although there is much disagreement as to how to interpret many of the images.'

Antonio nodded. 'Just as there are conflicting accounts of the mythical ruler of the Toltecs, Cē Ācatl Topiltzin, who is often referred to as Topiltzin Quetzalcoatl or just Quetzalcoatl. Over the years, the accounts have become so badly garbled it's difficult to know what to believe. For instance, some insist he was a mythical figure with no basis in history. Others claim he was the first ruler of the Toltecs. Still others say that he was believed to have been the divine reincarnation of the original Quetzalcoatl, the premier deity of Mesoamerica.' Antonio pointed to a collection of carved depictions of a stern man with a large head and what appeared to be a beard.

'It's all very confusing,' Sam agreed. 'Especially the beard. Unknown among American native people, right?'

Maribela smiled. 'Correct. And made more difficult

by the few Spanish accounts of Aztec lore and the civilization's history. We know that these were heavily altered versions of the oral tradition. Another problem is that there were no doubt some interpretation problems. Many of the existing documents were created by the Franciscan monks or the conquistadores, who quite simply botched the accounts.'

Antonio moved next to his sister. 'Not to mention that some records were secreted away because they contradicted the official histories. We know the Spanish tended to remove anything that they thought might lead to legendary treasures. Not that it did them much good, but it shows a systematic approach to looting the legacy of the Mayans and Aztecs for both financial gain and to curry favor with the King of Spain so that further expeditions could be funded.'

'Throughout history, money has played a part in driving human behavior,' Sam agreed.

Antonio nodded. 'There's little doubt that some of the official accounts are pure invention based on confusion over the original Quetzalcoatl the god and Quetzalcoatl the Toltec ruler.'

'What happened to the more accurate records that were taken by the Spanish, which might have hinted at significant sites?' Remi asked, careful to avoid the use of the word 'treasure.'

'All the surviving codices are more mundane. A few made it to Spain, some went down on ships that were routinely lost making the passage, others disappeared.'

'Have you tried to locate any?' Sam probed.

Antonio shrugged. 'Of course. We've made several trips to Spain, but there was nothing there that isn't part of the public domain. And there are some in Cuba, but that government's hard to deal with, even for us as Mexicans. They're very secretive. Maribela and I were there about four years ago for several months working with their museum. We were shown some pictographs and a manuscript that was said to be written by a conquistador relating to the Aztecs or Toltecs. They refused to allow us to study them closely or even to take photographs. We've approached them many times to gain access, or to have them returned to Mexico, but we're always stonewalled. It's a shame because that's our heritage, not theirs.'

'A manuscript? What did it say?' Remi asked.

'I couldn't tell you. It was unintelligible – probably some sort of cipher, which wasn't unusual in those days for sensitive documents. Without time to go through it line by line and figure out the code, there's no way of knowing. But I clearly remember that there were detailed drawings of Aztec, and possibly Toltec, icons, including one of Quetzalcoatl.'

'Have the Cubans tried to decrypt it?' Sam asked.

Antonio shook his head. 'I don't think so. It's just an old manuscript to them. I got the sense that it's been there so long that nobody is much interested – until we wanted to take it with us, at which point it became a national treasure.'

'And where do they keep all these Mexican relics?' Sam's voice was even, no hint of anything but polite curiosity.

Maribela eyed Sam. 'In Morro Castle, at the mouth of Havana Harbor. They have a small museum on the grounds, and I guess this stuff got relegated to the basement. I got the feeling that it's stored there because that's where it was stored hundreds of years ago, probably after the British handed the island back to Spain.'

Remi took a series of photos. She turned to Antonio. 'I can certainly see why everyone's excited – the tomb network sounds remarkable. You must be thrilled.'

'Yes, it's one of the first new discoveries in a long time that pertains to the Toltecs – and, given its location, it's a surprise. It was thought that the Toltecs only built in Tula, but now that must be reinterpreted.' Antonio paused. 'We know from legend that Quetzalcoatl was driven from Tollan and embarked on a journey to the farthest reaches of civilization, including the Mayan cities in Mexico and Guatemala, and perhaps even beyond.'

'Do you think the legend of Quetzalcoatl's tomb has any substance?' Remi asked.

'No, that's more from some questionable mentions in one of the more obscure codices, as well as some letters to the Spanish King. A wives' tale.'

'So you don't think there's any tomb?'

'It's doubtful. Everyone from the Spanish to present-day adventurers have hunted for that phantom, only to come up dry,' Antonio said dismissively. 'No, the true treasure of the Toltecs is their history, and, unfortunately, that's just as lost as any burial chamber for a quasi-mythical ruler. Besides which, think about some of the lore surrounding that story. You've heard it, right? I mean, come on – an emerald the size of a man's heart? That would have had to come from Colombia, and there's no evidence that the Toltecs ever traveled that far south, much less traded there. I've concluded that, like so many of the legends from that era, it's based more on high hopes than anything factual. Sort of the Mexican equivalent of the Holy Grail, and about as likely to exist.'

The inspection of the artifacts took the rest of the afternoon, and Sam and Remi agreed to meet Antonio and Maribela at the Four Seasons for pickup the next morning to explore the underground crypts. In the taxi back to the hotel, Sam called Selma on his cell phone and murmured into it as traffic whizzed by them.

'Selma, I want you to pull up anything you can find on Spanish artifacts in Cuba. Both public and anything rumored.'

'Cuba? Okay. I'll get right on it.'

'Oh, and for a real long shot, see if there's anything like an online blueprint for Morro Castle in Havana.'

'Will do. I'll e-mail you with a progress report when I have something.'

Remi caught his eye as he hung up and dialed another number from memory. 'What now?' she asked.

'Well, the Cuba thing has me thinking. Who would have more access to info on Cuba than . . . Rube?'

'Rubin Haywood? Good idea. I'm sure the CIA has a whole wing devoted to it.'

The SUV hit a particularly nasty bump, jostling them. Remi clutched the seat for support and moved her free hand to the gold icon at her neck. Sam waited as the call rang and whispered to her.

'We could use some of that scarab luck right about now. Can you rub it and make a genie appear?'

They laughed, and then Rube's distinctive voice came on the line.

'Rube. It's Sam. Your old buddy and pal.'

'Sam! Long time. What, are you in D.C.? Want to buy me dinner?'

'Have to take a rain check on that, Rube. No, this is more of a fact-finding call.'

'What is it this time?'

Sam took him through what he was looking for, and Rube remained silent for several seconds after he finished.

'It might take a while, but I can put an analyst on it. I hear they can do some amazing things with computers these days.'

'Data's only as good as whoever fed it in.'

'Ain't it the truth. So that's it? You want to know about any Cuban archaeological caches in Morro? Kind of an obscure area of inquiry, even for you . . .'

'I'm just trying to keep our relationship fresh and spontaneous.'

'*Ahem.* I'll have you know I got a promotion.'

'Really? Congrats.'

'Thanks. I'd tell you my new title, but then I'd have to kill you, so best to not ask.'

'Good to know.'

'All right, buddy. I'll put the elves to work. Still got the same e-mail?'

'Some things never change.'

When Sam hung up, Remi slid closer. 'What did you think of our new associates? That Maribela is a stunner, isn't she?'

'Who? Oh, the sister? I hadn't noticed.'

Remi elbowed him. 'Did you know when you're lying, your eyes give a telltale flicker?'

'Who are you going to believe, me or my lying eyes?'

'I was just saying . . . She's not what I expected.'

'Neither's the brother. Not as ugly as the sister, but still.'

They rode past the colorful façades of stores and apartments in silence, both lost in their thoughts, which now centered around a mythical ruler and his final burial place and the hurdles they would have to surmount to have any chance at finding it.

14

A slate sky drizzled on the windshield of Antonio's Suburban. The morning mist was a regular occurrence that time of year in Distrito Federal, or DF, as the inhabitants referred to Mexico City. Traffic was a snarl as they made their way north of the city center into the impoverished *colonia* of López Mateos.

Antonio turned, and a block up they found themselves facing two military vehicles flanked by heavily armed soldiers, their M4 rifles at the ready.

'This is our protection,' Antonio explained as he slowed the SUV. 'The police requested backup from the military when shots were fired at them last night. Probably just kids, but everyone's on edge.'

He pulled up on to a crumbling curb next to a corner market covered with spray-painted gang tags. Heavy grids of rebar were bent across its broken windows. A soldier bearing sergeant's stripes approached as Antonio opened the driver's door and presented his identification to the hardened veteran, who peered distrustfully at it before waving him forward. Maribela turned to look at Sam and Remi.

'It's showtime – isn't that how they say it?'

'Indeed,' Remi said.

Yellow tape cordoned off a brown-dirt slope leading into a chasm beneath the street. Sam and Remi held their breath at the stench of accumulated sewage as Antonio disappeared into the gloom. The distinctive roar of a gas generator started up, and two portable lights flickered to life inside.

'Come on. It's about fifteen feet farther in,' Maribela called.

Remi swallowed hard, almost gagging, and then followed the two Mexican archaeologists, Sam immediately behind her.

Ahead was a breach in a stone wall, where the rocks had collapsed inward into the space beyond. Antonio climbed through the opening and the three of them followed. Another light was set up on a tripod positioned at the junction of three passages.

Antonio waited until they caught up with him and then explained, 'Each of these passageways leads to a burial vault. Probably the most significant one is just ahead. You'll see the pottery and other items – they're numbered, and we've left them where we found them so we can do a more careful examination in the next few days. Be careful as you walk – the floor's uneven.'

They approached the first crypt as a group, their footsteps echoing in the confined space, the air filled with the scent of wet earth and decay. Antonio bent over and flipped a switch box lying by his feet. A bank of work lamps illuminated the end of the tunnel, their eerie glow reflecting off the chamber walls.

Remi gasped as a root brushed her shoulder.

Sam took her hand. 'Little creepy, isn't it?'

The room was small, no more than twelve by twelve, with a stone podium that had been the final resting place of a Toltec dignitary at the far end. Pots, ceramic figures, masks, and obsidian tools lay strewn on either side of it, with grid lines of white twine now strung over them to accurately map their positions. The most striking feature was the pictographs that covered every inch of wall space – the entire room was a Toltec art treasure. Sam stopped short of the pedestal, taking in the breathtaking display, and felt Remi inch closer, as their eyes roved over the tableau.

Maribela said, 'These possessions were likely collected in an orderly pile, but, over the centuries, earthquakes have had their way with them. Although the crypt is in remarkably good shape, what's most surprising are the carvings. Very much like the other Toltec sites we've mapped . . . but I've never seen them in this abundance.'

Sam and Remi approached the nearest wall. Sam took a small flashlight from his pocket and twisted it on.

A somber face glowered back at him, an elaborate headdress atop its head, a stylized club in one hand and a serpent in the other. Sam moved to another, where a jaguar stood ready to pounce in front of a depiction of a temple. Next to it, a procession of warriors. Below it, men leading animals on leashes. Figures constructing a towering pyramid. On and on, scene after scene.

'Amazing, isn't it?' Remi whispered. 'The condition's remarkable.'

Antonio nodded. 'We're hoping that as we excavate, we'll find even more. The mud you see on the floor is from leakage over time, which is inevitable. But most of the area is as pristine as I've ever seen.'

'What's your theory on who the mummies were?' Remi asked.

'Probably priests, but very highly placed – possibly the religious leaders of their era. Why they're buried south of Tula is a mystery.'

'Was it customary to entomb the religious leaders in such elaborate crypts?'

'Little is actually known about their civilization, so there are still more questions than answers. It will take many months, if not years, to fully document this find – assuming that the city doesn't shut us down. The street running overhead is a problem, although we can probably buy one of the nearby buildings and create an entrance there. But that takes funds . . .'

They moved to the other crypts, which contained more carvings and more artifacts. Remi took photographs of all the images for later study, amazed by the sheer quantity. The amount of work involved had to represent years of skilled artisan time.

After three hours of exploration, Antonio signaled that they were going to take a break and return to the surface.

Maribela led the way.

'We have a group of students coming in this afternoon to help us with the excavation. You're welcome to stay, if you like, but it will get crowded. And, frankly, you've seen most of what there is to see so far. Perhaps you'd like to spend some time at the Institute with the artifacts there?' Maribela suggested. 'I can drive you while Antonio takes care of things here.'

'That would be great,' Sam agreed. 'We don't want to get in your way. And there's certainly enough to see in the Institute vaults to keep us busy.'

Remi nodded her assent, and the group stepped carefully back out to the stinking street, where the sun was now burning through the clouds.

Sam's phone rang on the journey to the Institute. He glanced at the screen and answered it. 'What's the good word?' he asked.

'I may have something promising for you,' Rube said, 'but it's both good news and bad news.'

'What's the bad?'

'Cuba's about as secretive as the Chinese, so everything we have is hearsay and innuendo.'

'Meaning "unreliable."'

'Correct.'

'What's the good?'

'There's apparently a store of Spanish antiquities in Havana that the Ministry of the Interior controls. Part of their museums group.'

'I don't suppose I dare ask how you know about it.'

'Defector. Floated over along with fifty others on a makeshift boat forty years ago.'

'So the information's that old?'

'That's not your biggest problem.'

'Why do I suspect that you saved the best for last?'

'Am I really that transparent?'

'Just give it to me straight.'

'It's located in the subbasement of Morro Castle, which has a contingent of military guarding it round the clock.'

'Do you have any details on the layout?'

'Check your e-mail. But Sam? Just a little advice. The Cubans play hardball, and they don't like Americans. So if you're thinking of doing anything stupid, my advice is don't.'

'That's not very encouraging.'

Rube exhaled noisily. 'When I hang up the phone, you're on your own, my friend. I won't be able to help you if you pursue this and run into trouble, and I'd advise strongly against doing anything rash.'

'Noted. Thanks again. I owe you one.'

'Be careful, Sam. You have to be alive for me to collect.'

15

After spending the afternoon analysing the material at the Institute and comparing it to the photos from that morning, Sam and Remi called it a day at six and returned to the hotel. Sam logged on to his in-box and spent several minutes studying Rube's e-mail, which consisted of a set of crude blueprints of Morro Castle, obviously hand-drawn, and a description of the military contingent guarding the fort. Built in 1589 to protect Havana Harbor, Morro was a national landmark, now relegated to a tourist attraction.

Remi sat on the bed while Sam finished up and then raised an eyebrow when she saw the drawing.

'Sam Fargo, I hope you haven't dreamed up some crazy scheme.'

'Of course not. I was just thinking what a nice time of year it would be to visit Cancún.'

'Which is only an hour flight from Cuba, is it not?'

'What? Really? That's all?'

'You have a lousy poker face.'

He nodded. 'Then it's just as well I don't play cards.'

'I knew when you heard about an encrypted manuscript, you wouldn't be able to resist.'

'Well, now that you mention it, it does seem an awful

shame that something as potentially important to the Mexican people is being hoarded by a foreign power.'

'We don't know that it *has any import*ance. For all we know, it's a recipe.'

'With a bunch of pre-Columbian illustrations?'

'Don't forget the letters from seamen. Not exactly promising. Besides which, the Spanish conquest of Mexico went on for, what, a hundred and eighty years? So it could refer to basically anything, not necessarily the Toltecs.'

'Fair enough, but do we have anything better to go on?'

'Not yet, but we're just getting started analysing the reliefs. Maybe there's something in the new find that will point us in the right direction –'

'Which will still be here when we get back.'

Remi frowned. '*If* we get back.'

'Oh come on. All I'm thinking is that we sneak in, take some photos, and are gone before anyone figures it out. Where's the harm?'

'It's a fort, Sam. As in, *fort-i-fied*. By a regime that's more hostile to the US than any in this hemisphere. Something tells me that if we get caught, we're going to be in really hot water.'

'Which is why no part of the plan involves getting caught.'

Remi sighed. 'For the record, this is a bad idea. But I can see there's no point in arguing with you, is there?'

'Maybe to get better at it?'

'I've had years of practice and it doesn't seem to do any more good than it did when we first met.'

'Then we fly to Havana, scope out the fort, and slip into the vault in the dead of night.'

'Right . . . And just how are you going to do that?'

'I haven't completely figured that part out yet.'

'Call me when you do.'

That evening, three e-mails came in from the team, but none of them contained anything that Sam and Remi didn't already know. There was an encyclopedia entry on the legend of Quetzalcoatl's tomb, describing a casket of jade, mountains of gold, priceless ornaments, and the Eye of Heaven, which to Sam's trained eye read like the wishful thinking of a teenager. All hidden in a secret tomb in a sacred place, safe from desecration by heathens, which to the Toltecs meant anyone besides themselves.

Next was a doctoral student's report on a 1587 search expedition that had followed in the footsteps of the original one in 1521. While the group discovered many of the larger Aztec and Toltec cities, it came up empty on the tomb. But the unique fever that accompanies the promise of priceless treasure had taken hold and generation after generation of adventurers sought Quetzalcoatl's final resting place – as well as the legendary Seven Cities of Gold – and, in South America, El Dorado . . . all to meet with ruin, disease, and, ultimately, death.

In the early 1920s, according to a third article from a

popular journal, another group scoured the temple cities of central Mexico in search of the elusive treasure but never returned from their quest – presumed killed by bandits in a largely lawless land.

After a leisurely meal at the hotel, Sam checked on flights from Cancún and learned that there were several every day to Havana. He read up on entry requirements and discovered that they could easily make it into Cuba with paper visas inserted into their passports, to be removed once they'd left, so there would be no evidence of their ever having been there. After Sam explained the travel arrangements to Remi, they agreed to at least try a mini Cuban vacation and take a hard look at Morro Castle.

Sam's first act the following day was to send news of their plans to everyone in La Jolla and ask them to find someone reliable in Havana to help them while there.

Next item was the trip to Cancún. Sam instructed Rex to file a flight plan for that evening. Finally, he booked a flight for the next day from Cancún to Havana, after being assured that he could get visas in short order from the Cuban consulate in Cancún.

The afternoon at the Institute went by quickly. They'd already seen most of the carvings online, so there were no surprises. Traffic to the airport was a misery, taking almost as long as the flight to Cancún. When the G650 touched down and the fuselage door swung open, muggy heat flowed into the cabin, the humidity close to ninety per cent. A courtesy car whisked them away to the

Ritz-Carlton, where, after checking in, they dined at Fantino, the hotel's upscale restaurant. Remi started with the sweet pea and butter lettuce soup with scallops and chose the black cod for her entrée, and Sam went with the seared ahi tuna appetizer and the porcini-crusted filet mignon, all washed down with a bottle of 2006 Adobe Guadalupe Serafiel Cabernet/Syrah blend.

Sam reclined as the staff whisked away the plates, swirling the last of the wine in his goblet before taking a long, appreciative sip. 'Wow. Who knew they made wine like this in Mexico? It's amazing.'

'I know. Quite a mouthful. Almost a meal by itself.'

He took in the reflected light from the chandelier dancing in her eyes. 'You have to admit – so far, this isn't so terrible.'

'It's no Baffin Island, I'll give you that much . . .'

After dinner, they had tequila brandy at the pool bar and watched the surf crash on to the white sand beach, the waves phosphorescent in the moonlight.

'This is wonderful, Sam. I just hope that tomorrow finishes as nicely as tonight.'

'We'll be in Havana. We can find someplace that makes a decent mojito and soak up the local color. How bad can it be?'

'You realize every time you say that –'

'Something goes wrong,' Sam finished for her. 'I retract the "how bad" question.'

'I don't think it works that way. It's out in the universe now.'

'Nonsense. We're on the most beautiful beach in the world. And I'm with the prettiest girl in town.'

Remi edged close to Sam. The strumming of the Mexican bar band and the harmony of the singers perfectly complemented the intoxicating brandy they were sipping. They returned to their room, the future as uncertain as ever but their present as pleasant as any they could wish for.

Sam called Selma, anxious for word on her hunt for a Cuban guide. Kendra answered Selma's line.

'You're in luck. Selma's got a suggestion from one of her contacts: a doctor in Havana who agreed to show you around and who I've been assured is as resourceful as they come.'

'She vouched for him?'

'She did. He's a fan of several of her articles and they've corresponded for years. When do you leave?'

'Tomorrow afternoon.'

'Good luck.'

Sam paused. 'How's Selma doing?'

'Still rolling with the punches, but the physical therapy takes its toll on her.'

'It can do that. Is she following the doctor's instructions?'

'I think so. Probably doing more than she should. She told me yesterday that she just wants to get back on her feet as soon as possible.'

'Tell her she's in our thoughts.'

'I will.'

16

On their way to the Cuban consulate, it became clear that the taxi driver had no idea where it was. After asking three pedestrians for directions, he finally deposited them in front of a run-down white residence two blocks off the main street, which he assured them was the 'new' location of the elusive Cuban headquarters.

The hot waiting area was barely ventilated by a struggling stand-up fan that predated the combustion engine. When the woman at the counter finally held up their travel documents, they gratefully approached her, and, after paying the token fee, they couldn't get to the exit fast enough.

The pair ambled down the long blocks, the tropical sun beating down on them. When they made it to the main street, Sam was soaked through. He scanned the shops and pointed to a hardware store.

Ten minutes later, they emerged, several hundred pesos poorer but with a bulging sack of supplies. They flagged down a taxi to return to their hotel.

Lunch by the pool, along with a final margarita, revived their flagging spirits, and when they arrived at the airport, they checked their luggage and supply bag through security without a problem. Their previous evening's positive sentiment lasted until they were informed by the Cubana Air hostess that the flight was running an hour late due to unspecified delays. The departure area was as far from the Ritz pool as one could get, but Sam made the best of it with a cold Tecate beer and a bag of potato chips while Remi sipped a bottle of water.

One hour turned into two, and by the time they were in their plane seats Remi had mentioned several times that she didn't have a great feeling about the trip.

'Relax. What could –' Sam started and then caught himself.

Remi glared at him. 'I warned you. You're going to bring bad juju on us.'

'I didn't say it.'

'You thought it.'

Sam had no comeback to that, so he just gazed out the window at the palms baking on the edge of the tarmac. The ancient jet lumbered across it in preparation for takeoff, and then they were rumbling down the runway, the plane shaking alarmingly as it struggled to propel itself into the sky.

José Martí International Airport in Havana was larger than they'd expected, with three terminals and a host of planes on the ground. Remi noted quietly to Sam that the interior was as shabby as the gray concrete exterior. The customs agents were serious and unfriendly, frowning determinedly before waving them through.

Sam changed four hundred dollars at the currency exchange window and pocketed the Cuban bills. When they walked out on to the sidewalk to make their way to the taxi line, the heat hit them like a blow. Hot and more humid than Cancún, even the breeze was uncomfortable as it blew from the surrounding jungle. A line of new Mitsubishi cabs waited under a rusting steel awning, where a cadaverous man in a faded blue uniform blew a whistle with all the enthusiasm of a mortician.

The ride into Havana took forty-five minutes, first through countryside and then the outskirts of the city. Sam and Remi were surprised by how many of the vehicles were modern – they'd been expecting a fleet of 1950s-era junkers, based on the movie depictions. Apparently, the Cubans hadn't studied the same films because their appetite for Nissan and Honda seemed as insatiable as anywhere in America, although there were still plenty of aging Fiats and Ladas belching blue exhaust as they rolled down the streets.

When they arrived at the Iberostar Parque Central Hotel, a uniformed bell captain held Remi's door open as Sam paid the driver. The hotel was located in an elegant colonial building across the street from a park, a huge green square that served as the downtown city center – buzzing with activity as evening approached. A saxophone player blew a haunting riff to the accompaniment of revving car engines and peals of laughter from loitering groups of teens. Sam paused for a moment to listen before turning and accompanying Remi into the hotel lobby.

Once they were in their room, Sam called the contact Selma had provided: Dr Lagarde. When he answered, he immediately switched to passable English after hearing the telltale American accent in Sam's hello.

'Ah, I presume this is Selma Wondrash's friend?' Lagarde said.

'It is. We're in town. I wanted to touch base and see what your schedule looked like tomorrow,' Sam said.

'I shall arrange my affairs around your requirements, of course. I have some flexibility in that regard. I'll let the hospital know I won't be in.'

'Thank you. I hope it isn't too much of an imposition.'

'Of course not. Any friend of Selma's is a friend of mine. I hold her in the highest regard.'

They arranged for Lagarde to meet them at the hotel at nine the following morning.

'So where are we eating?' Remi asked from her position by the window, where she was watching the activity in the square across the street.

'I found a promising name online. My idea is we wander around a little, get a feel for the town, then eat a late dinner. Maybe around nine.'

'Works for me.'

After making a dinner reservation, they stepped out on to the street – a busy avenue that ringed the square and stretched from the famous *malecón* that ran along the ocean's edge all the way to the far edges of the city. They followed the Paseo del Prado down to the sea wall and found themselves across the harbor channel from their objective – the Castillo de los Tres Reyes Magos del Morro, or Morro Castle.

'It's certainly imposing,' Remi said, gazing up at the fort's towering stone walls. 'How do we get to it?'

'There's a tunnel that runs under the harbor for automobile traffic.'

'So we're not going to have to swim the channel?'

'Not tonight.'

'You want to go over there right now?'

'We can tour it tomorrow. Tonight we're sightseeing. Taking in the city's sights and sounds.'

A group of young women passed them on the *malecón*, their perfume lingering on the light wind. Remi and Sam followed them, having no special destination in mind. They walked east along the waterfront and then turned up a small street into the historic section of old Havana, a lively area where locals and tourists wandered along the sidewalks. Bricks poked through battered building façades like skeletal bones, the mortar long ago eroded away, lending them an aura of seedy disrepair.

They rounded a corner and nearly collided with a wizened man sporting a panama hat, his skin as dark as a well-worn saddle, puffing on a cigar almost as big as his arm. He smiled, a flash of pink gums, his teeth long ago sacrificed to age and circumstance, and muttered a sandpaper *'Perdón'* before continuing on his way, trailing a cloud of pungent smoke behind him.

'Are you sure about this, Sam?' Remi asked in a whisper.

'Absolutely. All the guidebooks say this section of town is as safe as the womb.'

As if to underscore the point, two soldiers with machine guns approached, their eyes watchful, studying the surroundings with the vigilance of a patrol in a war zone.

'There, does that make you feel any better?' Sam asked.

'It might if they were over sixteen.'

'Everyone's a critic.'

They stepped around a pool of stagnant water gathered in a low spot among the ancient cobblestones.

Remi pointed to a small yellow sign fifty yards to their left. 'Look. There's one of Hemingway's haunts. La Bodeguita del Medio.'

'I regard that as an omen. It's the universe commanding us to stop.'

'According to Papa, this is the best mojito in Havana.'

'That's good enough for me. Lead the way,' Sam said.

The bar was crowded and smaller than expected. Its walls were covered with autographs of the notorious, the famous, and the forgotten. Obligatory photographs of Che Guevara and Fidel Castro glared at them from dingy frames. A stool freed up and Sam elbowed through the tourists and held it for Remi, who took the seat gratefully and caught the bartender's eye.

'*Dos mojitos, por favor,*' she said, holding up two fingers.

The man nodded and moved to make the drinks, crushing the mint leaves with focused concentration before pouring a liberal slug of rum into a stainless steel shaker. He added lime juice, sugarcane syrup, and soda and then shook the concoction with sincere intensity, making a production out of the cocktail preparation while several cameras clicked behind Remi's head.

The drinks arrived on the scarred wooden bar, each with a sprig of mint atop it. Sam held his sweating glass up in a toast that was met by Remi.

One mojito led to another and soon they were chatting with a Canadian group bound for Varadero the next day — a beach resort seventy-five miles east of Havana famous for its hospitality and its sun-drenched shores. As the crowd got louder, Sam glanced at his watch and gestured to the bartender for the tab.

Outside, the darkened street seemed more ominous than when they'd arrived at dusk. They hurried along with other tourists, making their way from the waterfront toward the city center. When they arrived at a large hotel, Remi approached one of the loitering taxi drivers and asked him how far the restaurant was. The old man looked her up and down without expression.

'San Cristobal Paladar? Too far to walk. Maybe ten

minutes, maybe less, by car. You want me to take you there?'

Sam nodded and they got in.

The restaurant was in a colonial home in the middle of town and the food was divine – an unexpected treat. When dinner was over, the owner called a taxi for them and waited by the front door for the vehicle to arrive, chatting with Remi about the ups and downs of operating a business in a Communist country.

Back at the hotel, Sam convinced her to have a nightcap in the lobby bar. They savored snifters of aged Havana Club Gran Reserva fifteen-year Añejo rum as a tuxedoed musician stroked the keys of a grand piano in the atrium.

'Well, so far, I have to say this hasn't been terrible,' Remi conceded.

'Good food, good drink, and good company. Always a winner in my book.'

'I just hope we don't have hangovers tomorrow from all the rum.'

'It's common knowledge that when you drink it in the islands, you never get a hangover.'

'Interesting. I hadn't heard that. Sounds like another Sam Fargo invention.'

For a few short hours in their usually hectic lives, the world was perfect, the mood tranquil, the music hypnotic, the trade winds blowing outside, as they had for centuries and would for countless more.

17

The next morning Dr Lagarde was waiting for them in the hotel atrium lobby. A short, paunchy man in his sixties, with a dense gray beard and round spectacles, he wore a white tropical-weight linen suit and a pale blue button-down shirt, a seemingly mandatory panama hat perched on his head.

'I'm honored to meet you,' Lagarde said, shaking first Remi's hand and then Sam's.

'Thanks for taking the time out to play tour guide,' Sam said.

'Please, you're on my island. It's the least I can do for guests.'

'That's very kind of you,' Remi said.

'*Bueno.* So what would you like to see first? There is much of interest here, depending upon your tastes.'

'We're really here to study Morro Castle, Doctor.'

'Please, call me Raphael.'

'And we're Sam and Remi. Can you tell us about the castle?'

'Of course. It's a national treasure. Everyone in Havana knows its history and most have been there a hundred times. In the old days, it was free – for the people.' Raphael sighed and shook his head. 'Like so much, that, too, has changed and we must now pay to see our own history.'

'Can we go there and have you show us around?'

'Absolutely. My car is parked around the corner. Although we may want to take a taxi because parking there will be a problem.'

Remi nodded. 'Whatever you think is best.'

Seven minutes later, the cab dropped them off at the base of the hill. The fort loomed above them, the ugly black snouts of cannons jutting over the walls, pointed at the channel that any invaders would have to pass through. Raphael led them through the gates, where Sam dutifully paid their entry fee.

Like so much of Havana, the fort's walls were crumbling, their surfaces marred by centuries of storms and blistering sun.

Dr Lagarde removed his hat and fanned himself with it for a moment. 'The fort was designed by an Italian engineer, Juan Bautista Antonelli, who was rather well known at the time. His design was approved by the Spanish and construction started in 1589. Up until then, the hill only had a few cannons, and a stone hut for the guards, which was inadequate to protect the town as it grew from a small village to the main Spanish trading hub for the New World. There were constant threats by pirates, and after building the first lighthouse, the governor appealed to the Crown to build a proper fortification. It took forty years to build the fort, which was armed with sixty-four cannons.'

'But the British took it at some point, didn't they?' Sam asked.

'Indeed they did. In 1762. They held Havana for a year and it was returned to Spain as part of an end to the Seven Years' War. Immediately after that, construction began on La Cabaña, which is the larger fort you can see just past the point. That took ten years to build, and, together with Morro Castle, it made Havana impervious to attack.'

'There are certainly a lot of people wandering the grounds,' Remi noted, gazing at the crowd.

'It's one of the more popular destinations in Havana. Iconic. Even more so at nine every night when the symbolic firing of the cannon takes place. Originally, it signaled that the gates of the city were being closed. Now it's just one of those traditions that we've kept from Spanish times.'

Remi pointed at a doorway surrounded by a throng. 'What's that?'

'A museum. It features weapons and nautical relics from the castle's past.'

'Can we go inside the dungeons?'

'Of course. There are only a few sections at the lowest levels that are closed to the public. Old vaults, I believe.'

'Really? You'll have to show us the entire complex. I find it fascinating,' Remi said.

They spent the day walking the grounds and had lunch at one of the two restaurants, where a trio played salsa music for the patrons' entertainment. Sam sampled several beers, including the lighter Crystal and the amber Bucanero. When they returned to their hotel at four, they were both sunburned and tired but agreed that they wanted to go back to the castle that night for the nine o'clock cannon ceremony – a convenient pretext for observing how quickly the crowds thinned out so they could plot how to best access the vaults below. The blueprint Rube had sent showed crude air ducts from the vaults to the upper levels for ventilation – a possible entry point if they couldn't breach the doors.

Security was lax, but there were still soldiers and police patrolling the grounds – and it would only take one of them to sound the alarm and Sam and Remi would be in deep trouble. The wing that housed the vaults was closed off, a heavy rusting-iron barrier sealing off the stone hallway leading into the castle's depths.

Sam studied the drawing for another hour, searching for anything he might have missed, but there wasn't much to offer hope. The place was a stone fortress designed to repel attempts to enter it. Even from the inside, breaching it was a tentative proposition, assuming in the wee hours there were few or no patrols for long stretches of time in the vicinity of the vault. And they'd both noted surveillance cameras in the inner passageways, although not in the vicinity of the barrier – but that meant that if they were discovered, their likenesses would be there for all to see and their chances of getting out of Cuba would be nil.

At eight-fifteen they took a taxi to the Morro Castle

and mingled with the large crowd waiting for the cannon ceremony. The grass field where the cannon stood was almost completely black, any moonlight blocked by clouds. The soldiers in dress uniforms from the present and past went through the nightly ritual, to the popping of flashes and snicking of lenses. Excitement washed over the crowd as the master-at-arms yelled commands to his subordinates, who went about their assigned tasks with robotic efficiency as still more soldiers marched in formation on to the green.

The explosion was deafening and greeted with a cheer, and then the group seemed to deflate, the ceremony over, leaving everyone to find their way to the exits. Remi edged to the doors that led to the barrier at the lower level and, after glancing around to confirm that nobody was paying attention, eased one open and slid through the gap. Sam stayed in position, feigning interest in his cell phone and ignoring the policeman who walked by, whose attention was drawn more by the young women in short skirts than by Sam.

Five minutes turned into ten, and then another ten. Sam's resolve had just about cracked when Remi reappeared.

'You had me worried,' he said, relieved.

'Nothing to worry about. If you don't count the armed patrol I had to dodge.'

Sam studied her face. 'You're kidding.'

'Do I look like I'm kidding?'

'Not really. How did you avoid them?'

'I heard their boots and ducked into one of the jail cells down the hallway. I'm just lucky it was out of camera range.'

'So what did you discover?'

'Fortunately, the guards are sloppy and not paying attention. There's a large iron grid over the ventilation duct, which is so badly rusted I was able to break off pieces with my fingers. Five minutes with a crowbar or bolt cutters and we'd be through, but I don't think you'd fit. If we're going to get through using the vents, it's going to have to be a solo act for me. And there are still the cameras to consider.'

Sam shook his head. 'Absolutely not.'

'Okay, then, I guess we can go home now?'

'I don't like you trying this alone. There has to be another way.'

'I took a closer look at the lock on the barrier and it's a Soviet-era padlock. Case-hardened, so I don't think it can be cut – and that's assuming we could wander in with a bolt cutter, and further assuming that the guards wouldn't notice that the lock was cut off and start shooting the second they came through the barrier.'

'We've figured out a way in and out of trickier scenarios than this. We'll find a way. You think you could jimmy it?'

'It looks doable, but I've never picked a Russian lock before and there could be a learning curve that would throw our timing out the window. And let's not forget that any patrol would see it open if we both went in. I took a photo so we can research it online.' She paused. 'I still think the air vent is the best option.'

'Out of the question. I'm not going to just stand around while you take all the risks.'

Remi's face softened. 'That's one of the things I love about you.'

'My courage? My gentlemanly nature?'

'That you get us into a really dangerous situation and then pretend that there's no risk for you. I'm pretty sure if I got caught, you wouldn't be leaving the country anytime soon.'

'Yet another reason to not get caught. I wouldn't do well in a Cuban prison.'

She put a cool hand on his face. 'No, you wouldn't. Not with that pretty face of yours.'

'You always manage to say the right thing,' Sam said, and then something attracted his attention at the end of the walkway. A man with a baseball cap pulled low over his brow quickly turned away and lit a cigarette, shielding his features from view, and moved around the corner, smoke lingering where he'd been.

'I saw that guy earlier. I think we might have picked up a tail,' Sam warned, his voice low.

'For what? *We* don't even know what we're doing here.'

'It could be nothing. I just caught a glimpse of him before and I'm trying to remember where,' Sam said, his senses on sudden alert following the man's abrupt departure. Then his face changed. 'He was on the edge of the crowd. I noticed him because he was staring at you. Let's see if we can catch up to him. Come on.' Sam began walking briskly toward the corner. Remi matched his pace, but when they arrived at the junction, they were confronted by a sea of departing backs as the last of the cannon-firing spectators moved to the gates.

'Do you see him?' she asked.

'No ... Wait. There. Black baseball cap. Blue short-sleeved shirt. Thirty yards up, on the right. By that shop doorway.'

The man caught Sam staring at him and stubbed out his cigarette. The crowd surged as it neared the exit, and he melted into the stream of departing pedestrians. Sam broke into a trot and Remi trailed him, wondering what her husband planned to do when he caught up with the man.

Which never happened. When they reached the main gates, there was no sign of their quarry. Sam scanned the figures walking down the hill but without success. The man had disappeared like a mosquito in a darkened room.

They spent another two hours walking the fort, returning to the lower-level doors every few minutes, trying to time the entry of the guards, and they estimated that the patrol would enter the passageway every thirty minutes. By eleven-thirty, the rush of people had thinned to a trickle, and other than a few late-night revelers leaving the restaurants, Sam and Remi were the only civilians in the fort. Even the street vendors selling curios had packed up their trade for the evening.

Back at the hotel, Sam was still concerned by their brush with the tail. Remi suggested that they duck around the block and soothe Sam's brutalized psyche at another Hemingway haunt: El Floridita, the birthplace of the frozen daiquiri.

They sat at the bar and ordered, Sam with a watchful eye on the door, and it wasn't until his drink was almost drained that he seemed to relax.

'Sam, I'm not saying that the man didn't stare at me. If you say he did, I believe you. I just can't figure out why anyone would be following us. Maybe he was a pickpocket? Looking for some easy tourist targets?'

'That could be. I mean, who knows we're here? Nobody. And even if they did, what would be the point? It's not like we've located a gold-laden galleon off the coast.'

'Exactly. I think we're so sensitive to being followed that we notice things that would be lost on others. Which isn't a bad thing.'

'Maybe. Besides, all anyone following us would learn is that we're interested in historical sites and where to get the best drinks in Havana. Not exactly priceless information.'

Remi smiled. 'No, it actually seems pretty innocent, put that way.' She finished her drink and sighed contentedly. 'Since you've been so good today, I'll escort you back to the hotel. We've got to figure out how to deal with our little fort problem or the whole trip will have been for nothing.'

18

Three days later, Sam and Remi checked out, leaving their suitcases with Raphael for safekeeping. They'd traded them for a pair of black backpacks, their valuables tucked away in watertight bags in inner compartments, and each carried only a change of clothes and travel documents. It had taken forty-eight hours for Kendra to arrange for everything they'd requested, and the plan was for Raphael to send their bags on to them with the next person he knew flying to Mexico.

They slipped out the back door of the hotel, anxious to lose the shadow that they were now convinced they'd picked up. As far as they could tell, it was a three-person team – two men and a woman – who rotated, changing their appearances for each new shift. Remi had persuaded Sam to favor evasion over confrontation, to exchange his normal hard-charging approach for one with more subtlety.

After switching taxis twice to ensure they weren't being tailed, they took a third to the castle. This time, they ate a late dinner after the cannon ceremony at one of the restaurants on the castle grounds, taking their time to linger over the meal, waiting for the spectators to clear the area.

When they finished dinner, they browsed along the battlements, keeping a sharp eye out for the armed patrols. At midnight, they made their move into the building, inching the outer door open and listening for any signs of life before hurrying down to the barrier one level below. They passed a single security camera, but there was no way to avoid it and, because the area they were in was open to the public, they hoped it wouldn't trigger an alarm.

Remi stood sentry while Sam retrieved from his pocket the two pieces of an aluminum cola can he'd carefully cut and formed earlier. He slipped one rounded stub over the padlock post and slid it down until the tab was fully inserted, gave a twist, and was rewarded with a small click. He repeated the exercise on the other post and pulled the lock open.

'Showtime,' he whispered. Remi moved to his side as he squirted oil on the rusty hinges and clasp.

'Ready?' she asked, lifting the clasp.

'Always.'

She pushed the lever to the side, which squeaked like a wounded animal in spite of the lubricant, and then ducked inside. Sam listened for any hint of a patrol but didn't hear anything, and then felt his phone vibrate as Remi called from inside.

'Not good. There's a cam here in the hallway by the door, so I'm busted. Time to engage Plan B. Lock it up and get out of there. We'll rendezvous as we agreed.'

'Nope. Change of plans. I'm coming with you.'

'Sam, they've got me on camera. Any second now, there will be soldiers on their way. I don't have time to argue.'

'Then don't. Is there a way to lock the barrier from the inside?'

A moment of silence greeted him, and then Remi's hushed voice from his phone: 'Yes. A clasp. Like on your side.'

'See you in a second. You better get moving on the vault door. I'm hoping all your lock-picking practice will pay off.'

Sam pulled the door open and edged through. He closed it again quickly and slid the padlock into the clasp, snapping it shut. With any luck, it would hold the guards for a little while – the barrier looked strong even if it had been designed only to keep tourists out rather than fortify the corridor. And, as with all security doors, it opened outward, so you'd have to kick the whole frame in, not just the door. He guessed the Cubans wouldn't be stupid enough to try to shoot their way through it because of the danger of ricocheting bullets.

The hallway was gloomy, a single incandescent bulb in a caged fixture providing dim illumination. Sam hurried to where Remi was on her knees in front of the vault door. He moved past her and stopped beneath the ceiling camera, fishing in his backpack until he found a can of black spray paint. After peering at the mirrored globe, he popped the top off and hit the camera with a burst.

'They're blind now. How's it coming?'

'It's not as complicated as I thought. Should have it open in a second,' Remi answered. They heard running boots at the far end of the corridor on the opposite side of the barrier, followed by a crashing from the heavy iron slab as the guards tried to demolish it.

'Now might be a really good time to open the door, Remi.'

'I'm almost there,' she whispered between gritted teeth, and brushed the first makeshift pick lightly against the posts inside the lock as she applied pressure with the second pick she'd fashioned from a bobby pin. Sam had been dubious of the simple tools she'd created until she'd demonstrated her abilities with them by opening their locked hotel door in fifteen seconds, at which point he'd decided that it was time for a little more faith in his wife's talents.

'We're in,' Remi whispered as the dead bolt clicked open with a twist, and she stood. 'Ready?'

More slamming echoed from the metal door, accompanied by shouts and the blow of rifle stocks against it.

'You go. I'll wait out here and deal with the light. I don't want them getting any ideas about shooting down the corridor if they can punch a hole in the iron.'

As she pushed the door open, a Klaxon siren blared. They'd discussed the possibility of an alarm, either silent or audible, but it was still jarring. Sam stuffed foam earplugs in place as he hurried to the lamp. When he was directly beneath it, he took the paint again and sprayed the bulb and soon the hallway was pitch-black, the only light coming from a distant ventilation slit in the ten-foot-thick walls.

A gunshot exploded from the barrier, followed by a scream and yelled instructions. Apparently, the soft lead bullet hadn't penetrated; judging by the commotion on the other side, it had hit one of the guards, which would hopefully dampen their enthusiasm for more gunfire.

The crashing resumed within ten seconds, this time steel on steel. Sam's guess that the fire axes he'd seen in cases around the fort would come into play had been a good one. He had no illusions that the door would be able to stand up to a sustained assault. He crept along the passage back to the vault.

'Are you done?' Sam shouted through the vault doorway, momentarily blinded by the flash of Remi's digital camera.

'Almost! Three more shots and we're out of here,' she yelled back at him, the siren drowning out her voice as she continued to take pictures.

A beam of light appeared from the barrier. They'd pierced it. It would be only a matter of seconds until the shooting started.

'They're through. Let's go. Now!' Sam called. Remi didn't hesitate. They sprinted for the far end of the passageway, where they knew from the blueprint there would be a curve and then a junction. He prayed that the diagram was accurate and that a bright mind hadn't decided to seal their escape route at some point over the last forty years – that could ruin their night.

Sam reached the junction just as gunfire erupted behind them. Slugs whistled through the air, whining as they glanced off the stone walls and ricocheted in every direction. Both he and Remi dropped and crawled the remaining five feet, setting a new record for military-style scrambling. The gunfire continued until the shooter exhausted his clip.

Sam pointed at a dark chamber fifteen feet away and inched toward it, sticking to the floor in the event of a stray bullet bouncing off the rock walls. After what seemed like forever, they reached the doorway. The air was a bouquet of rot and decay, but also the most welcome odor in the world – salt air. From the far side of the room the crash of waves breaking against the rocks below the castle's foundation greeted them and they both leapt to their feet and felt their way toward the sound.

There, at floor level, were three chutes that opened out on to the sea, barely large enough to accommodate a human body. The iron bars imbedded in the stone had been mostly eaten away by the elements. Sam pulled a penlight from his pocket and then reached into his bag and extracted a tire iron and rope. He swung the beam around the room in search of anything to tie the line to. There – a stone sink sat at the far end of the small space, attached to the wall. He quickly wound the end of the rope around it several times before fashioning a climber's knot and giving it a firm pull.

'Let me break the bars, and, when I'm through, follow me down,' Sam instructed. He lowered himself to the cold stone floor, the surface slick from condensation and mould, and slid down the chute, arms first, playing out rope with his left hand, the crowbar gripped in his right.

The iron grille was little more than rust. It took less than half a minute to create a gap he could squeeze through. Chunks of iron dropped down the sheer wall outside and struck the rocks below. Sam flipped around and followed them down forty-five feet to a slim outcropping, where waves struck it and exploded in bursts of spray before retreating back into the black of night. The rope above him vibrated as Remi descended quickly; the clump of her rubber-soled boots landing on the rocks filled him with relief.

'Be careful! These boulders are slippery, and the barnacles will cut like razors if you slip,' he called, pulling out the earplugs and pocketing them as he eyed the dark castle wall above. 'We need to hurry. They'll be through soon enough, and if we're not gone by the time they figure out how we escaped, we'll be trying to outrun bullets and radios.'

Cautiously they began inching along the shoreline, going as fast as they dared. Remi slipped once and Sam caught her arm and steadied her. Five minutes later, the castle was behind them and they were jogging east on a rocky beach.

'How much farther?' Remi asked, easily keeping up with Sam.

'Should be no more than a hundred yards,' Sam said. 'Lucky for us they never sealed up the toilet chutes . . .'

'Please. I'm already going to have to take ten showers just to get the feel of the mould off me. I don't need any reminders about what the last things down the chute were.'

'They haven't been used for years – probably at least twenty. Thank goodness for indoor plumbing, right?'

'If you say so.'

They continued loping down the beach, anxious to put distance between themselves and the castle.

'How did it go?' he asked as he slowed, eyes roving over the coastline, seeking their objective.

'I got shots of everything, including the manuscript. It practically disintegrated in my hands when I unrolled it. A shame nobody cared enough to store it under better conditions.'

'We're fortunate there was anything left. Could you make out the writing and illustrations?'

'I did. But I'd say right now that's not our biggest problem,' she said as flashlight beams glimmered from the castle base. 'Our pursuers just figured it out. I sure hope Selma was good to her word or our troubles have just begun.'

'Look. There it is,' Sam said, pointing at a line tethered to a rock on the shore. He ran to it and pulled as hard as he could, and an ancient black inflatable boat came bouncing through the mild surf.

'You've got to be kidding,' Remi said.

'Hey, it's Cuba. What do you want? This is probably pretty modern for here,' he said as the dinghy washed up on to the beach. He snapped open his Swiss Army knife, severed the line from the rock, and coiled it up and tossed it into the tired little craft.

'Get in and I'll push it out until we're clear of the breakers,' Sam said.

Remi checked her backpack again to make sure that it was sealed tight, the camera safe in the waterproof bag, before helping push the boat a few feet into the water and climbing in.

Sam waited until another wave surged in and heaved the tender away from the sand, turning his back to the incoming surf as it broke over him. Lights from shore swept the beach as soldiers followed their path along the rocks. The bottom fell away from Sam's feet and he climbed aboard and, after a concerned look at the pre-1960s outboard, jerked the cord to start the engine.

Nothing.

He tried again and was rewarded with a feeble cough and puff of exhaust.

'Remi. Grab the oars and row us farther out. This might take a while.'

As she complied, he didn't need to turn to face her to read her expression. Instead, he focused on the outboard, which finally sputtered to noisy life on the eighth try.

'There. Told you it wouldn't be a problem.'

The moonlight glinted off the gold scarab hanging from Remi's neck as she peered into the gloom, where she could barely make out the sound of men yelling to one another. 'I'd put it into gear because we're still in range . . . and will be until we can't see the shore.'

As if to underscore her point, slugs splashed into the water behind them, followed by the sharp report of automatic rifle fire.

'Let's hope nobody's got a night vision scope. Keep your head down,' he said, and then goosed the throttle. He was rewarded by a groan as the motor almost died; then it revved and the boat surged forward over the small waves. More gunfire slapped into the sea around them, frustrated volleys rather than well aimed, and soon the noise of the gunfire receded as the little craft bounced its way north.

'How far?' Remi asked.

Sam pulled a small waterproof GPS from his backpack, powered it on, and squinted at the screen.

'Mile and a half due north. Now we'll be racing the Cubans' ability to get a helicopter into the air. If they're as *mañana* about that as about other things, we should make it. It's almost 1 a.m. on a weekday, and we shouldn't show up on radar. I like our odds.'

'What about the rendezvous boat?'

'Once we're aboard, we'll be in international waters

soon enough. It'll do an honest fifty knots on fairly flat seas like these, and in a pinch, can top out at over a hundred. Besides, I don't think the Cubans are going to cause an international incident over thrill seekers breaking into some old storage room. We didn't even take anything, which a quick inventory will show. Let's hope they lose interest when they figure that out.'

'Lots of hoping going on. I don't need to remind you that's not a great strategy,' Remi chided.

'The fastest craft the Cubans have tops out at thirty-six knots, assuming everything's operating perfectly, so we've got an advantage if there's a chase. They'd never even get close.'

'But their rockets might. It would be nice if we knew where the nearest Cuban ship was.'

'Our boat should have radar.'

'"Should"? Back to hope, are we?'

'So far, so good.'

19

The inflatable bounced along at a good clip, the swells two-footers, the breeze barely stirring their crests. Sam kept an eye peeled on Havana Harbor for any fast-moving lights, but none appeared, and in a few more minutes the dark hull of an oceangoing speedboat appeared on the horizon.

'That's it,' Sam announced as he pointed the bow in the direction of the waiting vessel. Soon they were on board the fifty-foot Cigarette Marauder, its three Mercury 1075 engines rumbling as they settled in. The captain, a tall silver-haired man with twinkling blue eyes, patted the dashboard as the three of them watched the dinghy sink out of sight, its life now over. He zipped his light windbreaker over a blue Hawaiian shirt and ran a large hand through his hair as he peered at the Cuban mainland in the distance.

'How long will it take us to get to Cay Sal?' Sam asked.

The captain glanced at his watch's orange face and smiled. 'If nature favors us, couple of hours max. My tanks are topped off, and I've got another boat waiting there to refuel me for the trip home. Of course, if we have to evade one of the Navy boats, we could be there in a little over an hour at full throttle. Either way, we'll be out of Cuban territorial water within ten minutes, maybe less. Run this baby up to eighty knots and it'll make short work of that.'

'Eighty knots? That's flying.'

'You aren't kidding. Might want to strap in because at that speed we might lift off.'

'Good idea,' Remi said. 'Let's get going. No point in waiting for the bad guys to get their act together.'

'Aye, aye, little lady. Hang on tight.'

The captain engaged the transmissions and pushed the throttles forward. The big engines roared, the boat leapt into motion, and thirty seconds later they were tearing over the waves at almost eighty knots. They rocketed across the sea, the low windshield barely breaking the rush of air as they hurtled northwest.

The captain placed a finger on the radar screen and tapped a blip on the outer reaches. 'That's probably a Navy ship!' he shouted over the scream of the engines. 'Looks to be twenty-two miles west. Let's see if he picks up his pace or not. He may not even have us on radar. It's pretty hard to track this baby, especially at night on moderate seas.'

They watched the pulsing glow of the dot he'd pointed out as they pulled north of it like it was standing still. The captain squinted and shook his head.

'It's moving fairly fast. Looks like around thirty-five knots, which is really hauling for a ship that size. Of course, we're doing more than double that, so by the time he reaches the limits of his territorial waters we'll be halfway to Cay Sal.'

The swell size picked up when they were fifteen miles from Cuba, the island's lights a glimmer on the horizon. The captain throttled back to fifty-five knots, which, while racing, felt almost stationary after the open-water run at close to double that. The bench seat slammed their lower spines, coming off each wave, and by the time the captain eased back to forty-five knots Sam and Remi felt like someone had been beating their kidneys with a board. Their host appeared unfazed; if anything, he seemed to be enjoying the nocturnal run, the wind whipping around him as he leaned forward into each wave.

They'd now been aboard for two hours and were approaching the leeward side of Cay Sal. The captain made a hushed call on his radio before piloting nearer the shoals. A flashlight winked in the darkness, and he deftly pulled the big boat alongside a waiting Cessna T206H Stationair and eased to a halt in the calm water next to it.

'Ahoy, Cap'n! Watch your step, you two. Come on, take my hand,' the pilot called out over the drone of the plane's idling engine as he tossed a line to Sam so he could pull the boat closer. Remi went first, leaping across the chasm with ease. Sam turned to the boat captain.

'Much obliged, sir,' Sam said.

'Safe travels to you and your lovely lady. May you

make it wherever you're headed with smooth air and an easy landing.'

Sam nodded and turned his attention to the plane. 'Here I come,' he warned.

Remi watched through one of the windows as he jumped on to the pontoon. Sam caught hold of the door and climbed into the aircraft. The boat's engines revved and it pulled away, ready for its rendezvous before making its way back to whatever port the boat called home. Sam peered at the transom as it faded from view.

'*Mistress of the C*. Odd name for a boat, don't you think?' Remi commented.

'After that ride, I'd say he can call it whatever he wants as long as it's available again if we're ever in a similar scrape.'

The pilot, a spry man whose dark brown goatee was sprinkled with silver, hoisted himself in and pulled the door closed. 'Welcome aboard,' he said, offering a grin. 'Buckle up for takeoff.'

They were pushed back in their seats as the plane accelerated, bouncing across the small waves until it lifted into the sky for the four-hour trip to Cancún, where their G650 awaited.

20

Once back in Mexico City, Sam and Remi set out to study the images they'd taken at such risk and found themselves viewing a collage of artifacts and four photographs of the manuscript. They'd already discarded the letters from the sailors, which were of historical significance but not much else, and focused instead on the jumble of apparently random letters in the mystery document.

The first thing they did was to send it all to Selma and the team for analysis, although it was with mixed feelings. Selma might have full faith in her niece's abilities, but Remi wasn't so sure. It had been a heated topic of discussion and one that had led them to disturbing conclusions.

'She and the team were the only people who knew we were in Cuba, Sam. That's fact. And we know Selma, Pete, and Wendy are trustworthy.'

'No, so did Lagarde. We have no idea who else he might have told.'

'It's possible, I suppose, but I have misgivings about Kendra. I have since the very beginning . . .'

'Which might be coloring your perception,' Sam

observed. 'We can't just assume she's feeding someone information about us.'

'I'm not assuming anything. I'm just saying there's no other way whoever was tracking us could have known where we were staying or about our interest in Morro Castle.'

'Except Lagarde. And everyone he talked to. Come on, Remi, which is more likely? That Kendra's working for the dark side or that someone in Cuba has a big mouth?'

They had to agree to disagree, but it was with hesitation that Remi sent off the shots of the manuscript, along with the images of the icons, with instructions to subject the manuscript to a comparison of all known sixteenth-century codes.

The photos of the artifacts were of little help. They appeared to be pictographs shipped to Cuba, presumably for either safekeeping or forwarding to Spain – which in this case obviously had never happened. The images depicted a procession of warriors and priests, various examples of the deity Quetzalcoatl – a fairly common icon in both Toltec and Aztec symbolism – and finally several tableaus of a pyramid belching smoke into the sky.

There seemed to be no rhyme or reason to why the artifacts had been taken from the mainland nor any indication of what was sensitive or valuable enough about them to warrant the effort. There were similar pictographs covering virtually every Mesoamerican city in Mexico, Belize and Guatemala.

The first day back, there were no answers, and they decided to pack it in early, still exhausted after their escape from Havana.

'I suppose it's a pretty safe bet that we'll never get invited to look for sunken galleons around Havana Harbor,' Sam said as they walked to their waiting taxi outside the Institute.

'It wasn't like we were on anyone's shortlist for that.'

'How about we order room service and get a good night's sleep? Does that sound reasoned and logical?' Sam asked.

'You make a compelling argument. But first I have a date with a long, hot bath.'

'Whatever the lady wants, the lady gets. That's my new motto.'

Remi gave him a skeptical look as he held the taxi door open for her. 'What did you make of the pictures?'

'Nice composition, decent lighting . . .'

She nudged him as he got in next to her. 'You know what I mean.'

'Ah, if you're referring to my hopes that they would lead us to our elusive friend's final resting place, I'm afraid they aren't really the equivalent of an X on a map, are they?'

'That's what I thought. They don't really make a lot

of sense to me. Seems like just more of the same,' Remi griped.

'Maybe we should get Maribela and Antonio involved tomorrow. They're really the experts. At least they can narrow down whether they're Toltec or Aztec. That would tell us if they're even relevant.'

'I'm reluctant, but it doesn't seem like we're seeing whatever the pattern is.'

'No. But that could also be because we just came off twenty-four hours of breaking and entering, being chased and shot at, traversing the ocean in a speedboat, flying across the Gulf in a prop plane, and jetting to Mexico City.'

'Don't forget sliding down an old toilet chute,' she reminded him. 'I won't anytime soon . . .'

'If you think of it as a water ride, it's more palatable.'

Remi crinkled her nose. 'Yuck! Just yuck.'

They rode back in comfortable silence and enjoyed dinner in the room. Sam surprised her with her favorite, pomegranate margaritas, and rewarded himself with Don Julio Blanco on the rocks with salt and lime. When they were done, Sam called Selma to see what luck she'd had with the manuscript. Kendra answered the call and the news wasn't positive.

'No hits so far. We tried an automated run and that didn't yield anything, so now we're doing it manually. But it doesn't look good. According to Pete, the auto-mated sequence would have picked it up if it was a known cipher. So we could be looking at something that hasn't been seen in that period, which is a whole different kettle of fish.'

'It also could be tied to a different document, in which case we'll never figure it out,' he said.

'Selma's going to run it through her sources and see if anything comes up. But most of the ciphers are well understood now, and those that aren't . . . well, they're keeping their secrets.'

'Stay on it, Kendra. I'll touch base again tomorrow. Has anything else come in?'

'A progress report from Canada. A Dr Jennings indicated that the preparations are coming along nicely. He said you would understand what he meant and that he's returning to Montreal as the cataloging continues so he can start raising funds for the restoration. He asked me to thank you for putting Warren Lasch from the CSS *Hunley* effort in touch with him – apparently, he's been a godsend.'

'Oh, good. I thought he might be able to help.'

'He's flying to Canada for a few weeks to assist with the infrastructure preparations and the transport of the ship.' Kendra hesitated. 'Oh, and I sent the progress report to your e-mail account, too.'

'Good. Thanks for all the hard work. We appreciate it.' Sam paused. 'How's Selma?'

'Fighting the good fight – you know her, she's a trouper. She's getting stronger and more mobile every day, but still needs painkillers at night sometimes if she overdoes it.'

'Is she there?'

Kendra hesitated. 'She's resting right now. Do you want me to go wake her?'

'No. Of course not. Let her sleep. I just wanted to say hello. It can wait.'

'Okay. Is there anything else?'

'No, Kendra. I'll call again at nine tomorrow morning your time.'

'I'll be here.'

Remi watched as he ended the call and saw his frown.

'Nothing?' she asked.

'Not yet.'

'Ever the optimist.'

'All part of my childish naïveté.'

'How's Selma?'

'According to Kendra, holding her own.' Sam relayed the gist of the conversation.

Remi sat in silence for a long moment and then kissed Sam's cheek. 'You're a good man, Sam Fargo.'

'Fooled you again. My evil scheme is working,' he said, and kissed her back.

'More like fatigue and the margaritas.'

'Gotta love those margaritas . . .'

21

The throbbing of the massive diesel engines vibrated the yacht's salon floor. Janus Benedict paced its length, a snifter of cognac clenched in his hand as he listened in quiet fury on his cell phone. Off in the distance, the white-and-blue buildings of Mykonos dotted the island's hills as the big ship approached for a week of revelry and meetings with Middle Eastern clients who were willing to pay top dollar for difficult-to-acquire arms.

'Two amateurs gave your professional Cuban intelligence service team the slip? How is that possible? Explain it to me,' he seethed.

'They were tracking them round the clock, but the Fargos must have somehow stumbled across the surveillance because they literally vanished into thin air when they should have been at the hotel,' Percy said.

'Which is an excuse. You know how I feel about excuses instead of performance.'

'Indeed. I've already made my displeasure known in the strongest possible terms to the locals. They won't be getting paid.'

'I'd prefer they were fed to the sharks.'

'Quite. But I'm afraid they rather frown on that sort of thing, even in Cuba.'

'Paying through the nose for poor results is becoming somewhat tedious, Percy.'

'No question.' Percy took a quiet breath. 'I did get a rather interesting report from a different Cuban source, though. That same night, someone broke into Morro Castle. The footage from the security cameras captured your friends in the act. The Cubans are livid at being made fools of – the castle is a fortified area, with a military and police presence, and yet your amateurs made it in and out without any effort, from what I can gather.'

'Unbelievable. What did they take?'

'Well, that's the odd part. According to the locals, everything's accounted for. As it is, the vault in question held only some naval odds and ends and a few documents. Oh, and some carved stones. Bloody rubbish, all of it, from what I can see,' Percy said.

'Not if they risked breaking into a guarded stronghold. If there's one thing I've learned, it's that those two don't do anything by accident. I want a complete inventory of that vault. Now would be good –'

'I anticipated your request. If you'll pop into your e-mail account, you'll find a list, with photos. Although some of the documents have degraded pretty severely after being stored in a dungeon.'

'Is everyone a complete idiot on that side of the pond? Why on earth would they house something valuable in a room where it would rot?'

'Apparently, they've got their hands full carrying on with the noble Communist Revolution.'

Janus grunted. 'Very well. I'll look it over and get back to you.'

He punched the call off and continued pacing, his stomach churning as he weighed his options. He'd heard from his Mexican contact earlier: the Fargos were back in Mexico City and had spent the day at the Institute, where at least he could keep a better eye on them. They hadn't spotted the surveillance, likely because the Mexicans were using a larger team. He made a mental note to caution his Mexican conduit to avoid doing anything to make them suspicious.

Janus entered his lavish office and checked his e-mail in-box and read the inventory list with interest. Something had been worth risking everything for.

No matter. Unbeknownst to even Percy, he had a secret weapon. One he had cultivated with care and which looked ready to finally pay off. He was confident he'd know as much about what the Fargos were working on as they did, just as he'd been able to track them around the globe.

Janus shut down his computer and rejoined his brother and the entertainment up on the pool deck. For this trip, he'd arranged for five stunning Spanish models, three of whom were blondes. He knew his clients' tastes well and blondes always eased the way for difficult decisions to be made about expensive ordnance. He ascended the stairs to the upper deck, his hand-crafted Italian moccasins soundless on the hardwood steps. Janus approached the table, arms open, a beaming smile on his face, as he eyed the young beauties, his to do with as he pleased before his clients arrived in a few hours.

'Ladies, please. It's rude to keep all the fun to yourselves. Slide over. The captain wants to spend some time with his new friends.'

The girls tittered nervously at his sudden appearance but relaxed when they saw his face. They were experienced and they knew that expression well. An unthinking hunger that was their stock-in-trade.

As old as the Greek hills they were steaming toward.

Maribela and Antonio gazed at the Fargos' Cuban photographs in disbelief, having stopped at the Institute that morning before making their way to the crypts, where excavation was under way.

'Absolutely remarkable. How on earth did you get these?' Antonio asked.

'Apparently, friendly persuasion works wonders. You just need to know the secret password and the Cubans couldn't wait to give us photos,' Sam said. They'd agreed to show Maribela and Antonio the snapshots of the artifacts but not the manuscript.

Remi sat nearby, her face impassive.

'Well, you have a career as a politician ahead of you if you want,' Maribela said, the admiration in her smile a little too warm for Remi's liking.

'I'm not nearly unscrupulous enough, I'm afraid.'

Maribela's musical laugh was like nails on a chalkboard for Remi and she all but groaned as she got to her feet and moved next to Sam.

'What do you make of the pictographs?' she asked.

Antonio edged nearer and studied the images. 'I'd say definitely Toltec, but the images are unlike any I've seen. We'll need to study them further, of course, but I'm sure.'

'Is there anything about the subject matter that strikes a chord?' Remi asked.

'Not really,' he said. 'A procession. Quetzalcoatl. Priests or dignitaries. The usual jaguars and eagles. The most unusual is the depiction of the pyramid or temple.'

'But it doesn't mean anything to you?' Sam asked.

'Part of the problem is that much of what we believe is really interpretations, which are subject to change based on new information. We've already made some discoveries in the crypts that have us reconsidering our earlier assumptions about the Toltecs.'

'We'd love to see what you've been up to in our absence,' Remi said.

Antonio nodded. 'Of course. We'll be heading up there after this meeting. You're welcome to come along.'

'It's still quite grim,' Maribela said, 'but now that water service has been restored to some of the affected area, the tension level has receded since you were last there.'

'Then it's a date,' Sam agreed, and quickly busied himself with his notes until he caught Remi glaring daggers at him.

When the siblings had departed to their office, Remi moved away from Sam, her shoes clicking on the linoleum floor.

'What is it with you every time Maribela's in the room?' she asked.

'What are you talking about?'

'You know exactly what I'm talking about, Fargo.'

He shrugged. 'No, really, I don't.'

'She opens her mouth and it's like you're a teenage boy at the prom.'

Sam's eyes widened. 'Why, Remi, is that the green-eyed monster surfacing? You? Really?'

'Don't try to deflect. I see how you're behaving.'

'You mean how I keep pawing at her?'

'It's not funny.'

His expression softened. 'You should know by now it's you and nobody else.'

She eyed him distrustfully. 'Are you just saying that to make me feel better?'

'If I was, whatever I said would also be to make you feel better. So if I said no, it wouldn't be the truth.'

'See? That's what infuriates me about you. You can never give me a straight answer.'

'I just did. Now, can we return to the treasure of a lifetime? Not that I mind living in a Mexican soap opera or anything . . .' Sam pretended to twirl a nonexistent mustache, and, in spite of herself, Remi laughed.

The ride to the site took forty minutes through the

city's bustling streets. When their SUV pulled up to the crypt entrance, a different contingent of soldiers was guarding the opening. The familiar formality of handing over identification was repeated and soon they were underground, where a dozen earnest students were whisking at pottery with brushes and photographing the finds.

Antonio led them through the passageway to the largest chamber. 'You know, one of the carvings you showed me reminds me of several here. I didn't want to say anything until I saw them again, but I'd be interested in your opinion.'

As they arrived, he said something in Spanish to three students who were tagging artifacts. They promptly left, making room for the four of them.

'Which carving?' Remi asked.

'I think . . . Yes, here it is. Right here. It's quite small, so you'll have to get close to see the detail,' he said, tapping an area of the pictograph with his finger.

Sam and Remi drew near and studied the area he'd indicated. A group of warriors and priests were paying homage to a pyramid. Above it, a cloud hovered.

Maribela squinted at the carving. 'I could go either way on that. It's inconclusive.'

'Looks like some sort of devotional or prayer-related motif,' Sam said. 'You can see where the gathering is supplicating, bowing to the pyramid. Is that type of thing typical of Toltec art?'

Antonio shrugged and frowned. 'No more than in Mayan or Aztec. Although we have far more of both of those to evaluate than we do of the Toltec.'

Remi peered at the pyramid for another moment and then stepped back. 'Let's assume for the moment that this representation is recording the same, or a similar story, to the Cuban carvings. What would that tell us?'

'Unfortunately, nothing.' Antonio paused. 'Except that some unknown party almost five hundred years ago felt there was significance to the depiction. That's about it.'

Maribela nodded. 'Whether there is actually any meaning attached to it is another matter altogether. I don't suppose you were able to convince the Cubans to give you the manuscript that was stored there? Maybe some photographs?'

Sam felt Remi stiffen and stepped in. 'We're working on it, but you know how that goes. We're lucky we got what we did. If something changes, though, you'll be the first to know.'

Maribela held his gaze for a moment and then returned to scrutinizing the procession memorialized in the stone. 'We don't even know whether it's linked to any of this or not, so perhaps it's not the end of the world. It could be someone's inflated account of the riches of the New World or an appeal to the Crown for more money . . .'

'But didn't you say it had illustrations of Aztec or Toltec figures?' Sam asked.

'Yes, but that wouldn't be unexpected if it was a coded progress report or the author thought he'd stumbled across something that later turned out to be a false lead,' Maribela explained as she turned from the carving.

Sam and Remi spent the remainder of the morning poring over the pictographs. At noon, Maribela drove them back to Mexico City while Antonio continued his work. After she dropped them off at the Four Seasons, Sam called Selma's line as they made their way to their room. Kendra answered the phone again.

'Oh, I'm glad you called. Selma wants to talk to you,' Kendra said after they'd exchanged pleasantries. 'She's right here.'

'Well, put her on.'

Selma wasted no time getting to the point. 'I'll make this short and sweet. I ran through the manuscript all night and came up empty. Whatever it is, it's not a common code. I also ran some small chunks of it by several academics who specialize in that sort of thing and they couldn't make heads nor tails of it, either.'

'Where does that leave us?'

'I was thinking about it this morning. I talked to your old Cal Tech professor, George Milhaupt, to see if he had any ideas. I know he's dabbled in cryptology and knows everybody.' Selma hesitated. 'He brought up a name and I'm not sure you're going to like it. He said that probably your best chance is with Lazlo.'

'Lazlo Kemp?' Sam said, his heart sinking.

'The one and only.'

An uncomfortable silence hung on the line, like the aftermath of a bad joke's failed punch line.

'But he's ... indisposed, isn't he? Since his, er, mishap?'

'Yes, ever since the scandal, he's been off the radar. But I did some digging and apparently he's given up the hallowed halls of academia for fieldwork. Last anyone heard, he was headed into the Laotian jungle in search of some lost treasure he believed he'd got a lead on.'

'He always had the personality of a treasure hunter, not a professor,' Sam said. 'I'm not surprised.'

'Well, perhaps once he became effectively unemployable, he figured he had nothing left to lose and decided to emulate your success.'

'He'd mentioned it a few times. But I always thought it was idle chatter.'

'Obviously, not so idle if the reports are true. Anyway, George said he would be the very best at deciphering your manuscript.'

'I can't fault that assessment. He does have a gift,' Sam agreed.

'I tried to reach him, but none of his numbers work. I even tried his daughter and she hasn't heard from him for years. Which, by the way, she wasn't too broken-up about, judging from her last statement before she hung up on me.'

'Ouch.'

Selma cleared her throat. 'If you want to get to the bottom of the manuscript's message, you're going to have to find Lazlo. Somewhere in Laos. Maybe. With him, you never know.'

Sam exhaled noisily and studied the ceiling before making a decision. 'All right, Selma. Thank you. Please put Kendra and the gang on this. I'll need to know everything I can about where he was last seen, who he was working with, who outfitted him, when he last communicated with anyone . . .'

'I figured. They're already on it.'

'You're a goddess, Selma.'

'Hardly.'

Sam paused. 'How's everything going with you?'

Her voice sounded serious. 'I wouldn't recommend this if you can avoid it. Hopefully, it won't take much longer. It's no joyride.'

When Sam disconnected, Remi was staring at him from across the room.

'Did I hear Lazlo's name mentioned?' she asked.

'My old professor said that he's about our best chance at decrypting the manuscript.'

'You've got to be kidding.'

Sam gave her a pained expression. 'I wish I was.'

'What's he doing after . . . the incident?'

'Well, he was fired. Nothing like a juicy scandal. Selma says he's off in the Asian jungle trying to find some treasure he has a lead on.' Sam shrugged. 'Why he had to pick the daughter of one of the most powerful newspaper magnates in England to . . . share his company with . . . is beyond me. Talk about bad decision making.'

Remi frowned. 'I'll say. Wasn't she about eighteen? And what was he? Fifty?'

'I think more like late forties, but the booze, well, isn't kind after a certain point. She was one of his freshmen students,' Sam confirmed. 'And she was barely eighteen. But they both said it was consensual . . .'

'I'm sorry, Sam, but he deserved everything he got. And I'm saying that as someone who liked him.'

Sam nodded, noting her use of past tense. 'And a drunk. No question. But he's also a wiz at ancient documents, which is why George recommended him.'

Remi shook her head. 'Don't tell me we're –'

'Going to have to find him.'

'The man's a menace. He's a walking disaster area. After sticking me on the ice and having me slide down a toilet chute, you're going to ask me to go in search of some self-centered lush in . . . Where did you say he was last seen?'

'Laos.'

'As in Laos, a sweltering, dangerous hellhole on the other side of the world? *That* Laos?'

'I hear there are parts that are lovely,' Sam countered.

'Absolutely not. Not a chance. You are not going to

sweet-talk me into going into the Golden Triangle to find him.'

'Remi . . .'

'Have you lost your mind? IT'S NOT GOING TO HAPPEN. End of discussion, Fargo. I mean it.'

The G650's tires screeched when they touched down on the scorching runway of Wattay International Airport in the Lao People's Democratic Republic. The flight from Mexico City had taken almost twenty-four hours, with a refueling stop in Hawaii. Kendra had arranged for the necessary permits for the plane to enter Laotian airspace and spend as much time as required on the ground there. The flight crew would remain in Vientiane, the nation's capital, for as long as needed.

A car from the Salana Boutique Hotel was waiting at the terminal when they cleared customs. The room was adequate, not lavish, with marginal but functional air-conditioning. After long showers, they ate a light dinner and went to bed early, the half-day time difference between Mexico City and Vientiane hitting them both hard.

When they awoke after eleven solid hours of sleep, Sam called Kendra, who had found a guide to take them into the hills of Laos to the last place Lazlo had been seen. From what Selma had discovered, he'd arrived in Vientiane and spent a week getting outfitted, visited an acquaintance at the university there, and then gone north in search of whatever had captured his imagination. His last contact with the world had been a collect call to his estranged brother, made from a pay phone in a small town on the banks of the Nam Song River, which was their ultimate destination: Vang Vieng.

The brother had reluctantly relayed the discussion to Selma. Lazlo had begged him to wire two thousand pounds to the Western Union in Vientiane a month and a half before to help fund his ongoing search and get him out of a 'spot of trouble,' as Lazlo had put it. When pressed, he'd said that he'd run afoul of the law in Vang Vieng and would be escorted to Vientiane by the police so that he could pay the outstanding fine he owed. His brother had sent the two thousand with the warning that there would be no more money. Lazlo had assured him it would be more than sufficient and that he was close to a discovery which would end his ongoing financial difficulties forever and make the whole family rich.

Since then, there hadn't been any communication, and the brother was afraid that Lazlo had finally got himself into a situation he couldn't readily get out of.

Their guide turned out to be a young man in his mid-twenties named Analu, who spoke passable pidgin English in a high-pitched, excited voice. He proudly escorted them to his vehicle: a ten-year-old Isuzu SUV with fading red paint and questionable tires. When Sam told him they were bound for Vang Vieng, he smiled, offering a dental display that was every oral surgeon's dream.

'You backpacking? Tubing?' Analu asked.

'Uh, no. We have a friend who we think might be up there.'

'Lots of people go and get hurt on river. Some die. Every year. Used to be crazy.'

'Used to be?' Remi asked.

'Yeah, uh-huh. Big tourist town, many kids party. But now not so bad.'

'What happened?' Sam asked, curious.

'Government tear down all river bars.'

'So there's no drinking?' Remi said. 'That sounds like hell on earth for Lazlo . . .'

'Still plenty drinking. Lots in town. Same-same but different. And few bars rebuild on water. Friends of police. Family, cousins, brothers, yeah?'

'I think I understand. So you know the place?' Sam asked.

'Yeah, sure, uh-huh. I take you now?'

'How far is it?'

'Three, maybe four hour. Road pretty good. No rain. Not so good in rain.'

'Are there hotels up there?'

'Sure, uh-huh. Plenty good hotels.'

'Well, then,' Sam said, 'let's get going. The day's not getting any younger.'

They piled into the SUV and the engine started with a cloud of ominous black smoke and then began idling roughly on its three remaining cylinders. Sam silently wondered where Kendra had got the tip for their new friend.

Analu pulled into traffic with a casual disregard for the oncoming vehicles – an effort that was rewarded with ample honking. He floored the pedal and made a gesture through his open window that Sam interpreted as a sign of friendly acceptance. The little SUV lumbered forward like a losing boxer at the end of the eleventh round after swerving to avoid a delivery van by a matter of inches, which didn't faze Analu in the least.

Ten seconds later, a black Nissan sedan rolled from the curb half a block behind and took up a trailing position, the two Laotian men in it serious, their attention focused on the SUV. The passenger made a call, as their quarry took the on-ramp to Route 13, and, after a terse discussion, gave instructions to the driver, who dropped back another fifty yards.

Once out of the Vientiane area, the road became a flat, two-lane strip in marginal condition, with swarms of motorcycles buzzing past each time the Isuzu neared a town. As far as Sam could tell, there were no discernible rules of the road and by the second hour he'd grown accustomed to near misses and kamikaze riders racing toward them in the wrong lane, pulling to one side to safety moments before impact.

To their surprise, lush farmland with almost neon hues of green stretched for miles on either side of the highway. They'd been expecting jungle and rain forest and instead seemed to be in a tropical agricultural strip that went on endlessly, the wind blowing twisted waves of ripples across the fields.

For all their misgivings, Analu avoided killing either them, or any other drivers, and offered a running commentary on the various communities as they drove north. Some of his asides were humorous, some sad, but all world-weary, the result of living in a society where poverty was endemic and corruption was an expected aspect of any form of authority.

As they neared their destination, Remi pointed to a string of mountains thrusting into the sky. 'Oh, look. That's really beautiful, isn't it?'

'Karst formations. Limestone eroded away by the river over time,' Sam said.

'It's like something out of a movie.'

Traffic increased as they drew closer to town and soon they were part of a long line of cars inching forward like a frustrated concertina as they waited for a herd of cattle to cross the road ahead of them.

'What first stop? We almost there,' Analu chirped, leaning on his horn occasionally to break the monotony.

'The police station.'

Analu stared at Sam with wide eyes in the rearview mirror. 'You sure?'

'Never more so. And we'll need you to translate if they don't speak English,' Remi said.

The expression on Analu's face clearly indicated he wished he'd asked for more details about their errand before accepting the job. As a native, he'd been raised to understand that going to the police station was right up there with juggling hatchets in terms of prudence. Still, he put on a brave show and nodded as though he hadn't a care in the world. Which would have been more convincing if his face hadn't blanched at least three shades lighter.

When they reached the town center, Analu made a right turn and drove up a block, then parked in a muddy lot in front of one of the few concrete buildings, the rest fashioned out of wood and painted gaudy colors. He shut off the engine, which wheezed like a chain-smoker before expiring with a shudder, and they climbed out into the muggy swelter. Sam eyed the building, which seemed barely large enough to house a few desks and a cell. He motioned for Analu to lead the way.

Inside, two wiry men with thick heads of greasy black hair sat behind a counter, smoking hand-rolled cigarettes, their uniforms stained with sweat despite the fan blowing a tepid stream of air their way. A portable radio on one of the desks blared a pop song that would have been insipid in any language. They looked up with drooping eyes as Analu made a cautious introduction. One of the officers stood, went into the back, and emerged after half a minute with a short, plump man in his forties who looked like he'd just woken up. The man buttoned his uniform shirt with clumsy fingers and then barked an annoyed question at Analu, who smiled with trepidation and embarked on a rambling explanation of why he'd interrupted the captain's afternoon rest.

The captain mopped at his perspiring face with a soiled cloth handkerchief and grunted and then asked another question, this time with a distinct tone of menace. Analu nodded like a buffoon and turned to Sam.

'He want to know what you looking for. I tell him you important guests of Laotian people and have questions, yeah?'

Sam cleared his throat. 'Tell him that we're looking for a British man who was either in custody or owed money to the police here about a month or so ago. The gentleman's name is Lazlo Kemp.'

The plump man's eyes narrowed at the mention of Lazlo's name. Analu translated and the captain waved him away with an abrupt gesture, then fixed Sam with a calculating stare.

'What you want with him?' the man demanded in fractured English.

'We're friends of his. We haven't heard from him for months. We're worried. And we have news for him,' Remi said. The official ignored her, waiting for Sam to speak.

'We need to talk to him and we were hoping you might know how to reach him,' Sam said. 'I'd be extremely grateful if you could help. *Extremely*.'

The man glanced at Remi and returned his attention to Sam, his expression now more one of cunning than annoyance. 'You friend?'

'Yes. A *generous* friend whose problem you might be able to solve.'

'How generous?'

'A hundred American.'

The Laotian official scoffed and the negotiation began. 'A thousand.'

Sam shook his head at the preposterous figure. 'Hundred and fifty.'

Three minutes later, Sam counted out two hundred and fifty dollars and handed the bills to the captain, who showed absolutely no concern at his extortion being viewed by his subordinates. He took the money and fingered each note as if suspicious that Sam had printed them that morning and then they disappeared into his pants in a blink. He pulled a pen from his shirt pocket and scrawled an address and a name on a scrap of notepaper.

'Talk to Bane. Maybe he see English,' he said, and handed the slip to Analu, who looked at it like it was a live scorpion.

Back in the car, Analu turned to them with concern etched across his face. 'This not good.'

'No, my suspicion is it won't be,' Sam said. 'But we need to find our friend.'

Analu coaxed the engine into life and they set out up the highway, turning toward the river on to a rutted dirt road after a hundred yards. They bounced along before they stopped at a complex of structures that looked ready to collapse under their own weight at the slightest breeze. Analu stared at the entry and shut off the motor with a shake of his head.

'We here. Need to pay again for information. Man who owns this very dangerous.'

'Remi, why don't you stay here this time?' Sam said as he swung his door open.

'And miss all the fun?'

'I think I'll pay a lot less if I don't have a beautiful woman with me.'

'Always looking for the bargain, aren't you?'

'It's my nature.'

'Fine. Just don't get yourself killed. I'd have a lot of explaining to do to Selma and the gang.'

Analu knocked on the flimsy slab of plywood that served as a door and after a full minute a wizened man with long white hair and a scraggly beard peered at them from within. Analu spoke in Laotian and the man grunted. After scrutinizing Sam, he pulled the make-shift door open and stepped back to let them enter.

Sam could barely make out the bodies lying on filthy cots along the walls in the gloom. The interior was broiling, but the sleepers seemed not to notice. They passed into another room, where two men sat at a folding metal card table with a metal lockbox and an array of pipes. Analu bowed respectfully and stated his case, and the elder of the two, an ancient birdlike man with scarcely any muscle on his bones, pursed his lips and looked Sam up and down.

After extended haggling, during which Analu almost walked away three times, Sam presented a hundred-dollar bill like a first-class ticket to New York. The opium dealer reached out with an emaciated arm, held it up to the light filtering through a filthy window, and murmured to his companion. The man who'd shown them in smiled in a way that reminded Sam of a Komodo dragon. Analu shivered involuntarily.

The old dealer leaned forward and spoke in raspy but understandable English seasoned by fifty years of smoking opium. 'Crazy Englishman hang out at Lulu's. One klick north. Probably there now,' he said with the solemnity of a clergyman delivering a eulogy.

Sam turned to Analu, who looked terrified. 'Do you know Lulu's?'

'It bad place.'

Sam nodded at the dealer and thanked him for his assistance. Sam and Analu could make out the men inside cackling through the paper-thin walls as they returned to the Isuzu.

'I'd say that went well,' he said to Remi as they slid back inside the baking steel box.

'I thought I heard laughter. What was the joke?'

'Who was it that said that if you're sitting at a poker game for fifteen minutes and you don't know who the patsy is, it's you?'

Remi glanced at the building. 'A wise man.'

The engine caught on the third sputter, and, a few minutes later, they were easing to a stop in front of a long rectangular shack with a thatched roof that made most of the hovels in the world look like palaces. Two motorcycles rested on rusting kickstands near the door, where a rooster stood, head swiveling, searching for anything edible. Music drifted from inside, and female laughter pealed over the melody, which to Sam's ear sounded like an out-of-tune children's recital with an aggravated bird of prey screeching over the din. He and Remi exchanged glances and then Sam took her hand and led her to the darkened doorway. A shabby pale green sign overhead announced that they'd arrived at *Lul's* – the last *u* having rubbed off at some point.

The interior was no surprise, given the curb appeal of the roadhouse, but, even so, Remi was taken aback. Soiled straw littered the dirt floor, which was dotted with six white plastic tables, all devoid of patrons. A wood-and-bamboo bar lurked at one end of the gloomy room, where a rail-thin man in his fifties sat watching a black-and-white television, behind which stood two decrepit refrigerators. At the other end, a local woman in garish red stretch pants sat drinking at a wooden table littered with empty beer bottles. Her companion was a Caucasian man with the unhealthy jaundiced complexion of a hobo, who stared at the newcomers with the blurry, unfocused gaze of a man who thought he was hallucinating.

'Lazlo. Nice place you've got here,' Sam said, fake cheer in his voice as he approached the table.

'Good heavens. Most remarkable. Sam . . . Fargo. What on earth are you doing here?' Lazlo asked with a slur. 'And if I'm not mistaken, with the lovely Rami?'

'*Remi,*' she corrected. 'And no, you're not mistaken.'

Lazlo made a valiant attempt to stand, an ambitious act that appeared to exhaust him. He sensibly downgraded his chivalry to a wave of his limp hand. 'Please, have a seat. Bartender, drinks all around!' he called. The man behind the counter looked up as if registering the newcomers for the first time and raised an eyebrow.

'A beer,' Sam said over his shoulder, while Remi shook her head. Analu stayed at the door, looking ready to run at any moment. A creaky fan with cracked plastic blades suspended from a beam twirled overhead, blowing Lazlo's cigarette smoke at the young woman, who appeared to be twenty-something going on sixty.

The bartender opened the nearest refrigerator and extracted a bottle of Beerlao Original, then padded over on bare feet and placed it on the table in front of Sam, showing no interest in clearing away Lazlo's empties. Lazlo raised his half-full beer in a toast. Sam clinked his bottle against it, taking in Lazlo's dilated eyes as he did so, as well as the three drained shot glasses next to the dead soldiers.

The beer was surprisingly cold. Sam took a long pull before setting it down and waiting for Lazlo to ask what they were doing there. Lazlo drank the rest of his beer in three gulps and dropped his smoldering cigarette down the neck, watching it extinguish with a damp fizzle before setting the bottle next to its empty brethren. Remi shifted uncomfortably on her hard chair and Lazlo finally got the hint. He regarded his female friend and rattled off a rapid-fire sentence in passable Lao. She finished her drink, rose, and teetered off toward the bar on high heels that left little doubt as to her vocation.

'So good to see you, old chap. Really. Whoever would have thought . . .' Lazlo began, but quickly seemed to deflate. 'Bit under the weather at present, though. Not my usual effervescent self.'

'I can see that, my friend. But it's good to see you, too,' Sam said as he leaned back in his chair. He fixed Lazlo with an amenable look. 'What's a nice Brit like you doing in a place like this, Lazlo?'

Lazlo offered a humorless grin and fumbled in his shirt pocket for his smokes, then lost interest. 'It's a long and sordid story. As are most involving yours truly.'

'We traveled halfway around the world to find you, so take your time.'

Lazlo cleared his throat. 'You've obviously heard about my little . . . indiscretion.' He shot Remi a cautious glance. 'Yes, of course you have. A monumental mistake by anyone's yardstick. But no matter. Once I got that all . . . reconciled, I decided to, well, sort of reinvent myself. Opportunity knocks often for the curious among us – and I'd been looking over some scrolls from the Khmers. And I'd always intended to get out into the world someday and make my fortune, but it didn't work out, so here I am.'

'Here you are,' Remi echoed.

'What happened, Lazlo?' Sam asked softly.

Lazlo felt in his breast pocket and pulled out a crumpled packet containing a solitary cigarette. Both Sam and Remi noticed that his hand trembled as he lit it.

'It all started well enough. I had some promising locations mapped out and three chaps to help me in the brush. We spent a few months searching . . . but nothing. But I still kept at it. I mortgaged the flat to pay for this expedition, so I had to make it work. But that wasn't quite what the gods had in store for me.'

'What were you looking for?'

'Treasure. What else? When the Khmer empire imploded in the fifteenth century, a remarkable store of gold and jewels was spirited out of what's now Cambodia and hidden in a cave somewhere in Laos. At least that's what I gleaned from the accounts, and I was convinced I could find it. Turns out that was a little optimistic,' Lazlo said, his voice brittle. He seemed to collapse in on himself, empty. 'So here you find me . . . for my sins . . .'

'Why here?' Sam asked.

'Why not? It's as good a place as any to wrestle with your demons. Why not in the wilds of Laos? What better place?'

'And that's it? You gave up? Or you discovered there was no treasure?'

'It wasn't so much that I gave up as my nature caught up with me. I had everything under control, but as my funds ran ever lower and I was no closer to finding the Khmer treasure than I was at the outset, I returned to the embrace of my waiting mistress: the bottle. It wasn't long before my passion for the treasure metamorphosed into smoking the local opium and chasing it down with a bottle of the natives' rice whiskey – *lao-lao*, it's called, and an absolute bargain at less than a quid a bottle.' Lazlo gave Sam a hunted look. 'Two quid a night for a guesthouse room, a handful of coppers for a night's supply of dragon smoke . . . A man can get lost for a long time at such enticing rates.'

Sam hunched forward. 'You're better than that, Lazlo.'

Lazlo shook his head. 'Not anymore, I'm afraid, not anymore. The old days are over. Can't take back the ticking of the clock.'

Remi cleared her throat. 'We have a proposition for you.'

Lazlo wheezed a lusty laugh. 'I'm truly flattered. Or, at least, I think I am . . .'

Remi ignored the clumsy innuendo. 'We have a project. Something we need your help with. But you need to be straight. You'll be of no use like this.'

'A project?'

'An ancient Spanish manuscript,' Sam interjected. 'We got it in Cuba. But it's in code and we can't crack it.'

'There are few codes that can't be cracked.'

'This one doesn't resemble anything we've seen.'

Lazlo blew a cloud of nicotine at the fan and closed his eyes. 'I sincerely doubt I have it in me anymore, Sam.'

'Nonsense. Of course you do. You're just throwing yourself a pity party,' he said. 'Killing yourself – one of the brightest minds of its kind – because you drink too much and do stupid things.'

Lazlo opened his eyes and smiled again – a maudlin apparition. 'Guilty, old friend. Guilty as charged. And better that you leave me to serve my sentence in this backwater of purgatory. I'm just not up to snuff.'

'Meaning you're too far gone to be able to solve the riddle? Or you won't because it will take you away from all this?'

'A little of both, I expect . . .'

'Lazlo, look at me. I said we have a proposition. Don't you want to hear it?' Remi asked.

He stubbed out his cigarette and his eyes finally met Remi's. 'Fine, young lady, fine. What have you come to discuss, assuming it's not my spectacular fall from academic grace?'

'Help us with the manuscript and we'll assist you with your Khmer hunt. Help us find ours and we'll help you find yours. Whatever it takes. Funding, personnel . . . We'll even go into the jungle with you. It's a no-lose proposition. Give us what we need and we'll give you what you need. Look at me, Lazlo. Listen to what I'm saying. Do this and we'll do what we have to in order to make your dream come alive.'

Lazlo sat back, his befuddled brain grappling with what she'd just said. 'You're . . . you're serious, aren't you?' he stammered.

'I'm dead serious,' Remi said. 'This is your big chance. To turn it all around. To mount a proper expedition. To make a significant find. With money no object. A once-in-a-lifetime chance.'

Sam nodded assent. 'Only a fool would turn this down. And you may be many things, but you've never been a fool.'

'There are some newspapermen who would argue against that most convincingly, I'm sure.'

Remi softened her tone. 'That's over and done. This is now. We need your help. Say yes and we'll get you out of here, clean you up, and put you to work. Whatever needs to be done.'

Lazlo shook his head. 'That might not be so easy. I've been doing this for some time.'

'We'll find you a good clinic. They'll wean you off. You'll be right as rain before you know it. You don't have to be this, Lazlo. You've got everything to gain by making the right choice.'

Lazlo's face crinkled into a sneer. ' "For once." That's what you were going to say, isn't it?'

'No. But if it makes it easier, then I will. Make the right choice *for once.*'

He didn't say anything for a long time and then his

shoulders shuddered and he buried his face in his palms. When he looked up, his eyes were red and moist.

'I don't deserve this. You're far too good for the likes of me.'

Sam shook his head. 'Nobody's better than anyone else. We're just in a position to help you right now. Just as you're in a position to help us. It's a simple transaction. We both get what we need. The basis of all working relationships.'

Remi stepped back and Lazlo wiped his eyes with the back of a grimy sleeve. 'Be careful what you wish for, Sam.'

Sam smiled and caught Remi's eye.

'I always am, Lazlo.'

23

Lazlo was living in a hovel near the river that would have been at home in the slums of Calcutta. Sam helped him with his few belongings, and soon they were rattling down the road back to Vientiane. Lazlo dozed off after the first leg and awoke only when Sam got cell coverage and left a message for Kendra, asking her to locate a suitable rehab center in the region that could handle both opium and alcohol withdrawals. Two hours later, Selma called – at 5 a.m. California time.

'I've located a place in Bangkok, if you can get him there. I gather you found him?' she asked.

'Selma!' Sam said, surprised. 'I was expecting Kendra. Quite a bit later, actually.'

'I saw her voicemail light blinking and took the liberty, figuring it was probably you. I was up, anyway. Here's the info. It's a first-class establishment. Apparently, the rich in Thailand regularly contend with the same issues Lazlo's facing. The website looks like a five-star hotel's, and it's part of one of Bangkok's top hospitals.' She gave him the particulars, which he repeated aloud so Remi could memorize them.

They had Analu drop them at the plane after calling

the crew and alerting them that they'd need to fly to Bangkok immediately. When they arrived at the airport, the G650 was already humming for the short flight. Sandra greeted them with a gleaming welcome smile. Sam had called the clinic and confirmed that they could accommodate Lazlo. They'd warned him what to expect and explained that he could have a drink on the plane to avoid the risk of convulsions, but not to allow more than one strong cocktail.

Sandra prepared a double Finlandia and tonic at the request of Lazlo, who perked up after he'd swallowed it like a parched man at a desert oasis. Sam and Remi made small talk with him during the flight, and a car from the clinic met them at the airport.

The facility lived up to its web presence. After completing a long application and signing his name to it, Lazlo was led into the depths of the clinic by staff, while the administrator, a handsome Asian woman in a dark blue business suit, explained their procedures to Sam and Remi.

'Believe it or not, the opium withdrawals are the least of his issues. We deal with that problem using drugs that cleanse the opium from the opiate receptors while he's under deep sedation, so if he's only been smoking for a few months and not injecting, that will be dealt with in a matter of hours. The alcohol is a different, and potentially more serious, complication. Your friend appears to be a long-term alcoholic and that can be quite dangerous to wind down.'

223

'He's been drinking for as long as I've known him,' Sam said, 'which is at least a decade.'

'Then it will be a rough ride for the next three to four days, and possibly longer. We use nitrous oxide and vitamin regimens to reduce the withdrawal effects, but every patient is different. Additionally, the physical withdrawal process is only the beginning. He'll need ongoing care for at least thirty days and he should enroll in a program.'

'We're already making arrangements for him in Mexico City. He'll be well looked after,' Remi assured the woman.

'Very good, then. Will you be staying in town for the duration?'

'Yes. We're at the Mandarin Oriental,' Sam said. 'I jotted our cell number on the information form.'

The administrator stood and shook their hands. 'Try not to worry. We'll do everything we can to make this as comfortable as possible for him.' She hesitated. 'I wouldn't stop in during the detox period – he's not allowed visitors until that phase is over.'

Remi nodded. She and Sam had looked up 'alcohol withdrawal' at the plane terminals while en route and she could well understand why the patient was off-limits for seventy-two hours or longer.

Four days went by quickly. Every meal was an opportunity to test the various restaurants the concierge had recommended. They took a tour of the city on the second day and spent long hours after that walking the streets of the teeming downtown whenever the sky was clear. When they returned to the clinic, the administrator showed them to Lazlo's room and then left.

'How did it go?' Sam asked.

'Far worse than expected,' Lazlo said with a troubled but clear stare. 'Wouldn't want to have to go through that again. Rather like being dragged through broken glass after having been roasted on a spit. No, actually, that might be more pleasurable, come to think of it.'

Sam nodded. 'The good news is that's a once-in-a-lifetime event if you're careful. How are you feeling now?'

'Certainly not a hundred per cent but could be worse, all things considered.'

'Have they got you on anything?'

'Valium. Said there's a danger of dependence, so it's a mixed blessing. But it's got the worst of the symptoms under control.'

'Have they indicated when you'll be fit for travel?' Remi asked.

'Haven't asked. I assumed I'd be working from here. Is that not the case?'

Sam and Remi exchanged a look. 'We thought it might be better if you came with us to Mexico.'

'Good heavens. Mexico? I must admit that's a pleasure I've yet to experience.' Lazlo paused. 'I was rather hoping that you could get me high-resolution scans of the document in question, as well as a computer, so I could begin my analysis while incarcerated. It's an awfully tedious place, this.'

'I have them on a flash drive,' Remi said. She ferreted around in her purse and extracted a notebook computer, pretending astonishment. 'And, oh, what's this? Just a computer. We thought you might want to get started.' She set the notebook on his bed and the drive on the table next to it before rooting around in her bag and finding the power cord. 'Voilà! You're a one-man cryptology department on wheels.'

'Good show. Good show indeed. Now all I need to do is find the on switch.'

Lazlo's hands were unsteady as he lifted the computer and set it on his lap, but that wasn't surprising given his state when he entered the clinic. They both knew he would be in fragile shape for some time to come, having already arranged for a clinic in Mexico City to supervise his ongoing treatment.

After another ten minutes, they left him to his new project with a promise to see him again the following afternoon. Next they met with the administrator, who approved him for discharge and travel in forty-eight hours, but with a stern caution to keep the plane dry so as not to present temptation. Neither of them had a problem with that, and, on the way back to the hotel, Remi passed the word to Sandra.

Checkout from the clinic two days later was a paperwork-intensive ordeal. Everyone sighed in relief when they were finally rid of the building and on their way to the airport. Sam and Remi had enjoyed the unexpected downtime but were itching to get back to Mexico, their sense of being under the gun more intense than ever. Lazlo was being tight-lipped about any progress he'd made on the manuscript, as was his fashion, although at times he would smile like a mischievous child, which they generally took to be a positive sign.

The flight across the Pacific was an hour shorter due to a strong tailwind but still exhausted them by the time they arrived in Mexico City. A representative from the clinic where Lazlo would take up residence met them at the airport and ferried them to the clinic's building in an upscale area of downtown near the business district. Sam and Remi checked back into the Four Seasons, where their luggage had been sent from Cuba courtesy of Lagarde's friend.

That evening, they had dinner with Carlos Ramirez, who was a charming host and took them to one of Mexico City's top restaurants – Pujol – where they dined like royalty on the chef's tasting menu and a host of rare tequilas.

Carlos told them that progress at the new find had been slow, hampered by the weather – it had rained for three days in their absence, as a massive front had moved across Mexico, flooding the whole area in its wake. The marginally accessible streets had become impassable, so Maribela and Antonio had been unable to resume their work until the previous day. Carlos said that they were excited by the images Sam and Remi had brought back from Cuba and had found a few more similarities between the artifacts in the crypts and the carvings in Havana.

By the time the evening wound down, Sam and Remi were satiated and optimistic about their chances now that Lazlo was on their team. They both agreed that they were lucky to have Carlos helping them and were sorry to see the night end. Carlos bade them goodnight and offered to drive them back to the hotel, but they declined, preferring to linger over after-dinner drinks. When they left, Sam held the restaurant door open for Remi, admiring her Hervé Léger black cocktail dress and the way it clung to her curves.

'The dress looks magical. Great choice, as always.'

'Why, thank you. I wasn't sure you'd noticed.'

'Are you kidding? I'm the envy of every male in Mexico City. And the shoes are incredible, too,' he added, going for bonus points.

'Jimmy Choo red pointy-toe pumps.'

He grinned. 'You had me at Choo.'

24

Janus Benedict set his coffee cup down on the teak table and gazed at the islands off the port side, their bluffs rising from the water in defiance of erosion and man-made progress. They'd gone ashore the prior evening with his guests: three gentlemen from Syria, who seemed most interested in his surface-to-air missile selection, as well as the availability of the Russian Ka-50 Black Shark helicopters that he regularly brokered for the cash-strapped Russian manufacturer. Of course, their negotiations would be lengthy and ongoing, and no religious beliefs were allowed to get in the way of their enjoyment of the Greek islands' pleasures, nor their appreciation of Janus's supplied entertainment, both chemical and feminine.

Janus's head was fuzzy from the extra two glasses of grappa he'd consumed against his better judgment, but sometimes one made sacrifices in order to make one's guests feel welcome. The Syrians seemed to have had a wonderful time, and Janus was confident that would translate into a higher price for the arms than they'd have been willing to pay had he provided sodas and sandwiches.

He checked the screen of his iPad and confirmed

that all three were still sound asleep in their staterooms. The hidden cameras came in handy for more than creating insurance for himself should something turn ugly; they also enabled him to be a consummate host and anticipate his guests' every desire before they even felt them.

For now, the staterooms were quiet, and Janus was confident that he'd have at least another hour or two to himself before he'd have to become the entertainment committee again.

Reginald stumbled up the stairs, a pair of Dolce & Gabbana sunglasses shielding his eyes from the worst of the morning glare, a cigarette dangling from his lips, as he sat down across from his brother and pointed at his coffee cup. A white-uniformed steward scurried from the bowels of the salon and poured him a generous measure of dark roasted coffee, and then, after registering Reginald's nod, he returned with a snifter of Baileys and poured it into the cup.

'I suppose I don't need to ask you how you're feeling this morning,' Janus said, watching his younger sibling raise the cup to his lips with an unsteady hand. 'Little jittery, I'd say.'

'It was a demanding night. That Sophie —'

'Yes, quite — spare me the gory details. We do what we must to make the clients feel at home. And we acquitted ourselves with aplomb. I think these chappies are clay ripe for the potter's wheel.'

'With the amount of coke they went through, they

'bloody well ought to be,' Reginald said, his face drawn from the aftermath of his own overconsumption.

'They seemed amenable by the end of the evening to reconsidering the value we add to their assumed prices for the helicopters, direct from the manufacturer.'

'Not that they'd be able to buy them direct in the first place.'

'Ah, but it's not so important that they grasp ugly realities as that they're happy about the deal. And I'd say, based on their enthusiasm and stamina until the small hours, they'll be as happy as men in their positions can be. After all, it's not as though it's their money. It's all part of the dance. They need to assure whoever they report to, their accountants or backers, that they got the best value available. Our job is to help them do that while making their visit as pleasant and diverting as possible.'

'Then mission accomplished.'

'Yes. And good news, old boy. You won't need to endure any more moments of amusement. I've got the jet in Athens waiting to take you to Mexico later today. After breakfast, Simon will ferry you ashore, where I've made arrangements for you to catch the first flight off the island.'

'Mexico? Good heavens. Why on earth would I want to go to Mexico? Beastly place full of bandits, isn't it?' Reginald complained.

'That may well be, but our clients there purchase a large amount of our product, and have expanded globally, so when they want to discuss updating their ordnance it's a lucrative priority. That, and those two meddling pests, the Fargos, are back in Mexico City. I want to be prepared if they've discovered something and I'm not willing to lose the day it would take me to fly there if they have. So I'm sending you to hold talks with the Los Zetas cartel about their expansion requirements and to personally supervise any action required with the Fargos.' Janus took another taste of coffee. 'And, Reginald – these are very important customers. Quite volatile, I should add. You'll be on their home turf, as they say, so I'd caution you to behave accordingly. Don't do anything that would anger them or this could well be the last I see of you.'

'Brilliant. You're sending me into psycho country to parley with a bunch of gun-happy lunatics.'

'They're not that bad. And, as I underscored, rather profitable and worth caution in your approach. I'm sure as long as you keep a level head, you'll get along swimmingly. As for the Fargos, don't do anything rash. If action is required, consult with me first. Do I make myself clear?' Janus warned in a menacing tone.

'You don't need to speak to me like I'm a five-year-old.' Reginald finished his coffee and signaled to the invisible steward for another. 'I understand. I'm to play nice with the peasants and act as a paperweight with the Fargos. Should any thinking be required, I'm to leave that to you. Did I miss anything?'

'Reginald, I'm serious. There will be no impulsive

outbursts. This is a personal matter for me now. Don't muck it up.'

'Message received. I'll be impeccably behaved as I trade beads with the natives. You'll never know I was there.'

Janus's eyes narrowed and then he nodded. It was as close to capitulation as his brother would come. Hopefully, it would be sufficient. Janus knew Reginald was itching to prove himself but still had youthful impulsiveness to outgrow. Besides, the regional head of Los Zetas he'd be meeting wasn't much older than Reginald, so perhaps they'd get along well. And, of course, there was little downside Janus could see to having his brother on the ground if the Fargos required attention.

The following day, Sam was shaving in the bathroom when his phone on the nightstand rang. Remi stirred at the sound and rolled over to answer it.

'Hel . . . Hello?' she said, her voice thick with sleep.

'Remi, it's Lazlo. I must say, I'm surprised to find you still asleep at 7 a.m. when there's treasure to discover . . .'

'Uh . . . good morning, Lazlo.'

'How soon can you be at this miserable prison to meet with me?'

'I thought it was rather nice.'

'Beside the point.'

She checked her watch. 'Depending on traffic, maybe an hour.' She cleared her throat and sat up. 'Why?'

'Oh, nothing. I thought you might be interested in what I did during the depths of the night.'

'Which is . . . ?'

'Pondered my miserable existence with genuine remorse and not a small dollop of anxiety. Oh, and decrypted the manuscript.'

'You're kidding.'

'No, I've cracked it. Of course, you'll need to work out what it all means. Something about a temple and snakes with wings. Odd bunch, the Spanish.'

Sam came out of the bathroom when he heard Remi's voice. She waved him over and handed him the phone.

'Lazlo?'

'Top of the morning to yer, young man!' Lazlo said with a passable Irish brogue.

'You're awfully cheerful.'

'I've decoded the manuscript. I invited your better half to come and join me for coffee while we go over it. The invitation extends to you, of course, unless you're otherwise occupied.'

Sam blinked twice and glanced at Remi. 'That's great news. You're a magician. We'll be there in two shakes.'

'Take your time. I've no pressing engagements now that I'm purer than a nun's prayers.'

'Or sober at least.'

'That also. See you soon.'

Sam tossed the phone on the bed. 'Just a suggestion, but today might be a good day to hurry in the shower.'

'I'll be ready in five minutes,' Remi said, already on her way into the bathroom. 'This is exciting. I love this part. When it all comes together.'

Sam smiled. 'Me too.'

25

Lazlo was sitting on his room's small brown sofa when they arrived. He rose to greet them and moved to a circular table in the corner, where the notebook computer was displaying its screensaver.

'Please, take a seat. I suspect you'll be here for a while,' he said, indicating two folding chairs he'd obviously requested in anticipation of the meeting.

'You look better, Lazlo,' Remi said, studying his face, noting the clarity in his eyes.

'Thanks, Remi. You're a persuasive lady – in the best possible way, I mean.'

'So what have you got for us?' Sam asked as he sat next to Lazlo.

'Ah, where do I begin? First, the code. It was a substitution cipher and the original underlying text was written in Latin – or every other word was, alternating with Spanish. That's more than a little unusual, but it suggests to me that the author wasn't a conquistador – rather, he was a member of the clergy or an educated nobleman. I won't bore you with all the technical details; the short version is, I've only encountered anything similar from that era once before and that was an encoded document intended for the Pope's eyes only. I entered it on my list purely out of habit and thank goodness I did. Because when I ran the text through that program, it identified the encryption pattern. And, from there, it was child's play.'

'Interesting. So it was a priest?' Remi asked.

'You'll have to be the judge of that.'

'Why didn't it show up in our database?'

'Probably because you haven't spent the last two decades compiling the most complete list of encryption techniques ever assembled,' Lazlo said with the slightest hint of a smile.

'So what does it say?'

'Once I translated all the Latin into Spanish, it seems to be a report on an oral tradition the author dragged out of a highly placed Aztec prisoner – a holy man. Perhaps one of the most esteemed. Anyway, this man told the author about a supposedly great treasure that was to be found in sacred ground. Gemstones, rare icons, and something given to his predecessors by one of their gods.'

'A god?'

'That's what it says. Loosely translated, I took it to mean "the Eye of God."'

Remi sat back. 'No. It's "the Eye of Heaven," although the Toltecs didn't have a specific belief in heaven that we can determine. Too little's known about them, though, to say that with conviction. But I can see how in grappling with a concept like an afterlife, Christians would naturally use words that were the most familiar to them.'

'God, heaven – to my ears, it amounts to the same.'

'Does it offer any direction to where this Eye of Heaven can be found?' Sam asked.

'In a roundabout way. Near as I can tell, it's in the burial chamber of one of their supreme beings. Unpronounceable.'

'Quetzalcoatl,' Remi murmured.

'That's close enough.'

'And does it say where this chamber is?'

'Near a holy place dedicated to the god, of course.'

'It comes out and says that?'

'Well, not in so many words. More amid ramblings about winged snakes and suchlike. Haven't got the foggiest whether you'll be able to make anything out of it, but I made a copy of my rough transcript and saved it to the flash drive you gave me. It's all yours, and I hope it points you in the right direction. Although you'll just give the treasure to the natives rather than pocketing it like any sensible fellow would.'

'That's right. It's not about the money. Any percentage that Mexico offers us, assuming we find anything, will go into our charitable foundation,' Remi said.

'I don't suppose you'd adapt your charitable model to include broken-down, disgraced ex-academics, would you?'

Sam smiled. 'Why don't we take it a day at a time?'

'Can you take us through this line by line?' Remi asked. Lazlo nodded.

Thirty minutes later, they all sat back, a look of puzzled consternation on Sam's face, Remi's expression neutral, Lazlo positively beaming with accomplishment.

'It doesn't really tell us where the tomb is, does it?' Sam said.

Lazlo smiled. 'You mean something like "Walk fifty paces from the old oak tree, west by northwest, and when you see the split rock, dig"? Not as such . . .'

'There can't be that many temples dedicated to Quetzalcoatl,' Remi mused.

Sam shook his head. 'Actually, there are. The Toltecs, the Aztecs, the Mayans . . . they all worshipped him. So, depending on when the tomb was constructed, the body could have been placed in an existing tomb or a tomb being built at the time of the burial. The manuscript doesn't clarify the timing, does it?'

'No. It just says "a chamber beneath a pyramid,"' Lazlo said, pointing to a passage in the translation.

Sam shook his head again. 'There are dozens . . . hundreds, assuming that it's not one that has yet to be discovered. Seems like every year, they're finding more Mayan ruins in the Yucatán.'

'Or that it wasn't one that was destroyed. Like Chulula,' Remi added.

'Not that I wish to dishearten you,' Lazlo said, 'but there could also be some confusion in the translation from the original language to Spanish. It could well be that it wasn't a temple dedicated to this Quetzalcoatl but rather a holy site where he was worshipped alongside others.'

'So what does that leave us?' Remi asked.

'Looking for a chamber beneath one of hundreds of pyramids,' Lazlo said. 'At least it was clear that the chamber was beneath the pyramid and not incorporated into the walls.'

'Which assumes that was accurate. It sounds like the Aztec priest wasn't sure about the exact location, either.'

Lazlo nodded. 'True. The manuscript states pretty clearly that it's founded on hearsay. As are most of these accounts, really.'

Sam groaned and stood. 'Nobody said this would be easy, did they? Lazlo, you're a prince among men. Seriously.'

'Good show, old chap. If only my sanctuary here afforded the odd gin and tonic for toasting purposes . . . but I suppose Nurse wouldn't allow that.'

'It's for the best, Lazlo,' Sam said softly.

'I expect that even if I don't live any longer, it'll seem like an eternity – and an arid one at that,' Lazlo teased, and then gave them both a look of resigned acceptance. 'Seriously, though, I appreciate your help in all of this.'

'We have an ulterior motive. We're hoping we can convince you to look over our shoulders and help us find the tomb. Maybe peruse the photos from the earthquake site, see whether you concur with our interpretation of the pictographs?'

'I'd be delighted, of course. You have but to ask.'

'That's the spirit.'

As their taxi drew near the Institute, Remi took Sam's hand in hers and exhaled quietly. 'Don't worry. We'll figure it out.'

'We usually do, don't we?'

'Kind of our thing, right?'

'Exactly. But we might need some help on this one. How do you feel about approaching Carlos about it?'

'I'd rather not. Let's see what we can come up with on our own first. And don't forget our secret weapon – the one and only Lazlo,' Remi said, her tone not entirely confident.

Sam nodded and squeezed her hand. 'Maribela and Antonio certainly seem like they could narrow it down for us if anyone could . . .' Sam glanced at the side mirror, as he'd been doing periodically since leaving the clinic. 'Do me a favor, would you? Tell the driver to keep going past the Institute,' he said quietly.

'What?'

'I've seen the same car behind us on the way to the clinic and now here. A black Toyota. I think we're being followed and I want to find out for sure.'

Remi leaned forward and had a brief conversation in Spanish with the driver, who nodded and continued south.

'What did you tell him?' Sam asked.

'To take us to the best breakfast restaurant he knows in the area.'

'An enterprising choice.'

'Hopefully, tasty too. I could use some eggs and a cup of strong coffee.' She glanced at the mirror on her side. 'What do we do if we are being followed?'

'Good question. Maybe try to corner them and find out who it is and why they are following us?'

'That hasn't always worked out well in the past, has it?'

'Fair enough. Then what's your vote?'

'We go about our business and lose them when it matters. I don't see much harm in anyone knowing we're at the hotel or that we're doing research at the Institute. It's not like we're an unknown quantity in Mexico.'

'Nice to have the brains of the operation thinking clearly. My instinct is to charge in, guns blazing,' Sam admitted.

'Which has its merits in some circumstances, I'll grant you. But we don't have any guns.'

'Always pouring cold water on my fun, aren't you?'

'It's my life's work.'

They continued on for another six minutes and then the driver coasted to the curb in front of a popular restaurant, judging by the crowd inside. They walked in and the hostess showed them to a table by one of the large picture windows. The tantalizing aroma of freshly cooked food and dark coffee permeated the room.

Sam's mouth started to water as he took his seat. A glance at the street confirmed that the Toyota had taken up position fifty yards down the block, ending any arguments about its role.

'Sam, I know you don't like hearing this, but there's only one person who knew we were in Cuba and now here.'

He nodded. 'Not really. Lagarde knew. He had our bags delivered, remember?'

'It's not Lagarde, I'm telling you. It has to be Kendra.'

'Let's say you're right. That's a difficult situation.'

'What are we going to do?'

'Stop relying on the office until Selma's back full-time.'

'Why don't we just fire her?' Remi said. 'It makes me furious that she'd spy on us and sell us out. Selma's own family . . .'

'How do you think it would make Selma feel if we let Kendra go? No, I think we have to keep it to ourselves and offer as little information as possible from now on. I don't want to break Selma's heart.'

A waitress arrived and Remi ordered coffee for them both. Sam pretended to study the menu.

'Know what you're going to have?' Remi asked.

'Huevos rancheros. Those are on the menu, right?'

'Might help if you weren't holding it upside down.'

'Come on, my Spanish isn't that bad.'

'If you say so. Just let me order or you'll wind up with a hard-boiled pig snout or something.'

243

'Bacon makes everything better.'

'So we don't fire Kendra?'

Sam shook his head. 'And no pig snout.'

'Phooey.'

26

Sam and Remi spent a long day at the Institute scrutinizing the relic collection for anything that might be a clue as to which pyramids showed the greatest promise. Dusk was approaching when they were surprised by Maribela's arrival. Remi was by Sam's computer, pointing at a photograph of a temple, and realized too late that the manuscript was still up on her screen on the opposite side of the lab table. Before she could switch the image to something more innocuous, Maribela was staring at the scan with bewildered shock.

'You got it! You're amazing. I thought we'd never see it again,' she exclaimed as Remi hurried back to her station. Remi threw Sam a resigned look and then turned to Maribela.

'Yes. Sometimes we get lucky. The Cubans have been most forthcoming. Perhaps it's all in the approach . . .'

'I recognized the document immediately. But it's still gibberish. That could take years to decode.'

'Actually, we've already decrypted it,' Remi said, her tone only slightly arch.

'Really! That's . . . unbelievable. You really are miracle workers. What does it say? Anything interesting?'

'We were just discussing it. Basically, it's an account

by a Spanish priest or educated nobleman that tells the story of Quetzalcoatl's hidden tomb and of the treasure associated with it.'

Maribela seemed taken aback. 'I've seen the other mentions of the legend, but this was written specifically to relay information about it?'

'In a manner of speaking. The problem is that it's typical of the era and very vague. If there is a tomb, it's buried beneath a holy pyramid. That's the best we've been able to figure out.'

Sam moved from his position over to where the two women stood. 'We were going to ask you and Antonio to look over the text and help us narrow it down. That is, if it won't interfere with your current project . . .'

'But of course! I can speak for my brother. We'd be honored to look at it and offer our thoughts. He's up in his office. I'll go get him.'

Maribela hurried from the room and Remi sat down in her chair and glared at the monitor. 'That was sloppy of me.'

'We weren't getting anywhere. Maybe this isn't the worst thing that could happen.'

'Then why does it feel so wrong?'

'We're territorial animals. And fiercely competitive. It's natural to resist sharing "our" discovery.'

'It's not a discovery yet. It's only a manuscript. Which may or may not amount to anything.'

'Which is why there's probably no harm. Besides,

Maribela and Antonio would likely be working the dig, anyway, assuming there's anything to it.' Sam shrugged. 'Frankly, if there *is* a tomb and it's buried beneath a pyramid, we'd need to get the government's permission to excavate in a historic site. It's not like we can just take a backhoe to their national treasures.'

Maribela returned with Antonio and they huddled around Remi's monitor. Sam couldn't help but notice that even after a day in the field, Maribela looked like she'd just stepped off the runway in Milan. Remi glanced at him as though able to read his thoughts as she brought up the decoded text on the screen.

They spent the next two hours going over it with the siblings.

'It's been a long day,' Sam announced as he stood and stretched, glancing at his watch. 'Shall we resume this tomorrow?'

'Absolutely. Would you have any problem if we took a copy of both the manuscript file and the decryption so we can study it at home?' Antonio asked, holding up a flash drive on his key ring.

Remi nodded. 'Sure. Just treat it as confidential, please. This could be an extremely important find, if we can figure out which pyramid it is.'

'Of course. We'll limit it to just me and my sister. And Carlos. As the director, his approval is needed to invest man-hours in researching it.'

'That's fine. Is he still here?' Sam asked.

'No, but I'll be in early and will tell him all about it.' Antonio glanced at his Panerai. 'When would you like to meet tomorrow? Nine?'

'That would be perfect,' Remi said with a smile directed at Antonio.

Sam extended his hand to Antonio for the flash drive. 'I'll go make a copy.'

Their taxi arrived fifteen minutes later. On the way back to the hotel, Sam turned to Remi with a smile.

'Do you want to eat at the hotel or seek out some local fare? I don't care as long as it's soon. I could eat a horse.'

'Which you might be doing if we don't dine at the hotel. Breakfast didn't sit well with me.'

'It was probably the pig snout.'

'Right. Maybe it wasn't fresh.'

'That's the worst. Snout past its prime,' Sam agreed, and they both laughed. 'Still having regrets about letting them in on it?'

'No, I'm over that. As much as I hate to admit it, you were right. I was being a big baby.'

'Not really. Like I said, I could see myself doing the same thing.'

'But I expect you to behave like a toddler.'

'It's part of my naïve charm.'

'You bet it is.'

Dinner was quiet, with Remi agreeing that one margarita never hurt anyone. After enjoying their huge entrées, they returned to their room, both wondering silently whether they'd really done the right thing by handing over the result of so much hard work and if, in the end, any of it would even matter.

The next morning they awoke to their windows rattling from sheets of wind-driven rain lashing the hotel.

'I thought Mexico was all about warm weather and blue skies,' Sam said.

'Well, it's been warmer than back home.'

'And rained enough to give Seattle a run for its money.'

'Probably the time of year. Hey, do we have time to grab coffee and a roll?'

Sam looked at his watch as he edged by her into the bathroom. 'If I don't shave my legs.'

'I'm willing to overlook it this once.'

The drive to the Institute was slow and miserable, the streets awash with floating trash and overflowing manholes. By the time they made it to the office, it was half past nine. Maribela was waiting for them with an excited expression. It was all she could do to restrain herself when they walked through the door.

'Good morning, Maribela,' Sam said, running his fingers through his wet hair, the result of the run from the cab to the front entrance.

'Good morning.'

'How did your night go?' Remi asked.

'I didn't get much sleep. Neither did Antonio. But I have good news. Antonio thinks he knows which pyramid it is,' Maribela blurted.

'Really?' Sam said. 'That's great! How did he figure it out?'

'He discarded the Mayan ruins that didn't fit the criteria or if their story came from an Aztec religious figure. The Aztecs had limited interactions with the Mayans, so it's unlikely that a secret this important would have been imparted to an Aztec priest. Also, back then, travel would have been difficult into the Yucatán from here, and there's little chance that any pilgrimage made would have stayed secret for long. And last, unless the body was somehow preserved, it would have been buried around the time of Quetzalcoatl's death – the ruler, obviously, not the deity. Which narrows the field considerably.'

'Makes sense so far,' Remi agreed.

'That leaves us with pyramids that were in existence at the time of his death – which is uncertain but which we can estimate to be between AD 980 and 1100. Either way, while that's a decent number, it's not huge. And it rules out all the Aztec sites.'

'But what if the tomb had been constructed later and the body moved?' Sam asked.

'Possible, but that's not the way the text reads if you adjust it for the nuances of the Nahuatl language. The person who wrote the manuscript was recording what he thought the Aztec was saying, but that's probably not what he actually said. It's a record of how a Spaniard would interpret what he said. Make sense?'

Remi nodded slowly. 'But because that's your area of specialty . . .'

'Exactly. Our interpretation can adjust for what might have been lost in translation. If that's the case, and there's no guarantee, then the site is one of the ruins north or east of Mexico City.'

'Which are Teotihuacan, Cholula, and Tula, right?'

'No, Cholula was south, near where Puebla now is.'

'And you've definitely ruled out the Mayan cities?'

'As much as anything can be excluded. It would have been impossible to keep something like the construction of a secret tomb beneath a sacred pyramid secret. No, we're looking at either Teotihuacan, which was uninhabited by the time Quetzalcoatl died, or Tula, where he ruled but from where he was exiled late in his rule. The likelihood is that it's Teotihuacan because it would have been empty, so anyone working in secret could have performed the excavation and built the chamber without being discovered.'

'Sounds like a lot of manpower,' Sam said.

'Yes, but the manuscript mentions a secret order that worshipped the ruler Quetzalcoatl as a living god and later dedicated itself to the protection of the sacred tomb. If the followers were suitably zealous, it's entirely possible that they could have done the construction and then taken up residence in the area, keeping their secret through the generations.'

'Then it's the Temple of the Feathered Serpent in

Teotihuacan?' Remi asked. 'We've been looking at that as one of the candidates, but it seems like it's too obvious.'

'Sometimes the most obvious place is the best place to hide something of immeasurable value. We have a dig going on there right now. A tunnel system has been discovered beneath the temple, but it was filled in around AD 250 and it's taking forever to excavate it.'

'Then you would have discovered the secret chamber, too, if it was there,' Remi said.

Antonio entered and approached them.

'Maribela was just telling us about your theory about where the temple might be located,' Sam said.

'Ah, yes. Well, it's all speculative, but, for my money, it would be somewhere beneath the Temple of the Feathered Serpent,' Antonio said.

'But there's been sonar done after the tunnel discovery,' Remi said, 'and it didn't reveal anything more. Maybe the tunnel connects to it?'

'Doubtful. One of our colleagues heads up that dig and nothing's been discovered or hinted at or we would have heard about it. No, if it's there, it's somewhere other than the obvious. And the sonar scan that was performed concentrated on that one quadrant after this latest tunnel was found. If it's in one of the other quadrants, or if it's deeper than the tunnels, it could be a decade before anything's found.'

'Then how do we locate it?' Sam asked.

'Based on our interpretation of the manuscript, it

seems to point to some fairly specific areas once you narrow it down to that pyramid. Of course, that would have been all but impossible for a sixteenth-century exploration, which may well be why the search was eventually abandoned.'

'How do we get permission to excavate?'

'Well, you'd need a permit from the Ministry. Which I just got finished discussing with Carlos. He's going to put in a request and see if he can fast-track it.'

'How long will that take?' Remi asked.

'If no resistance is encountered, maybe a week,' Maribela said.

'And there's the question of funding the undertaking,' Antonio added. 'We're always low on money, and the new find has taken a hundred and ten per cent of our discretionary fund.'

Sam and Remi smiled at the same time.

'We could make a donation, if that would smooth the way,' Sam said. 'Just tell us what you think it would take and we can put the wheels in motion. We've funded other digs, so why not this one? Making the discovery is worth more than the cost of a small excavation team . . .'

Antonio nodded. 'That's very generous of you. Perhaps you could relay that to Carlos? He handles the finances for the Institute.'

Sam and Remi went upstairs to Carlos's office and knocked. He came to the door and beamed at them before welcoming them into his suite. They first discussed the likelihood of a tomb beneath the Temple of the Feathered Serpent and he seemed genuinely excited about the possibility. When talk turned to logistics and their participation, he was reticent to commit to a time line but then noticeably relaxed when Sam floated the idea of a donation to cover the excavation expense.

'That's extremely generous of you. And I'd imagine it will make it much easier to approve if we have funding in place,' he said.

'That's what we were thinking,' Sam said. 'We don't want to delay exploration. Say the word and we'll arrange for a wire transfer to the Institute's account. It can be there by tomorrow.'

'I don't think it would be overly expensive if you have a specific location in mind. Really, we're talking about a few workers, a supervisor, possibly some excavation equipment . . .'

'And a scanner, if you think it would help,' Remi added.

'Probably not, but it doesn't hurt to budget for it. Figure, mmm . . . fifty thousand American dollars would more than cover it, including the permit. The scanner must be flown in from the United States and operated by a trained technician from there.'

'Consider it done.'

When they returned to their temporary office, Antonio was scrutinizing satellite photography of the location and Maribela was pointing to an area near one of the corners at the pyramid base. 'This is the likely spot,' she said, tapping the monitor. 'All of the elements in the Aztec's account are there . . .'

'This may seem like a silly question, but is the actual pyramid, this Temple of the Feathered Serpent, solid or hollow?' asked Remi, the thought just occurring to her.

Maribela sat back. 'It appears that it's hollow, but far deeper than could have been reached with any ease from the exterior. What happened is that successive pyramids were built over the prior temples, incorporating them inside. Archaeologists tunneled into it and discovered over two hundred skeletons, as well as human remains at each of the four corners. And they've been over it with sonar. There's no chamber inside.'

'Yes, but sonar has its limitations. I'm all too aware of them,' Sam said.

Remi nodded. 'And what about the Adosada platform in front of the pyramid? Have we excluded that as a possibility?'

Antonio shook his head. 'That was built at a later date than the pyramid. The Adosada was probably constructed to supplant the pyramid as the place of worship. The manuscript doesn't discuss it, but, you're right, it could also be a location. Maybe a sort of sleight of hand of the tomb builders – a misdirection. Or we may be interpreting it incorrectly and it's none of these.'

'So you think the Temple of the Feathered Serpent

pyramid in Teotihuacan is the best candidate?' Sam summarized.

'That's our belief,' Antonio agreed.

Sam rubbed his face. 'Maybe we should go out to the site while we're waiting for the permit.'

Remi looked out the window. 'Once it stops raining. It's not that far, is it?'

'It's about forty kilometers away.'

'Then that's what we'll do,' Remi said. 'Unless anyone's got any better ideas?'

Sam shook his head. 'Sounds like a plan. Here's hoping for clear skies sooner than later.'

27

It rained all of the following day, so Sam and Remi immersed themselves in studying everything they could find on Teotihuacan, focusing on the Temple of the Feathered Serpent. The history of the city was fascinating, as was the speed with which it had ceased to be viable – at one point, it was the largest in the world, but it was abandoned around AD 700 and destroyed by fire fifty years later. A city that at one point was larger than Rome had become a ghost town. And as little is known about its builders as about the Toltecs, whose own city was only sixty miles north.

They didn't see Carlos all day but assumed that he was at his other office and would contact them about funding the project when he'd got approval for a dig. The day dragged by slowly and by five o'clock they were both more than ready to leave.

Morning brought the blessed relief of the sun and, with it, travel to Teotihuacan to see the layout for themselves. Even though they'd studied it, nothing could have prepared them for the grandeur when they exited their taxi and stood in front of the huge stone figure that acted as a greeter near the museum gates.

They moved with a small group of German tourists

and walked on to the long, wide Avenue of the Dead, which bisected the city and terminated at the Pyramid of the Moon. The Temple of the Feathered Serpent was at the opposite end of the unearthed portion of the city, with the Pyramid of the Sun between the two landmarks – an incredible sight and the third-largest pyramid in the world after those in Egypt and Cholula.

Sam indicated the surrounding buildings. 'You get a sense of how vast it was and how evolved the civilization must have been. One of the most amazing things is how geometrically precise the layout is. The front wall of the Pyramid of the Sun aligns with the points where the sun sets on the equinoxes, and the Avenue of the Dead points at the setting of the Pleiades. Astronomy played a huge role in this society.'

'The other thing I wasn't prepared for is how hot it is. I guess no shade anywhere has its drawbacks,' Remi said as they walked up the famed avenue, taking in the city's size. 'And here I was complaining about it being cold just a few days ago on Baffin.'

They strolled along in silence, and, after they had moved halfway along the Avenue of the Dead, Sam held his phone up, as if checking for a signal, and then spoke softly. 'Don't turn around, but our tail's about two hundred yards behind us.'

'Are you sure?'

'See for yourself.' Sam had been filming as he held the cell aloft. He quickly rewound and handed the phone to her. The footage was bouncy, but he'd caught an image of a Hispanic male in his thirties, walking alone, looking out of place. He obviously hadn't been expecting to have to walk miles in the heat and was dressed differently than the other visitors, to his detriment.

'Doesn't look very happy, does he?'

'He was probably thinking he'd be sitting all day, not going on a hike.'

'You know, you've just inspired me to pick up the pace and spend twice as much time walking the site as we'd planned,' Remi said, handing the phone back to him.

'Bad day to be in the "Follow the Fargos" business.'

'Let's make him earn his money, shall we?'

'You're a hard woman, Remi Fargo.'

'Aye, that I am, kind sir. That I am.'

The Pyramid of the Moon loomed before them, with smaller temples on either side lining the avenue. They stopped at the Palace of the Jaguars, so named because of the colorful frescoes to be found throughout its interior, and savored the shade from the corrugated-metal roof before trekking to the Palace of Quetzalpapalotl, which owed its name to the illustrations on its walls of a mythical butterfly creature. It had been renovated and stood in most of its former glory. They took their time inside, fully aware that their tail was out in the harsh sun. When he finally followed them inside, they left and made for the Pyramid of the Moon, forcing him back outside.

'I almost feel sorry for him,' Sam said quietly as they started ascending the steps on the front of the pyramid along with a few other hardy tourists.

'Not me. Nobody's forcing him to tail us.'

'He definitely got the raw end of the deal. Did you see? He's wearing black leather dress shoes. Not a good choice for this kind of thing. He'll be lucky if he can walk by the time this is over.'

'And there's so much more to see. Wow, look at this view,' she said, then pulled her phone from her pocket and took some photos of the entire city spread out before them. The buildings shimmered from the heat rising off the pavement as Sam and Remi took in the awe-inspiring panorama.

'Where to next?' Sam asked.

'Oh, I think we need to see the Pyramid of the Sun, don't we? And then we can finish up in the Citadel, which is the section with the Temple of the Feathered Serpent over on the far end.'

'Good thing we ate a big breakfast. We won't be out of here until two or three at this rate.'

'And our tail will be limping on stumps by then. Didn't his mom ever tell him that sensible shoes were important?'

'And sunscreen. Bet he wishes he'd brought a hat, at the very least. Should be a mean burn. We are at seven thousand feet. Ouch.'

'Now even *I'm* feeling a little sorry for him,' Remi said, 'but not enough to wind this down. Am I correct that there were temple structures on top of each of those smaller pyramids before the city was destroyed?' she asked, pointing to the row to her left.

'That's the assumption. Same for the top of this one, as well as the others.'

'Makes you feel very small and recent, doesn't it? To think that all this was thriving fifteen hundred years before we were born. And now it's largely mounds of dirt.'

'Nobody gets out of this alive. Which is a good reason to make the most of it while the sun's shining. Which it definitely is today, as our friend can attest to.'

Remi took Sam's hand. 'Come on, let's get to the big pyramid. Our boy down there seems like he's getting way too much rest. And how long can he stare at the other buildings before he stands out even more? This is the main attraction, and everyone else has climbed the steps.'

The smaller temples along the way were large when viewed from the ground, the terrain beyond them rising nearly to their summits. When excavation had started, the city had been bumps of land with an occasional structure peeking from the landscape, the earth seemingly eager to reclaim it as though wiping any trace of Teotihuacan from its surface.

They climbed the steps to the Pyramid of the Sun and gazed down at the rest of the complex two hundred feet below.

'Poor Quetzalcoatl's pyramid's kind of puny compared to this. He got shorted. Those feathered snakes get no respect,' Sam joked as a welcome breeze tousled his hair.

'Let's stop in at the museum. No doubt it has air-conditioning. Let's cool off there and then finish up with Snake Boy, shall we?'

'Sounds like a good plan. Especially the AC part.'

The museum was filled with artifacts that had been uncovered during the hundred years of archaeological exploration of the site and included a map and a simulation of what the city had looked like in its prime. All the buildings had been covered with plaster and bright paint, decorated with frescoes to honor the gods and celebrate important moments in the civilization's history. They browsed for fifteen minutes, enjoying the cool of climate control, and then made their final way to the area called the Citadel by the Spanish, which they had thought was a fort but was actually a plaza that housed the Temple of the Feathered Serpent.

As they approached the temple, it didn't look particularly impressive compared to the two larger pyramids. But once they'd mounted the steps of the platform in front of it, they could see the detail of the carved snake heads and the elaborate depictions of serpents winding their way around each level.

'It's certainly all about snakes,' Sam said.

'Go snake or go home. That's my new motto.'

'You're in the right place, then. All snake all the time.'

'But with feathers. Don't forget the plumage.'

'Of course not.'

'Looks like it's closed off to visitors,' Remi observed. 'And they're working on some of the heads.'

'I have a feeling this is a bit like owning a bridge. You're never really done with maintenance.'

'Then this was the center of the city?'

'That's the thinking. But the rest is under that farmland over there.'

'And that shopping center.'

Remi pointed to the pyramid. 'So you think our chamber could be along the back side? Can we get over there?'

'Doesn't look that way. It's cordoned off. Besides, once we have a permit, we'll be out here for days while we excavate. I'm sure there's nothing to see until then — just more dirt.'

After twenty minutes looking over the Citadel, they headed back to the main entrance, where a row of taxis waited in the sweltering heat for exhausted visitors. As they took the first in line, Remi sneaked a peek behind them, where their shadow was hobbling as fast as he could to the parking lot.

'Should we wait for him?' she suggested.

'No. Why make anything easy?'

'I wonder who he is? Or, rather, who put him up to it?'

'Someone really frustrated about now. Don't worry. We'll ditch them once we have the permit. There are small hotels around here we can stay where we'll never be found. The trail will end with an empty bag.'

'I hope you're right.'

The trip back took an hour, and, after a late lunch at a nearby restaurant, they went to the Institute. Outside, two police cars were parked at the curb, with a few curious students standing near them.

'I wonder what this is all about?' Remi muttered as they entered the building.

Maribela was standing at the security desk, talking with a police officer in hushed tones. When she saw them, she disengaged and approached, strain evident on her beautiful face.

'What is it, Maribela?' Sam asked.

'It's Carlos. He's disappeared. The police say he's been kidnapped.'

'Carlos?' Remi blurted.

Maribela frowned and nodded. 'It's a regrettable part of living in Mexico City. Kidnappings happen all too often.'

'That's terrible. What are the police doing?'

'They're going through his office to see if there's anything that could help identify the kidnappers, but it's purely a formality. These are usually organized criminal gangs that do it for the money. They target the wealthy and the powerful. I'm afraid that Carlos is a little of both, between his family fortune and his position with the government.'

'Do . . . do the kidnappers usually harm their victims?' Remi asked.

Maribela's face clouded further. 'Sometimes. There's no way of predicting it. But we'll pray that there's a swift resolution to this and that Carlos is returned to us unharmed. I'm afraid that's all we can do.'

28

Over the next two days, they learned their permit had stalled with Carlos's kidnapping. Without his pushing to get it done, it had been sucked into the great black hole of Mexico City's bureaucracy. Antonio visited the Ministry to see what progress had been made, but after a half day there, he returned with a dour expression.

'Nobody knows anything about it. So I made a new request. But we've lost almost a week.'

'That's frustrating. It doesn't sound like there's much we can do about it,' Sam said.

'No, unfortunately, this is the system. It's a bad one, but it's the one we must work with.'

'How long do you think this application will take?'

'Could be as much as a month. Although I high-lighted that we have a commitment for funding, which I told them was time-sensitive, so I'm hoping that hastens it along.'

'A month is too long. Carlos felt he could get it done in a week.'

'Which he probably could. The problem is that Carlos isn't here, so we don't have his contact base to draw upon. He could pick up a phone and take the right person to lunch. I'm afraid I don't even know who the right person is. I've spent my time in academia and in the field.'

Remi shifted in her seat. 'Is there anything we can do to help speed things up?'

Antonio frowned. 'I sincerely wish there was. But I can't think of anything.'

Antonio left them and returned to the new find. Sam continued studying the images from the tunnel discovered under the Temple of the Feathered Serpent while Remi pored over the pictographs from the tombs north of town, unearthed during the earthquake. At one o'clock they took a break for lunch and Sam called the clinic to see how Lazlo was faring. The administrator, Isabella Benito, came on the line, and, after exchanging pleasantries, Sam cut to the questions that he and Remi had discussed the previous night.

'How is he?' Sam asked.

'Physically, he's getting stronger, and has made a nearly complete recovery. He's put on three kilos, and is taking part in the clinic's exercise program every day.'

'And mentally?'

'Ah, that is always a more difficult process. The psychological dependence on alcohol is insidious, and it has been a major part of his lifestyle for many years.'

'I understand.'

'His self-image must be revised so he can imagine a future without alcohol. That, as they say, is the hard part. Unfortunately, many patients don't make that important transition and instead fall prey to old habits.'

Sam sighed. 'In your opinion, is he stable enough to work on a project with us?'

'That depends on what you require of him. If you are asking whether he can work here while he's recovering, the answer is a cautious yes. It could well prove therapeutic.'

'What about going into the field with us?'

'Into the field? You mean leaving the clinic before his course here is done?'

'Only temporarily. Perhaps a day here, two there. What's your assessment?'

Benito hesitated as she considered the question. 'We're nearing the point where we would slowly reintroduce him into the outside world. Small steps to acclimatize him to a noninstitutional setting. But that would be under carefully controlled circumstances and supervised at every turn.'

'Then he's ready to reassimilate?'

'Yes, but I'm describing going to a restaurant with several of the other patients, accompanied by a counselor. Taking a shopping trip. It sounds like you're proposing something more . . . demanding.'

'Señora Benito, Lazlo is foremost an academic. It's what he lives for. Intellectual stimulation is like oxygen for him. What I'm proposing is to involve him in a project that will fully engage his attention. That will give him a purpose.'

268

'If you wish to do so, I have no objection, but you'll have to take full responsibility for him.'

'Yes, I appreciate that. If I'm understanding you correctly, you're saying that he's probably up to it, but you can't guarantee that he won't . . . backslide.'

Her tone was cautious. 'I can't see anything negative, but honestly, Señor Fargo, none of us can predict a patient's outcome with complete accuracy, especially at this stage. It's still very early.'

'I respect that. Thank you for your candor.'

'You're welcome.'

'We'll be coming by this afternoon to look in on him.'

Sam hung up and filled Remi in on the discussion. She shut down her computer, a look of concern on her face as she gathered her things.

'I don't know, Sam. I mean, he's delivered a small miracle with the manuscript, but it sounds like he's still on thin ice.'

'No question. But I think it would be good for him to work with us, and it certainly won't hurt to have another set of eyes on the data. What's the worst that could happen?'

'There you go again.'

'Sorry.'

Remi sighed. 'Let's grab something to eat and go see how he's doing. If he seems fine, we'll make the call then, okay?'

Sam nodded. 'You bet. But just in case, you might want to put together a care package for Lazlo.'

She held up a flash drive. 'I'm way ahead of you.'

Aware of being followed but now resigned to it, they made their way across town to the clinic. Lazlo was sitting up in bed, reading a book, when they arrived.

'How's the life of leisure?' Sam asked, rounding the bed as Lazlo stood and shook his hand.

'I'm about bloody ready to crawl the walls with all this clean living. Who knew that virtue could be so boring?'

Remi smiled. 'You look good.'

'Flattery will get you whatever you desire, young lady. Please. Have a seat. Tell me all about how the hunt for your tomb is going,' Lazlo said, motioning to the sofa. 'Can I offer you some water? I'm afraid that's all I've got, unless you want me to ring for some coffee. I've given up on a proper cup of tea.'

They explained their theory. Lazlo followed along, seemingly without effort, asking direct, probing questions that were as precise as they were relevant. After half an hour of back-and-forth, Sam and Remi exchanged a glance, and she leaned forward, hands folded in front of her.

'Lazlo, we could use some help. How would you like to look over what we've gathered and give us your expert opinion?'

'Well, I'm not sure how expert it is compared to all of you, but if there's anything I can add to the party, why not? It's not as though I'm figuring out cold fusion at the moment.'

Remi reached into her purse and extracted the flash drive. 'These are photos of all the material we've collected. Pictographs from the newly discovered Toltec tombs, everything that's relevant from the Institute archives, URLs for anything in the public domain, maps – the whole shooting match.'

Lazlo took the small device. 'Well, this should keep me busy for a time, I'd imagine. When are you planning to do your dig?'

'We're still waiting for the permit. There was a complication,' Sam said.

'Oh?'

He told Lazlo about the kidnapping and the effect it had had on their project. Lazlo frowned and shook his head. 'Bloody bad luck, that. So you're stalled?'

'I wish I could say otherwise, but that's what we are.'

'Only ray of light is that it will give me time to get up to speed. Doors closing and windows opening, and all that.'

'Yes. Well, hopefully, we'll get the go-ahead soon. When we do, we want you with us,' Remi said.

Lazlo raised one eyebrow. 'You think my jailers will allow that?'

'If you swear to be on your best behavior, I think they might.'

'My best behavior is usually everyone else's worst . . .'

Sam smiled. 'But this is the new you, my friend. And helping us with this find would be a big step in establishing your credentials as a field expert rather than an academic.'

'Well, if you can convince the dragon lady to let me loose on the world, how can I say no?'

'That's what I was hoping you'd say. For now, give everything a look, and get in touch if anything occurs to you. We'll start with that.'

'Will do.' Lazlo paused, and when he spoke again, his voice was soft. 'I appreciate everything you're doing.'

Remi smiled. 'You're helping us. It's a two-way street.'

Lazlo looked toward the window, where motes of dust drifted lazily in the afternoon sun. 'I won't let you down.'

The ride back to the hotel was a quick one, the plaintive lament of a distraught tenor on the taxi radio battling with a mariachi horn section that sounded like it had started happy hour early. Remi gazed at the side mirror as she edged nearer to Sam.

'They're still following us.'

'At least they're consistent.'

She furrowed her brow. 'What did you think of Lazlo? He seemed lucid to me.'

'You heard the administrator, it could go either way. But for now, my money's on Lazlo. I think he wants a new lease on life . . . This is it. Lord knows it beats a hut in some mudhole.'

'I hope you're right.'

Selma called as they were preparing to go out to dinner, her tone excited. 'I spoke with an old friend at the

State Department who knows someone who knows someone. They're going to contact the relevant Mexican ministry tomorrow and see what can be done to put your permit on the fast track.'

'That's great news, Selma. Didn't take you long.'

'I had to promise a case of good champagne. She's a connoisseur, so none of the cheap stuff.'

'If she can make this happen, she'll get Dom Pérignon.'

'Oh, she'll make it happen. She's got a lot of influence with foreign aid programs, including those that are directed at Mexico. Everyone there wants to do her favors. I wouldn't say it's a lock, but it's as close as you can get to one.'

'Then it's Dom on the menu for her as soon as I can order it.'

'I'll take care of it. Feels good to actually be doing something useful.'

'Then spare no expense, Selma.'

'Will do. Have a good night.'

'And you as well,' he said quietly and smiled for the first time in what felt like forever.

After a somber dinner Sam and Remi went to sleep early. Several hours later the jarring ring of Sam's phone shattered the silence of the room. He groped for the lamp switch, groggy, and, after switching it on, stabbed the little cell to life.

'Hello?' His voice was hoarse.

'Sam, old boy. I've reviewed the translation of the

manuscript and looked over your snaps of the pictographs and I have to say I'm not convinced at the reasoning that puts the tomb where you think it is.'

'Lazlo, do you have any idea what time it is?'

'None whatsoever. Sorry if it's late. I thought you'd want the bad news.'

'Can we discuss this in the morning?' Sam squinted at the LED display of the bedside clock. 'Or later this morning?'

'Absolutely. I just wanted you to know. And I'd very much like to go to the recently discovered tomb to see the pictographs in person. Photos aren't all they're chocked up to be.'

'Noted. I'll call you when it's light out.'

'Good show. I'll be waiting.'

Sam switched the light off as Remi shifted beside him. He exhaled softly and she moved closer.

'Still think this was a good idea?' she murmured.

Sam was already asleep.

29

A battered 1970s-era blue Ford truck loaded with cast-off wooden beams lurched up the dirt road that ran alongside the grounds of the building-supply warehouse on the outskirts of Mexico City. Inside the high cement wall that ran along the lot perimeter sat three vehicles, even though the warehouse was closed to business for the week – a black Cadillac Escalade, a white Lincoln Navigator, and a lifted burgundy H2 Hummer with oversize tires.

Inside the smaller secondary building, Carlos sat bound to a wooden chair, naked from the waist up, his face a brutalized mass of contusions, the chair back barely supporting his slumping weight as he struggled for breath against the ropes. Reginald paced in front of him, his cigarette smoldering, his face contorted with unthinking anger as he weighed the information he'd just received.

Reginald moved back to Carlos and punched him again, the tops of his black driving gloves slick with drying blood. Carlos gurgled; the blow barely registered after having survived so many from his enraged captor.

'I thought you told me that the permit was killed.

You lied to me. You'll regret that,' Reginald hissed, the menace of his threat obvious in every syllable.

Carlos leaned to the side and spat on the floor near Reginald's handmade shoes. 'It . . . was. When you kidnapped me, it . . . should have . . . stalled indefinitely,' he managed, blurring in and out of consciousness as pain ravaged his body.

'Apparently not. Our sources just told us that a permit for the Fargos, in partnership with the National Institute of Anthropology and History, is being walked through and has received the highest priority.'

'I . . . different permit . . . not mine. You . . . had me . . . days. Must . . . be . . . new,' Carlos mumbled, the words barely distinguishable, and then his chin lolled on to his chest as he blacked out.

Reginald punched the side of his head for good measure and then shook his own hand, which was sore from the blows. His fury gradually abated as he studied the unconscious archaeologist. He paced again for a few moments and then he stripped off the gloves and threw them on the floor in disgust before stalking from the room.

In the office next door, a dark-complexioned Hispanic man in his mid-thirties, acne scars pocking his features, regarded Reginald with pig eyes from his seat behind a cheap metal desk. Two younger men sat near the door with Kalashnikov AKM assault rifles in their laps and stared off at nothing.

'Well? Did you learn anything?' asked Ferdinand

Guerrero, the Mexico City chief of the Los Zetas cartel, the most violent in Mexico – an international criminal enterprise with tentacles that reached as far away as Africa, Europe, and South America, as well as every major city in the US

'No. He claims it's not the same . . . issue . . . I was concerned about.'

'Maybe he's telling the truth?' Guerrero asked, his soft voice out of place with his thick, fight-flattened nose and customary sneer.

'It doesn't matter. His absence hasn't bought us enough time to get our permit approved.' Reginald kicked the side of another metal desk in frustration, the sound like an explosion in the small space. Their source had got them the manuscript and translation. And a little money spread to an assistant with a drug problem and in over his head to Guerrero had got a copy of the lost permit, so they knew exactly where in Teotihuacan to target.

'What do you want us to do with him? Let him go free? If his usefulness is at an end . . .' Guerrero said, shifting behind the desk to study the silver tips of his burgundy Lagarto ostrich cowboy boots.

Reginald fought for control of his emotions and then waved a hand nonchalantly. 'I presume you have a means to dispose of him?' He paused, thinking. 'He can identify me.'

Guerrero laughed, a phlegmy sound devoid of humor. 'You could say we do. Any special timing concerns?'

'Let's wait till the end of the week so it looks like a kidnapping gone wrong. In fact, if you have someone who could contact the family and make a large ransom demand, that could be money in your pocket,' Reginald suggested. 'Easy money for your trouble.'

Guerrero's eyes narrowed. 'I told you the price for arranging this.'

Reginald saw the danger and instantly backtracked. 'Of course. Which we'll be happy to discount from your organization's next order. I meant additional money – more of a performance bonus.'

Guerrero laughed again and slapped the tabletop. 'Ha! You're a funny man. Much more than your brother, eh? But you talk the same way. A performance bonus!'

The two bodyguards, uncertain what had amused their boss, grinned, but didn't dare go as far as laughing. Guerrero was notorious for mercurial mood swings. If he imagined an insult from a subordinate, it could be a death sentence. And his volatility wasn't improved by his prodigious cocaine and methamphetamine intake, making him as dangerous as an armed grenade.

Guerrero nodded slowly and Reginald ventured a wan smile, choking back the tremor of unease that the cartel killer's gaze induced. 'Good show, then. I'd say wait until the end of the week, then do what you like with his body.'

'*No problemo, jefe,*' Guerrero said, his tone now neutral.

'Quite.'

Reginald paused by the door and one of the gunmen pulled it open for him. As he walked back to the SUV that Guerrero had thoughtfully provided for his use, he weighed strategies for keeping his latest scheme from his older brother, who would be livid if he found out about the kidnapping. Janus was too conservative, Reginald thought, and sometimes it was best to adapt to a situation on the ground as it developed. If things had gone as planned, the permit they'd applied for would have made it through the system while the Fargos' application languished, and they'd have been able to supervise the dig themselves.

As long as Guerrero didn't speak to Janus about it, he saw no downside. And his brother wouldn't have any appetite for discussions with the homicidal sociopath who ran the Mexico City Los Zetas. Reginald would bring his brother a price for approval that included the discount he'd promised and assure him that was the best he could do – after trimming off a few thousand quid for his own bank account, of course. Janus was family, but he treated Reginald like a petulant child, as he had most of his life, and the resentment ran deep.

He stepped outside of the darkened warehouse. He slid his sunglasses on and waited for his eyes to adjust to the bright light as he studied his slightly swollen knuckles. With a glance at his white gold Patek Philippe World Timer, he approached the Lincoln, humming a song that the mariachis had played the evening before while he was entertaining the sixteen-year-old dancer Guerrero had arranged for.

It looked like it was going to be a beautiful afternoon.

Antonio and Maribela entered the Fargos' work area two days later, beaming like they'd got raises.

'The permit. It's done. We can start whenever we want,' Maribela announced, waggling a single sheet of paper in the air.

'That's wonderful, Maribela,' Remi said. 'Will you be working with us on this?' she asked, her doubts about Maribela lingering.

'Of course. It's too important a potential find to entrust to anyone else.'

'But what about your new one? The crypts?'

'That will be months, possibly years, of painstaking effort. We've got one of our trusted associates heading up the team. So we're all yours,' Maribela said with a good-natured toss of her incredible hair.

Remi fingered the gold scarab dangling from her neck and offered a wan smile, which Antonio returned. 'That's a beautiful necklace. I don't think I've ever seen anything quite like it,' he said, eyeing the pendant.

'Thank you. It's my lucky talisman. From Spain,' she said lightly.

Sam cleared his throat, not delighted with Antonio's admiration of Remi's bauble. 'Let's get this show on the road. I'll arrange to have some money wired immediately. We'll need to make a list of equipment and personnel we'll want. If the wire goes out today, we should be able to source whatever we need tomorrow and be at the site by the following day.'

'That's great,' Remi said. 'It feels like we've been waiting months. I know it's only been ten days, but still . . .'

Antonio nodded. 'Yes. I just wish Carlos were here. He would have made an exception to his schedule to participate in a dig of this magnitude.'

'Has there been any news?' Sam asked, choosing his words carefully.

'No. Nothing. It's taking too long. His wife's out of her mind with worry. As you can imagine.'

'Is that kind of delay unusual?' Remi asked.

'Yes. Most criminals want their money as quickly as possible,' Maribela said. 'Waiting does them no good and increases their risk. So it's most unusual.'

A tense silence hung between them, and then Antonio rubbed his hands together. 'No point in dwelling on what we can't affect. Better to focus on what we can, eh?'

'Indeed,' Sam said, staring at his iPhone's screen. 'I'll make the call on the money. I still have the account information Carlos gave me.'

'Then I'll leave you to it.'

The remainder of the afternoon was spent making lists and outlining the best approach to the dig. They were eager to excavate but had to proceed cautiously to ensure they didn't damage any artifacts.

Two days later, they'd slipped out of the Four Seasons, taking a side entrance, before ducking into a waiting car driven by one of Ferrer's people. They'd checked into El Oasis, a motel six blocks from the ancient city. While the accommodations were primitive, the air conditioner and shower worked, if grudgingly, which was more than they'd expected. Now they were standing beneath a tarp that provided welcome shade. The rear of the Temple of Quetzalcoatl pyramid loomed before them.

Lazlo had joined them on his first outing from the clinic and seemed relieved to be out of the controlled environment, obviously preferring being in the field. The late-afternoon sun beat down on them as workers dug along a forty-foot section of the pyramid's base. The laborers earned their meager pay, working ten hours and moving a surprising amount of soil.

The foreman was about to wrap it up when one of the men, his yellow T-shirt soaked through with sweat, called out. Everyone rushed to where he was standing, in a deep trench a full story below ground level. Remi held her breath for a few moments when she saw what he'd hit with his shovel – the unmistakable shape of a man-made stone surface.

'This is it,' she said in a whisper.

Sam moved to the crude wooden ladder that stood nearby. All five of them lowered themselves into the trench and Antonio barked an order. The man carefully scraped more dirt away, and he was quickly joined by two more laborers.

An hour later, a ten-foot section of what was clearly the arched roof of a chamber stood revealed, the workers now leaning on their shovels, panting from exertion.

'It will be night soon. We can continue tomorrow,' Maribela said, but Remi shook her head.

'No, the men can go. They've earned their rest. But we've come this far, and I know I won't be able to sleep if we don't at least try to find a way in.'

Sam nodded. 'We can handle it without the workers. We've got some small experience with this kind of thing,' he pointed out.

'Very well,' Antonio said. He had a quiet discussion with the foreman, who stood like a supplicant, straw hat in his hand. The crew scrambled up the ladder, taking their shovels with them. Sam studied the stone surface and then raised his gaze to the darkening sky.

'Can we get a few of those work lights turned on?' Lazlo asked.

'Of course,' Maribela said. She quickly ascended the rungs to ground level and spoke with the foreman, who was talking to the security guards.

Sam called up from the excavation, 'Oh, and we'll need flashlights, pry bars and rope.'

Ten minutes later, they were feeling along the mortar seams of the large stone bricks that formed the structure's roof, looking for a way to work one loose. Antonio called out from his position at the edge and they moved to where he stood, looking down.

'Think you can get one of the bars in that?' he asked, pointing to a gap in the joint – a crack running around the stone where time had degraded the mortar.

Remi slipped her bar into it. 'Sam? Try to get yours in, too.'

Sam joined her, but the fissure was too tight. He began scraping the mortar with the sharp edge of his tool, and in a half hour the stone was loose enough to shift. Lazlo joined them, and Antonio got his crowbar into the crack as well, and between the four of them they worked the stone from its setting, leaving a two-foot gap, the darkness below inky and damp. Remi directed her flashlight beam into the cavity, which swallowed the light like viscous mud. She squinted, trying to make anything out.

'Get the rope. I'll drop down inside and look around.'

Sam shook his head. 'No. I'll go.'

'You think you can fit through that? It'll be tight.'

'I work out.'

'Lately, by lifting tequila and enchiladas. But if you think you can make it . . .' Remi teased as Antonio uncoiled the nylon cord.

Antonio handed Sam one end. 'There might be snakes. Many in this region are quite poisonous, as are the scorpions and spiders. We might want to wait until morning. I can get a fiber-optic scope from my associate in the tunnel dig, and perhaps one of his robots to explore the chamber.'

Sam grinned. 'And lose out on all the glory? No chance. I live for this kind of thing.'

'But the snakes . . .' Maribela cautioned.

'I eat 'em for breakfast.'

'Hopefully, none of them have the same idea about you, old boy,' Lazlo said.

Remi rolled her eyes as Sam wound the rope twice around his waist. 'Tie this to something up top that will support my weight – one of the vehicle bumpers would work. I'll lower myself until I'm inside. Then I'll let out rope. Slowly. If I'm screaming in pain, that would be a good signal to pull me up and get some antivenom ready.'

'We don't have any antivenom,' Antonio said.

'No plan's perfect. But the "If I'm screaming . . . pull me up" part's still a good one.'

Remi took his hand. 'Be careful, Tarzan.'

'I'd do the jungle call, but it might scare the snakes.'

'And horrify the bystanders. As well as your wife,' Lazlo said.

Antonio carried the rope up to ground level and returned a few minutes later. 'You're secure.'

'"All right," as Evel Knievel used to say, "here goes nothing."'

'Five bucks says he never said that,' Remi countered.

'Under his breath.'

Sam sat at the edge of the hole and dropped his legs

in; then, with a final tug of the rope, he leaned his weight against the side and slid his lower body into the abyss. He fed out line slowly, disappearing beneath their feet. Remi moved to the edge and shined her flashlight beam down at him.

'Any snakes?' she asked, watching her beam and his play across the stone floor.

'Nope. No lawyers, either.'

'Sounds safer than out here.'

His feet touched down. He slowly swept the interior of the chamber and then played out more line as he moved cautiously to a stone entryway.

Above him stood Antonio, his leg twitching with nervous energy, and Sam could just make out the heads of the two security guards peering down the hole. The sky was now almost black, with the occasional twinkle of stars glimmering overhead.

Maribela paced from one end of the trench to the other, chewing at a fingernail, while Remi swept her beam into the far reaches of their discovery from above.

A minute later, the rope tightened again, and Sam called from below. 'Pull me up.'

Antonio called out to one of the guards, who hurried off to start the truck and back it up, raising Sam in the process. The rope went taut, and then Sam appeared, his hair dusty and a spiderweb stuck to his face. Antonio yelled and the truck stopped. Sam hoisted himself the rest of the way and untied the rope from around his waist.

'Well?' Remi asked expectantly.

'Not good news. Looks like grave robbers got here a long time ago. As in centuries. Many centuries. You can see where the entry rocks were knocked in. That would have been before the surrounding terrain had covered it, so we're talking pre-Columbian. Maybe even a thousand years ago. Even the skeletons are gone.' He shook his head. 'Whatever this is, if it was the hidden tomb, it wasn't that well hidden. There's no treasure. Nothing. Just a couple of small empty rooms and a few carvings – nothing more.'

Remi's shoulders sagged, as did Lazlo's. 'Not even any snakes?' she asked.

'Nary a one.'

She brushed his shirt as he swept the spiderweb aside. 'So a big letdown, huh?'

'Only if you were expecting something besides a hole in the ground.'

'Much ado about nothing, then . . .' Lazlo said. 'Ah, well, it happens, I suppose.'

Sam peered into the opening. 'Although we still might learn something. But if you're asking whether it was worth missing dinner over, the answer's no.'

Remi smiled at him. 'My big, brave explorer. I bet you worked up quite an appetite down there, didn't you?'

'And thirst. Don't forget drinks.'

Lazlo snorted and then covered it with a well-timed cough.

She turned to Antonio. 'Are there any good places to

eat in town? We can post a security guard here and explore the chamber in the morning.'

'Yes, there are several very good traditional Mexican restaurants.' He gave them the names of two of the most popular as they filed up the ladder, disappointment evident in everyone's demeanor.

'How about we get you cleaned up and fed and then we can commiserate over a few margaritas about what went so horribly wrong?' Remi suggested to Sam. She turned to where Antonio was helping Maribela from the ladder. 'Antonio, Maribela, you're welcome to join us. You too, Lazlo.'

Antonio exchanged glances with his sister. 'No thank you, we still have to drive back to Mexico City. But we'll see you back here tomorrow morning. Say, nine o'clock?'

Sam shrugged. 'Sure. There's no hurry now. We found what there is to be found.'

'I've learned to never turn down the offer of a meal, if you don't mind my sober company,' Lazlo said.

'There's nothing we'd like better,' Sam replied.

Mexico City, Mexico

A dark brown sedan rolled slowly down the deserted street in the Cerro de Xaltepec barrio of Mexico City, near the base of Sierra de Santa Catarina mountain, one of the worst neighborhoods in Mexico. Violence, drug trafficking and human slavery were an everyday occurrence, as were murders that the police rarely spent time investigating. The philosophy was that if you were in that area, you were either looking for trouble or were a predator and probably deserved what you got. Pools of stinking water ringed the intersection where the sedan eased up by a gray cinder-block home with a corrugated-metal roof, the entire structure covered with graffiti, no lights on inside nor on the street.

The back door of the slow-moving sedan flew open and a form tumbled on to the filthy pavement. The door closed with a thunk and the driver sped up, traveling two blocks before he turned right on to a larger road and illuminated his headlights.

Carlos's lifeless eyes stared uncomprehendingly into the eternity of the night sky. It would be many hours before a coroner's van appeared to scoop up his remains, escorted by several trucks with heavily armed police to ensure that nobody shot the technicians as they went about their work. It would take two more days to make an identification, a typical occurrence in one of the most populous cities in the world – par for the course for a police force that was woefully under-budgeted and understaffed and had to make do with antiquated equipment already old at the turn of the new century.

Teotihuacan, Mexico

The two security men Antonio had deployed to guard the tomb took a break from their monotony and moved far away from the trench as an SUV eased to a stop near it. They'd been well compensated to make themselves scarce for thirty minutes and to see and hear nothing and they had gladly complied, each pocketing a month's pay for a paltry half hour of disinterest.

Janus Benedict exited the passenger side and walked to the edge of the excavation, joined by Reginald. The driver remained in the vehicle with the engine running.

'This is it? Doesn't look like much,' Reginald said, annoyed to be awake at 4 a.m. to waste his time in some armpit well away from the refined comfort of his five-star Mexico City hotel.

'Looks like for once the Fargos came up empty. Which I'm thrilled about. But also a little intrigued by.' Janus sighed. 'I suppose even the best of us comes up short every now and again. Bound to happen.'

'Then what are we doing here?'

Janus peered down into the trench again and then shook his head and returned to the car. 'Since I flew halfway across the bloody globe, I thought I'd see it for myself.'

'Looks like a hole in the ground to me.'

Janus glared at his brother. 'Nothing slips by you,

does it?' he snarled as he climbed back into the passenger seat.

Reginald muttered an oath when the door shut, angry at his brother's barb but knowing better than to confront him. Nerves were close to the surface, with the temple having been found, and he didn't want to risk an outburst from his jet-lagged sibling.

The tires crunched on gravel as the big vehicle backed away, and when the security guards returned fifteen minutes later, the site was calm and empty, which would be their report the following morning, now only a few hours away.

30

'What is it?' Sam asked as they took a taxi from their motel to the site.

'I don't know. Something just doesn't feel right. I can't believe that that was it. It just feels so . . . I don't know, so incomplete.'

'Of course it's disheartening, but at least we solved the riddle of the manuscript and located the chamber,' Lazlo said.

'That's what's bugging me. I'm not convinced we did. We found *a* chamber; but the question is, did we find *the* chamber?'

Sam turned to her. 'What are you saying?'

'Isn't it possible that we got something wrong?'

'We found it. Right where we thought it would be.'

'Not where *we* thought it would be – where Antonio and his sister were convinced it would be. But what if they are wrong?'

'And we just happened to find a crypt by accident?'

'They've been finding new tunnels and chambers around those pyramids for years. Nobody dug that area up before, I'll bet. We excavated a huge stretch of the base. The odds of finding something aren't as high as you'd think. And what did we actually find? A looted tomb. That's all we know. Did you see a lot of images on the walls that would lead you to believe that it was the final resting place of a ruler revered as a god?'

'Well, actually, now that you mention it, it was rather simple. But still . . .'

'If you were going to construct a hidden tomb that was legendary for its riches and contained the remains of the most important ruler your civilization had ever known, would you consider that a fitting final resting place?'

Lazlo nodded from his position in the front seat. 'She has a point.'

Sam studied her face. 'Is that what's got you jittery? That it's so . . . unimpressive?'

'I think it's that, and that I've never been a hundred per cent convinced that their assurances were right. I've had my doubts since they first told us. Don't ask me why. Call it intuition. But some part of my brain was going, No, that's not right. I don't know what I saw that led me in a different direction, but whatever it was, I did, and I've learned to trust my instincts.'

Sam's face grew serious. 'Wait. What did you just say?'

'Didn't you hear me?'

'Of course. You said you don't know what it is you saw.'

She looked perplexed. 'Right.'

'What do you mean you *saw*? Where could you have seen something that would lead you to a different conclusion? What did you see that's convinced you they got it wrong?'

Remi thought in silence and, as they approached the gate, shook her head. 'I don't know. It's just a figure of speech.'

'I've known you for a long time. You're very precise with your use of language, whether you realize it or not. You said you *saw* something. Now my question is what?'

'Sam, I'm really trying to think, but I honestly don't know. It's baffling.'

He nodded. 'Let your brain work on it. Don't keep concentrating. Let it come up with the answer on its own. It'll come to you when your brain figures it out. Brains are good that way.'

'Since when do you know so much about brains?' she asked, eyeing him skeptically.

'That's how mine works. I figured yours might operate the same way.'

'If that were true . . .'

Lazlo was silent, lost in thought during the exchange. When the taxi rolled to a stop, he looked around, as though startled, before climbing out of the cab.

Sam paid the driver, and they began the walk to the temple from the entry gates. The morning air was cool, a light overcast providing some relief from the sun's blaze. When they arrived at the site, Antonio was standing under the tarp, studying an image on a large monitor.

'What's that?' Sam asked as they approached him.

'Ah, good morning. This is a feed from a robot that I wrangled from my colleague for a few hours. They're using it at the other tunnel, but I figured it would speed up our work to have the interior of the chambers filmed before we go crashing around in there.'

'Excellent idea. Where's your sister?'

'She's down in the trench, operating the remote. It's on a cable, so she was limited by length.'

They watched the images flickering on the screen, and Lazlo shook his head when the lens slowly roamed over the carvings. 'What do you make of those?'

'Pretty average for Teotihuacan.'

'Do they look Toltec?' Remi asked.

Antonio took a closer look. 'Not particularly, but it's so hard to tell until we have a chance to really –'

'But your first impression is that they look more like the others here?'

Antonio slowly turned to face Remi. 'What are you getting at?'

'Something tells me that this find, while interesting, isn't what we were looking for.'

His eyes widened. 'What?'

She explained her reservations to him, taking him through her thinking process. When she was done, Antonio didn't look quite as confident as he had when they'd arrived.

'But you don't know what it was you saw that made you question the location?'

She frowned. 'Not yet. But it's a strong feeling.'

Sam moved toward the excavation. 'Good morning,' he called down to Maribela, who was staring at a smaller monitor set up on a card table near the crypt entry, maneuvering a joystick to direct the robot beneath her feet. She pressed a button and looked up at him with a smile.

'*Buenos días* to you as well.'

'You didn't happen to find an incredible treasure while we were running late, did you?'

'No. Anything of value was taken long ago.'

'What's your impression of the carvings? I only saw a few.'

'Too early to say.'

'Did they strike you as appropriate homage to a breathing incarnation of a god?'

'What do you mean?'

'My impression from yesterday was that they're pretty humble.'

'Mmm,' she said noncommittally. '"Humble" . . .'

Remi approached, trailed by Lazlo. 'Sam, I know what it was.'

Maribela regarded them with confusion.

'What?' Sam asked.

'The Cuban carvings. The pyramid. With the cloud over it. In both that image, as well as the one at the new find of the same scene, there's always a second building.'

'There is?'

'Yes. A smaller temple.'

'And?'

'Why?' Remi asked with a satisfied tone. 'Why is there a smaller temple?'

Sam paused. 'You're going to tell me, aren't you?'

Lazlo cleared his throat and took over. 'Because the pyramid is an orientation point, not the actual location of the tomb.'

Maribela eyed him skeptically. 'How do you know?'

Remi stepped forward. 'There's the pyramid and the cloud. But barely visible in the cloud is the same thing: the moon. The cloud obstructs most of it, but it's there.'

'Okay . . .'

Remi shook her head. 'We got it wrong. It's the Pyramid of the Moon that's the location. We were so fixated on Quetzalcoatl, we were looking for snakes. And the depictions are confusing. Just like the account in the manuscript.'

'Are you sure?'

She gazed into Sam's eyes. 'I've never been so sure about anything in my life. We've been looking in the wrong spot.'

Lazlo glanced around before speaking. 'I think it's about time that I take that trip to the earthquake site I've been requesting and take a hard look at the pictographs in person. With all due respect, before we continue down this road it would be nice to know that we haven't missed anything else.'

Remi nodded. 'I agree.' She turned to Antonio. 'Do you think we could get access today?'

'I don't see why not. Let me make a call and alert the team that we're on our way. I'll drive you myself.'

Maribela eyed the dig, hands on her hips. 'I'll stay here and supervise the workers.'

Antonio checked his watch. 'All right, then. I'll call from the car. No point wasting any time.'

31

The roads to López Mateos were clogged with late-morning traffic as the big SUV rolled past the deteriorating buildings into the center of the district, now largely recovered from the earthquake. The little street with the tomb entrance was still closed to traffic, and a contingent of soldiers was standing guard. Antonio displayed his credentials and they were allowed on foot down the well-trodden path into the dig site.

The leader in charge of the project approached Antonio and shook hands, and, after a short discussion in Spanish, moved past the group into the sunlight. Antonio squinted as his eyes adjusted to the gloom in the crypt, and he turned to Lazlo and the Fargos.

'Sam, Remi, you've been here before, so you know the precautions to take. Lazlo, most of the areas have been cordoned off so as not to cause any damage as we excavate and document the findings. I'll ask you to respect that and to avoid touching anything. I've instructed the crew to take lunch early so the site will be all yours for the next two hours.'

'Of course. You'll never know I was here,' Lazlo assured him.

'And thank you again for doing this,' Remi said.

'Hopefully, it'll yield positive results.' Antonio motioned with an outstretched hand. 'This way. We'll start with what we're calling the main burial vault.'

They moved slowly down the passageway to the junction, and Antonio led them into the largest of the rooms. He switched on several more lamps, so they could better study the pictographs, and stood back.

'Again, be careful of the areas on the ground with the stakes and chalk around them. Those are artifacts that remain to be unearthed,' he reminded the group, and they nodded as he neared the first of the elaborate carvings that spanned the wall.

Remi joined him and pointed at the pictograph. 'Here's the procession, you see? Exactly as in the photos.'

'Really remarkable in person, isn't it?' Lazlo murmured, taking in the entirety of the image before moving closer to study the detail. 'Must have taken them ages. Incredible handiwork . . .'

'And there are more on the burial platform, as well as on the other walls. But this one is repeated in all the chambers, so it no doubt had significance to the Toltec,' Antonio said.

'See? There it is. Obviously, the Temple of the Feathered Serpent,' Sam said, pointing to the ornately carved depiction of the six-level step pyramid.

'Yes, I'd wager so . . .' Lazlo agreed, eyes narrowing as he inched nearer.

Remi began photographing the pictographs again in case she'd missed something on her earlier pass, and Sam edged to the far wall to study the carvings there. Lazlo spent several minutes poring over the depiction of the procession, muttering softly to himself, before joining Sam.

'That's the one repeated in all the rooms?' he asked.

'Yes.'

'I'll just have a look, then. Might as well since we're here.'

'You should go with Antonio. He'll show you the way.'

'Of course. Wouldn't want to get lost or wander into a local watering hole.'

Lazlo and Antonio moved down the stone corridor to the next vault as Remi stared at the images of pyramids with furious concentration, as though through sheer force of will she might have a breakthrough that would shed light on the true location of Quetzalcoatl's tomb.

'It's pretty obvious that it's Teotihuacan now that we've been there, isn't it?' Sam said.

'Yes, so we're in the ballpark. That's something.'

'And that's got to be the Pyramid of the Sun.'

'I'd think so, based on its size.'

Sam shook his head. 'Then the Temple of the Feathered Serpent can't be the correct spot. Look at the orientation.'

'I agree. But again, Antonio and Maribela are the experts and they thought –'

Sam was interrupted by Lazlo, hurrying back into the vault. Remi turned to look at him, taking in the excitement on his normally placid face.

'I think I've got it, dear boy. Took me a while. And fiendishly clever, whoever carved these. Frankly, if you didn't know what to look for, you'd never figure it out. Certainly not from the photographs – no offense.'

'What are you talking about?' Remi asked.

'The pictographs are slightly different in each of the tombs. It's subtle, but they are.'

'Are you sure?' Sam asked.

'Absolutely. Come on, I'll show you.'

Lazlo led them into the chamber next to the one they'd been in and pointed to the pictograph. 'See? The dignitaries are positioned differently, and so are the landmarks. That pyramid is more to the right.'

Sam frowned. 'That could be natural variation. Just a result of the materials available or the artist. Meaningless.'

'True. But now let's go into the next room. You'll see yet another slight difference.'

'If the artists were carving from an illustration, as they most likely were, there's probably no significance to any of it,' Antonio said from the threshold.

'Normally, I'd agree with you. But humor me. Let's go to the next one.'

Everyone filed into the third vault, where two lamps bathed the carvings in light.

'Yet more variation, do you see?'

Remi nodded slowly and took several photos. 'I do. But what does it mean?'

Lazlo's face cracked into a wry grin. 'That's really the question, isn't it? To know the answer, you have to get a little lost.'

Sam and Remi exchanged a puzzled glance.

'Sorry. I'm not following you,' Sam said.

'I wanted to confirm my suspicion, so I went to look at the fourth tomb. There, in the dark antechamber, I could make out carvings on the wall at nearly ceiling height – above eye level. There was no lamp, which made it hard to see, so I borrowed Antonio's penlight. And what do you think it was?'

Sam shook his head. 'GPS coordinates?'

'Ha. Close. Come. Have a look.'

He led them into the narrow stone corridor to the far tomb and stopped before entering. Remi directed her penlight beam at the carving Lazlo was pointing at. 'Look familiar?' he asked.

'It's the procession again.'

'Indeed it is. Except look closer. Do you see something that isn't in any of the larger carvings?'

Sam stepped nearer to Remi, nodding.

'Well I'll be . . .'

Remi looked up at Sam's profile, realization written across her face.

'Those are planets and stars.'

Lazlo nodded like a proud father. 'Yes, they are. And with the celestial waypoints, we should be able to decipher where the true location of the tomb lies.'

32

Back in the second tomb, Antonio gestured at the procession pictograph. 'In this one, there are faint outlines of the moon and several stars, too. But almost as an afterthought.'

'Yes, as there are in one of the others. Only the constellations are as different as the drawings, I'm afraid,' Lazlo confirmed.

'Then I don't understand. How will we know which of the depictions is the correct one?'

Lazlo stood mute for a moment, thinking. 'I can't help but believe that the repeated pictograph has meaning. I'm guessing that it's an astronomical depiction – a clue to those who were adept at reading the stars. Maybe . . . Maybe the reason that the position of the landmarks is different in each rendition is because the images are representations of the same thing at different times of the year. Major events. Summer solstice, winter solstice . . .'

'How will we decide?' Remi asked.

Lazlo's eyes widened. 'You have images of the manuscript and the pictographs from Cuba, right?'

'Of course. But they're back at the motel.'

'Then that's where we need to go next,' Lazlo said.

'Why?'

'Because, if I'm not mistaken, the manuscript holds the final clue that will enable us to unravel this riddle. Remi, take another series of photos of each room's pictographs, in order, as we'd see them if we were moving from the primary vault to the final one. Try to get them from the same angle in each. Finish with our new find in the antechamber.'

Within ten minutes, they were back in the SUV, moving down the uneven streets, back toward Teotihuacan. An hour later, they stopped at the motel and Remi ran inside, emerging moments later with a flash drive in her hand.

Once back at the dig, they gathered around the monitor as Lazlo studied the Cuban pictographs and the manuscript. Nobody said a word as he gazed intently at the images, flipping between them, before finally settling on the series from the tombs.

'The Cuban pictograph and the manuscript narrow it down to the second in the series. See the moon there? It matches the position in the Cuban carvings. The rest are red herrings, as you say in the colonies.'

'You're correct. That's a depiction of the moon. Faint, and I would never have noticed it with all the rest of the glyphs, but there it is,' Antonio conceded.

'Now the question is, which temple is it? The smaller one over there?' Sam said, pointing to a lower building to the right.

Lazlo didn't say anything and then stepped back. 'It's

not as hard as you think, now that we know what to look for.'

'What is it, Lazlo?' Remi asked.

'The other symbols point the way,' Lazlo nodded. 'Teotihuacan is organized in a very specific manner. The city was designed according to astronomical events. The movement of the sun, the stars, the moon – all of these played a huge role in its layout.'

'Right . . .'

'Look up at the sky in the carving. Above the moon. That one star is bigger than the rest. Which would make it the North Star. Polaris.'

Antonio grunted assent. 'That would fit, based on other Toltec images we've analysed.'

Lazlo sighed. 'Now I'm afraid the really hard work comes in. We'll need to simulate the movement of the moon and the stars until we come to a point where they fit the positions in that carving. When we do, we'll be able to calculate the tomb's location.'

'It may not be so hard after all,' Antonio said, and then walked them slowly through the other astronomical symbols. After conferring with Lazlo, he jotted down a few notes before typing on the laptop's keyboard at a furious pace. They watched as he deleted one word and entered a different one into a blank search box and then pressed a series of keys.

'I have a program that will analyse the position of the moon, stars and sun based on rough coordinates. It'll take a while to process all this. Lazlo's assuming that the final procession would have been at a key celestial event. Something monumental. Fitting for the burial of the greatest ruler of his time. So I entered in all the possible obvious events. The equinoxes, other alignments that are viewed in Mesoamerican cultures as significant.'

A screen popped up. He and Lazlo studied it and then overlaid it on a model of Teotihuacan. After changing the screen several times, Antonio stepped back.

Lazlo tapped the screen. 'There's your temple. The first one on the right as you face the Pyramid of the Moon.'

Remi looked to Antonio. 'Have there ever been any excavations there?'

Antonio shook his head. 'I don't believe so, other than clearing the land away on the front side so you can see the temple. The secondary pyramids were considered trivial in the scheme of things, so resources went to the larger buildings.'

'Then they've never been thoroughly explored,' Remi said.

'We only have limited resources —' Maribela bristled.

Antonio held up his hand, cutting her off.

'I don't think Remi is saying we've been negligent. I think her intent was to establish that nothing much is known about them since all the serious digs focused around the more spectacular sites.'

'That's right. So there very well could be a tomb

there. Either under it or along one of the bases,' Remi said.

'Actually, if you look at how things line up, you'll see the rear of the temple on the axis.'

'How long is that side?' Sam asked.

'They're all about thirty-six meters square. So almost a hundred and twenty of your feet.'

'Not that much smaller than the Temple of the Feathered Serpent.'

'A little more than half the size, actually, but you're correct that it's a large area.'

'Let's go over and have a look. Would we need a new permit?'

'I think as the senior functionary of INAH here, I'd say no.'

They piled into Antonio's official Suburban and crawled the length of the Avenue of the Dead, taking care to avoid the scattered groups of tourists taking in the sights. When they reached the temple, they climbed the slope behind it, which had only been partially cleared, and stared at the rear of the smaller pyramid as if they could intuit where the lost chamber was with instinct alone.

'Call it ninety feet to excavate. But this is considerably more dirt to move. Could we get a backhoe here?' Remi asked. 'Just to do the gross-level clearing and then we could have the crew take over . . .'

'I don't see why not,' Antonio said. 'There are numerous places in town that rent equipment and a man to operate it. Perhaps we could get one this afternoon. And with sufficient financial incentive, the man would probably be willing to work late. We might get it done in a day or so, then move in after that with the men as you suggested.'

'Then let's stake out an area to clear.'

A huge backhoe arrived at two and worked till nine, doing so by the glow of the work lights once the sun set. Sam, Remi and Lazlo left when the operator did and took a taxi to the restaurant where they'd eaten the previous night. The food was good and the mood excited, the sense of having made significant progress palpable, as they discussed the project in hushed tones.

The next morning the excavation started at eight and by two-thirty the entire back section of the pyramid base was ready for the waiting men to begin the more careful digging with picks and shovels. The crew went to work, continuing till dark.

They resumed the following day, clearing the dirt under the relentless glare of the hot sun. At 6 p.m., one of the picks broke through the hard clay into a cavity below. The hole was widened enough to allow entry. This time, Remi insisted on being the first one in, and after similar warnings as Sam had got before, she was lowered into the opening with a high-powered portable light and a radio.

'What do you see?' Sam asked after thirty seconds.

'It's a crude tunnel. It goes under the temple.'

'How far?'

'That's what I intend to find out,' Remi said, her tone short. Sam decided to leave her in peace and allow her to explore until she felt a desire to communicate. After a long pause, the radio crackled again with her voice. 'There's an entryway. Stone, and carved far more elaborately than any we've seen before. But it's blocked with smaller rocks mortared in place. We'll need something to break through. And it would probably be a good idea to shore up the tunnel, although if it hasn't caved in over the centuries, it's probably okay for now.'

Sam passed the information on to Antonio, who was standing by the opening with Lazlo, staring into the void. He ordered the men into action. The foreman brought a tall ladder, and three workers dropped into the dark. The rest stayed above and passed down wooden beams and boards to build primitive shoring.

'I'm coming down,' Sam said, and after the first wave of workers was clear, he descended, a pick in his free hand, followed by Lazlo, Antonio and Maribela, all carrying heavy iron pry bars. Their flashlight beams played along the clay walls until they saw Remi around a bend in the tunnel, facing a crudely mortared rock wall framed by carved stone – the carvings much like those they'd all seen in the crypts at the find in López Mateos.

'Look. The pyramid with the moon,' Remi said, pointing at the procession depicted at the top of the doorway. 'This is it. It has to be.'

Sam nodded. 'Stand clear,' he warned. 'Let's see if we can get through this rock, shall we?'

Everyone stepped back. He swung the pick and it connected with stone. A chunk of mortar flew off. He swung it again and another, bigger piece dropped at his feet. 'This will work. It'll just take a little time.'

'Let's have the laborers do this,' Maribela suggested.

Sam shook his head. 'No way. Just give me a few minutes.' He continued beating at the wall, and, after several dozen blows, one of the rocks fell into the empty space beyond. 'We're through! I'll knock out a few more of these and then let's put those crowbars to use.'

Two crudely squared stones collapsed inward after his next blow, then another on his next. He dropped the pick by a side column as Lazlo and Antonio moved in with their crowbars, the area too limited for Remi or Maribela to help. More of the rocks dropped into the space, and then the lower part of the wall collapsed in a heap of rubble. A dust cloud rose from the pile.

'I think Remi should do the honors,' Sam said.

Antonio motioned to her with a small bow of assent. 'Absolutely. Señora?'

She lifted the bulky portable light and held it in front of her and then leaned into the newly open area and glanced around. 'It's a vault.'

Remi climbed through the opening, light in tow. They heard her gasp, and a shiver of fear went up Sam's spine.

'Are you okay?' he demanded, shining his flashlight into the dark.

'Perfect. I think it's safe to say we found the tomb.' She paused. 'There's a body covered in jade on a stone platform, and several mounds of offerings around it. They're dusty, but I see some glinting, so probably gold. And jade masks.'

'Gold? The Toltecs didn't have any gold,' Maribela said.

'Perhaps they traded for it? Obsidian, too. And Toltec pottery. Ceramics.'

'Any reason I can't come in?' Sam asked through the hole.

'No, but be careful. This will be a significant find and we don't want to crash around like buffalo.'

Sam eased himself through the gap. Maribela and Lazlo followed him in, trailed by Antonio.

They found themselves in a twelve-by-fifteen-foot chamber of carved stone walls. Remi stepped gingerly around a pile on the ground and leaned down, holding the lamp in front of her. The LED bulbs illuminated the interior of the crypt in an eerie white glow. She lifted a small figure from the mound and held it up. 'Gold.'

Sam and Lazlo were standing by the figure on the platform. The mummy's skin was desiccated, the color of coffee and the texture of beef jerky. Lazlo peered at it and did a quick calculation. 'Looks like he was no more than five feet tall, so clearly indigenous. Not exactly the tall, imposing, bearded figure of the legends, is he?'

Maribela moved to his side, gazing down at the body. 'But the robe is consistent with the stories. White, or what was once white, animal hide. The robe of a prophet . . .'

'Or a god,' Antonio whispered.

'But no Eye of Heaven,' Sam said.

'Alas, probably part of the legend that grew over time,' Maribela said. 'As you know, the enormous riches could have increased in these tales with the telling, along with Quetzalcoatl's height.'

Remi had moved past the offerings and was studying the symbols on the wall. 'Look, almost all of them are snakes. Quetzalcoatl. And here – the procession theme is reprised, but they're carrying the body of a feathered serpent in this depiction. A funeral procession.'

They spent another hour inside the chamber as the workers continued propping wooden beams along the tunnel's length, and then Remi set her dimming light down and brushed a hand through her dusty hair. 'I think we've had a productive day, don't you? It's probably time to leave this to the experts.'

Antonio nodded. 'It's one of the most significant discoveries in the last hundred years. You should be very proud of yourselves. The discoverers of Quetzalcoatl's final resting place. It's an incredible honor to work with you both.'

Maribela smiled. 'Yes. It's a remarkable achievement.

The Mexican people owe you a tremendous debt for restoring an important piece of their history to them. *Another* tremendous debt,' she added, referring to the Mayan Codex the Fargos had retrieved only months before.

'The honor is ours,' Sam said, 'for being allowed to explore a sacred site. And you should be congratulating yourselves as well. This will be a huge event in the archaeology community. Quetzalcoatl's lost treasure and his body all in one day. Most don't have that kind of a find in a lifetime.'

Remi cleared her throat, the dust thick in the air. 'What we've found we couldn't have done without you,' she said graciously, although the truth was more complicated.

Lazlo was staring at the mummy, shaking his head.

'What is it, Lazlo?' Sam asked.

'We're still missing something. I don't know what, but we are.'

Maribela chuckled. 'Lazlo, you did it. If the find isn't what you'd hoped for, that doesn't mean anyone's missing anything.'

'Perhaps. But I want to do a careful inspection of the interior. Just as the information that led us here was overlooked in the López Mateos tombs, my sense is it's too early to assume we've cracked this nut.'

Antonio stepped forward.

'Of course we'll do a detailed analysis of the find and go over every inch of it. We're all after the same thing, and I think Lazlo's instincts should be respected. It's always possible that there are more secrets here and that Quetzalcoatl hasn't revealed them all to us yet.'

When they were back at ground level, Antonio placed calls to arrange for more security as night fell. They wanted to take no chances with a room that contained gold and priceless artifacts. In a rural area of Mexico well away from the reaches of the police departments, Antonio was naturally cautious – enough of the workers had seen what lay in the chamber for rumors to begin and an armed presence was the sensible precaution.

Antonio's cell phone chirped and he excused himself. He listened for a few moments and his face went white. When he returned, he looked shaky.

'What's wrong, Antonio?' Remi asked.

'It's . . . They found Carlos's body.'

They fell silent, the excitement over the find now muted by the reality of their colleague's violent demise. Antonio shared the slim facts he'd been given, which explained nothing. Another senseless death in a brutal world and a good man taken from the Earth for no reason. As the daylight waned, a hot wind blew across the ruins like the breath of an angry god, moaning through the surrounding structures, a funeral dirge for their departed friend. After contemplating the news of Carlos's passing, Sam and Remi packed their backpacks as the siblings issued instructions to the two security men.

When Antonio was finished, he approached the Fargos, his mood somber.

'I'm going to stay here until the additional security shows up. I've asked for a contingent of soldiers from the nearby military base.' He checked the time. 'They should arrive in an hour. Are you leaving?'

'We'll come by tomorrow to see what's being unearthed, if that's okay,' Remi said.

'It would be my pleasure.'

They followed the last of the straggling tourists down the Avenue of the Dead, moving toward the entry gates on automatic pilot. Remi and Lazlo were quiet on the way back to the motel.

33

The next morning Lazlo, Remi and Sam rode an INAH-supplied golf cart toward the Pyramid of the Moon. Antonio's SUV was parked near the research tent that was being erected by a sleepy crew. When they approached, he was giving an orientation to a group of earnest-looking students. Maribela stood at the edge of the gathering and her eyes brightened when she saw them roll up.

'*Hola!* You're here early,' she called out as she walked over to them, her stride as fluid as a dancer's.

'We wanted to get a second look at what we found,' Sam explained.

'Very good. We're just going over the protocols with the team. We've been assigned a dozen helpers. We want to ensure we don't harm anything as we document the contents of the crypt.'

'We'd like to spend some time inside, photographing everything as it was found before it all gets shifted around.'

'Of course. Come this way and I'll get you some gloves and brushes in case you spot anything you want to clean off.'

'Thank you, but we're mostly interested in the

carvings. We're hoping to find something that will shed some light on why Quetzalcoatl was described in a number of accounts as a tall, bearded white man. The mummy is anything but . . .'

'Ah, yes, the legends,' Maribela said.

'It never hurts to be thorough,' Remi said, her voice even, her tone firm.

Lazlo sensed a rising tension between the two women and moved quickly to diffuse it.

'How much longer before your brother's done with the lads?' he asked Maribela.

'He's been at it for fifteen minutes, so I think he'll be finishing up pretty soon.'

Antonio joined them once he wound down his orientation and greeted them like visiting royalty.

'There they are! Come to celebrate?'

'We wanted to get photos of the find before everyone really gets to work.'

Sam glanced at the six soldiers standing in a loose ring at the site perimeter, their M4 rifles hanging from shoulder straps, not one of them more than nineteen.

'I see you've got the big guns in. Literally.'

'It wouldn't do to have Quetzalcoatl's treasure walk off, would it?'

The day went by in a blur of photographs and dusting of carvings to get all the detail. Sam finally came up for air, done with the crypt. Remi joined him under the tarp, where Lazlo was methodically poring over the photographs on the big monitor with rapt concentration, seemingly oblivious to the noise around him.

'Did you get everything you wanted?' Sam asked.

'I think so, although I was struck by the same sensation I had yesterday. Not much of a treasure, really, compared to some.'

'The Toltecs probably weren't a rich people.'

'True. But the legend just seems so overblown compared to what's down there,' Remi said, her fingers brushing her gold scarab. 'Maybe it's just my lucky charm sending out skeptical vibes.'

'I'd say it's been pretty lucky so far. Still, vibes or no vibes, I'd count it as a win. We solved another of history's riddles. Not a bad day's work.' Sam glanced at Lazlo. 'You about ready to pack it in, Lazlo?'

Lazlo seemed only then to register them. 'We're missing something. I don't know what, but we are.'

'I start to get worried when you and Remi agree on so much,' Sam joked. 'But, come on, it's been a long day. The photos will still be there tomorrow and your eyes must be burning out of your head by now. You hungry, Remi?'

'When am I not? But you look like you could use some freshening-up.'

'You haven't looked in a mirror lately, either, have you?'

They said their goodbyes to Antonio and Maribela and, having checked out of the motel that morning, took a taxi to the St. Regis in Mexico City, first dropping

Lazlo off at the clinic. They agreed to regroup the following morning and drive out to the site together, once they were rested and fortified, the hard work now done.

Teotihuacan was deadly still at 3 a.m. The towering pyramids were almost invisible against the deepening vault of the night sky, the ancient city's wide boulevard an inky strip devoid of life. A sliver of moon peeked through the patchwork of clouds, giving barely enough light for the soldiers guarding the newly discovered crypt to see one another's faces. A hardened sergeant roamed the temple perimeter, ensuring that his dozen men were alert and vigilant. Although they were only twenty-five miles from the hum of Mexico City, this was another world, the glimmer of lights from the nearby town of San Martín de las Pirámides as unlike the capital's neon brilliance as water and wine.

A corporal stood near the barricade that had been erected to make the excavation area more manageable, telling a joke in a low tone to one of his men. He stiffened when he saw the sergeant approach and fell silent – their commander was known as a hard case, a career soldier who'd spent fifteen years in the service stationed all over Mexico during the upheaval of the drug wars. He took this dull guard duty dead seriously, whereas his men, most of whom were barely old enough to shave, viewed it as yet another in a long string of boring postings that seemed random and pointless.

The sergeant opened his mouth to speak, a look of reproach on his face, when his cap blew off along with half his skull. The corporal took a second to register what had happened – the final second in his short life as a tiny red dot danced over his sternum and then two rounds slammed into his chest. The private he'd been telling his story to was swinging his weapon up to fire at the invisible assailants when a slug tore through his throat and he collapsed in a heap, his dying breath gurgling as he shuddered, his rifle now lying uselessly by his feet.

From the surrounding field, eight men clad in black moved toward the site, their passage stealthy and practised. Three more soldiers succumbed to the puffs of the sound-suppressed 9mm pistols, their subsonic ammo making them as quiet as air guns, and then a cry went up from one of the remaining soldiers when he spotted the huddled body of one of his squad near the edge of the field. The leader of the attacking group murmured into his earbud and all eight of the black-clad figures opened fire on the remaining soldiers, making short work of them.

The battle was over before it began; the soldiers had been mown down without getting off a shot. The leader of the intruders rose from his crouched position and moved through the carnage, stopping occasionally to fire into one of the moaning wounded. When he was sure the area was secure, he fished a cell phone from his black windbreaker pocket and pushed one of the speed dial buttons.

Two minutes later, three large vehicles approached – SUVs running with their lights off. The lead truck pulled to the edge of the site and all four doors opened. Guerrero stepped out and waited for Reginald, who was only a moment behind him.

'It's done. But we should hurry. I have no idea if they have to radio in to the base on a regular schedule or what their protocol is,' Guerrero said, eyeing the corpses, his expression calm – the sight of dead Mexican soldiers an everyday part of his business.

Reginald nodded. 'Have the men bring the holdalls. We'll want the gold, of course, but also any icons or ceramics. There's a thriving market for those if you have the right contacts.'

'Which, of course, you do.' Guerrero grinned, and a stray moonbeam glinted off a gold-capped incisor, lending him a demonic cast in the gloom.

'Rather makes me the ideal partner, doesn't it? This could be worth a fortune.'

'Then let's go see what we got, eh? Lead the way,' the cartel chief said.

Reginald picked his way around the bodies to the ramp that had been excavated for easier access to the tomb. Inside, he flicked on his portable lamp, as did Guerrero, and soon the other men had joined them. Four remained above to ensure their looting wasn't interrupted. Reginald entered the crypt and knelt by one of the three mounds. He carefully lifted a gold figure and hefted it with a grunt and then wrapped it carefully in a towel before sliding it into his bag.

'There isn't as much as I'd hoped, but this alone weighs at least two kilos. No question this will be a profitable night. Let's take everything – this will hardly fill four or five bags, so there'll be more than enough room. But remember what I said: careful with everything and don't just throw things into the bags. Wrap each item completely. We'll take inventory once we're well away from here.'

The men went to work. One dug out the priceless artifacts and his partners wrapped and stowed the goods. The vault was cleared out within twenty minutes. Reginald stared at the mummy before glancing at his watch.

'That's it. Our business here is concluded,' he said, taking a last sweep of the crypt to ensure he hadn't missed anything. Satisfied, he joined Guerrero, who extended a hand in an offer to carry Reginald's bag.

'What do you think?' Guerrero asked as he took the heavy sack's handles from Reginald.

'No way to tell at this point, but I'd guess millions. How many is really determined by the market and how long we need to let the inventory cool down before offering it to a few discriminating collectors.'

'Why don't we just melt the gold and convert into cash immediately?'

Reginald shook his head as if appalled by the notion.

'Good heavens no, old boy. The value in those icons is in their history, not the weight of the gold. They're likely worth a thousand times more than the raw value of the metal.'

Guerrero gave Reginald a skeptical look. 'Remember the deal: fifty-fifty. No tricks or there isn't a corner of the planet remote enough to hide in.'

'Wouldn't have it any other way,' Reginald said, doing his best to sound every bit the honest upper-crust Brit to this pretentious savage. Of course, no matter what the trove brought, he would ensure that at least seventy per cent stuck to Janus and him. The cartel thug would have no way of knowing the actual terms of each sale, and, if necessary, Reginald was confident that he could do side deals for secret payments over and above what was wired to his account.

He couldn't wait to see Janus's expression when he appeared with the treasure. While his older sibling slept, Reginald had taken the initiative and made them a small fortune. It had occurred to him to cut Janus out altogether, but the truth was that he needed his brother's expertise to value each piece, as well as needing his network. Perhaps in another five years he would know all the players, but for now Janus ruled that roost whether it rankled Reginald's pride or not.

With any luck, they would be safely back in Mexico City by the time roadblocks barred the surrounding roads and vehicles were searched in a manhunt that would be too little, too late.

Reginald could only imagine how the Fargos would react when they discovered their thunder had been stolen, that their big find would be remembered as an unmitigated disaster.

A wolf's grin flashed across his face as he envisioned their expressions.

Payback time.

34

Lazlo was waiting in the clinic lobby when Sam and Remi's taxi pulled up outside the imposing building the next morning. He practically ran from the doorway when Sam got out of the car and waved and within minutes the three of them were comfortably ensconced in a booth at a nearby restaurant.

After they'd ordered breakfast, the discussion turned to the tomb.

Lazlo took a sip of his black coffee. 'I want to take my time going over the location today. I'm afraid that your Mexican colleagues are a little too quick to declare victory, for my liking.'

'They just aren't as naturally suspicious as you are,' Sam said.

'Years of poor behavior and cynicism mould one, in that regard,' Lazlo agreed.

Sam's cell trilled as their meals were delivered. He glanced at the number, puzzled, and answered it as Remi and Lazlo dug into their eggs. After a hushed discussion, he hung up and placed the phone on the table next to his plate, the blood drained from his face.

'Sam. What's wrong?' Remi asked.

'It's the site. It's been attacked. Everyone killed, the treasure gone.'

'How is that possible?' Lazlo asked incredulously.

'Late last night. Someone murdered the soldiers and raided the crypt. All the artifacts . . . everything gone.'

'How many soldiers were there?' Lazlo asked.

'A dozen. That was Antonio on the phone. He's absolutely devastated, as you might imagine.' Sam went on to fill them in on what Antonio had relayed. When he was finished, they stared at each other in stunned silence, the reality of the attack taking a while to settle in.

'So there's nothing left?' Remi finally asked.

'At least they didn't take the mummy.'

'Who even knew about the find? Had it been reported?' Lazlo asked.

Remi shook her head. 'No. But, obviously, somebody talked. Could have been one of the laborers or one of the students or even one of the soldiers. Way too many fingers in the pie.'

'Antonio says that the place is crawling with *Federales* and TV crews. He said we were welcome to come up but to wait till the end of the day so the cops can do their thing.'

'This is unbelievable. We're only rock-throwing distance from Mexico City . . .' Remi said, her thoughts a blur.

'Are there any theories on who perpetrated it?' Lazlo asked.

'A criminal gang. Cartels. Take your pick. But whoever

it was had to be very, very good. Nobody heard anything until the day shift showed up at seven. Which means the attackers killed a dozen heavily armed soldiers in silence. None of the soldiers had even fired their weapons. It had to be almost instant.'

'Like SAS. Commandos. Nigh on impossible, I'd have thought.'

'They're taking tire impressions, but Antonio didn't sound positive. Something tells me that the *Federales* aren't TV-style CSI.'

'No, I wouldn't expect so,' Remi agreed.

Sam's shoulders sagged. 'I've pretty much lost my appetite.'

Remi pushed her plate away. 'Me too.'

Lazlo continued plowing through his food as Remi sipped her coffee. After a final forkful of omelet, he sat back and gazed through the picture window at the traffic on the street outside.

'You know, one of the things I was studying last night was accounts of these sorts of tombs. For all intents and purposes, if you're going to hide something, you should keep it a secret. But even so, secrets can leak. So if you have a treasure that's unlike anything anyone's ever seen before and it's buried with your glorious leader . . . what would you do?'

'I give up.'

'Well, in a few instances, there's been a decoy tomb. The one that makes everyone stop looking because they think they found it. Typically, with adequate riches to satisfy everyone that it's the real thing. Ingenious buggers, some of them were.'

'You think this could be . . . a head fake?'

'Anything's possible, isn't it? It's just an observation – based on what you were expecting and what you found.'

'You've seen the photos. Does this strike you as a treasure fit for a king? Even by Toltec standards?'

'Not really. I think that's rather my point . . . and yours.'

'But if it's not the real tomb, then why memorialize it in the carvings?'

'That's what's got me thinking. Perhaps the location's correct, but the crypt we discovered . . . was designed to be discovered so that any hunt for it would end there.' Lazlo sighed. 'Which, you have to admit, it effectively did.'

Remi considered the idea and looked at Sam. 'Didn't I tell you that Lazlo is a genius?'

'Well, the jury is still out, but still . . .' Sam replied, smiling.

'No, seriously.'

'Interesting, and it does make a certain sense. But, frankly, the Mexican government probably isn't going to be thrilled with us digging randomly in the hopes that maybe that hunch is valid. We have nothing to go on,' Sam said.

'But there has to be a way.'

'I didn't say there wasn't. Just that they won't let us excavate in a proven historical find just for giggles.'

Remi studied his expression. 'But you have an idea, don't you?'

'I do. One of the things Antonio told me on the call was that the sonar finally showed up, albeit too late to do us any good. Only, I'm thinking maybe it's not too late after all.'

Sam paid for breakfast and they stepped out on to the street. Remi waved at a cab and waited as it pulled to the curb, traffic surging past it.

'Does this mean that our glorious stay at the St. Regis is over? Back to the Teotihuacan motel?' Remi asked.

'Only if you want to give this one more go.'

'Of course I do. Lazlo's instinct is the same as mine on this one. We may have discovered the only chamber and it's just a wildly exaggerated tale or we fell for a tricky Toltec ruse.'

'Human nature hasn't really changed in a thousand years, has it? Anyone normal would have found this, seen some treasure and a body, and called it a day,' Lazlo agreed.

Sam held the rear door open and slid in next to her while Lazlo climbed into the passenger seat.

'But we're not normal, are we?' she said.

Sam smiled. 'Thank goodness, no. We'd be bored to death.'

La Jolla, California

Kendra leaned back in her chair, another long day of research concluded, and sneaked a glance at Pete, who was shutting down his computer. Wendy had taken off a half hour earlier, leaving the two of them to their devices as they worked on their latest assignment.

'Any luck?' Pete asked as he stood, a two-day dusting of stubble on his face. He brushed a boyish lock of hair off his forehead and smiled at Kendra, who shook her head.

'No, but we weren't really expecting any miracles. This is going to take a long time. Nothing's jumping out at me,' she said.

'That's why they call it a job, right?'

'Beats flipping burgers.'

Pete approached her desk. 'Are you speaking from experience or in a hypothetical burger-flipping way?'

Kendra batted her eyes. 'I'm not going to give up all my secrets so easily. A girl's got to have her mysteries . . .'

Pete seemed suddenly uneasy and shifted from foot to foot before clearing his throat. Kendra raised one eyebrow, waiting for his next utterance.

'You have any plans for tonight?'

'I was going to get another tattoo. Why?'

That threw him, but he continued now that he'd begun his pitch. 'Oh, nothing. I was just thinking about heading into Old Town and grabbing a beer at a new microbrewery that opened up. I read about it online. It's supposed to have awesome pizza.'

'I don't eat carbs or dairy or drink alcohol,' Kendra said and then offered a grin. 'I've always wondered what I would sound like saying that. I've heard it so many times it makes my head want to explode. Now I know.' Pete looked confused and Kendra sighed. 'It's a little humor, Pete. I love pizza and beer. What red-blooded American girl could resist an offer like that?'

'So no tattoo?' he asked, relieved and happy she'd accepted his invitation.

'Depends on how many beers I have. You buying?'

'First round's on me.'

She clicked her mouse on an icon and shut down her computer, then stood and slid the shoulder strap of her slim purse over her head. 'There. I travel light. Two cars or one?'

'That's up to you. I don't mind dropping you off later if you only want to take one.'

'Sounds like a deal. Lead the way. I'm actually starving – I kind of forgot to eat lunch today.'

'I thought I was the only one who did that around here.'

'Like minds think alike.'

As they walked to the door Kendra held up a finger and mouthed the name 'Selma,' and then she moved across the darkened floor to Selma's door. Seeing light beneath it, she rapped lightly on the heavy wood.

Zoltán let out a protective bark from inside and then Selma cracked the door open and smiled when she saw Kendra.

'I'm just heading out of here, Selma,' Kendra explained. 'Do you need me to get you anything in the morning on my way in?'

Selma shook her head. 'No, darling, thank you. I'm fine. Have a good night. And remember to set the alarm when you leave.'

'I will. Are you managing any better?'

'Isn't there an expression? "That which does not kill us . . ."'

'Nietzsche had a way with words, didn't he?' Kendra said with a smile.

'He did indeed. You take care of yourself,' Selma said, then spotted movement in the shadows. 'Oh, Pete. You still here?'

'Yes, Selma. I was just walking Kendra out.'

Selma gave Kendra a knowing glance before her face assumed its customary neutral expression. 'That's very chivalrous of you. All right, then, it's time for this old lady to hit the sack. You kids have a nice time.'

Kendra leaned forward and gave her a light kiss on the cheek. 'Take care and sleep well.'

35

Mexico City, Mexico

Janus Benedict fought to control the simmering rage that was threatening to explode as he watched Reginald's smug face describe his nocturnal tomb raid. Reginald was high on more than adrenaline, Janus thought, as well as excited at having made off with the treasure under Sam's and Remi's noses.

Reginald's self-preservation instinct kicked in toward the latter part of his account as he registered the flat look in Janus's eyes – a look he knew well, even if he didn't understand why his brother wasn't happy at the news.

When he finished, Janus stared at the ornate ceiling of the Mexico City villa he'd rented for the week, lost in thought.

'Well, aren't you going to say anything?' Reginald demanded. 'We got the treasure.'

'Quite. But let's expand on that a little. You orchestrated and participated in a night attack on a historical location with members of the Los Zetas cartel and slaughtered a dozen soldiers in the process?'

'Yes, I told you. But we got away clean.'

' "Got away clean." You murdered a dozen men and have made yourself and me part of it.'

'Part of what? We have the treasure.'

'Ah. The treasure. Which is hardly the stuff of which dreams are made, looking over your photos. And where is it, pray tell?'

'I told you. Weren't you listening to anything I said? Guerrero has it in a safe house.'

Janus stood and moved to a window to gaze out at the park. When he turned, his face was impassive. 'You don't have any idea what you've done, do you?'

'Well, actually, I do rather know what I did. I got the bloody treasure, didn't I?'

'No, what you did was partner with the most vicious bunch of lowlife murderers on the planet in a blood-bath that will have the Mexican government scouring the Earth for those artifacts for years to come. So you've not only ruined any ability to market the goods, but you've made me a bedfellow with killers who would just as soon cut your heart out as eat breakfast. Instead of being a disinterested vendor who supplies these animals with what they require on the arms side, you've made me a partner with them. Oh, and if any of these thugs ever gets into hot water and wishes to barter information, they now have something they can exchange – not only about their chief but also about you and, by association, me.'

'I . . . I didn't think . . .'

Janus's explanation was like a blow to Reginald's face. 'That's the first sensible thing you've said. You didn't think. At all. If you had, you would have spoken with me and I would have explained why your idiotic scheme was dangerous and stupid. I would have arranged to have the cartel execute the raid without you there, with us merely on the receiving end of the goods. If they were successful, with no expectation of immediate financial gain on our part.'

'What's the difference?'

'The difference is that I know these parasites and they'll want their money. They won't be interested in why it could take several years for this to cool down. Which, because I'm their partner now, I'll have to cover or risk their ire. So, you dim fool, you've not only exposed us both to considerable danger, now and in the future, but you've also cost me a pretty penny, which I may or may not ever recover.'

'But we have –'

'Hell's bells, Reginald! We have nothing. Los Zetas have a bunch of trinkets we won't be able to market and whose very existence endangers you. We have customers who will now believe they're our partners in crime. We have an ongoing risk that one or all of them is eventually arrested and gives you up in exchange for leniency. And guess what? Most places in the world will extradite a mass murderer, you bloody imbecile.'

'But I didn't kill anyone.'

'Your word against theirs. Do you want to protest it while rotting in a Mexican jail? I simply can't understand how you thought this was a good idea.'

'Well, it's done and there's no undoing it,' Reginald said, arms folded over his chest, his tone truculent.

'I can't believe I allowed you into my affairs. Really. You don't have any idea what you're doing and yet you still think you're the smartest chap in the room. Unbelievable.'

'See, Janus? This is exactly the kind of thing I'm getting sick of. You dressing me down like a schoolboy.'

'You're getting sick of it?' Janus took a series of deep breaths, his hands shaking with rage, his pulse pounding in his ears like a bass drum. He willed his heartbeat slower. 'Reginald, you've embarked us on a disastrous course. And, worse, you still don't know what the Fargos are really up to.'

'What do you mean "up to"?'

'They're still here. In Mexico City. And I have it on good authority they're back at the site. Which doesn't sound like predictable behavior if they'd found their treasure and were calling it a day, does it?'

'But there's nothing left except for that old stiff. Maybe they're gathering their equipment or having a last look before buzzing off?'

'Perhaps. Of course, if you hadn't gone on a rampage, we'd still be watching and waiting with the advantage ours. Now they're warned and are sure to be even more cautious. A dangerous state of affairs.'

Reginald lit one of his cigarettes before moving to the bar to pour himself a healthy slug of Scotch. He downed it in two swallows and turned to face his brother.

'I'm sorry, Janus. I just thought I could surprise you . . .'

'You've certainly surprised me, that's for sure,' Janus spat and then shook his head. 'Call Guerrero. I want to meet with my new partner as soon as possible to discuss our options moving forward.'

Teotihuacan, Mexico

The area around the Temple of the Moon had been closed off by the police and yellow crime scene tape fluttered in the breeze as Lazlo and the Fargos neared the smaller pyramid next to it. The authorities looked to be finishing up their investigation, the bodies long since hauled to the morgue, any evidence already collected. The remaining officers stood around chatting. The excitement was over and they simply were running out the clock until the end of their shift.

Maribela approached as Remi was explaining their presence to two uniformed police standing sentry by the entry, a gap in the tape, and after a few terse words they were admitted. She led them to the research tent, where a dejected Antonio was sitting on a collapsible blue camp chair, his students sent home that morning after they'd arrived at what was now a war zone.

'Ah, there you are. The police are just winding things up. Shouldn't be long now and then we can go in and survey the damage. I'm having the mummy carefully removed today to keep the jade intact and taken to the Institute for further study. Seems safer to have everything out of the crypt in case someone sees the news articles and thinks there may be some easy money in selling Quetzalcoatl's remains on the black market to the highest bidder.'

Sam nodded. 'Probably best. So now there's just the empty chamber?'

'Yes. Of course, the chamber itself is historically significant, as are the carvings, but they're not portable. We can arrange to have a locked gate installed over the next few days. That's what many of the other areas have and it seems to work.'

'What about security at night?' Lazlo asked.

'We'll have a small contingent of soldiers, but there's nothing left to steal, so it's purely for show. I'll arrange for a construction crew to erect the gate tomorrow and we'll only need the site security after that.'

'Which is what, exactly?' Remi asked. 'The security, I mean?'

'A few cars, golf carts, and six men at night. Teotihuacan is a big area to patrol and they mainly spend their time making sure there's no vandalism. Their presence is more a deterrent than anything else.'

'They didn't discover the dead soldiers?'

'No, they'd been told by the Army to stay out of their way so they wouldn't get shot by accident. The site was under military control. Not that it did a lot of good.'

'Any leads on who did this?' Lazlo asked.

'None they're sharing. I'm just an academic who roots around in dirt for a living. Nobody tells me anything,' Antonio complained.

'Well, that's about to change. But let's wait until everyone leaves, shall we?' Remi said.

Maribela and Antonio looked at her strangely.

'Is this the sonar?' Sam asked, standing by two black Anvil road cases emblazoned with *Fragile*.

'Yes. That one is the monitor and sensor units and the other is the tricycle contraption.'

'I haven't seen one of these in a while,' Sam said as he opened the cases.

'They used them on some of the other locations. But the range is limited. The Muon detectors are more effective.'

'Still, it will penetrate, what, thirty to forty feet and give reasonably accurate readings? I recall those are the specs.'

'Of course. But it will be going back tomorrow. I told them not to bother sending out the operator. A delivery truck will be by in the afternoon to pick it up.'

Sam and Lazlo exchanged a conspiratorial look. 'That should be more than enough time.'

'Time? For what?' Maribela asked, edging closer.

'I'll fill everyone in once the police have cleared out and it's just us,' Sam said, then returned to examining the device, Lazlo beside him, the pair exchanging hushed whispers.

Antonio turned to Remi, who just shrugged. 'Don't look at me. I married a crazy man.'

The *Federales* departed at six-fifteen, when a jeep with six armed soldiers arrived – the night shift, who were understandably on edge after their predecessors' fate. The men gripped their weapons nervously, on alert but with no obvious threats to defend themselves against.

As dusk fell and the pyramids' shadows lengthened, Sam pulled up a camp chair and faced Antonio and Maribela while Lazlo and Remi perused the latest images from the vault. He took them through his suspicions and he told them what he wanted to do: use the sonar to perform a clandestine search for another chamber while nobody was around.

'I want to do it this way to avoid any leaks. There were far too many people here when we found this site. Somebody talked. The only way to ensure a secret stays a secret is to keep it between us.'

'You really believe there could be another chamber?' Maribela asked in disbelief.

'It's a possibility. One I don't want to overlook. And it seems we have the perfect chance to work with the sonar without an audience tonight. Let's do it. If we don't find anything, it's only an evening of our lives. But if we do . . . I just don't want to get on a plane and fly out of here not knowing.'

Antonio nodded. 'How do you want to do this?'

'We'll get the sonar unit down into the crypt and I'll push it along,' Sam said. 'Any cavities beneath the surface will show up as interruptions of the normal pattern on the scope. It's fairly simple detection but should do for our purposes.'

The system comprised a folding stand with a single wheel on the front and two at the back, like a modified baby stroller. An operator console with a screen rested at chest level in front of the handlebars, with the sonar detection array suspended just above the ground near the front wheel. The soldiers watched them with mild curiosity as they pushed the assembled cart to the dirt ramp. Antonio stopped and chatted with them, explaining that they were conducting measurements below and not to worry. Nobody seemed interested, and soon Sam was fiddling with the device controls to calibrate the sensitivity.

'See that? Solid earth,' he said, pointing at the screen, which was a sea of static.

'How will we know if it's not solid? Or if it's structure?' Remi asked.

'That's where the art comes in. It will all depend on the operator's deft touch.'

They inched slowly along the passageway toward the crypt, and Sam turned knobs as they progressed.

Three-quarters of the way to the chamber, he stopped and adjusted the screen.

'What is it?' Maribela asked.

'Looks like something below us. Yes, there's definitely something there.' He pointed at the screen. 'See that? The disturbance in the field? It's a hollow area. Could be a cave . . . or a tunnel.'

'A cave?' Remi asked.

Antonio nodded. 'Yes, much of the city was built above caves. The Pyramid of the Sun, for example, has a naturally occurring cave beneath it that was used for sacred rites.'

'So how do we know whether it's man-made or natural?'

'Lazlo, would you take the chalk and mark this position? We'll come back to it later,' Sam said, indicating a tin of yellow powder. Lazlo made an X on the dirt floor, which everyone was careful not to disturb as they continued toward the chamber. Just outside, the floor became stone blocks and Sam had to recalibrate the system again.

They passed over the threshold and carried out a methodical grid search of the tomb area, but there were no more readings like the one in the passageway. After twenty minutes of careful scanning, Sam wiped a bead of sweat from his forehead and motioned to the tunnel.

'The only thing I'm picking up is that one anomaly on the way in. That's it.'

'It didn't seem that big, did it?' Maribela asked.

'No. No more than a couple of meters.'

'How far below us?' Lazlo asked.

'Looked like maybe two, two and a half meters. We'll be able to narrow it down once we go over it again,' Sam explained, and then pushed the cart back into the passageway and stopped at the chalk mark on the ground.

'There it is. It's two meters directly beneath us. Looks irregular – wider than it is long. Could be just about anything, but it's definitely there if you're feeling adventurous.'

Remi's eyebrows rose. 'What did you have in mind?'

He studied the image one final time before shutting the system off.

'I was thinking a little exercise might be invigorating.'

36

Sam, Antonio and Lazlo grunted as they swung picks at the hardened clay, having hit a rhythm over the half hour they'd been working at it. Twice they'd stopped and cleared away piles of soil, and they were now half-way to whatever awaited them, standing in a hole roughly eight feet square. Remi and Maribela piled the dirt evenly along the wall, to be filled back in once they'd satisfied their curiosity about the mysterious cavity beneath the corridor.

The earth below the men's feet began to shift and before they could climb out of the pit it gave way. They found themselves falling in a shower of dirt and then landing on a stone floor hard enough to knock the wind out of them. Remi's voice drifted down to Sam from above.

'Are you all right?'

Sam shook the dirt off and sat up, probing his ribs before calling out to her.

'I think so. Lazlo? Antonio?'

Antonio shifted next to him. 'I'm okay. Just . . . stunned.'

'No way to treat guests, I'll say that much,' Lazlo muttered, brushing dirt off his face.

'I thought we'd have more warning than that before the floor gave way,' Sam said.

'Sometimes it's an imprecise science, no?'

Sam coughed and looked up. 'Remi? Could you toss down some flashlights?'

Sam felt something scuttle across his leg and shivered involuntarily, the snake warnings suddenly not so funny. Above, he heard footsteps and then Remi called out.

'Look out below!'

Three aluminum flashlights landed on the mound of dirt between the men. Remi's voice echoed off the walls of whatever space they were in. 'Well? What's down there?'

Sam switched on his light and shined it around where he was lying, the air still thick with dust. Seconds went by. 'We're in another tunnel,' he finally said.

Sam waited for her response, and Antonio and Lazlo flicked their beams on as well. The tunnel was eight to ten feet wide and stretched into the gloom.

'Hang on, then. I'm coming down,' Remi said. The end of a rope dropped next to Sam, and Remi's slim form descended, accompanied by more loose dirt from the hole.

Sam flashed his light across Remi's torso. 'Nice of you to drop in. What did you tie the rope to?'

'Our mummy friend's platform. Maribela's staying up there in case we need help – doesn't seem like a good idea for all of us to be down here without a sure way to get back up, does it?'

'Maribela?' Antonio called.

'Yes?'

'Can you get the soldiers to bring one of the ladders down? A tall one?'

Sam shook his head. 'No. I don't want anyone but us to know about this yet.'

Antonio nodded and winced from pain in his neck and then looked up at the opening. 'Sam's right. Can you bring the tall aluminum ladder here? It doesn't weigh much. And some more lights, if possible. But no soldiers. Just you.'

'All right,' she said. Her footsteps echoed down the upper passageway, leaving them with the sound of their breathing and nothing more. Remi's light played over the walls of the tunnel, and she pointed to their right.

'Do you see that?'

'Yes. Looks like an antechamber of some kind,' Sam said.

'Look at the carvings. They're Toltec. The same as the ones in the crypt. But these are more exotically detailed.' Remi moved down the tunnel to the stone walls of the larger area. A massive stone frame around the passageway threshold displayed the distinctive pictographs of the crypt above – but carved with considerably greater detail and obvious care. 'Here we have the same funeral procession. Same pyramid, but the moon isn't obstructed by any cloud. And Quetzalcoatl . . . Look! He's depicted here differently than in any of the others. Here he's got long hair and a beard.'

348

'Promising,' Sam said.

Remi eyed the passageway. 'The builders certainly took their time on this, given the length of the tunnel and the detail of these carvings.'

'I wonder what's down the other way?' Sam asked, looking over his shoulder to where Lazlo had wandered.

'Only one way to know,' Remi replied, and returned to the caved-in spot. She stopped a dozen yards farther along, where Lazlo stood with his flashlight beam playing over a mass of dirt and rocks where the tunnel ended.

Lazlo eyed the ruined passage. 'Looks like the builders collapsed the tunnel after they were done. They really didn't want anyone making their way in here, did they?'

Sam studied the debris. 'There's no indentation above. So this was deliberate. They caved it in or filled it and then smoothed out the terrain above so there would be no trace of the entrance.'

They were startled by the clatter of the ladder being lowered by Maribela. Antonio wedged the base into the dirt below and tested it for stability before giving her the go-ahead to descend. She came down using one hand, the other carrying the more powerful battery-powered LED work light they'd used in the crypt above.

The lamp's harsh white glow illuminated the tunnel like an approaching train, and the siblings quickly joined Sam and Remi in the antechamber. Maribela took it in without comment. Lazlo pushed by them and moved slowly into the chasm. Remi motioned to them and led the way deeper into the subterranean passage, which extended considerably farther, bisecting the tunnel above before turning under the pyramid.

'Hold on. Everybody stop,' Sam said as they neared another bend. The group froze and Remi edged closer to him.

Lazlo looked around, unsure of what to do. 'What is it?'

'There. That section of the floor,' Sam said, pointing to a depression. 'I've seen that sort of thing before. It's a booby trap. The Toltecs used reeds or something similar to create a false floor over a pit and then put dirt on top of the matting. Over the centuries, gravity has exerted its pull, but . . .'

Lazlo took a shaky step back. Sam inched forward and knelt in front of the six-foot-square depression and then turned to Remi. 'Do you have your knife with you? Afraid I left mine at the motel,' he confessed.

'No well-dressed girl goes tunnel crawling without one,' she said, and handed it to him. He unfolded the five-inch blade and locked it into place, then leaned forward, one hand steadying himself against the edge of the depression, and stabbed it into the dirt in front of him. The knife penetrated into the ground. He sawed with it, then removed the knife and handed it back to her.

'Whatever it is, it's too hard to cut.' He took the

handle of his long aluminum flashlight and pounded on the ground. The unmistakable hollow sound of a cavity answered him. After a final thump for good measure, he stood and nodded.

'Let's get some wood from the research tent and put it across this area. What do you want to bet when we excavate it, we'll find a deep hole with a lot of very sharp objects at the bottom? Obsidian blades or spears? It's a drop trap.'

Antonio and Sam went for the planks left over from the shoring project while Lazlo, Maribela and Remi waited by the depression. They returned with four planks, easily long enough to span the area. Lazlo helped Antonio set them in place, and Sam tested the makeshift bridge before walking across.

'Mind that you don't slip off. Could be fatal,' Lazlo warned.

At the end of the tunnel they found themselves facing a large carved doorway sealed with stone bricks, carefully mortared in place rather than the haphazard rockwork of the other crypt. Antonio and Lazlo went back to the ladder, mounted it in search of tools, and returned with the picks.

The brick barrier proved more solid than the other, but in half an hour the first stone block shifted, quickly followed by three more. They redoubled their efforts and soon had an aperture large enough to squeeze through. Remi and Lazlo led the way, Maribela behind them with the lamp, while Sam and Antonio relaxed.

'Oh my . . . this looks like the real thing,' Remi said, her hushed voice still audible in the confined space. Sam shouldered his way into the vault, where Remi was gazing at an ornate sarcophagus resting on a pedestal – but unlike the platform above, this one was covered in carved figures. Sam approached her and regarded the top of the coffin while Lazlo did a slow scan of the otherwise empty room, his flashlight eventually coming to rest on the pictographs adorning the sides and top of the sarcophagus.

'Who wants to help get this open?' Sam asked.

Antonio and Lazlo moved to the opposite side and nodded at him. Lazlo set his flashlight on the stone floor. 'Ready when you are, old boy. But it looks heavy.'

'Hey, your sister and I can help, too. Move over, Fargo,' Remi said, and slid next to Sam. Maribela joined Antonio and Lazlo on the other side and, on Sam's nod, they heaved.

The lid moved a few inches. They tried again, and then again, each effort edging it farther open. When they'd cleared two feet of space, they stopped and Remi directed her flashlight inside.

Remi gasped, as did Maribela. Sam let loose a low whistle and stepped closer.

'The legends were true,' he said quietly, his hand on Remi's shoulder.

The figure was mummified, but his long red beard and hair were intact, carefully braided in an ornate style, with small jewels woven into the strands. He wore a tunic of chain mail, a classic Viking helmet, and had a steel sword clenched in one hand and a spear in the other. A battle-axe rested by his side and a shield covered his lower legs.

Antonio regarded the length of the sarcophagus. 'What do you think he was? Hundred and eighty centimeters? Assuming his body stretches the full length of the coffin.'

'More like six feet something. He was tall, that's for sure. A Viking,' Sam said.

Maribela looked at him strangely. 'You seem so sure.'

Sam told them about the longship on Baffin Island and their eyes widened.

'So that's why you were so interested in the legend,' Antonio said. 'You knew it likely corresponded with fact.'

'Yes,' Sam admitted. 'And now we have further proof that the cultures overlapped in ways nobody's ever imagined.'

'Look at this,' Lazlo said, shining his flashlight on the underside of the coffin lid. 'There's an inscription.'

'What does it say?' Remi asked.

He studied it for several long seconds before answering. 'I can't be sure. My runic alphabet's a mite rusty, but, on first glance, it looks like a eulogy of some sort. I'll need to see the entire thing to be able to do a reasonable translation.'

'Could you do it from a photograph of the interior lid and another one of the part that's exposed at the foot of the sarcophagus?' Remi asked.

353

'I suppose so. Care to do the honors?' Lazlo invited. Remi slid her phone into the spacious coffin and took several photographs, then repeated the process with the exposed underside of the lid. When she was done, she photographed the entire exterior of the sarcophagus as the rest of them studied the carvings on the walls.

'Bit odd that there's no booty, isn't it? Didn't the legend specify an emerald the size of a small car?' Lazlo asked.

'It did. But that could be an exaggeration. I don't see anything in here. Do you?' Sam asked. Both Antonio and Maribela shook their heads. Maribela played her light across an elaborate pictograph.

'This appears to tell the story of Quetzalcoatl's conquest of a large Mayan city. Maybe Chichen Itza.'

Antonio pointed to the series of carvings next to it. 'And here . . . It'll require further study, but it seems like this chronicles the move of the Toltec capital, or perhaps it's the seat of power, to the Mayan city. And look! This symbolizes Quetzalcoatl's exile from the Toltec capital . . . and . . . his death.'

'Lazlo, if I haven't told you yet today, you're absolutely brilliant,' Remi said.

'I never get tired of hearing it, although it's a bit of an overstatement,' Lazlo said, pinpoints of color blossoming on his cheeks.

Sam turned to Remi. 'It would have never occurred to us that the other tomb was a decoy.'

Antonio shook his head in awe. 'This is really

incredible. The more I study these pictographs, the less I feel like I know about the Toltecs. Their trading sphere was apparently much more extensive than we believed.'

Remi tapped the side of the coffin. 'Remember that the legend says that Quetzalcoatl wandered in the wilderness for years after leaving Tollan.'

'Figuring all this out will be a life's ambition. A dream, really, for both me and my sister,' Antonio said.

Lazlo smiled. 'Well, I'd say you more than have your work cut out for you.'

They admired the carvings for several more minutes and then Sam glanced at his watch. 'I suggest that we wind this up for the evening and return tomorrow morning to do a more thorough inventory and catalog all of the carvings. I don't see anything else, do you?'

Antonio shook his head. 'No. Still, this is a historical treasure without precedent. It will change the history of my people. Whether or not there's an Eye of Heaven, today is a miraculous day by any measure.'

Lazlo nodded. 'Yes. Well, quite.' His stomach rumbled audibly. 'Sorry about that. Nature calling for sustenance – nothing to be done about it.'

'Let's get you boys fed and we'll take this up tomorrow,' Remi said, and Sam grinned.

'All this tomb raiding does make me a little peckish.'

'We don't want either of you to waste away to nothing.'

'Come on, then, I'll buy the first celebratory Coke,' Lazlo agreed.

Once they were back at ground level, Antonio gave the contingent of soldiers exacting instructions, forbidding anyone from entering the tomb while Remi transferred the photographs she'd taken first to her flash drive. When she finished, Antonio offered to give her, Sam and Lazlo a lift to their motel, which they gratefully accepted. A harvest moon glowed orange from between the scattered clouds as they rolled down the broad avenue of the dead metropolis, the find of a lifetime behind them. At the motel they waved as Antonio pulled away and, after cleaning up, rendezvoused at the nearby restaurant.

'I don't suppose you'd let the shots of the coffin lid out of your sight this evening, would you?' Lazlo asked as their plates were being cleared away.

'You're reading my mind again, Lazlo. You have to stop doing that,' Remi said.

'What's the hurry? I'd say after a day like today, you can take the rest of the night off,' Sam said.

Lazlo shrugged. 'Oh, no particular hurry, I suppose. I just thought you might like to know where the treasure's hidden, that's all.'

'What are you talking about?'

'The inscription. My Old Norse orthography isn't as rusty as I pretended.'

Remi's eyes narrowed as she passed the flash drive to him. 'What did you see, Lazlo?'

Lazlo paused dramatically. 'If it's all the same to you, I'd just as soon translate it before the madding crowds descend on the tomb tomorrow. Not to get everyone's hopes up, but the last line said something about the Eye of Heaven. Which, given the inscription's location, would seem about as good as a treasure map to this dusty old academic.'

37

Lazlo was subdued the following day at breakfast. Dark circles ringed his eyes, lending him the look of a haggard raccoon, and it was obvious to Sam and Remi that he hadn't spent much of the night sleeping. After his third cup of coffee, he sat back and fixed them with a fatigued stare.

'The answer to your question is yes. Yes, I translated the inscription. And, yes, it tells an incredible tale. Unfortunately, the one thing it doesn't describe is where to find the Eye of Heaven,' he said.

'What does it say?' Remi asked. Lazlo pulled a piece of worn notepaper from his pocket and unfolded it. He slipped it across to Sam and Remi, who read it carefully.

You see the body of Knut Eldgrim, son of father Bjorn and mother Sigrid. I came from Gotalander with 200 men and 4 ships. I was their leader and navigator. After 30 days' sail across a calm sea we came on to a strange sandy shore by a rock cliff beneath a mountain that jutted straight into the sky. The land around was covered by lush forest.

We met strange people unlike any we had ever seen. They were friendly and led us a long way inland to their village, Tollan.

I helped heal a large gash on their ruler's right leg from a jaguar. I used the medicine we had brought with us should we find ourselves in battle. In gratitude the King made me his chief adviser.

I aided other villagers with injuries and sickness. My crew was given many rare objects and precious stones for digging a canal to bring water from a river to their village.

One year later the King died. Just before he left us he ordained me as the new leader of the people and gave me the name Topiltzin Cē Ācatl Quetzalcoatl. He bequeathed a headdress of the great feathered serpent god. He gave me an amulet as a symbol of my power as ruler and god, a large green stone from the south that glows with the life of the sun: the Eye of Heaven.

In the years that followed I showed the people how to smelt iron, lay masonry, and carve sculpture, to grow food and build roads and waterways.

Under my rule our empire grew. We conquered the Mayan city of Chichen Itza. I moved the capital of our vast lands to this city and there I built a temple to the feathered serpent like the one in Tollan.

As I lay dying the people of this land wept and said that my brother, the god Tezcatlipoca, was casting me out but that I will return to them.

My warrior comrades have returned to our homeland laden with the wonders of this world, with plans to return. A marker has been built where my ships came ashore. When my people of Gotalander return they shall return to these people with the Eye of Heaven, marking my return to them.

Sam and Remi puzzled over the final line as Lazlo watched their reaction. When Sam looked up, his expression reflected the frustration Lazlo felt after spending half the night on the translation.

'So there's a marker near a rock cliff beneath a hill or mountain. Piece of cake. That only leaves, what, several thousand miles of Mexican and Central American coastland? And a marker that could have well disintegrated long ago,' Sam said.

'Assuming it wasn't a casualty to one of the earthquakes that have reshaped the coastline and decimated cities in Mexico over the last thousand years,' Remi added.

'Or hurricanes. Let's not forget the hurricanes.'

'Although it does say that a marker had been built. Not erected or carved. Built. I take it to mean that it must be referring to a structure. Where the ships landed,' Lazlo said.

'Oh well, in that case forgive my pessimism. All we're looking for is a marker that was *built* on the coast a thousand years ago. Which could mean anything from a pile of rocks to who knows what,' Remi corrected.

Sam appeared lost in thought. He took a long sip on his coffee and then stopped, the cup frozen in midair as he turned to Remi.

'On the ship. The Baffin find. There was a rune stone aboard. Do you have a picture of it?'

She nodded. 'I think so. But I'm not sure where. Probably on one of the flash drives.'

'We never bothered to translate it.'

Remi pushed back from the table. 'Oh . . . my . . .'

'If I might be so bold, I'd love to get a look at that photo sooner rather than later,' Lazlo said.

Remi almost ran back to the room. The waitress cleared the plates out of the way and Sam was laying down several large-denomination peso notes when Remi returned, holding a blue flash drive aloft in triumph.

'How long will it take you to translate it?' she asked as she handed it to Lazlo.

'Depends on how much text there is. How big was the stone?'

'Maybe two feet by three. I honestly thought it was ballast the first time I saw it in the hold.'

'Let me get to work. Shouldn't be more than an hour or two. Certainly not after all the practice I've recently had.'

'We'll wait here for you.'

'No need. If you want to go to the dig, I'll meet you there once I have something to report.'

Remi nodded. 'One thing, though. I think for now it would be best to keep our discoveries to ourselves. This could well lead us to the Eye of Heaven. I don't want to broadcast that and become targets. Or get beaten to the punch. So mum's the word,' she said.

'My lips are sealed,' Lazlo agreed as he rose. 'You can tell the lads I slept in, should anyone have a burning desire to consult with me about the price of tea.'

'The man needs his beauty rest,' Sam agreed.

'Good luck, Lazlo,' Remi said.

Lazlo gave her a pained smile. 'Luck will have little to do with it.'

Antonio and Maribela were already at the tomb site when Sam and Remi got there, supervising what seemed like a phalanx of archaeologists and techs from the Institute, all outfitted in newly issued white lab coats, while a cadre of armed soldiers looked on. Antonio waved when he saw them and the guards let them through.

'Good morning. Where's your partner in crime?' Maribela asked with a sunny smile.

'He should be along anytime,' Sam said. 'What have you got planned for today?'

'We're going to begin mapping the area and go over the lower tomb with the sonar before we send it back – just in case,' Antonio explained. 'And I've just briefed everyone on the protocols for documenting the find with video and photographs.'

'Sounds like you've got everything under control,' Remi affirmed.

'As much as anything of this scale can be managed. But make no mistake – this will be a multi-year endeavor. It dwarfs any of the other excavations we have going.'

'Do you have a team working on the casket inscription?' Sam asked.

'That will be processed in due time.'

'We can help with that, if you like,' Remi offered.

'We appreciate it, but, honestly, you two have done

more than enough,' Maribela said, her tone cordial but her glance dismissive. 'Which reminds me. We'll be doing a press release and a conference later and would love to have you there.'

They were interrupted by a harried-looking scientist carrying a clipboard and a radio, and Sam and Remi used the disruption to move away from the command center. Sam held one hand over his eyes, shielding them from the morning sun, and watched the activity near the mouth of the tomb.

'You have any interest whatsoever in doing a press conference?' he asked Remi.

'Not unless someone's holding a gun to my head.'

'So we'll beg off?'

'Absolutely. We can claim one of us got food poisoning.'

'Works every time. Want to flip a coin?'

Remi shook her head. 'No, I'll be the fall guy this time.'

Half an hour later, Lazlo arrived and, after running the security gauntlet, headed directly for them, barely contained excitement playing across his face. Maribela watched him march toward the Fargos, and Sam moved to meet him before he gave anything away.

'I say, I think I've –' Lazlo started, but Sam cut him off.

'We have a lot of folks paying attention to us today. Maybe we should take a nice, slow stroll around the pyramid while you tell me what the rune stone says?'

363

'Ah, quite. I see. Well, lead the way. Sorry. Didn't mean to give away the game.'

'No problem. Remi, will you join us?'

'You couldn't stop me.'

Once they were out of earshot, Lazlo quickly gave them a rundown of what he'd discovered.

'The rune seems to have fairly specific instructions on locating the Eye of Heaven. It doesn't refer to it as such, but it does say the pride of the New World resides beneath a temple. And then it goes on to describe landmarks. A jutting peak just south of it. A nearby lagoon. Cliffs. A small nearby island. I think that there's enough to go on. With a detailed examination of the coastline along the Gulf of Mexico, we should be able to narrow it down – assuming that the landmarks are still roughly the same.'

Remi's eyes lit up. 'Why, Lazlo, that's wonderful. Do you have a written translation for us?'

'Of course.' He slipped her a folded piece of paper. She slid it into her rear pocket and exchanged a conspiratorial look with Sam.

'Lazlo, we're going to bow out, claiming stomach problems. You're welcome to stay or you can join us back in Mexico City while we research this.'

'Much as I enjoy standing in the sun turning into a lobster, I think I'll err on the side of caution and accompany you. Do you mind?'

'Of course not.'

Sam and Remi moved back to the staging area and,

after a brief discussion with Antonio, begged off the media circus in favor of returning to their motel. Antonio had one of his assistants drive them back, and by noon Lazlo was back at the clinic and Sam and Remi were checked into the St. Regis.

Sam's first call once they had settled into their room was to Selma, who agreed to stand by for receipt of the translation so the team could go to work on locating the area. Remi quickly typed it into her computer and sent it off, and as she watched the confirmation of receipt appear in her in-box, smiled at Sam.

'It's only a matter of a few days before Antonio and Maribela get around to translating the inscription, you know.'

'Yes, but nobody has the message from the longboat except us.'

'What about Antonio and his sister? How do you feel about involving them?' Remi asked.

'I think once we have an idea what we're looking at, we can make that call. Right now, the fewer people with all the puzzle pieces, the better. There have been too many leaks already. Why tempt fate?'

38

Isla Mujeres, Mexico

Janus Benedict carefully lit the Cohiba cigar he'd been saving for after lunch and puffed contentedly, taking in the turquoise waters off Isla Mujeres from the lower deck of his yacht. The glass-and-steel buildings of Cancún's skyline sparkled in the distance. A steward approached with a cell phone and, after apologizing for the intrusion, set it on the teak table and disappeared. Janus lifted the phone to his ear.

'Yes?'

'The Fargos have managed to pull yet another rabbit out of their hat.' The speaker went on to describe the Viking find, culminating with the news conference that would be broadcast later that afternoon.

Janus processed the information in silence and, after blowing a cloud of smoke at the sky, issued a set of instructions. When he was finished, he hung up, his face untroubled, to all the world a man with no cares.

With the find at the Pyramid of the Moon, he knew the Fargos well enough to understand that if there were treasure to be hunted, they would do so with the tenacity of leeches. All he needed to do was be patient and remain vigilant. From his current position he could be anywhere in Mexico in a matter of hours, and when he was alerted that the Fargos were on the move, it would be child's play to intercept them.

Reginald was still in Mexico City, where his quarry remained. Janus would watch and wait, allowing the irritating pair to do the work for him. A relatively simple scheme had already been made far more complicated by his brother, and Janus didn't want to involve him again unless absolutely necessary. Guerrero's participation as more than a hired gun was an irritant and subjected Janus to undue risk, but there might come a time in the near future when his brutal approach would come in handy.

Janus looked up at a pair of pelicans circling off the transom, eyeing the surface of the sea for any signs of bait fish. Predators feeding. The natural order of things.

An immutable law of nature that the meddlesome Fargos would soon experience firsthand.

Mexico City, Mexico

Selma reached Sam the next day. Her voice sounded stronger than it had over the last few weeks – the old Selma, brimming with efficiency and stamina.

'We've been working on the landmarks you gave us, and we've narrowed it down to several likely areas. One's on the Caribbean coast, near Belize; the second is in the Yucatán north of Cancún; and the third is north of Veracruz, on the Gulf of Mexico.'

Sam closed his eyes, envisioning the geography. 'How many miles from Teotihuacan is the one by Belize?'

'About seven hundred and fifty miles.'

'Mostly jungle, I'd guess.'

'It would be, yes.'

'What about the Yucatán location?'

'A little farther.'

'I can't see a group of Vikings traveling that distance overland, through jungle, can you?' Sam asked.

'Anything's possible, but I'd say they would have needed a pretty good reason.'

'Hmm. And how many miles is the Veracruz spot?'

'About a hundred and seventy. But there's a mountain range between Teotihuacan and the coast, a natural barrier of sorts.'

Sam thought for a moment. 'I can see them crossing the mountains with a guide. I can't see them trudging through dense jungle.'

'Then the Veracruz location is your baby . . .'

'I hear a *but* in your voice, Selma.'

'Well, there is a small wrinkle.'

'And what's that?' Sam asked.

'It's on or near the grounds of a nuclear power plant.'

The silence stretched over the line as Sam absorbed the information. 'You're kidding.'

'You know I don't kid.'

Sam sighed. 'I suppose I do.'

'Depending on the precise location, it could be just outside the perimeter security area. But there's no way of knowing until you're on the ground. I looked at all the satellite footage and it's inconclusive. The only way to tell for sure is to go there.'

'Well, at least it's not too far.'

'That's a positive. Although it's also in a region that has a lot of security issues.'

'More than Mexico City?'

'Oh yes. There's only one highway north along the coast from Veracruz – the main port on the east side of the country. Which is also, not coincidentally, where much of the cocaine from Colombia enters. So that area is the primary distribution artery for trafficking cocaine north to the border states – which until recently were considered outside of the government's control, effectively operated by the cartels.'

'Tell me this gets better.'

'I figured you'd want to know what you were looking at.'

'Thanks, Selma. I'm guessing it would be pretty close to impossible to slip in there without a permit and dig around, what with the nuclear power plant.'

'That's probably a safe assumption.'

Remi returned from the spa an hour later and Sam filled her in, pointing out the area on their laptop.

'Look at the bright side. At least we've got a likely spot for the temple,' she said.

'Sure. Crawling with cartel killers and nukes. And we

can forget about secrecy – we're going to have to bring Antonio and Maribela into this if we're going to get a permit.'

Remi sat on the bed and brushed her fingers through her auburn hair. 'Doesn't sound like we have much choice. I mean, we don't have to tell them that we think the Eye of Heaven's there. Just that we have a lead and want to look for ruins in that area.'

'A lead on what?'

'Well, on something related to the Vikings. That based on information we gleaned from the longship, we believe that was where they came ashore and that there might be some evidence. Keep it vague.' She rose. 'I'm going to take a shower. Think about it some and then we can call Antonio. After discovering Quetzal-coatl's tomb, I don't see how he'll say no.'

'I don't, either. But I also don't see how he won't want to accompany us. It's relatively close and he's been with us so far.'

'You're probably right. And that means his sister, too.'

'They seem to come as a pair.'

'No comment.'

Antonio was polite but cautious when they spoke on the telephone that afternoon. He was still in Teotihua-can, where he would remain until he was satisfied that the excavation was well under way and a team leader had been put in charge.

'I'll have to check to see what restrictions there are.

We're dealing with the nuclear regulatory authority and they're a law unto themselves. Part of the power company, but because of the risk posed by reactors . . .'

'I understand, Antonio. It would really mean a lot to us.'

'I can tell you that if it's on their grounds, it will be much more difficult. Imagine if you wanted to conduct archaeological research on the grounds of one of your nation's reactors . . .'

'Well, let's hope that it's not. There's no way of knowing until we go out there. Maybe we should assume that it's not within their perimeter fence – would that make a difference?'

'It might. Let me make some calls and see what we're up against.' Antonio hesitated. 'How important is this? Is it something urgent?'

Remi laughed, hoping her light tone would disarm him. 'Well, we'd like to knock it out while we're still in Mexico. I would consider it a huge favor if we could.'

'Well, I hate to disappoint a lady. I'll get back in touch when I know more.'

'Thank you, Antonio.'

Remi hung up and smiled at Sam. 'He's going to do everything he can.'

'No surprise there.'

She considered him for a moment. 'Why, Fargo, is that a hint of jealousy?'

'No. My stomach's still uneasy from the food poisoning.'

'That was an invention.'

'Oh. Right.'

Remi slid next to where he was sitting on the bed and took his hand. 'You're the only globe-trotting treasure hunter for me, Sam Fargo.'

'You probably say that to all the adventurers.'

She kissed him on the cheek. 'Only the ones willing to wear chicken suits.'

'At least I've got that going for me.'

She kissed him again. 'That's more than enough.'

39

Veracruz, Mexico

The Gulfstream's wheels touched down on the runway of Veracruz International Airport and taxied to the private terminal at the southern end of the runway. Lazlo smiled at Maribela, who was seated across from him. She looked out the window at the morning mist hovering over the airport instead of returning the smile. Antonio caught his eye and shrugged. Sam and Remi unclipped their seat belts as the plane coasted to a stop and, moments later, they were inside the terminal. Antonio spoke into his cell phone briefly and then turned to them.

'The cars should be here in five minutes.'

'"Cars"?' Maribela asked.

'Ah, yes. Well, a concession I made with the power company was that we would be accompanied at all times by three of the local police force. It's for our protection, as well as to ensure we don't trespass on their property. If we determine that we need access within the plant's perimeter, that will be a different discussion.'

'That's not a problem as long as they can keep quiet about what we're doing,' Sam said.

'It wasn't negotiable. And frankly, with all of the violence lately, it's not a bad idea.'

Lazlo looked uncomfortable. 'I say, did you just mention violence?'

Remi nodded. 'It's not that big a deal, Lazlo. They've just had a few beheadings recently.'

'And gun battles,' Sam confirmed.

'Oh, and the grenade attack. Or was that somewhere else?' Remi asked innocently.

Lazlo blanched. 'I do hope this is all for my benefit. Jolly good. Quite amusing, I assure you.'

'Come on, Lazlo, you only live once,' Remi joked.

'Which I've grown quite fond of in my own way, even if dry as the desert wind. I'd hate to have my winning streak ended by a machete blade.'

Antonio waved at them from the glass terminal doors. 'They're here.'

Two silver Chevrolet Suburban SUVs sat at the curb. Three uniformed police officers stood by the vehicles, submachine guns dangling from shoulder straps, deployed as though they were expecting to be attacked at the airport. Everyone's demeanor grew serious as the reality of the danger there was driven home by the men's alertness, and any urge to joke about it further died at the sight of their weapons and the flat look in their eyes.

'I'll ride in the lead vehicle with the officers and Lazlo,' Antonio directed. 'Maribela, you ride in the second vehicle with the Fargos.'

Their baggage and equipment was loaded and they were out of Veracruz, on the coastal road north, within fifteen minutes. Shimmering fields of tall green grass undulated in the light breeze as they rolled past. When they left the city limits behind, the landscape transitioned into farmland, with acres of crops stretching to the base of the foothills in the distance. Half an hour from Veracruz, a massive array of mocha sand dunes lined the coast.

'That's amazing. It looks like the Sahara,' Remi said. A four-wheel-drive dune buggy shot over the crest of one of the nearest dunes, throwing a cloud behind it as it tore along parallel to the highway and then raced back toward the sea.

Ten more minutes and they passed a lagoon, the rippled emerald water dented by the wind, ringed by palm trees and brightly painted cinder-block buildings with thatched roofs. Sam pointed off to their left at a peak, jutting into the sky like a monolith.

'That's promising. I seem to recall that described rather well, actually. Looks perfect for rock climbing, if that's your thing, what with the sheer face and all.'

Maribela glanced at him in the rearview mirror. 'That's El Cerro de los Metates. It's well known in Veracruz. There are Totonac tombs nearby in Quiahuiztlan, along with substantial ruins on the hill. Let me know if you'd like to see them. The turnoff is up ahead.'

Remi shook her head and Sam shrugged. 'Maybe once we're done looking around on the coast. Would

375

there have been Totonac settlements around here at the time Quetzalcoatl arrived? Around AD 1000?'

'Without a doubt. The region has been inhabited for thousands of years,' Maribela confirmed.

'Interesting. For whatever reason, I imagined this stretch as relatively desolate back then,' Sam said.

'Well, it's more a question of semantics. There were definitely cities in the area, but they were small compared to modern standards.'

'So this would still have been remote?'

'Except for fishing camps, I'd say that would be correct.'

Four miles farther north, the brick-red towers of the Laguna Verde nuclear power plant came into view. Maribela turned her head slightly toward the rear seat.

'Our destination is on the other side of the plant. As you can see, it's a large complex. It's been in operation since the mid-nineties.' They passed the buildings, and Maribela pointed at a deep teal lagoon on their right, between the highway and the Gulf of Mexico. 'That's Laguna Verde – the "green lagoon" the plant gets its name from. The road we'll take runs north of it to the shore.'

The lead Suburban's brake lights illuminated and signaled a right turn. Dust rose into the air as it turned on to the dirt track, and their SUV followed. They passed several homes and then made another right and followed the road until it became little more than a trail. Antonio's SUV stopped by a dense thicket and he got out, along with the armed escorts, and waited as the driver parked.

Everyone gathered next to the rear cargo doors and waited as Antonio pushed aside the assortment of picks, shovels, pry bars and lamps to get at the smaller items and hand them out. Sam hefted a machete and regarded the blade before sliding it back into its canvas sheath.

Antonio cleared his throat. 'All right. The police will stay with the vehicles to ensure nothing happens to them in our absence. You all have canteens and machetes – my only word of warning is about snakes. There are plenty of rattlers around here, so tread carefully. And do not be in a hurry. They should be more afraid of you than you of them, but you never know, so best to give them plenty of warning that you're coming.'

'Nobody mentioned snakes, either,' Lazlo reminded Sam, who shrugged.

'He just did.'

Remi took over from Antonio. 'We're looking for the ruins of a temple. Exposed to the weather, it may be only remnants. I'm not sure, but if you come across anything that appears man-made, yell. I'd suggest we spread out, ten meters apart, and work our way south from this point.'

'Again, how do we keep from being bitten by snakes?' Lazlo asked.

'By moving slowly and watching your step,' Antonio said.

'Prayer might also help,' Sam added.

'Ready?' Remi asked.

They began working their way up the rise toward the summit, accompanied by the sound of the surf crashing against the rocks at the base of the cliff ten stories below. The brush was thick and untamed, covered by a canopy of tree branches, nourished by the plentiful rain and sun. Late morning transitioned into afternoon, the sun beginning its slow descent behind the Sierra Madre Mountains, when Remi called out from the edge of their line.

'I found something!'

'On my way!' Sam yelled as he moved toward her.

'It's overgrown, but it looks like part of a wall.'

Lazlo joined Sam and they hacked their way toward Remi; Maribela and Antonio approached from the inland side, and soon they were all standing by a rise from the natural terrain.

Remi tapped it with her blade and the steel clinked against rock.

'I scraped away a foot of soil in a couple of places and it's stone underneath. Looks like it rises about fifteen feet above the surrounding area.'

'Which would be more than enough for a small temple,' Antonio confirmed. 'After a thousand years of storms and runoff and soil buildup, you'd expect it to be a big lump – exactly like this is.'

Sam stepped forward and dug at the dirt after pushing away the tangle of plants growing out of the sloping face. 'We're going to need those shovels and picks from the trucks.'

Antonio and Lazlo went for the tools while Sam, Remi and Maribela hacked at the thick foliage with their machetes, trying to clear the perimeter of the mound. All three were exhausted by the time Lazlo and Antonio returned and they took a break as the cooling breeze blew from the edge of the cliff only a few short yards away.

'Approaching ships would definitely have been able to see this from the sea. What do you want to bet that those left behind lit a signal fire every day as part of their duties?' Sam asked.

'That would make sense,' Remi agreed. 'It might also explain the cloud over the pyramid in some of the depictions. That could have been a smoke cloud – a veiled reference to this temple.'

Maribela eyed Remi. 'Perhaps you can tell us what it is that we've found?'

'Lazlo was able to translate a rune stone from the Viking longship,' Remi explained. 'It spoke of a marker on the shore – a temple that would lead the Norsemen back to the New World to colonize it in the name of their leader who was buried there. There's probably a trove of historical data we can glean from it.'

Sam rose from where he'd been crouched and hoisted one of the shovels. 'Let's get some of this dirt off and see what's underneath it, shall we?'

Antonio joined him with a pick, and they began

working on the center of one side of the mound while Maribela and Remi dug into another. After an hour of hard work, Sam stepped back and examined the cleared area he and Antonio had created.

'Remi? Come check this out. It looks like an entry. But it's been sealed off.' Sam tapped the area with the tip of his shovel. They'd managed to expose a rectangular opening with a stone lip, but their way was barred by a mixture of rock and crude mortar. 'And you'll want to get a picture or two for our scrapbook of the depiction carved into the rim.'

Remi joined him and leaned her shovel against the dirt. Maribela arrived a moment later and gasped when she saw what Sam was pointing at.

Etched into the granite frame over the doorway was a death's head – wearing a war helmet adorned with the head of a snake, its fangs exposed, its feathered wings spread wide, as it prepared to strike.

40

Maribela looked at Antonio with astonishment.

'I don't . . . understand. That's unlike any of the Toltec images we've ever come across.'

'Yes, it's more typical of the sort of thing the Vikings were known for,' Remi said, her camera clicking as she captured multiple angles. 'Look at the skull. It's got a beard. I think we're seeing the first example of Viking iconography ever found in Mexico.'

'The juxtaposition of the indigenous art and the Viking is . . . striking, to say the least,' Maribela said.

'Not particularly welcoming, is it?' Lazlo commented.

'It definitely makes you stop and think twice,' Sam agreed. 'I wonder why they sealed the temple entry?'

'Perhaps they got tired of waiting for the ship to return?' Lazlo said.

Sam nodded. 'There's only one way to find out what's inside. Might as well see if we can break through this while we've still got some light to work with.' Sam turned to Antonio. 'What do you think? Do you have any problem with us creating an opening here?'

'I'd say your instincts have been quite good so far.'

'All right, then. Let's see what this mud is made out of, shall we?'

The mortar had hardened to the consistency of rock, and the sun was sinking below the mountains by the time their picks had punched the first hole. The sight of the gap widening encouraged them, with mortar crumbling away in large chunks, and within minutes they'd cleared the entire entryway.

Maribela had brought flashlights from the SUVs and she flicked one on and handed it to Sam. He squinted and peered inside. Remi edged next to him, bringing her beam to bear on the interior.

'This wasn't what I was expecting,' she said, and stepped back so that Antonio and Maribela could see inside. Lazlo approached and looked over their shoulders as they played their lights over the interior.

'This is another first. I've never seen a mass burial in a temple like this. How many skeletons are there?' Maribela asked. Antonio counted quietly in Spanish.

'A dozen. But look at how they're dressed,' he said as he took a tentative step down the single stair into the temple. Maribela followed him in, trailed by Lazlo. Sam and Remi nodded to each other and joined them. The chamber was larger than it had looked from the outside – at least twenty feet square. The skeletons sat against the walls as though waiting for something. Each had on a chain-mail tunic, and several had Viking helmets sunk over their skulls, decayed teeth grinning into eternity, swords and battle-axes by their sides.

'Look! There,' Remi said, pointing to several objects near the entry stairs. She trained her flashlight on the long wooden trough and the tools near it. 'That's where the mortar came from.'

'Bloody hell. They walled themselves in,' Lazlo exclaimed.

Nobody spoke as the weight of what they were seeing sank in. There was no way of knowing how many of the skeletons belonged to men who had been alive when the doorway had been sealed, but the tools were ample evidence that at least one, and probably more, had lived long enough to complete his grim work before spending his final time on Earth trapped in his own tomb.

'Look at the pictographs. They're cruder. But look at what they're portraying,' Remi said, gazing above the assembled bodies at the carvings.

A bearded warrior, part snake, part bird, was slaying a group of men attacking a small temple. Above the peak, a cloud hovered. The imagery was grizzly: the bodies hacked apart, several beheaded. Lightning bolts blazed from the warrior's eyes, setting fire to the surroundings, where still more figures burned in the flames.

'Not terribly cheery, is it?' Lazlo whispered. 'Bit Armageddon for my taste. Still, the message is clear.'

Sam nodded. 'I'll take it as a warning to anyone who tries to breach the temple.'

'Like we have,' Remi said.

Everyone was quiet until Antonio moved back

toward the doorway. 'It's getting dark. We should gather our things and have the police guard this overnight. I'll speak to them about it.'

'I'm not ready to leave yet. Let's get the portable work lamps from the trucks and set them up,' Remi said.

'But there's nothing that can't wait until morning,' Maribela protested.

'I'm not tired. If the guards are going to be here all night, I see no reason we can't work through the night, too. It wouldn't be the first time. The batteries should last at least that long.'

Sam gave Antonio a weary look. 'You heard the lady. I just follow orders.'

'I don't understand what the urgency is. We can just come back tomorrow. Everyone will still be dead,' Maribela said.

Remi glanced at Sam. 'There's more at stake here than just the temple.'

'What do you mean?' Antonio asked.

'Somewhere inside may be the Eye of Heaven. Left for the returning Vikings so they could claim their position as the leaders of the indigenous people of Mexico.'

Maribela blinked in astonishment. 'Are you serious?'

'I didn't want to say anything until we found the site.'

'Then where is it?' Maribela asked. 'The Eye of Heaven?'

Sam shrugged. 'That's the problem. The language isn't specific. "Beneath the temple" is all the rune stone said. Which could mean below us in a chamber or vault, or in a cave somewhere down the cliff, or buried in some hidden corner of the temple. For all we know, there are more clues in these pictographs. Nothing about this has been straightforward and I see no reason to believe it will be from here on out.'

Remi moved into the center of the space. 'Which brings us back to our sense of urgency and desire for secrecy. This project has been plagued with problems and we'd rather avoid one out here in the middle of nowhere. The only people who know anything about this are in this room. But the longer it takes for us to find the jewel, assuming it really exists, the greater the likelihood that something goes wrong.'

Antonio nodded. 'I understand. We'll get the lamps and negotiate with the police to spend the night guarding the area. Tomorrow we can arrange for heavier security while we work – these men will have to go home and, when they do, they might talk, which around here could mean serious problems. Everyone's aware of the violence that's been an unfortunate part of the region's recent history.' Antonio didn't need to say anything more.

'Not to mention the snakes,' Lazlo added, lightening the mood only slightly.

Half an hour later, the three lamps were in place and one of the officers was sitting outside the temple, his companions back in the SUV, where they could spot approaching vehicles. Lazlo was pacing in front of the entry, scratching his head, as Sam and Remi tapped on the floor, Sam with the handle of his machete, Remi with her flashlight. Antonio and Maribela were taking photographs of the carvings.

Lazlo stopped midstride and stared at the wall. 'Sam? I just noticed something.'

'What is it?' Sam asked, still tapping.

'The walls. They don't end at the floor.'

'What are you talking about, Lazlo?'

'Look at the walls. The stone blocks. They're symmetrical. But the ones at the base are only a third as deep. So this floor isn't set on bedrock, as you might expect. Either that or the blighters dug a footer for the walls, which isn't likely circa 1000.'

'What's your point?' Sam asked.

'My point is that you'd expect to see this if there was more structure below us. Or as the rune stone said, *beneath*.' Lazlo unsheathed his machete and began scraping the floor, removing the film of dirt that had accumulated over the centuries. 'And if the entire thing's hollow below, you might not hear a difference by tapping. In fact, I'd wager it'll all sound the same.'

Sam eyed Remi and nodded, and soon they were all on their knees, working away. An hour passed, and then Antonio called out.

'I found a peg.'

Remi rose and went to him. 'A peg?'

Antonio tapped part of the floor. 'Do you have a pocketknife?'

Remi unfolded her knife and handed it to him. He used the point of the blade to clear dirt away and soon they were staring at a circle in the floor, six inches in diameter, crafted from stone.

'We've seen these in Mayan ruins,' Maribela explained. 'The builders would affix a movable slab, using stone pegs to prevent the slab from shifting – effectively locking it in place. There will most certainly be others.'

Antonio wedged the knife blade down the edge of the peg and wiggled it. The peg moved.

'Does anyone else have another knife? We're going to need at least two.'

Sam handed him his SOG Ae-04 Aegis folding knife and Antonio worked at the stone plug. He was able to raise it three-quarters of an inch, and Sam gripped the edges and pulled it free. He sat back, admiring the precise tapering of the granite cone, and then set it to one side.

'Let's find the rest of these.'

An hour and seven pegs later, the distinct outline of a stone slab, three feet wide by four long, was clearly evident. Lazlo and Antonio had gone in search of some saplings they could use as makeshift rollers, and Maribela had commandeered a bottle of motor oil to lubricate the edges, hopefully making it easier to break free. Once Antonio returned with two decent lengths of tree trunk, Lazlo following with two more, they placed the wood on the floor and went to work with the pry bars, wedging them along the slab's edges.

'Get this side lifted and I'll try to push it from the end using my bar,' Sam instructed. They worked at the stone rectangle, Remi and Maribela using the shovel tips for greater leverage as the men worked the bars, and one end slowly rose from the floor.

'Great. Hold it there . . . hold it . . .' Sam heaved on his bar and levered the slab, first one inch, then another. 'Lazlo, get one of the rollers under it. Watch your fingers!'

Lazlo pushed a sapling to the edge, directly beneath the lip, and they eased off the bars, lowering the slab. Antonio quickly rolled the other three in line, so as the slab slid farther it would roll along the trunks. Lazlo joined Sam and got his bar into the opening and heaved. The slab moved another few inches. Sweat dripped from their brows, and Sam paused to wipe it out of his eyes.

'I thought you had a bad back.'

'Bit miraculous, isn't it? I feel like a teenager again,' Lazlo said.

'It's a wondrous time. Now, let's get this thing out of the way so we can see what's under it.'

They pried together as Maribela poured the last of the motor oil on the grooves. Remi squeezed next to Sam and added her weight to the effort. The heavy stone covering lurched up on to the saplings, revealing a yawning opening. Maribela and Antonio rolled the slab toward them and it ground to a halt near one of the skeletons. Sam freed his aluminum flashlight from his belt and directed the beam into the inky gap. Nobody spoke until Lazlo broke the silence.

'I just hope there aren't any snakes.'

41

Remi brushed dust off her pants and moved to the far side of the gap, her beam shining over the long series of stone stairs leading seemingly endlessly downward. A gossamer film of cobwebs blocked the light, and a large black beetle scuttled away into a cranny. Antonio and his sister joined them in peering into the darkness, their additional flashlight wattage doing little.

'So who wants to go down first?' Lazlo asked.

Remi coughed. 'Sam?'

'I knew I'd get the job when I saw the spiderwebs.'

'Don't pout. You love this part.'

Sam grinned. 'Indeed.' He moved to where the first step descended into nothingness.

His scuffed boot landed on the narrow stone ledge and he wiped away spiderwebs, his flashlight gripped in his left hand. Another step, and then another, the thick soles silent as he placed each foot with care. Sam's breathing sounded like a bellows in the narrow passageway, and he instinctively stooped to keep from brushing against the ceiling. He stopped once at the eighth step and crouched down.

Remi called to him. 'What is it?'

'I thought it might be a booby trap. There's a gap on one side, but it's nothing.'

'Are you sure?'

'We'll know in a second.'

He put his weight on the step and nothing happened.

Sam continued down until he was barely visible from above. He reached out to steady himself but drew his hand back from the wall when he saw what looked suspiciously like snake holes. A brown millipede slunk along the rock face. The lamplight played off its chocolate exoskeleton and he shuddered involuntarily.

His balance restored, Sam took a deep breath and continued down. The air temperature dropped as he descended. Three stories below the temple he reached a small landing, the stone slab beneath his feet slick with mould. On the wall were more carvings, these different from those adorning the temple.

There was a passable etching of a longship, its square sail and dragon heads painstakingly detailed, cutting through huge waves. A bearded figure, wearing a billowing cloak and the winged serpent helmet, stood at the helm. Round shields lined the hull, and the ship was filled with warriors, their spears and axes exaggerated in the depiction. Floating in front of the boat was what appeared to be a sun or a planet, emitting waves of energy or light as it guided the ship to its destination.

Sam inched closer to it and saw that it wasn't a

celestial body at all. From its center, a stylized carving of an eye gazed down at the ship.

He turned, the glowing rectangle of the top of the stairwell seemingly a mile away, and called.

'I think this is it!'

'What?' Remi's voice answered, echoing off the stone walls.

'It's a pictograph. A Viking ship piloted by Quetzal-coatl, with a jewel the size of my head in the carving.'

Sam turned to where his voice was reverberating in a larger area to his right. There, at the end of a short passage, was a small cavern, worn from the earth over thousands of years by groundwater dripping through the stone. He brushed more cobwebs aside and felt something crawling on his arm. He froze and then slowly moved the flashlight beam down the length of his arm until he saw a black widow spider marching along his exposed skin.

Sam slipped the end of the flashlight between his teeth. He drew a deep breath to steel himself and brushed the arachnid away. The disgruntled spider landed on the stone floor and raced off into the darkness, and Sam closed his eyes for a moment and cursed silently. Then he directed the beam along the walls of the cave until it glinted off something at the far end, at the top of a stalagmite that appeared to have been lopped off. Sam swept the floor of the cave with the light, wary of booby traps, and when he saw nothing suspicious, placed one careful foot in front of the other as he approached the makeshift pedestal.

Thirty feet above him, Remi and Lazlo waited, their breathing shallow, as though any deep inhalations might disrupt whatever fragile balance was in play and bring about disaster. Maribela paced back and forth near the entrance, her anxiety obvious, as Antonio eyed the skeletons with curiosity.

'You can see these were Vikings from their size. They're all a foot taller than any of the mummies we've recovered in our digs,' he said.

Lazlo nodded. 'The last guard, waiting for their ship to come in, poor blighters. Must have been rough duty. Most of them have gray beards, so unless this was the geriatric cruise, they were here for many years.'

'We'll probably find evidence of a signal fire on the top of the temple when it's excavated,' Remi said, taking in the skeletons with a long glance.

'Imagine what it must have been like. Day after day, year after year –'

Lazlo was interrupted by Sam's voice from the passageway.

'You won't find that kind of dedication anymore, that's for sure,' he said, stepping from the opening as he wiped a spiderweb off his shoulder. 'Did I mention I hate black widows?'

'Sam! What did you find?' Remi asked.

Sam's expression was dejected as his gaze landed on

each of their faces. He sighed deeply and then his face broke into a grin.

'Oh, nothing. Just the biggest emerald I've ever seen. It looks Incan to me, but what do I know?'

42

Sam led them down the stairs, warning again about the suspect eighth step as everyone followed him to the vault where he'd found the Eye of Heaven.

'Be careful. Try to walk in my footsteps. I don't trust this floor. There could be a deadfall trap anywhere in here,' Sam cautioned. Remi took care to fit her feet into the prints Sam had left in the dust as she neared the glowing jewel. Lazlo followed, slightly more unsteadily, glancing around warily at the spiderwebs that drifted like ghostly tendrils from every surface. Antonio and Maribela were more confident in their approach, the environment their natural habitat after years exploring ruins.

They stood facing the stone. A decayed wooden chest rested nearby on the chamber floor like an afterthought. Sam cleaned off a thousand years of calcium that had accumulated on the emerald face with his bandanna and they took in the way the jewel refracted the light, glowing as if possessed of an inner energy. The stone was clear, nearly flawless, and easily the size of a grapefruit. It sat in a hand-beaten gold casing with stylized depictions of Quetzalcoatl on it.

'It's stunning,' Lazlo whispered. 'Like it has a life of its own. I've never seen anything like it.'

Remi moved to the side and crouched down to study the remnants of the chest, the wood long ago rotted away, only the rusty bindings hinting at its original form. 'I'd say it's safe to assume that the Toltec made it into Inca territory. The emerald would have had to come from the Inca empire in what's now Colombia. Look at these statues.'

Antonio nodded. 'This is truly a priceless find.'

'How many carats would you say the emerald is?' Lazlo asked.

'I wouldn't even know how to guess. Is "huge" a number?' Sam said.

'Close enough, old man. Well played, by the way, all around. Been a busy week for the Fargos by any measure.'

'Yes, we've been very fortunate,' Remi said, returning to his side. 'But now the real work begins. Antonio's team needs to take over and make sense out of all this. All we did was follow a few clues – which we couldn't have done without your help, Lazlo.' She paused. 'As I've said numerous times, you're a genius.'

'Never argue with a lady,' Lazlo said, beaming.

Maribela glanced at her watch. 'I just realized that with all the excitement we haven't eaten since breakfast. Does anyone want something for a late dinner? I can run to the nearest town and get something. The officers will want to eat, too.'

Sam turned. 'Good idea. There's not a lot more we can do here other than ensure nobody disturbs the site until we can get it properly secured.'

'I'll go while you're taking photographs. Are we planning on staying here tonight?' Maribela asked.

'I suppose so. No way I'll be able to get any sleep now,' Remi said. 'Tell you what, I'll go with you.'

'No need. It could take a while to find something that's open. Are chicken enchiladas good for everyone?' Maribela asked.

They all nodded.

'Perfect. I'll be back as soon as I can.'

'Do you want some money?' Sam asked.

'I'd say that you've made enough contribution to Mexico over the course of this adventure that we can buy you take-out food. It's the least I can do.'

When Maribela had gone, Antonio looked around at the cave. 'I'm going to get one of the work lamps from the temple so we have light.'

'Good idea. And while you're at it, see if you can arrange more security. Finding this changes everything,' Sam said.

'Will do.'

Lazlo moved to the chest and examined the icons, careful not to touch them. Antonio returned a few minutes later with an LED lamp and set it near the Eye of Heaven so Remi could get photographs of everything. Once she'd filmed each item in the cave, they moved back to the landing, where she repeated the process with the carvings. When she was finished, they wearily climbed the stairs to the temple, Sam leading, Antonio behind him, Remi and Lazlo bringing up the rear.

An explosion of gunfire erupted from above, sounding like cannon fire in the enclosed space. The body of one of the officers tumbled down the stairs, his rifle clattering next to him. Sam stopped the man's fall, checked his pulse, and grabbed the rifle as Antonio freed the man's service pistol. Nobody said a word, their ears ringing, the policeman's lifeless form blocking half the stairway.

Janus Benedict's voice called out from the temple above.

'Don't do anything stupid, Fargo. This isn't the hill you want to die on, old chap. I assume you're down there and by now have your hands on the guard's rifle. Just put it down, nice and easy, and come out with your hands up.' Janus Benedict's voice was calm and reasonable, like he was discussing a chess move.

Sam's eyes searched the opening. 'How do I know you won't butcher us like you did this poor man?'

'Not my style. But my local partners aren't as patient as I, so if you don't drop any weapons, you'll be facing a group you have no chance against. And they look jumpy.' Janus paused. 'And, of course, there's the Mexican woman. They're holding a gun to her head. If this goes any further awry, it's on you. Put down the pistol and it will all work out. You have my word.'

'Your word? A thief and a murderer?' Sam spat.

Janus's tone hardened. 'This is your last chance and then I'm afraid the lads here will shoot the young lady and toss her body down to you as an indication of their resolve. We don't have a lot of time to quibble now that there's been gunfire. Reinforcements will be here soon and I intend to be gone by then. So what's it going to be? Prove a point and the girl gets it, or be sensible and live to fight another day?'

Antonio exchanged a look with Sam and shook his head, but Sam rose and tossed the rifle through the gap. Antonio scowled and then tossed the pistol up.

'We're unarmed,' Sam called out and raised his hands.

'Yes. That's much better,' Janus said as Sam climbed out of the opening, followed by Antonio. Maribela was standing next to Janus by the tomb entry, Reginald holding a pistol, Guerrero behind them with his own handgun, its ugly muzzle pointed in their direction.

Antonio's face radiated relief, and then confusion, as Maribela smiled and stayed by Janus's side as he approached. Guerrero moved to the discarded guns, kicked them a few feet farther away, and took up a position next to Reginald, his weapon trained on them.

Sam locked eyes with Janus. 'Even for you, this is a low moment, Benedict. This is how you want to be remembered?'

'Not my doing, old chap. Really. But the locals do things differently and it's their ball, so to speak. When in Rome . . .' Janus said, shaking his head. 'Believe me, all the killing is as appalling to me as it is to you.'

'But you didn't stop it.'

'Couldn't. But I don't condone it. I requested that this be done as antiseptically as possible. But I'm afraid that there's a limit to how far I can influence the natives. A bloodthirsty bunch. Not my choosing, but there it is.'

'You'd have been right at home in Nuremberg.'

'Shut your filthy mouth or I'll add your body to the pile,' Reginald threatened, his pistol pointing at Sam. 'Who do you think you are, anyway? You're lucky you're still breathing, you ignorant American pleb.'

'What's this, Janus? Brought your brother along to do the dirty work? Didn't want to break a nail with the bloody stuff?' Sam taunted.

Reginald stepped forward and struck Sam across the face with his pistol. Sam grunted and held his hand up to where the butt had split his cheek open.

Janus turned to Reginald. 'Now, then, no need for that. I'm sure they'll be sensible.' He returned his attention to Sam. 'Where's your lovely bride, Fargo?'

Sam returned his stare but didn't say anything for a few beats. 'Rot in hell, Benedict.'

Janus shook his head, as if dealing with an ill-behaved child, and pulled an iPhone from his pocket. 'Never mind. Ah, I see she's down on the stairs. Hoping for one of your infamous Fargo miracles, I'd wager.' He cleared his throat. 'Remi? Be a dear and don't make me come get you. I know you're there. Come out and play.'

Sam's eyes widened. 'A tracking device?'

'You are a bright one, aren't you? Yes, I've been aware

of your every move since Spain. Your wife's lucky talisman is also my lucky talisman. Well worth the paltry sum it cost for the homing device.'

Several moments later, Remi moved from the gap, slowly, her flashlight gripped tightly, an expression of loathing being Janus's reward. Lazlo lagged behind, looking shocked, his hands raised over his head.

Remi sneered at Janus. 'I thought I smelled vermin. Should have known it was you, Benedict.'

'There, there. Don't be such a bad loser. Not becoming at all.' Janus shrugged. 'I love your necklace, by the way. You really have no idea how much.'

Remi tore the necklace off and tossed it on the ground. Maribela stepped forward and picked it up. 'Very nice. A little vulgar, for my taste, but I'll smile whenever I wear it.'

Remi started forward, fury in her eyes. 'You scum.'

Janus stepped toward her. 'Now, now, dear woman. I'd hate for your last breaths to be tarnished with unpleasantness.'

Sam spat blood on the dirt at his feet. 'Then you are planning to kill us. So much for the moral high ground. You're nothing but a two-bit thief and a murderer. Never bright enough to locate your own treasures, always reduced to stealing.'

Janus frowned. 'You've got quite an ugly mouth on you, haven't you? Both of you. I won't be doing any such thing. However, my colleague here probably isn't predisposed to leaving any loose ends, so I'm afraid that it doesn't look good for you celebrating another anniversary together. The brother will be spared, with the promise that if he speaks a word, both he and his sister will meet with untimely ends. But you two pose a problem for which there's only one obvious solution. If it's any consolation, I'll put in a request that it be swift and painless.'

Janus consulted his Patek Philippe wristwatch. 'Do try to enjoy your final moments.'

'You're cursed, Benedict,' Sam promised, drawing Remi to him.

43

Janus looked past the Fargos and eyed the stairway opening, taking in the slab off to the side. He moved closer and looked down into the dark space while Guerrero and Reginald kept their weapons trained on the group. After several seconds, he stepped back and turned to Maribela with the hint of a smile.

'Maribela, why don't you take Reginald down to see the emerald while I sort out this unpleasantness?'

'Very well, Janus. Reginald?' Maribela said.

Antonio stared at her, confused, and then he shook his head and cursed in Spanish. 'No. Why on earth . . . ?'

Maribela shrugged. 'Shut up, Antonio. This is for the best. We have the photographs. The actual emerald isn't going to do us any good – it's not like we're going to get a bonus for locating it. You yourself said that the treasure of the Toltecs was their history. We'll still have that.'

Sam shook his head. 'What kind of woman are you? Men died because of . . . what, greed? How much is he paying you? How much does it cost to betray everything you've worked for? I'm curious.'

Janus waved his statement off. 'That's none of your concern. Though I can't deny that the lovely Maribela will be handsomely rewarded for her efforts. Now, go. We don't have much time.'

Antonio looked devastated. 'Maribela . . .'

'Let it go, Antonio. Trust me on this. In a week, we'll be able to fund our own explorations and not have to beg for coins from the government. You may be fine living like this but I'm not,' Maribela said scornfully, and then pointed to the opening in the floor. 'Come on, Reginald. I'll show you the way.'

'Wait. I am going with you,' Guerrero snarled in heavily accented English.

'I'm not sure that's necessary,' Janus said. 'You're rather more in need up here, I should think.'

'I am going,' Guerrero insisted, eyeing Reginald distrustfully.

'Ah, well, then, I see. But who will take care of this lot in your absence?' Janus asked, his civilized demeanor cracking, if only momentarily.

Guerrero walked over to where he'd kicked the guard's Beretta pistol and scooped it up, then handed it to Janus, who held it like it was a live snake.

'You can. I'll be back. When I am, I'll finish the job for you,' Guerrero said with an ugly smirk. He called outside and a gunman holding an assault rifle filled the temple doorway. 'Come in and watch these two,' he ordered in Spanish. The gunman moved inside.

Guerrero turned to Maribela and switched to English. 'Lead the way. Your boyfriend's right about one thing – we need to hurry. It won't be long before the security force from the plant gets here, and we don't want to have to shoot it out with a squad of soldiers.'

Maribela stepped down into the gap. Reginald descended the stairs behind her, his pistol in his belt, a look of false bravado on his face as his eyes nervously tracked the tunnel ceiling.

'Don't worry. It's held up for a thousand years. It should be safe for five more minutes,' Maribela said.

'I'm not worried. I just don't much care for confined spaces,' he said, his voice cracking on the final words.

'Many people don't.'

They made their way to the cave, where the work light was still illuminated, and approached the emerald.

'Bloody hell. That's bigger than I thought it would be. Massive, isn't it?' Reginald said in awe.

Maribela nodded, her gaze locked on the stone. Reginald stepped closer to it.

'The Eye of Heaven. It's magnificent. Truly breathtaking,' he whispered, avarice and cunning in his eyes as he took in the priceless jewel.

'It is. There's no telling how much a collector will pay. Many millions. Perhaps hundreds of millions,' she said, calculating her likely cut.

Reginald drew his pistol and turned to Maribela. 'You really are a greedy bitch, aren't you?'

Shock and fear played across her face. 'No. I've . . . I've done everything you asked.'

'Which makes you stupid, in addition to greedy.'

She shook her head, panicked. 'Your brother gave me his word . . .'

'Yes, well, I didn't. I'll take care of Janus. He'll see the light when he's saved the twenty per cent he was going to pay you.'

The 9mm parabellum round struck Maribela in the center of the forehead. Her body stiffened and she collapsed, lifeless, to the ground. The sharp crack of the pistol reverberated in the stone chamber like a bomb detonating. Reginald slipped the weapon back into his belt and returned to the emerald. Guerrero grinned and clapped Reginald on the shoulder as they eyed the priceless jewel.

'So, *cabrón*, you like your money as much as I do, eh? Good. More for us!'

In the temple, the cartel gunman's eyes never left the Fargos, his finger on the trigger of his Kalashnikov rifle, ready to fire at a moment's notice. Janus held the Beretta on Antonio, distaste evident in his expression at having had to sully his hands with the vulgar task.

The deafening sound of Reginald's shot exploded from the stairwell, and then time seemed to compress and move in slow motion. The gunman instinctively turned to face the noise, if only for a moment – but long enough for Sam to pull his knife from his pants pocket and flip it open in a single move and fling it at the man's throat. It plunged into his neck, the three-and-a-half-inch razor-sharp blade slicing through his trachea. His finger reflexively jerked the trigger of the assault rifle, sending a volley of rounds into the skeletons. Ricochets whistled and whined in the space. Sam threw himself at the killer as he fell backward across the entryway threshold, where bullets from his murderous colleagues outside peppered his dead form.

Janus tried to aim the Beretta at Sam but Remi's booted foot connected with his wrist, sending the weapon spinning to the ground. He lunged for it, but Remi was a split second faster and he was almost on the gun when she grabbed it and slammed the butt into his temple. His eyes went out of focus and he slumped to the ground as Sam got hold of the cartel gunman's rifle.

Sam dove for the work light and switched it off, plunging the temple into darkness. More shots rang out from the exterior of the building, but Sam held his fire as he waited for his eyes to adjust. He knew that without the light to target him and the others inside, the gunmen would be firing blind at the entry – a slim advantage but the only one he had.

'Antonio. I'm betting the gunman had a pistol. You ever use one?' Sam asked.

'I'll figure it out.'

Guerrero's voice echoed from the stairs. 'Jaime! What's going on up there?'

Remi crept to Sam's side and murmured, 'I'll take them. You take the shooters outside.'

Sam quickly sized up the situation and nodded. 'Deal.'

He saw movement in the dim exterior moonlight

and sighted down the barrel of the rifle, then squeezed off three shots. Sam heard a grunt outside and crept forward to where the gunman's corpse lay on the step. More shots sounded from outside and thumped into the body. Sam gritted his teeth and ignored the fire, focused on reaching the man and checking his pockets. He reached the entry and groped with his free hand, the rifle pointed into the night as he felt for the telltale shape of a thirty-round magazine or a pistol. He found a revolver in the man's belt and pulled it loose, then slid it across the stone floor to Antonio.

Sam heard a rustle from the brush to the left of the temple and emptied the rifle into it. His fingers felt two magazines in one of the windbreaker pockets. He tore them free and rolled away as a hail of bullets blasted overhead. Sam ejected the spent magazine and slapped a new one in place and then chambered a round and squeezed off measured bursts at the killers outside.

Remi waited soundlessly near the stairwell opening, ears straining for any sound, the high ring from the gunfire dampening her hearing. Antonio crawled to her side and whispered, 'What should I do?'

'Shoot down the stairs when I do.'

She returned to listening, certain that Reginald and Guerrero were making their way up the passageway. And then Reginald, on the steps below Guerrero, switched on his flashlight to avoid falling. Guerrero hissed at him to turn it off, but it was enough – Remi had been able to make them out. She loosed four shots into the gap. Antonio fired three times beside her, the ricochets bouncing off the stone as the stairwell became a killing field. She heard a groan as a body hit the stones hard. She fired two more shots for good measure and was rewarded with a terse exclamation and then the sound of boots pounding down the stairs.

Reginald's distinctive voice cursed again and she heard a body fall, bouncing as it slid down the steps. Reginald had turned tail in the darkness, lost his footing, and fallen the rest of the way.

'Are you all right?' Sam called from his position by the entry.

'Never better!' Remi answered.

'I . . . think so,' Antonio said.

Lazlo moaned from near the skeletons. Remi peered in his direction.

'Lazlo,' she whispered.

'I . . . I'm . . . hit.' Lazlo's voice was a croak.

'How bad?' Sam asked.

'A bloody . . . bullet . . . hit me. How much . . . worse . . . does it get?'

'Where?'

Lazlo coughed, 'Shoulder.'

'Hang on. This will be over in seconds.' She turned to Antonio. 'Do whatever Sam tells you to, do you understand?'

Antonio nodded. 'What are you going to do?'

Another volley of shots pelted the temple doorway. Remi cringed and ducked her head. Sam's Russian rifle answered the fire, its staccato bark music to her ears. She glanced back at the stair opening and her eyes narrowed looking into the darkness.

'Finish this.'

44

During a lull in the shooting, Remi ran in a crouch to Sam and told him what she was planning to do.

'I'm going to take him down, Sam. We either wounded or killed the cartel guy, so it's only Reginald and Maribela. And I've got a score to settle with her.'

'Remi. Think this through. Just wait up here. Eventually they'll have to come up the stairs. Take them then.'

'I don't like them down there with the emerald.'

'It's not like they can go anywhere with it.'

She thought for a few moments and nodded. 'Fine. We'll do it your way. But for the record, I'm in favor of doing a Sam Fargo – going in with guns blazing.'

'Noted. And I'm not ruling that out. I just don't like a situation where you're on the stairs and Reginald is shooting from a position of safety. That's asking for it.'

'You made your point. What are you planning to do?'

'They've got us pinned down. It's a stalemate. We can't leave, but they can't get in. My goal is to hold them off until the guards show up from the nuke plant. It won't be much longer with all this gunfire.'

'Let's hope so. We don't actually know how long they'll take. And there could be more cartel goons on the way. In fact, the nuclear staff might be under instructions not to leave the grounds in case this is just a diversion for a frontal attack.'

Sam looked at where Antonio was crouched, pistol in hand. 'Antonio, does your cell phone work in here? Do you have a signal?'

He fished it out of his pocket. 'I do.'

'Call someone. Get the entire Mexican military here. Now. Explain the situation. We need the cavalry to come over the hill.'

Antonio punched in the emergency number and spoke in low tones as Sam and Remi kept watching the brush outside the temple. When he hung up, he didn't look confident.

'They wanted me to stay on the line. I told them I couldn't but that they needed to get an armed group presence out here immediately. And an air evac for casualties. The operator said she'd do the best she could.'

'That doesn't sound promising,' Remi said.

'They'll send someone – the only question is how long it takes.' Antonio hesitated. 'What are you going to do about Reginald and my sister?'

'All we can do is wait. It's suicide to go down those stairs.'

'But Maribela could be hurt. Or he could be using her for a hostage.'

Remi touched his hand. 'Antonio. Think. There was a gunshot that started all this. And only two people were on the stairs – Reginald and Guerrero.' She paused. 'I'm sorry, Antonio.'

'She might be wounded . . . like Lazlo.'

Sam nodded. 'It's possible. But there's nothing we can do right now. We need to hold off these men until help arrives. Then the professionals can take care of Reginald. We'll see how he fares against heavily armed soldiers in full battle gear.'

Lazlo groaned from the floor.

'How're you doing, Lazlo?' Sam asked, eyes continually scanning the grounds for signs of life.

'Not . . . great.'

Remi crawled over to him. She saw the bullet wound. 'Lazlo, help's on the way. It shouldn't be long now.'

'Good . . . show . . .'

More shooting slammed into the stone entryway, sending chips flying. Sam popped off a shot at the orange blossom of the shooter's muzzle blast as Remi returned. 'Let me have that thing. I'm the marksman, remember?'

'I've done pretty well so far.'

'They're still out there and shooting. Come on, I'll swap you. AK for a nearly new Beretta nine. Such a deal.'

Sam did as she asked and hefted the pistol. 'I'm not sure what I'll be able to accomplish with this peashooter.'

'Don't worry. Fire off a couple of shots, see if you can draw them out.'

Sam squeezed off two rounds. When the gunman outside opened up, Remi kept her head down until he was done and then fired three shots in quick succession.

No fire answered. She turned to Sam and gave him a small smile. 'Never send a man –'

'To do a woman's job. I know. You think you got him?'

'Pretty sure. But there may be more out there.'

'Want to risk trying a breakout?'

'It would be safer to stay here and wait for the military to show,' Remi said. She looked around. 'Where's Antonio?'

Sam turned to scan the darkened interior of temple. 'He was just here.'

Remi cursed. 'Idiot. He went down after Reginald. I knew it.' She handed Sam back the rifle. 'Give me the Beretta.'

'Remi. Just because Antonio wants to commit hara-kiri doesn't mean you should.'

'He's doing what I should have.'

'No, he's doing something really stupid you shouldn't be involved in.'

'Hold that thought, Fargo.'

'Remi . . .'

She covered the distance to the stairs in seconds and was out of sight before Sam could do anything to stop her. She felt her way along, gun held in front of her. There hadn't been any more shooting from below – at least that was a positive. She also didn't sense Antonio in front of her, which meant he'd turned the corner and was in the passageway to the cave.

Remi passed Guerrero's corpse, knelt down, and felt around until she found his pistol. She slid it into the waist of her pants at the small of her back and continued down the steps until she reached the landing. The faint glow from the work lamp was a little brighter there and she could barely make out the pictograph as she leaned against the stone wall and prepared to turn the corner.

She ducked around low, in a crouch, presenting as small a target as possible. Nothing. Step by careful step, she crept forward, eyes adjusting to the low light, gun scanning the passage as she made her way forward. She listened and heard only the soft dripping of water somewhere in the cave.

Remi swung into the cavern, leading with her gun, and froze when she saw Reginald at the far side, standing behind Antonio, his gun pointed at Antonio's head.

'Drop it or I blow his head off,' Reginald said.

'Shoot him. He killed Maribela,' Antonio hissed.

Reginald shook his head. 'It wasn't me. It was Guerrero,' he lied.

Antonio tried to struggle free. 'Shoot him.'

'Give me one reason not to, Reginald,' Remi said, taking another step into the chamber.

'I'll kill him. I swear I will.'

Another step. 'And why should I care? I drop my gun, you'll just shoot me.'

'This has all gone wrong. I just want to get out of this alive. Don't make me kill him.' Reginald paused, then shouted at Remi, 'You have five seconds and then you'll be wearing his brains!'

Remi lowered her weapon. 'Easy, Reginald. I believe you. If you shoot us, Sam will cut you down when you try to come up the stairs. You'll be deader than Elvis before you make it three feet.' She saw a flicker in his eyes.

'Shut up and drop the gun.'

'Shoot him now,' Antonio pleaded.

'I'm putting the gun down.' Remi slowly knelt, her eyes never leaving Reginald's. She saw the moment of triumph she'd been waiting for when she set the gun on the stone floor and began straightening up.

Reginald moved his gun from Antonio's head to point at Remi as he sneered in victory. 'You stupid cow —'

He never saw her other hand slip behind her and grip Guerrero's gun, all his attention focusing on her eyes and the hand that was placing the Beretta on the floor.

Her left-handed shot caught Reginald high in the shoulder, inches from Antonio's chest. He spun from the force of the shot shattering his scapula as Antonio threw himself on Reginald and started to beat him with angered fury at the death of his sister. Reginald's pistol dropped on the floor and Remi raced toward it as Antonio and he fell together. She kicked it out of reach as Sam's voice called out from the entryway.

'Remi. You're okay!'

'Of course I am, Fargo.'

Sam handed his rifle to Lazlo, who was leaning shakily against the passage wall, and moved to break up the fight. By the time he reached Antonio, he'd stopped battering Reginald, a glazed look in his eyes as he gripped the younger man's shirt.

Reginald's head slumped forward as he lost consciousness. Sam eyed Reginald and nodded at Antonio. 'Doesn't look like he'll be a problem anytime soon. How about you?'

'He killed my sister,' Antonio seethed.

'I'm sorry, Antonio. I really am,' Sam said. 'But you need to let the authorities deal with him.'

Antonio gazed down at Reginald's battered face as if coming out of a trance and released him. He stood slowly, looking at his swelling knuckles as if considering finishing the job on Reginald.

Sam stepped forward. 'This isn't the way,' he said. 'I need you focused if we're going to survive until help arrives. Pull yourself together.'

'I'm just shaken,' Antonio replied, slowly calming down. 'What about the cartel gunmen?'

'I heard two heavy vehicles arriving. If I were them, I'd be long gone. My hunch is that they're not going to want to take on whatever just showed up.' Sam studied Antonio. 'Let's head back upstairs just in case. Security should be here any minute. They're probably on their way from the parking area down by the road.'

Antonio looked around the chamber and his eyes locked on his sister's body.

Lazlo moved into the cave and stood in front of Maribela to break Antonio's concentration.

Sam leaned down and scooped up Antonio's revolver, pocketed it, and then took him by the arm. 'Come on. Let's go topside to greet the welcoming committee.'

Remi followed Sam and Antonio out and up the stairs. As they climbed the steps, Remi looked back.

'Lazlo? Are you all right?' she called.

His voice rang out from the doorway. 'Have no fear, I'm right behind you.'

When they neared the top, Sam switched on his flashlight, the pistol in his right hand sweeping the room. He stopped abruptly at the top step.

'Sam. What is it?' Remi asked in a hushed whisper.

Sam stood motionless before turning his head and whispering through clenched teeth, 'It's Janus. He's gone.'

45

'Gone?' Remi said.

'He was right here when I went down to get you. He must have come to. Either that or he was faking and waiting for a chance to escape.'

'You have to catch him. He can't get away with this,' Antonio growled.

'I'm way ahead of you. I'm going after him.'

Remi stepped out of the stairwell. 'Sam, are you sure about this? There are a lot of guns lying around out there . . .'

'He's not going to escape. If I know him, the last thing he wants is a gun battle. That's not his style.'

'What if you're wrong?' Remi demanded.

He handed her the guard's Beretta and removed the revolver from the guard's pocket. 'Here's more fire-power. If anyone but me or the police shows up, start shooting and don't stop.'

'You never answered my question.'

'I'll take my chances.'

Sam shut off his flashlight and moved to the temple entrance. He paused, trying to sense any menace, and then threw himself out, rolling on the flattened grass as he waited for bullets to pound the ground around him.

Nothing.

He scanned the area, noting now he was outside there was more moonlight than he'd thought, and, seeing nothing, considered which direction the Englishman would have taken.

It was no contest. Janus would never choose to walk into the hands of his adversaries.

Sam eyed the ground as he moved away from the temple and came across a dead gunman, his pistol case on his belt open and empty – confirming that Janus was now armed. Sam followed a small trail that the gunmen had used for their approach, stepping softly, careful not to provide Janus with a warning that he was being followed.

Waves pounded the shore below the cliff that was no more than ten yards away and he could smell salt in the air as he pushed deeper into the brush, stopping occasionally to listen in case Janus was blundering along like a wounded ox. But there was only the crash of the surf.

Sam plunged through vine-covered trees over a thick curtain of brush that eventually opened on to a small circular clearing. The clearing ended at the rocky cliffs, high above the pounding surf. Too late, he saw Janus up ahead in the eerie glow of the moon.

Janus stood facing Sam with a pistol aimed at his head, a mere thirty feet between them.

The mouse had turned on the cat.

In the blink of an eye, Sam raised the revolver to firing position. 'It's over, Janus. Throw down your weapon.'

'I don't think so,' Janus said, a tight smile across his face. 'We have what is appropriately called a Mexican standoff.'

'Call it what you may,' Sam said, 'you're still going to pay for your killing of innocent people.'

'I never killed anybody.' Janus's voice was clear, his tone frigid.

'Liar.'

Janus shrugged. 'Believe what you like. There's no blood on my hands.'

'Maybe you didn't personally murder anyone, but you're the cause behind a long trail of dead bodies.'

'Not my doing, old chap. Really. I wasn't in control of the situation – regrettably, my Mexican associate took matters into his own hands. Like I said, the natives here do things differently. Senseless. Most regrettable.'

'You could have stopped it,' Sam spat.

Janus shook his head. 'No, I couldn't. My position was compromised due to my brother's misstep. Could have been the death of me, too. I'm afraid there was a limit to my influence. Not my doing, but there it is.'

The distant beat of a helicopter came from the sea. Neither Sam nor Janus spoke as the sound became louder and a spotlight shot through the gloom, framing them in its glare.

'Mexican authorities,' said Sam. 'I hope you enjoy your ride to prison.'

To Sam's surprise, Janus laughed in a gloating tone. 'Yes, I'll enjoy the ride, but it won't end in a Mexican

421

prison. It will be to my yacht, which is in international waters.'

Sam was angered by the cocky reply, but when he saw the helicopter was bright blue instead of military khaki, he knew Janus wasn't bluffing. 'I can shoot you before you board.'

Janus stared at Sam in silence and then dropped his pistol. He shrugged and slowly turned to face the helicopter, his back to Sam. The helicopter set down and two armed men leapt from the aircraft, their weapons trained on Sam.

Sam continued to keep his weapon aimed at Janus even though he was outgunned. 'One day you'll pay for your crimes.'

Janus walked toward the aircraft. When he neared it, he stopped, turned to Sam, and called out over the noise of the rotor blades, 'As I said, I don't kill. Not even you, Sam Fargo.'

'At least you didn't get the Eye of Heaven.'

'True,' Janus shouted above the thumping sound. 'But there will come another time when a treasure will bring us together.' He turned and boarded the chopper as Sam stood frozen.

Sam watched as it lifted from the clearing and turned over the cliffs toward the sea. 'Yes,' he said softly to himself, 'there will come another time.'

Sam lowered the revolver as his eyes followed the darkened aircraft disappear into the night, leaving him alone on the bluff. The breeze tugged at his clothes as he made his way slowly back to the temple.

When he reached the entryway, Remi ran out and threw her arms around him. He hugged her for a long moment and then pulled back.

'He got away.'

Remi's eyes radiated confusion. 'He escaped? How?'

'I let him go. I couldn't shoot an unarmed man in the back even if it was Benedict.' He explained what had happened.

Remi reached down and took Sam's revolver from him. She peered at it in the moonlight, flipped open the cylinder, and then turned to him.

'Good thing. You were out of bullets.'

46

Sam and Remi watched as the heavily armed soldiers ringed the temple area and four medics came toward them. Remi pointed to where Lazlo was slumped against a wall and two of them went after a stretcher as the other two followed Antonio down the steps to Reginald.

Sam moved to Lazlo, who reached toward him with a shaking hand.

'Don't try to talk. They'll take care of you,' Sam said.

Lazlo motioned for him to come closer. Sam exchanged a glance with the medics, who shrugged as they stood, having stabilized Lazlo. Sam knelt by him and offered a grim smile.

'Save your energy, my friend. You're going to need it.'

Antonio burst from the temple, a look of alarm on his face. Remi glanced at him.

'What is it?'

'The Eye of Heaven. It's gone,' Antonio whispered, eyeing the dozens of soldiers who were milling around in the interior. 'This is a catastrophe.'

Lazlo coughed and winced. 'My . . . my jacket,' he said, turning his head to where one of the men had placed his bloody windbreaker.

'Are you cold?' Sam asked, alarmed.

'No. The . . . the jewel's in one of the pockets.'

'What?' He scooped up the jacket, feeling the weight, and retrieved the emerald.

'I thought it might . . . be best . . . to remove temptation . . . if we were expecting . . . a crowd,' Lazlo said and closed his eyes, exhausted by the effort.

Remi and Sam exchanged a glance and Sam handed the jewel to Antonio, who took it reverentially. 'Be careful, Antonio. That's an important piece of history you're safeguarding.'

Antonio nodded, a conflicted look in his eyes as he studied the gem, the memory of his sister clearly at the forefront of his thoughts as he held the treasure of the Toltecs in his hands.

Seven hours later, Lazlo regained consciousness at the military hospital in Veracruz after a two-hour surgery. The prognosis was good, and, with a little luck, he would mend, a puckered scar and a crescent-shaped incision as bragging rights.

Sam and Remi approached his bed as his eyes opened, his complexion still waxy and gray even after countless bags of blood and plasma. He cleared his throat and tried to talk, but Sam shook his head.

'Don't. We'll be back tomorrow. We just wanted to stick around until you came to. Looks like you cheated the Grim Reaper once again. Nine lives, the man has.'

'I . . .'

'Just take it easy. There's nothing that needs to be

discussed right now. We just wanted you to know we're here for you and we'll be staying nearby. Rest, and we'll come back tomorrow, all right?' Sam said, and Lazlo managed a weak nod, then closed his eyes and drifted off.

The area around the temple was cordoned off and a small military encampment had been set up blocking the access road. Sam and Remi showed their passports and, after a stony-faced corporal checked their identification against a list and radioed for approval, they were allowed on to the grounds. Another soldier pointed to an area filled with military vehicles, where they were to park. The trail leading the two hundred yards to the temple was now a dirt road, cleared and widened to get equipment and staff to the area. Armed soldiers lined the track every dozen yards or so, and Sam and Remi could see that they were taking the security precautions seriously.

They arrived at what had been a dirt mound only hours before. It now resembled an anthill, with workers crawling over it and clearing soil under Antonio's watchful eye. A large tent had been pitched nearby, along with a tarp suspended from four beams, under which technicians were setting up equipment accompanied by the steady drone of a generator.

'Antonio, did you get any sleep?' Remi asked as they approached the temple.

'A few hours. I knew I wasn't going to get much and there's work to be done here. As you can see, we're clearing the exterior, with another team working inside. It will take some time to catalog everything.'

'And the Eye of Heaven?'

'Under guard in the base commander's safe until we can fly it to Mexico City.'

'How long do you plan to be on-site here?'

'At least a week. I'll be commuting back and forth between Teotihuacan and this site for a while. Both finds are monumental. For which the Mexican people owe you a deep debt of gratitude.'

'The work is its own reward, Antonio,' Remi said and Sam nodded.

Antonio pointed at an area near the flat roof of the temple that had been cleared and called out to the workers in Spanish, then turned his attention back to his guests.

'How is Lazlo?'

'He'll recover.'

'Have you heard anything about Reginald?'

'Under arrest, being treated at the same medical facility. Reginald's in guarded condition from blood loss, but he'll survive,' Sam said.

'I wanted to talk to you about that. I don't feel comfortable asking but I have to for the sake of my parents. Is there any way you could leave Maribela's involvement with Benedict out of the official account?'

Sam and Remi smiled together. 'We've already discussed it. As far as we're concerned, she died in the line of duty,' Sam said.

'There's nothing to be gained by tarnishing her memory,' Remi added.

'I thank you. You'll never know how grateful I am.'

'We're both very sorry about how this turned out . . . about her untimely death.'

Antonio looked off at the sparkling surface of the Gulf of Mexico, a distant expression on his face. When he returned his gaze to them, his eyes were moist.

'In spite of it all . . . she was my sister.'

Sam nodded as Remi swallowed hard.

'I know, Antonio. I know.'

47

La Jolla, California

Four days later, and one good night's sleep, Sam and Remi sat in the kitchen, gazing at the cobalt blue of the Pacific stretching to Japan. Selma brought a pot of coffee and set it next to her tea. She cleared her throat as she sat down opposite and studied them. 'You two look tan and fit.'

'Yes, lounging around Mexico seems to agree with us,' Sam said.

'I'd say you had a healthy dose of Fargo excitement,' Selma commented.

'Oh, you know, the usual,' Remi said. 'Gunfire, cartel killers, hidden treasure. All in a day's work . . .'

Sam sipped his coffee as Selma filled them in on the news since they'd been gone. Kendra had finally been offered her dream job at the University of California at San Diego and would be starting the following week.

'That's wonderful, Selma. Thanks again for bringing her aboard to help.'

'I know she really enjoyed her time here. And she made a big point about how we could always call on her if needed.'

'That's very sweet.'

'She'll be stopping by tomorrow to get the rest of her things and say good-bye.'

'Good. I want to thank her personally,' Sam said.

'Oh, and did you hear? Antonio was named the new head of INAH. The youngest ever,' Selma said.

'He deserves it. He's a dedicated archaeologist and he's paid his dues,' Remi said. 'We'll have to send him a note congratulating him, Sam.'

'Of course.' Sam paused. 'And, Selma, may I say that you're looking great?'

'Well, thank you. I'm actually feeling pretty close to a hundred per cent. The doctors gave me two thumbs-up. They said I'll still need to be monitored, but the procedure and physical therapy have been a success. In fact, I'm taking up tap dancing. Doctor's orders. Something about it helping with the hip joints.'

Remi looked at her with a look of disbelief. 'That's wonderful. But tap dancing?'

'Tell me about it. But the bad news is that I'm fit for duty, so you're stuck with me.'

'The best researcher in the whole world,' Sam countered. 'Hardly "stuck."'

Color rose to Selma's face and she turned to look out at the ocean.

'What about Benedict and his brother?'

Sam frowned. 'Reginald's being held, pending trial. We'll probably have to fly back at some point and testify, but between our account and Antonio's he's going to be put in jail for the rest of his life.'

'There's no way for him to slip out of it?'

Sam shook his head. 'None. A major Los Zetas cartel boss was with him, along with a host of cartel killers. Ballistics and prints matched Reginald's gun to the bullet that killed Maribela. No, he's history, although there's some concern that he'll never make it to sentencing. Apparently, the Los Zetas are holding him responsible for Guerrero's death, so he's in solitary confinement for his own safety.'

'And Janus? Did he ever surface?'

'We've sworn out a complaint, but there's some question how that will play out – he's disappeared. The case against him is trickier because they can't show him actually pulling the trigger and the only eyewitness who could have confirmed his involvement was Guerrero – and he's not talking to anyone but the Devil.'

'But Janus was there. You can put him at the scene,' Selma said.

'I know. But it's complicated. If he was still in Mexico, it might not be, but since he isn't –'

'Then he might get away with it,' Remi finished.

'Antonio has taken a very personal interest in ensuring that neither of them walk. My money's on him doing everything possible to make the wheels of justice grind forward,' Sam said.

Selma sat back. 'Well, then. Another page in the

Fargo book turns. What's next? You mentioned something about Lazlo?'

'To be determined. He told us he's going to stay in Mexico and help Antonio for a while, but I suspect we'll see more of him around here,' Sam said.

'Assuming he's changed his ways, that could be interesting,' Selma said.

'A bullet tends to be a big attitude adjuster. I think he's on the right path.'

Selma's eyes narrowed and then she smiled.

'Well, as with everything, time will tell.'

48

Forty-five days later, Mexico City, Mexico

The National Museum of Anthropology was festooned with colorful banners announcing a new exhibition dedicated to the Toltec legacy, featuring the fabled Eye of Heaven – a jewel that had been the feature of countless magazine articles and television specials since its discovery. The undeniable presence of Vikings during the Toltec heyday was now established as historical fact and the jewel served to commemorate the intersection of the cultures.

Dignitaries from the government mingled with the upper crust of Mexico City society at what was being described as 'the event of the season.' A sixteen-piece mariachi band played favorites in the exterior courtyard as servers circulated through the crowd, offering appetizers and liquid refreshments.

Sam and Remi stood with Antonio, sipping champagne, near the entry to the hall, where two stern armed guards framed the doorway. Lazlo, also there, shifted from foot to foot, eyeing the crowd, a soda in hand.

'You clean up pretty well, I'll give you that,' Remi

teased. Lazlo hadn't stopped fidgeting with his tuxedo's bow tie since they'd arrived.

'All part of my evil plan to take over the country, you know,' Lazlo said with a wink. 'But you, my dear, are the envy of every man here.' Remi's beaded chiffon evening dress by Carolina Herrera danced under the glow of the outdoor lighting. Sam's smile was worth a thousand words.

'Your friend here has been invaluable on the dig. I even think he's starting to pick up a few words of Spanish,' Antonio shared with a smile.

'I'm glad to see that you've fully recovered – not that I believed that a bullet would slow you down much,' Sam said.

'Mad dogs and suchlike. And, yes, I feel tip-top. Although I wouldn't recommend the whole getting shot part of the experience.'

'All's well that ends well, as they say,' Remi said, and held her champagne flute up in a toast.

Antonio's face grew serious. 'I presume you heard about Reginald?'

'No. Don't tell me that he escaped,' Sam said.

'He was killed yesterday during a disturbance at the prison. It's still under investigation, but my sources tell me they believe it was a mini-riot that was staged to create a diversion so that several Los Zetas cartel enforcers could exact retribution. Apparently, it was brutal.'

Remi shook her head. 'Live by the sword . . .'

'Can't say the world's the poorer for it,' Lazlo said, at which Antonio nodded.

'And has there been any word on Janus?' Sam asked.

Antonio shook his head. 'No. It's like he disappeared into thin air. There's a warrant out for his arrest in Mexico, but it's difficult to enforce outside of our borders. He hasn't been convicted of any wrongdoing, so cooperation, especially against a man with considerable money and power, is . . . grudging, to say the least.'

The band stopped playing and an elegantly dressed matron approached the microphone and made an announcement in Spanish. Antonio offered a hushed summary when she was done speaking.

'They're going to open the doors in two minutes, and, for the first time in history, the Eye of Heaven will be on display for all of Mexico to see. It's an exciting moment. I hope you don't mind saying a few words inside and having a brief photo session with the jewel,' Antonio said. 'The papers have been clamoring for it.'

'Do we have to?' Sam asked.

'I'm afraid so. It is all part of the pageantry,' Antonio said.

'Can't Lazlo stand in for us? He's a far more persuasive speaker, and he's got the tux and everything,' Sam said.

'You look quite dapper yourself, old chap,' Lazlo said, eyeing Sam's navy blue Canali silk suit. 'No way out of it. Goes with being an archaeological rock star.'

Sam shrugged and turned to Remi. 'Well, Remi, looks like it's time to strut our stuff.'

Remi winked at Lazlo and then turned to her husband. He waited expectantly. Her eyes filled with mischief, she leaned into him and stood on her tiptoes, her lips inches from his ear.

'Pwuk-pwuk.'

49

Two years later, Montreal, Canada

The longship rested on handcrafted wooden wedges to keep it upright, its keel surprisingly sturdy despite being a thousand years old. Strategically placed lighting illuminated the craft, which had been lovingly restored by a crew that had worked tirelessly, often around the clock. Members of the press roamed the newly built structure adjacent to the museum that had been designed especially for the ship, photographing the imposing hull and the display of artifacts in illuminated cases along the walls, as the gala attendees murmured in hushed tones.

Dr Jennings approached Sam and Remi through the throng, accompanied by a tall, tanned man in a well-tailored Armani tux. The man's face cracked into a wide smile as he shook hands with Sam and gave Remi a two-cheeked kiss. It was their old friend Warren Lasch, who had flown in to meet them after investing months of his time helping with the restoration project.

Dr Jennings, Lasch and the Fargos walked slowly around the vessel's impressive length, admiring the care that had been taken in returning the ship to its original grandeur.

'It's really miraculous,' Remi said as they looked up at the glowering dragon head on the bow. 'You've done a marvelous job. It's an amazing achievement.'

'Even the shields look like they're in perfect condition. Bravo! Really,' Sam echoed.

Dr Jennings smiled. 'Thankfully, we had unlimited resources, due to a generous donation from an anonymous philanthropic organization, so we were able to take appropriate care to get her here intact and do a first-rate job.' He turned to Lasch. 'We couldn't have done it without Warren's considerable assistance along the way. He's been a guardian angel to us.'

'I'm afraid Jennings here is prone to exaggeration,' Lasch said.

'No, I don't think he is. And the showcases for the artifacts are really impressive,' Sam observed. 'This display should be the jewel in your museum's crown.'

'Yes. We've already had requests from Paris and New York to loan the smaller items for an exhibition in the coming years. But, frankly, and perhaps I'm being sentimental, but I can't imagine letting any of it out of my sight.'

'I know the feeling,' Remi said. 'You leave a little part of yourself in each find.'

A waiter approached and made a slight bow. 'Mr Fargo?'

Sam nodded. 'Guilty as charged.'

'I have a note for you, sir,' the waiter said, handing Sam a cream-linen envelope.

'A note?' Sam asked, puzzled. 'Who from?'

'The gentleman who gave it to me did not give his name. He merely said for you to accept his apologies for being unable to stay.'

'Gentleman? What did he look like?'

'Tall, very distinguished, with gray hair.'

Sam took a few steps away, turned his back, and opened the envelope. He read the short note and then rejoined the others, a slight scowl on his face.

Remi studied his expression. 'What is it, Sam? You look like somebody stole your bicycle.'

Sam sighed and passed her the note. 'It's from an old friend.'

Remi read the note out loud in a hushed tone: '"Looking forward to our next encounter. Enjoy our truce. It won't last long." It's signed Janus Benedict.' She eyed Sam. 'You look as though he got to you.'

'When I get the opportunity, I'll send him a reply that will burn his ears off.' Sam's gaze flowed over the crowd, the women in colorful fashionable gowns, the men in black tuxedos looking like a regiment of uniformed elite troops, but there was no sign of Benedict. 'I'm afraid he's made his exit.'

'The next time we meet, he won't be as charitable,' Remi said sarcastically.

Sam nodded. 'Not when he discovers our next expedition is a search for the Ark of the Covenant.'

Remi's eyes widened and a scowl spread across her face. 'Forgot to tell me, didn't you?'

Sam laughed. 'I hope Benedict has the same reaction.'

'Let me guess. This is another one of your devious ploys to mislead the wolf.'

'Yes. Our artifact-thieving friend abhors frustration.'

'You know, of course, you're beating a club against a hornet's nest.'

'I do.'

'Then where will we be when Janus is trying to find us?'

Sam grinned. 'Basking under the sun and swimming in a tropical lagoon in the Pacific, searching for clues to the ancient ruins of a lost civilization in the Solomon Islands.'

Remi ignored the roomful of people and put her arms around Sam's neck, pulled him down with smiling eyes, and kissed him.

'I'll say one thing, Sam Fargo, you know how to cozy up to a woman.'

He just wanted a decent book to read ...

Not too much to ask, is it? It was in 1935 when Allen Lane, Managing Director of Bodley Head Publishers, stood on a platform at Exeter railway station looking for something good to read on his journey back to London. His choice was limited to popular magazines and poor-quality paperbacks – the same choice faced every day by the vast majority of readers, few of whom could afford hardbacks. Lane's disappointment and subsequent anger at the range of books generally available led him to found a company – and change the world.

'We believed in the existence in this country of a vast reading public for intelligent books at a low price, and staked everything on it'
Sir Allen Lane, 1902–1970, founder of Penguin Books

The quality paperback had arrived – and not just in bookshops. Lane was adamant that his Penguins should appear in chain stores and tobacconists, and should cost no more than a packet of cigarettes.

Reading habits (and cigarette prices) have changed since 1935, but Penguin still believes in publishing the best books for everybody to enjoy. We still believe that good design costs no more than bad design, and we still believe that quality books published passionately and responsibly make the world a better place.

So wherever you see the little bird – whether it's on a piece of prize-winning literary fiction or a celebrity autobiography, political tour de force or historical masterpiece, a serial-killer thriller, reference book, world classic or a piece of pure escapism – you can bet that it represents the very best that the genre has to offer.

Whatever you like to read – trust Penguin.